1945

NEWT GINGRICH

1945

WILLIAM R. FORSTCHEN

Technical Editor,
Albert S. Hanser

1945

Copyright © 1995 by Newt Gingrich & William R. Forstchen

A Baen Books Original

Baen Publishing Enterprises
PO Box 1403
Riverdale, NY 10471

ISBN: 0-671-87676-7

Printed in the United States of America

Dedication:

*To the generation that fought
the Nazis in the real world,
especially our parents:*

Bob and Kitt Gingrich,
and
John and Dorothy Forstchen

Acknowledgments:

Many people have been most helpful in making this novel a reality, but particular thanks are due to Joseph Hanser, Bill Fawcett, and especially David Drake, who in more than one instance corrected our nomenclature, and for whom we stretched a point.

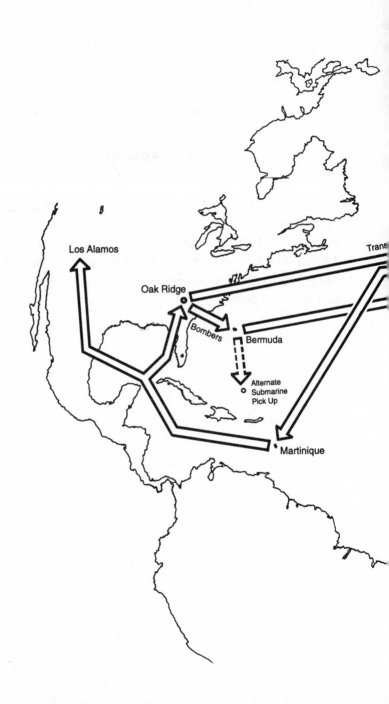

Los Alamos

Oak Ridge

Bombers

Bermuda

Alternate
Submarine
Pick Up

Martinique

Trans

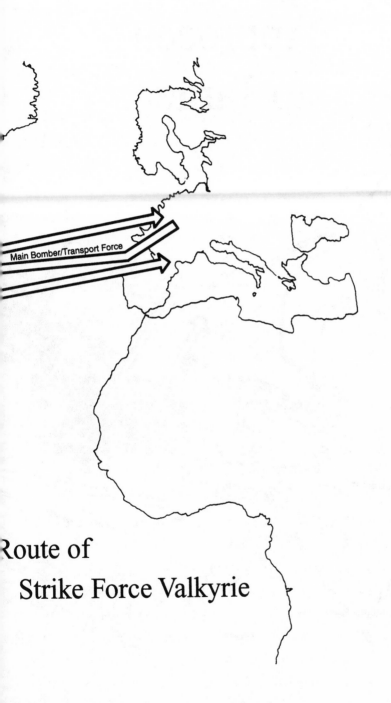

Approach
to Target

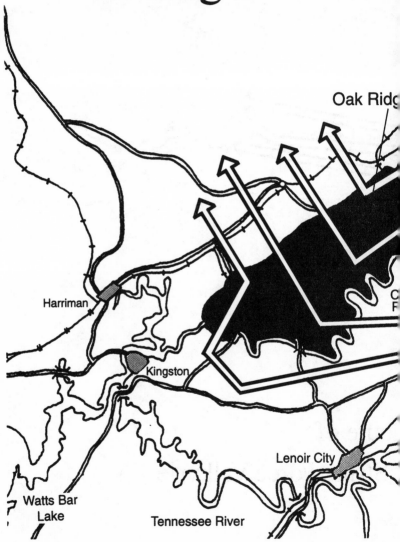

Oak Rid[g]

Harriman

Kingston

Lenoir City

Watts Bar
Lake

Tennessee River

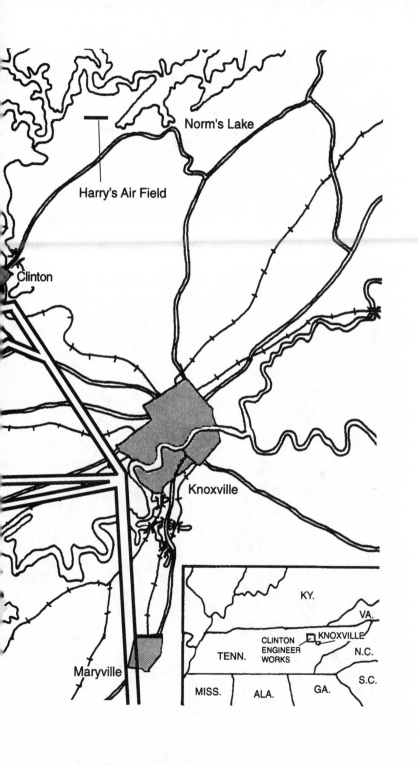

Norm's Lake

Harry's Air Field

Clinton

Knoxville

Maryville

KY.

VA.

CLINTON
ENGINEER
WORKS

KNOXVILLE

N.C.

TENN.

S.C.

MISS.

ALA.

GA.

Bomber and Transport
Runs on Target Area

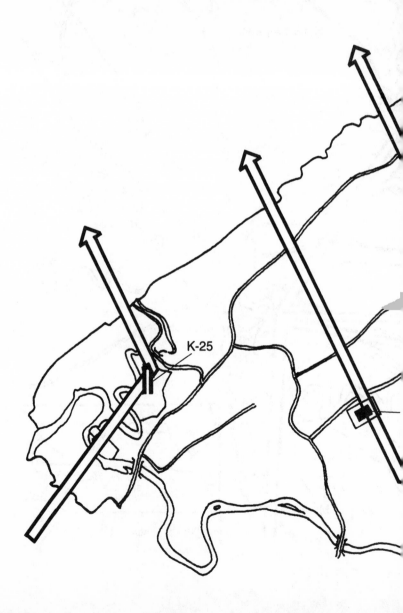

K-25

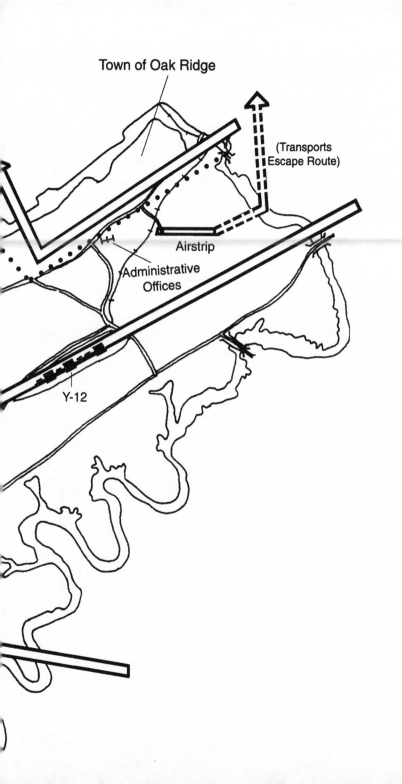

Town of Oak Ridge

(Transports
Escape Route)

Airstrip

Administrative
Offices

Y-12

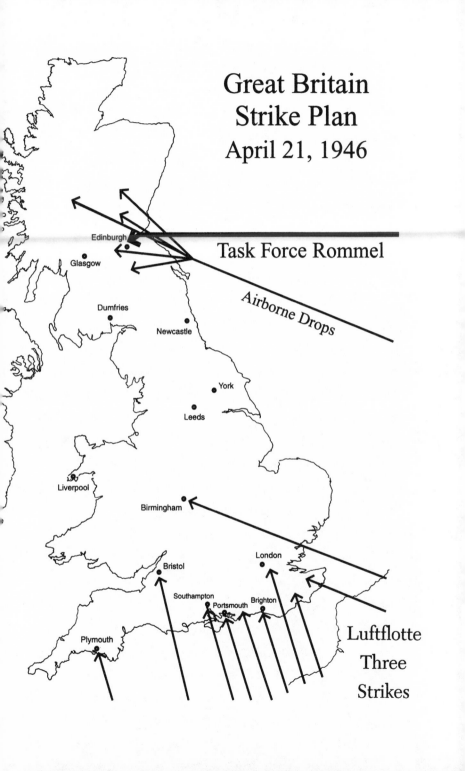

Great Britain
Strike Plan
April 21, 1946

Task Force Rommel

Airborne Drops

Luftflotte
Three
Strikes

Edinburgh

Glasgow

Dumfries

Newcastle

York

Leeds

Liverpool

Birmingham

London

Bristol

Southampton
Portsmouth
Brighton

Plymouth

PROLOG

September 1, 1945
Washington, D.C.

"But *darling*, Germany and the United States are not at war. What harm is there if we share the occasional bit of . . . gossip? Surely you don't think that I, a loyal Swede . . ." The question trailed off in a lethal pout as his beautiful and so very exotic mistress stretched languidly, mock-innocent appeal in her eyes.

Still, he mustn't let her see just how much she moved him. A relationship had to have *some* balance. He stretched in turn, reached over for his cigarettes and gold-plated Ronson on the art deco nightstand with its Tiffany lamp. Since he wasn't sure what to say he made a production out of lighting up and enjoying that first luxurious after-bout inhalation.

His continued silence earned him a small punishment.

"Darling . . . isn't it time for you to leave?"

Playfully, to drive home the potential loss, she bit his shoulder, then kissed it better.

"Aw, hell, I don't want to . . . I wish I could just *divorce* Mrs. Little Goodie Two-Shoes!"

"*I* like this arrangement." She laughed softly. "Mistress to the Chief of Staff of the President of the United States. Nice title, don't you think? *Such* a book I could write."

Mayhew shuddered at the thought. "Don't even joke about it." But he could trust her to be discreet. . . . He was sure he could trust her.

More to cover his moment of doubt than for any other reason, he harked back to her initial gambit. "One thing we really don't have to worry about is a war between Germany and the United States. It just isn't in the cards. There's no way it could happen within the next year or so, and after that—well, just take it from me, nobody is going to dream of messing with the United States, not even Adolf Hitler."

"I don't think there is going to be a war either, but you seem so sure. What is your big secret? You were so excited about it when you came in here, and now you won't *tell* me." Suddenly the pouting sex kitten gave way to Diana the Huntress. "Tell me," she hissed.

Mayhew looked at his delicious interrogator. For a moment her intensity almost frightened him. Then he was overcome by it, by her. His had been a strict and starchy upbringing, and his marriage had not been born of love but of political opportunity, though his wife didn't know that. So he capitulated. Besides, he wanted to tell. What good were secrets if you couldn't share?

"Okay. I surrender."

"Lucky for you," she purred, then laughed. "Such games we have," she whispered in his ear. "You play wonderfully. Now tell!"

Having given in, characteristically he stalled. "Sure you're not looking for a story for your Swedish newspaper?"

She just looked at him. He could tell she was tiring of the delay.

"Our interests are different," he announced as if he were the first to have that particular insight. "Germany won its war in Europe and will be busy consolidating its gains for years. Our situation in the Pacific is much the same: We've won; now it's time to consolidate. There just isn't any significant conflict of interest between us, and there won't be for a long time.

"Hell, by the time they've consolidated their hold on Western Russia and the Ukraine and practically all of Europe, we'll be looking at the next century. Same for us, especially now that we have this China mess to worry about. We have no reason to interact with each other. Our paths don't cross. It's that simple."

"What about the death camps we're hearing about?"

"What about them? It's a shame what's happening there, but it's not something to start a war over." Personally he couldn't care less about the camps, but he wasn't about to admit that aloud to anybody — not when his President felt about it the way he did. Continuing with that line of thought he added, "Even my boss isn't about to throw away millions of American lives over it, and even if he wanted to Congress would never allow it. Victory in a war with Germany would not be a sure thing. Remember 1918? Germans are tough. Right now the only thing that could move us would be an invasion of England. That might do it."

"Really?"

"I know it for a fact. I heard my boss talking about it with the House Minority Leader and the Speaker. They agreed. We don't dare lose England."

"This is so exciting. You really do hear about everything, don't you?" Her fingers twined the fur on his chest.

John maintained a smug silence.

"But there's something more. I know there is. Something that nobody else knows. Now you must tell. Or . . . "

"Okay! Okay! There is something more," he said hurriedly, laughing with just a hint of nervousness. He stirred at the movement of her fingers, which were no longer on his chest.

"Can't it wait just a little while?" he panted, suddenly wanting her very much.

"If you promise faithfully . . . "

"I promise. Everything!" She was truly an artist. . . .

His next coherent words were:

"We're making this new kind of bomb . . . "

CHAPTER ONE

October 3
Berlin

"The Nazis may be crazy, but they sure can throw a parade."

Lieutenant Commander James Mannheim Martel, head of Naval Intelligence at the American Embassy in Berlin, nodded silently in grudging agreement to Major Wayne Mason, his Army counterpart, then turned back to the spectacle.

The thundering engines of the Tiger and Panther tanks, the cheering of the crowds and the insistent beat of the "Horst Wessel," theme song of the Nazi party washed over him in waves. Martel hoped it wasn't his German heritage that set his pulse to pounding in response. The thought was deeply distasteful.

After a while the Waffen SS division *Leibstandarte Adolf Hitler* passed in review, flowed around the sides of the Brandenburg Gate and down the broad Unter den Linden thoroughfare in a dark gray torrent. These were the heroes of the Russian front, the victors of Stalingrad, Astrakhan, and Baku. On this, the second anniversary of final victory in Russia, they were still heroes of the present rather than aging icons of former glory. Now more tanks, rank after rank, three abreast, roared by. Dark clouds of exhaust fumes spewed heavenward. The thunder nearly drowned the roar of the multitude.

Across the boulevard a thin line of black-clad SS guards, arms interlocked, swayed back and forth in response to the pressure of the ecstatic mob. The SS men were friendly enough, but they were also beginning to look a little desperate; it would never do to have some of the most enthusiastic patriots of the Third Reich pulped beneath the treads of a Panther—especially in front of the Führer and the international press — something that could well happen if the crowd broke through. The scene brought to Martel's mind the absurd image of a cobra tenderly protecting a baby.

The last of the tanks passed by. Next came half-tracked APCs, armored personnel carriers. Their squads of camouflage-clad infantry sat at rigid attention, immobile as statues, until they turned as one to salute the Führer, who stood on the reviewing stand, right arm outstretched. "*Sieg heil!*" roared the crowd. "*Deutschland! Führer!*"

Hitler was surrounded by his entourage — Göring, slightly ridiculous in his robin's-egg blue uniform, Goebbels, the gnomelike master of propaganda, Himmler, bloodless lips pulled back in a sardonic grin as his elite armored division rolled past, the ever-present Bormann, dressed in the brown uniform of the Party. In a wider circle around them were the field marshals, generals, industrialists, and Party hangers-on. Victory Day was the holiest day of the Nazi liturgical calendar, and the high priests of darkness reveled in their celebration of all that they had done to the world.

Again Martel became uneasily aware of how his own blood was set racing by the sense of power and glory that drenched the entire artificial drama. It was like being aroused by a woman one despised. No matter the revulsion, despite the inner certainty that never would one yield, beneath all moral rectitude there lurked a dark, compelling attraction. Again he wondered: was it his maternal heritage that made him feel this way? He very much hoped the attraction was at a more universal level, and not something peculiar to his personal history.

But how his mother would have cheered. German pride, German discipline, the Germany nation itself reborn in victory, marching in perfect unison toward its true and glorious destiny.

Martel shuddered slightly and interrupted his dark musings to thank his God that he was an American like his father before him and, again like his father, an officer in his country's navy.

It had been when traveling as part of a US Naval delegation to the German Imperial Navy that Captain Jefferson Lee Martel had met Katerina von Mannheim, he an attaché to the legendary Admiral Sims, she the daughter of a German rear admiral. After a whirlwind courtship too romantic to be quite real, they had married. Not long after had been born unto them a son, their only child, James Mannheim Martel.

Martel had always been fascinated by the two so similar and yet so different traditions that he was heir to. Had his father been the German and his mother American he might well have been part of the crowd roaring beneath him rather than a foreign military observer.

As things had actually transpired, in 1917 his American father had sailed into the North Sea, where he might have been killed by Rear Admiral von Mannheim in battle. Instead his father had returned home safe from his passage through harm's way—while not long after taking part in the "mutinous" scuttling of the German fleet rather than transfer it to the Allies, his grandfather had died a suicide.

Little Jimmy Martel had been three years old at the time of America's entry into the Great War. Yet he would never forget how, when he walked down the street holding his mother's hand, people he had first met in his very own house would turn their backs on him and his mother rather than acknowledge the existence of the Hun amongst them. His mother had not taken it well. Among her class and nation the accordance of dignity and consideration to a forlorn female "enemy national"—to say nothing of the wife of an officer of the host nation! — would have been so automatic as not to bear comment. The naively close-minded patriotism of the American middle class did not charm her aristocratic soul.

Initially, Katerina had been determined to become the American wife of an American naval officer. After America entered the fray her attitude quickly became that of an enemy alien, a prisoner of war trapped by the existence of her son. And while she loved him and fulfilled her duty to him as she saw it, she did not hide her feelings. This small continuation of the Great War lasted until 1921 when she died of diphtheria, and the boy was sent to the Outer Banks of North Carolina to live with his American grandparents. During the years that followed his father spent as much time as he could with his only child, but he was much at sea.

For the sake of her memory Jim clung fiercely to his mother's heritage, even retaining German as his second language through constant private reiteration and practice. His grandfather had encouraged him in this. Being the son of a defeated Confederate naval officer, he understood how precious lost causes could be. There was nothing disloyal in it—quite the contrary!—and Jim's father and grandparents had even agreed to Jim's spending 1932, his last year of high school, in Berlin with his mother's family. That had been the happiest year of his life, even though he had lived it against the backdrop of the gathering Nazi darkness that had culminated in Hitler's final grab for power.

After Germany had come four years at Annapolis, where he graduated third in his class. Perhaps for that reason he was chosen to spend a further two years as a junior instructor. His senior thesis on the development of German naval air reconnaissance during the First World War (a field his grandfather had helped launch) also may have been a factor. Despite his expertise in aviation however, because he could so easily pass for a native German, his advisors at Annapolis had tried to push him into naval intelligence—but it was naval aviation that drew him. Perhaps that was inevitable; his father too was a pioneer in the new discipline, having been converted to air power as a result of the 1929 Panama fleet war games in which the new carrier *Saratoga* slipped through the covering lines of battlewagons and "destroyed" the locks. The umpires of the game were later pressured into reversing their decision but some observers, including the Japanese naval attachés, had paid attention.

His old man, as Jim fondly recalled, would lecture by the hour to anyone willing to listen about the revolution to come, even after — especially after — his forcible retirement due to a heart attack. Whatever his successes at converting the rest of the Navy, his son was hooked. After flight school came Jim's assignment to the *Enterprise* as a fighter pilot. His tour began on December 5, 1941, two days before Pearl Harbor. When compression fractures to two vertebrae, the result of trying to bring in a shot-up Corsair that quit a hundred yards short of the deck, ended his flying career, he was America's number-seven ace of the Great Pacific War.

After several months in traction, Jim emerged to find that the war in the Pacific was all but over, and now that fighter aces were a drug on the market some old dark spots on his personnel folder had come back to life. Like Billy Mitchell and his own father, Jim believed that the US military, including the Navy, was paying far too little attention to the *next* war. By the time Jim was at Annapolis, no one had any doubt as to the magnitude of air power's role, but to him it was obvious that far too little attention was being paid to advanced technology. In his superiors' view to merely vocalize such opinions was bad enough — and Jim had published.

The fact that he had published under his father's name in obscure professional journals had kept him out of the hottest water, but the true authorship was an open secret —his dad's iconoclasm had not extended to airborne radar vectoring (science fiction!) nor the accelerated reaction times carriers would require when confronted by jet-powered aircraft. So while his discretion had left the brass merely irritated rather than wildly outraged, still there were some in positions of power who thought him another loudmouthed maverick in the Mitchell vein who was badly in need of a lesson in patience, and why it was a good idea to keep superiors happy.

Besides, the Navy quite validly felt that Jim was uniquely well positioned to understand just exactly what lurked in the dark underside of Nazi conquest: Europe enslaved, concentration camps, labor camps still teeming with Russian POWs, the blood-spattered basements of Gestapo headquarters, and, still only whispered about, a nightmare called "the Final Solution." Let him spend a few years out of the way, fixed so he can learn to keep his mouth shut good and proper, the thinking had gone. And so had come the posting to Berlin. To Jim's way of thinking, the worst part of it was that he couldn't keep up with the details of cutting-edge research in the USA. On the other hand there was some pretty damned cutting-edge stuff going on right here in—

As the last SS battalion passed by, Jim was pulled from his reverie by a sudden high-pitched whine that quickly rose in volume to a wailing shriek as a group of Me-262 jet fighters grouped in the shape of a swastika came roaring in, their shadows racing them down the boulevard. Mason, who was also a pilot, looked up at them with hostile envy. Jim shared Mason's envy, but was more phlegmatic about it, perhaps because he knew the plane fairly well.

Behind the 262s came a formation of less familiar shapes, and Jim abandoned his camera for his binoculars to get a closer look. He hoped his companion, who was snapping away, was doing his job right. The Germans were building three carriers, and American intelligence was still trying to figure out which planes would be adopted for seaborne operations.

As he watched, the flight of Arado 234 twin-engine jet bombers swept by, breaking from their swastika formation to climb almost vertically up through the scattering of clouds. Compared to the 262s, they did not seem all that agile, but as torpedo attack planes they would be formidable, far different from the lumbering Avengers the Americans had flown during three years of combat in the Pacific.

Jim still kept as a souvenir a picture of a young American pilot, Lieutenant George Bush, standing on the wing of a splashed Avenger. He'd flown cover for the kid while he waited for rescue. Martel smiled as he thought about him. He had been one of the youngest flight leaders in the fleet, but by God if you needed someone to lead a group straight into enemy flak like they were on rails, he was your man.

After the 234s came the twin-engine Me-510s, prop-driven ground-attack bombers, their fifty-millimeter antitank guns looking like long ugly stingers slung under the nose. Either plane would be well suited for carrier-based operations, but the Germans were keeping that part of their hand close to the chest; none of the planes flown today had the necessary arresting gear for carrier landings.

"Here come their new heavies," Mason yelled as he pointed back up the street. Martel swung his binoculars around. Below, the crowd broke into wild yet inaudible cheers as a flight of Me-264 heavy bombers thundered overhead at rooftop level. Wait . . . this was a variant on what he'd expected. Longer . . . and the wings—were they larger too? There had been rumors of a new "stretched" 264E. Clearly this was it.

For the final two years of the war England had slowly increased the pressure of night bombing with their fleets of Lancasters. Though the destruction had never seriously hindered the German war effort, Hitler had not been amused—and Göring had sworn to his Führer that never again would Germany lack the means to retaliate in kind. Next time, Jim thought sourly, both sides could dedicate massive portions of their industrial capacity to the indiscriminate slaughter of civilians.

This Me-264 variant was massive, even bigger than the American B-29s they rather resembled with their glassed-over forward canopies. Unlike the American plane, however, these were a curious mix of prop and jet: four BMW 901G radial engines and two Jumo 004 turbojets. Mason was again busy with his sixteen-millimeter camera. Like any hunter, he had focused in on a single member of the herd and was clicking away.

Though fully briefed on the standard-version specs, Martel watched in silent awe as the fast and deadly behemoths passed overhead. Earlier wisdom had been that Germany would not build a bomber fleet capable of reaching New York. The Germans, analysts had argued, simply could not afford the fuel consumption: Five hundred bombers flying five missions a month would devour one sixth of all avgas produced in the Reich. In a classic example of the perils of depending on narrow-gauge experts for strategic decision-making, the capture of Russia's Baku oil fields had changed all that. Still, it could have been worse; Intel believed that only a few 264s had been built. So far they had been pretty competent at that sort of analysis, thanks to code breaking and in-country agents — and anyway, the conclusion seemed reasonable to Martel. German air doctrine remained focused on tactical support, not strategic bombing. Furthermore, they had enough *Arados* and older twin-engine stuff to keep England quietly in her place.

As the last of the 264s passed, another even higher-pitched whine made itself heard in rapidly increasing intensity. Suddenly, gone almost in a blink, batlike forms shot across the avenue at right angles to the thoroughfare. A few oddly empty minutes in which the loudest noise was the chatter of the crowd followed. Then, "There they are!" Mason shouted excitedly.

Martel looked up past the Brandenburg Gate where Mason was pointing. A few miles away the formation that had just passed overhead was swooping around in an impossibly tight turn to come racing up the boulevard in precise single file, literally below rooftop level. He had seen the early intelligence specs, and had been specifically instructed to photograph the Gothas if they appeared. Though he would have vastly preferred to continue direct visual observation, Martel dutifully picked up his own camera and started to mimic Mason's efforts, snapping off shots and trying to keep a single plane centered in the viewfinder as they passed.

To Jim the Gothas looked utterly bizarre, and very, very threatening. Based on a flying-wing design, they had no fuselage, and in place of a tail showed only two tiny vertical stabilizers mounted on the outside trailing edges. Except for their exhaust outlets, the planes' twin engines were invisible.

Their boomerang shape, Jim thought, would be entirely at home in a Flash Gordon serial. Scary as they looked though, he knew that the Germans had discovered some serious flaws inherent in the flying-wing concept; if the *Luftwaffe* had, as rumored, really achieved supersonic velocities, they hadn't done so with flying wings. But subsonic or not, the Gothas were fast, highly maneuverable, and presented a razor-thin target silhouette when approached from astern. Martel found the mere thought of going up against them in a Corsair or Bearcat chilling.

Not that the US had entirely ceased weapons development since Martel had missed the deck of the *Enterprise*. The Navy's new FD-1 Phantoms could go head to head with any German jet yet in production—it was more than a match for the 262—but so far only a few were actually aboard the carriers. As for designs not in production, part of his job today was to write up a detailed analysis of any new German craft glimpsed during the parade. One thing he already knew would go in that report: any prop plane the Navy flew would be in for a rough time if it stumbled on one of these jet-propelled monsters; it was time and more than time to move on to the next generation of aircraft.

A carrier fleet depended for its life on its ability to knock out enemy ship killers before they got in range. With Gothas to protect them even the older bombers became a major threat. As for the Arados, if the German admiralty could arrange for Gothas to arrive in the neighborhood simultaneously with that winged annihilation . . . with Gothas flying in support, Arados might as well have been custom-made carrier killers.

As the last of the bat-shapes swept past, Martel swung his camera around to the main reviewing stand and snapped off a final human-interest shot of the fat man waving at the planes and laughing with childlike delight as he pointed out his latest toy to his Führer.

Hitler himself grinned hugely as the last of the planes whisked past, then gave a final salute to the adoring multitude lining the streets. A sea of upraised arms answered his, and the avenue echoed with chanted *Sieg heils!* as the most successful mass murderer in the history of the human race turned and disappeared down a covered exit way, his entourage scrambling for position to follow.

"Quite a spectacle," Mason reiterated, as he put away his equipment.

"Nothing succeeds like success," Jim replied while packing his own camera bag. "If the ghouls up on that stand had lost, that mob would be spitting on their memory. Perhaps one day they will anyway." Martel knew in his half-German bones that along with the sort of thoughtless jingoists so well represented out in the street this day, there were scores of millions of Germans who were secretly repulsed by all that the Nazis represented.

Mason raised his eyebrows. "Lose? The Russians were finished the day it started. It just took a little longer than expected, that's all."

Martel shrugged and started down the steps of the reviewing stand to join the crowd swarming into the middle of the boulevard, delighting in the beautifully clear autumn afternoon, when the SS security guards finally released their arm locks.

"Hey, I want you to meet this guy," Mason whispered as he grabbed Jim's arm and guided him over to a knot of SS officers he had apparently just noticed. One of them, the tallest, nodded toward the descending Americans, and the rest of the group slowed and looked up. The one who had nodded was nearly six and a half feet tall, and had a build from a football fullback's nightmare. His pale blond hair was close-cropped, almost shaved, and his face was slashed with several dueling scars.

The scarified giant smiled at Mason's approach and, unlike his compatriots, saluted in the traditional military way rather than like a Nazi. Jim returned the gesture. "Good afternoon, Major! " Though he spoke to Mason, his cold snakelike eyes had fixed on Martel, who stared straight back.

"Colonel Otto Skorzeny, I'd like to introduce Lieutenant Commander Jim Martel." Skorzeny extended his hand. Taking it, Jim was startled and annoyed by the viselike grip that was meant to embarrass and almost did, before Jim, thankful for the free-weight training that was part of his therapy, bore down in turn.

As Skorzeny released with a faint look of disappointment, Jim briefly examined his companions. All three wore SS uniforms with paratroop insignia, and looked nearly as hard, competent, and well trained as their boss. The one standing just behind Skorzeny had a face marked by dueling scars as well. Another, with ghostly white hair, was scarless but had the mashed-in nose and puffy features of a battered prizefighter. The four of them might have been taken for professional athletes in the peak of training were it not for their indefinable aura of deadliness. Jim had killed more than a few in the Pacific War, and sometimes spent ghost-ridden nights because of it, but these were killers in a far different league.

"So what did you think of our display today?" Skorzeny asked the Americans, as he flexed his fingers just a little.

Mason let Jim respond. "A lot of new designs, hugely expensive ones, I should think. I thought by now you'd be easing off a bit on the armaments."

"Peace through strength," Skorzeny replied. "If we stay

strong, there will be no future problems. Remember, Russia is still waiting on the other side of the Volga."

Peace through murder and conquest, more likely, Jim thought to himself. "I doubt they'll be a problem," he finally said aloud. "Stalin's too busy fighting resistance groups out in Siberia to want a return match."

Skorzeny laughed. "Not immediately, in any event. But in ten years? You Americans have no idea of the service we have done the world. Without us, it would be you squandering your lives and wealth fighting the Red Menace. Without us, your forces in China right now would be facing a Communist tidal wave, rather than helping the Nationalists mop up the remnant of the Maoists. The suppression of Marxism is an accomplishment for all of civilized humanity, one for which Germany deserves the highest recognition."

He looked back at his comrades, who nodded their approval, and went on. "Poland had to go before we could come to grips with the real foe. If Churchill had only understood that, our differences with England never would have occurred. Be very sure that if the Russians try again, we will be ready."

When Jim still did not seem to feel the need for any reply beyond a slight shrug the officer with the battered face interjected coldly, "The Russians are not like the Japanese you so easily squashed. You Americans think that when a war is over your Johnnies can just come marching home to glory. Yours is a fool's paradise!"

Another chimed in: "You had a romp in the Pacific. We know war."

"Lieutenant Commander Martel made twenty-three kills," Mason interjected, "and Japanese pilots were every bit as good as those in your Luftwaffe."

"No air force is or was equal to ours," the battered officer replied heatedly. "And I would like to see your Martel's performance against the RAF. *There* was an enemy to be proud of."

"Hans, Hans, let us not bandy insults with our guests,"

Skorzeny said with an ironic grin. "Besides, some of the American pilots are quite good." The way he said it made the unspoken "but not good enough" almost audible.

Having made his point Skorzeny reverted to host mode. Casually gesturing at the wings and Navy Cross ribbon on Martel's uniform, he said, "I am a pilot too, you know. In that at least we can understand each other."

"Perhaps," Jim replied with a smile of his own.

"Yes, 'perhaps,'" Skorzeny replied softly.

There was a tense moment of silence, and then Skorzeny smiled again. "Well, we had best be going. I look forward to a time when we can meet again, perhaps under less . . . constrained circumstances."

Martel devoutly hoped that any such unconstrained meeting between him and this human attack dog took place at about 20,000 feet. He was ashamed to realize that under those circumstances he would go out of his way to give the German his wish. An old and painful image rose in his mind, only this time it was this tall SS officer rather than a Japanese naval pilot batting at himself as he tumbled out of his aircraft and began the long, long fall, drenched with burning gasoline. Skorzeny, it seemed, brought out the killer instinct in others as well. . . .

Almost as if reading Jim's mind, the SS colonel nodded drolly as he and his companions turned and merged with the crowd.

As they departed, Mason snatched his camera out of its case and snapped off a quick shot. "That is one scary son of a bitch," he said quietly. "He's head of the SS's number-one commando team."

Feeling himself begin to unwind, Martel realized he'd been in an adrenal state appropriate for combat. "The guys who snatched Koniev out of Leningrad?"

"The same. Runs his operations exactly the way he sees fit, answers directly to Hitler. Even field marshals have to step aside if Skorzeny wants something." Mason paused for a second. "That wasn't his only coup, either. He pulled half a dozen other ops in Russia in the last months of the war. As a matter of fact I saw a report that he was planning to 'drop in' on Stalin if the armistice talks fell through." Mason smiled and shook his head. "What glory, if he'd succeeded. I think he was disappointed that he didn't get the chance."

Skorzeny was nearly out of sight when he turned back to cast that same ironic smile—and was gone. 'The Cheshire Commando,' Jim thought, without the least bit of amusement.

As Wayne Mason continued to rattle off his information, Jim found that the professional in him grudgingly admired Skorzeny. He was the ultimate soldier, but lost without the scent of battle to follow; to men like him, the cause for which one was fighting became nothing compared to the pure flaming joy of combat. Skorzeny was most likely in his own private hell right now. Too long without a war and he might well go mad. Jim thought about that as he said good-bye to Mason and turned to drift with the crowds, on his way to his real task of the day.

There had been a taunting challenge in Skorzeny, the self-confident arrogance of a player on a winning team who had just verbally scrimmaged with someone he would meet and surely defeat come next Saturday afternoon. It was an interesting datum, something that he would note in the contact report. Strange that it had felt so personal. . . .

After leaving Mason, Jim continued down the boulevard, passing several of the new temples to the Nazi Reich. The central section of Berlin had been hit hard by the RAF in the closing months of the war, but the rubble had long since been cleared, and now Hitler's neoclassical monstrosities were beginning to dominate the skyline. To his right just ahead, the new Party headquarters, with the beginning of what would one day be a thousand-foot dome, was just starting to rise up out of the ground. Supposedly it would take another fifteen years to bring the hideous thing to completion. Next, also on his right, the new museum for the Volkische Kunst — for "Aryan Peoples' Art" — had just opened. Nearly all its displays leaned heavily toward the new German heroic style, which in practice seemed to mean a superfluity of iron-jawed young Teutonic knights battling the hordes of darkness, alternating with saccharine scenes of buxom peasant girls tending hearth and farm.

Craftwise enough to assume he was being tailed, Martel moved casually, taking in the sights. As he strolled down the middle of the boulevard a line of young boys dressed in the brown shirts and red neckerchiefs of the Hitler Youth marched past him. They were singing the latest popular hit about the heroes of the Eastern Front. It had been given great prominence on the airwaves in preparation for Victory Day. The main point of it was that the gods must love dead Slavs because they had helped the Reich make so many of them. Theirs was the kind of religion, Martel thought dryly, that gave atheism a good name. As they marched, the boys waved their Nazi flags in time to the song's catchy beat. It looked as if venomous red, white and black butterflies swarmed over their heads.

As they marched by, several of the children looked up at him, wide eyed at the sight of an American uniform. He smiled at them until one flung a comment about American Jews. How *his* Jews were next on the list. Shocked and angered, he turned away lest he strike the little monster and create an international incident.

"Jim! Good to see you!"

A German army officer had come around the corner and bumped into him, as if by accident.

"Willi! Good to see you!" Jim extended his hand, grabbing hold of the German major's in a grasp of genuine affection.

Major Wilhelm von Metz, adjutant to Major General Hans von Oster of Admiral Canaris's Abwehr, the German center for military intelligence and counterintelligence, patted Jim on the shoulder.

As it happened, Willi was Jim's cousin. Indeed the two of them might easily be taken for brothers, though Willi had the typical pale blue eyes, high cheekbones, and aquiline nose of the Mannheim family line, while Jim, whose nose was equally aquiline and cheekbones equally high and planed, had the dark hair and gray eyes of his father. During his high school year in Germany he had lived as a fully accepted member of Wilhelm's family. Willi's mother was Jim's aunt, and he had rather adored her.

It was a relationship the Navy had known about and wanted Martel to cultivate; the Navy had reason to hope that both Wilhelm and his superior Canaris hated the Nazis and might be willing to do something about it. Jim was able to confirm this; while living with the von Metz family he had witnessed their horror at the rise of Nazism, and had often heard his aunt privately denounce the "Nazi thugs." The Mannheims were German patriots and Junkers of the old school, and the von Metz's too were fiercely patriotic, and just as proud of their military heritage, which they traced back to the army of Frederick the Great. To such as they the Nazis were gutter sweepings that in an obscene twist of fate had seized control of the Fatherland. In Willi's case, this hatred was compounded on a personal level by the loss of two older brothers who never returned from Russia.

But huge as the stakes might be, and dark the backdrop against which their little drama was played, balancing against each other the intelligence jobs their respective countries had handed them was an amusing game in some ways. Willi had let Jim know early on that he had been given the task of playing upon Jim's German heritage and family relationships in order to turn him into an asset of German Intelligence.

To string the other side along, Jim would occasionally be cleared to "let slip" a minor detail about naval equipment or designs, and very occasionally, to keep the contact hot, something major that Navy Intelligence knew was already compromised. But in von Metz's case the turning was genuine.

"I was supposed to meet Lori here after the parade," von Metz said loudly enough that he could easily be overheard. "Have you seen her? I think we must have got our directions crossed."

Directions crossed. They were definitely being followed. Jim looked around as if to help out.

"Well, I'm pretty sure she hasn't passed me, so she probably went this way," Jim replied, pointing down the street, and the two set off as if in pursuit, pushing their way through the crowd, forcing their tail, whoever he was, to fall behind.

"We won't be seeing each other again for some time," Wilhelm whispered.

"Why, are we under suspicion?"

"Not 'we.' It's you. Certain people are more interested in you than they should be. Apparently there's something in the works to damage you. That's all I know."

"Me? Just me? You're my only contact!"

"I don't have any details and we don't have time to go into it," Wilhelm replied quickly. "Just be careful."

"Careful about what?"

"I don't know. Some kind of set-up maybe."

Clearly Willi was worried for him, which added weight to his next words: "But that's minor compared to the other. Something big is up. We don't know what, but security has been tightened. Also, training schedules for units inside Russia have gone to a wartime footing, and secret amphibious and airborne assaults are being rehearsed on the shore of the Black Sea."

He slowed down for a moment, turning around as if looking for his fiancée and then took off again, with Jim following. "Even Canaris is in the dark on this," he whispered. "Internal security is higher than it was before Operation Barbarossa." Barbarossa had been the code name for the launch phase of the Reich's attack on the

Soviet Union in '41. "Expect some major code changes at the highest levels in the near future, also some—what's the English phrase? False . . . herrings?"

Despite the tension, Martel couldn't help his smile.

"Don't trust anything you hear — and not just you personally. Your entire intelligence system can expect to be the target of major spoofing.

"Oh. And one more thing. The entire operation, whatever it is, is code-named 'Arminius.'"

"It's definitely aimed toward us?"

"We think so, but we're not sure. Jim, this is our last contact for a long time. Canaris ordered me to break off with you now so that he won't be questioned later about my part in the failed effort to turn you."

Jim nodded, smiling as if the two were exchanging a casual pleasantry.

Wilhelm looked past Jim, as if seeing something else.

"I think that's Lori over there," he announced, and he started to move away. Wilhelm paused and looked back, his blue eyes filled with a distant melancholy. "If you should ever get a message from me inquiring about your father, it's a clear warning that the show's about to start. Remember that, and . . . take care, my cousin." He reached out, squeezed Jim's hand, and disappeared into the crowd.

Jim made a studied effort to appear as if nothing at all had transpired between him and his cousin other than a friendly chat while looking for a misplaced girlfriend. Slinging his camera bag over his shoulder, he continued down the thoroughfare, pausing for a moment to look in a shop window where the new television sets were on display.

Berlin had opened the world's first full-time television station the month before, and a crowd was gathered around the window watching an old propaganda film about the start of the war with Russia four years ago. The image was grainy, and the picture tube no more than a hand's span across, but even so it had a certain hypnotic quality.

One of Jim's assignments was to track down leads on a rumored Nazi superweapon, which mated a television camera and maneuvering fins to a rocket bomb. The resulting weapon would be remotely guided to its target. . . . If the Nazis had managed such a trick they had also ushered in a revolution in warfare straight out of science fiction. He watched the picture, trying to image how a maneuvering target — such as, say, a US aircraft carrier, would look on the grainy screen.

After a minute or two he turned and continued on, pausing here and there to look in shop windows that were again filled with goods. Gasoline, rubber products, and anything that required copper, brass, or aluminum were still impossible for ordinary folk to find, but the food markets overflowed with loot: Russian sausages, bread, and vodka (which had become the cheap hard liquor of Germany); fruit from the Black Sea region; French wines and the latest Parisian fashions. Even silk stockings were coming back, though they generally sold out in a few hours.

Sadly, Jim had noted that hemlines were dropping again. To his mind the effect on hemlines of the tight rationing of cloth had been one of the few real wartime benefits, both in Europe and America.

But despite the lowering hemlines the people around him seemed relaxed and happy; clearly they were enjoying the fruits of German victory — even though, Martel supposed, they could not help noticing that there were far more female celebrants than male.

Other social changes the war had created were evident as well. Under Speer's wartime economy program, rushed into effect within days of Hitler's accident, German women had filled the factories. Germany had still been playing a guns-and-butter game up until then, but instantly when given the opportunity, Speer had changed that. Within eighteen months, the most essential military production was up three hundred percent, and the majority of the labor force was female, something previously unthinkable.

Women controlled the money now and spent it as they pleased. Jim wondered how, if Germany ever did demobilize, these women would react when the former masters of the house came back home and tried to reassert control.

As he passed a beer garden, loud and boisterous singing rioted through the open doors from an interior packed with soldiers in a happy mood after the parade. He continued on with the flow of the crowd, sensing from them the same self-satisfied contentment that emanated from crowds going home after Fourth of July and Labor Day picnics.

Martel wondered how that could be. How could they not know of the horrors being perpetrated in their name all over the Reich and in the conquered territories? Slave labor starved in the East while working to fill Berlin shops. Tens of thousands were dying of overwork, malnourishment and exposure as they labored like the captives of Pharaoh on the new *Autobahn* extensions that were pushing deeper and deeper into the Ukraine and Occupied Russia. And worst of all, the camps. On the other hand, in a climate where no one dared speak "sedition" except to their closest, oldest friends, information flow would be very slow. Especially if people did not want to know. But sooner or later murder would out, the atrocities become common knowledge. What of German pride then?

Coming to the corner that housed his destination, Martel turned from the boulevard and its obscene canopy of swastikas to Old Glory where it waved above the American Embassy. As ever, he felt a certain relief at the transition to American soil, symbolic though it was. Going through the outer doors, he returned as crisply as they were proffered the salutes of the Marine guards, stepped into the main corridor, and turned to sign in at the receptionist's desk, where to his surprise Betty was waiting to meet him.

"Hi, Betts. What are you doing out here?" Normally at this time of day Betty would be busy keeping the intelligence section of the embassy running. She was one of those incredible private secretaries who wind up running the show. "Sharon sick again?"

"They asked me to sit out here, so here's where I'm sitting. How was the parade, Commander?"

"The usual," he replied as he leaned forward to scribble his name. "Lots of brass bands and marching around." Much more quietly he added, "Wait till you see the pics. If this doesn't wake people up, I don't know what could." Jim was being mildly out of line talking with her even in such vague terms, not because she shouldn't know but because they were arguably in a public place, deserted though it was.

Betty McCann looked up at him with a smile. "Hey, Lover, one lieutenant commander, even one as gorgeous as you, can't take the whole weight of national defense policy on his shoulders."

When he hardly smiled in return, nor reminded her that though they might have an understanding they were not lovers, and by the way why not? she too turned serious. "You and I have gone over the specs for those planes, Honey. As far as our side is concerned we wrote the book on German jets. You've even drawn schematics. Surely just seeing them in flight didn't add that much?"

"Seeing them made it real. Betty, I'm telling you. We're in trouble, and if we don't wake up to that fact and do something about it, we could wind up fighting a war in the continental USA."

"Jim, it's not that bad."

"Not quite. Not yet."

For a moment Betty seemed at a loss for words, as if she wanted to reassure him, but not falsely. She understood too well the profound implications behind Jim's concern, and suspected that the vision of Nazi air power he had just experienced would have had a similar effect on her. "Nothing much we can do here, though, except stay on top of developments and do our jobs," she finally ventured.

"Betts, I think my dad might soon be moved to write another article, and this one not for *Defense Analysis Quarterly*."

Betty's face fell. "Jim, don't. They're mad enough at you already."

Jim shrugged. Frankly, he wasn't sure an article such as he had in mind would have any desirable effect, while he was pretty sure it would permanently blight his career. Also he realized that he would have to be awfully damned careful to avoid references to anything he had learned as a matter of performing his duties as an intelligence officer . . . which would include about everything that would give such an article credibility. "Oh, hell, you're as right as you usually are. I'd just cancel myself out of the equation without doing any good." He smiled lopsidedly. "When they assigned me to intel they really muzzled me good, didn't they? Good thing I have you. . . ."

"Me too." Betty smiled sympathetically, then turned impish: "And I have my sights set on an admiral of the fleet, my boy — an admiral who has done it all, up close and personal. I *don't* have my sights set on a defrocked flyboy history teacher stuck in some out-of-the way school because he resigned under a cloud!" Despite her attempted humor, clearly Betty shared his frustration over the way so many in high places would rather stick their heads in the sand than admit error, or even admit a failure in their own omniscience.

Looking at her, feeling both her emotional support for him personally, and her shared concern for their country, Jim regretted more than ever embassy policy on liaisons between staffers. He and Betty would be seeing a lot of each other as soon as they both were out of this place, and it was very damned irritating that in public they had to settle for a friendly bonhomie, while aside from a couple of carefully coordinated vacations their "private" times were limited to working over intelligence files. Once, on a Berlin street, while Jim and Willi were setting up a meet, Betty had happened upon them. Impulsively they had ducked into a shop for a cup of tea—and were asked about it the next day, with a strong hint that a repetition, even a repetition without Willi, would be frowned on very darkly indeed. As if it wouldn't be better for staffers to spend some lonely hours together rather than to be constantly subjected to temptation by the local talent, some of which was quite gorgeous. Not that the locals weren't equally forbidden, but still, the —

"Jim, could I see you for a minute?"

Jim's musings flash-evaporated as he looked over his shoulder at Steve Acres, the head of military intelligence. Supposedly Steve was a mid-level State Department functionary and came complete with the usual (though in his case phony) Yale credentials. In fact, in other times and places he would again wear the single star of a brigadier general of the US Army.

Something was wrong. Before Jim could respond to his request, Acres had turned away from him and was walking back to his office. As he followed Acres through the double doors into the heart of the embassy, Jim felt his hackles begin to rise. When (crossing the small reception area that held Betty's desk to do so) they had entered Acres's office and Jim saw that there were two others in the room, they rose even more.

One of them, Harriman, his name was, Jim vaguely recognized as an intelligence agent with the OSS. He wasn't around much, and didn't mingle when he was. The other was a complete stranger, though he seemed to recognize Martel—and looked at him as if he were a piece of rancid meat.

Without benefit of introductory niceties the stranger stated baldly, "You met with von Metz this afternoon." As he made this announcement he pointed peremptorily to a chair set in the middle of the room.

Jim looked over at Steve.

"Jim, this is Mr. Grierson. He's here to ask you some questions."

Jim sat, but otherwise ignored Grierson. "Steve, what the hell is going on here?"

"Lieutenant Commander Martel, I asked you a question," Grierson said grimly. "You would be well advised to answer it."

Still ignoring his interrogator, Jim continued to gaze levelly at his boss.

"Jim, you are to answer Mr. Grierson's question without hesitation."

Jim turned in his chair to face Grierson. "Sure. I met with von Metz. If you check the contact report that I turned in yesterday you'll see that I already had the meeting arranged."

"What did you discuss with him?"

Jim looked back at Acres.

"Sir, is there a problem here?"

"Martel, I'm asking you a question," Grierson snarled, "so stop looking to General Acres for help like you're Charlie McCarthy sitting on his knee."

Jim swung around and stood up. "Listen buddy, back off."

"Jim!"

Jim turned and looked back at Acres.

"You've been accused of a breach in security," Acres said. "Grierson came in this morning from the States to check it out. Just answer the questions."

Stunned, Jim looked back at Grierson, who now pointedly ignored him as he spoke to Harriman. "You followed Martel today?" Grierson asked.

Harriman nodded.

"After the parade he met von Metz. The two suddenly took off through the crowd and I fell behind. They talked for several minutes and then parted company."

"So? We should stand motionless, talking in loud clear voices? He had sensitive information. That was the point of the meeting!"

"And what was that information, Jim?" General Acres asked, holding his hand up for Grierson to be silent.

"Something is starting to move. Willi's not sure what. Training schedules for troops inside of Russia have been stepped up. Amphibious assault rehearsals on the Black Sea coast. Internal security is tightening up, the same way it did before they went into Russia. Their coding system is scheduled for a major overhaul. Even Canaris is being kept in the dark. One hard fact: The code name for this operation is 'Arminius.'"

"'Arminius,'" Acres repeated, looking back quizzically at Jim.

"You probably remember it from your Academy days. The German leader during the reign of Augustus. Annihilated Varus's legions in the Teutoburger Forest."

"What's the target?"

"Maybe us. Probably us. Von Metz wasn't sure."

Grierson laughed sarcastically. "That's it?"

Jim started to report on von Metz's personal warning, then decided to omit that for the moment. If he was suspected of a leak, then a leak there almost certainly was —somewhere. If word of a personal warning got back to German intel, it might be just what they needed to nail his cousin. "That's about it."

"Martel, we've been filtering reports like that since the war ended. Why should we take this one seriously? Hell, we're the last thing the Germans want to take on."

"What about this amphib report?" Acres asked the civilian. "Do the British know about this? With Churchill looking to be back in office the Germans might be having preemptive thoughts about England."

"We've been getting those reports as well," Grierson replied disdainfully. "Our assessment is that they're prepping a move into Kazakhstan for more oil. The amphib's for moving some divisions directly across the Caspian Sea; training in the Black Sea would be the obvious place."

Grierson turned and looked back at Jim.

"What did you and your German relative really talk about?"

"I told you."

"Nothing else?"

"Nothing. I was doing my job."

"I've already looked at the initial contact report for today," Grierson said, casually revealing that he had access to General Acres's files.

Acres barely flinched.

Grierson looked over at Harriman and nodded a dismissal. Harriman stood without comment and exited. As he watched him go, Jim felt as though he were watching something wet that crawled in the dark. The worst part of it was knowing that if the tables had been turned—as they easily could have been — he would have been the one doing the tailing and reporting. Suddenly he was hip deep in the filthy reality that underlay all cloak-and-dagger games. He didn't like it, or himself, much just then. He longed to be a pilot again.

As the door closed on Harriman, Grierson burst rudely in on Jim's thoughts. "Martel, are you familiar with recent developments in radar equipment used for spotting submarine periscopes and snorkels?"

"Yes."

"How and why?"

"I was briefed on it four months ago. One of my assignments was to find out if the Germans knew about our design, the frequencies we were using, and whether they had developed radar-detection gear for their submarines."

"What about acoustically guided torpedoes?"

"I wasn't briefed on that, but I *was* supposed to find out if they were developing submarine noise makers. That made it pretty obvious that we or the Brits were working on acoustical guidance."

"Why?"

Acres interjected. "Jim, we've gotten feedback from other sources —"

"General!"

"Mr. Grierson. He's the best operative I've got. This

whole thing is a bunch of crap. Chances are the Nazis got the information Stateside. Since the Pacific War ended it's become a damn sieve back there. This whole thing is most likely an FBI screw-up."

So Grierson was FBI. Very high-up FBI. No wonder Acres had hesitated to cross him.

"The leak originated here in Berlin. That points to one person. Him."

"Am I being charged with something?" Jim asked sharply. "If so I have a right to know—or are you picking up a few tricks from the Gestapo?" He regretted the words almost immediately, and not just because of what came next. He knew very well the difference between even a hardnose like Grierson and a genuine secret-police thug.

"Lieutenant Commander James Martel, under the Espionage Act of 1941 you are hereby charged with delivering classified information to a foreign power. You are under arrest. You will be escorted back to the United States where you will face a military court martial. Prior to that court martial some people in my division want to have a long, long talk with you. A plane is waiting at Templehof." Grierson went to the back door of Acres's office and, with a bit of flourish, knocked on it. The door opened and two more men in civilian garb stepped in.

"Martel, these two men will escort us to the plane and back to the States. They have been ordered to kill you rather than let you escape, and believe me, should the occasion arise they will happily carry out that order."

Stunned, Jim looked back at Acres.

"Just cooperate, Jim. I'll get things moving on my end. You'll be cleared of this within a week, maybe two." In the long months to come James Martel would often recall that empty promise.

CHAPTER TWO

November 6
Reykjavik, Iceland

President Andrew Harrison sat in his high, straight-backed chair waiting for his undiplomatically tardy opposite number. As he stared into the fireplace's contained conflagration he unconsciously attempted to impose some sense of order on the flickering shadows capering before him, but he had no more success in that than he had ever had in imposing a pattern on the remarkable series of events that had led to this meeting and whatever would follow.

Hardly more than a year ago he had been the Junior Senator from Nebraska. Now he was President of the United States. To this day, that title—his title, President of the United States — still evoked the image of Franklin Delano Roosevelt, and no other. But when the Japanese surrendered and The Great Pacific War was won at last, FDR suddenly announced his retirement and as a last exercise of his extraordinary political power had virtually anointed his own successor: Andrew Harrison III.

Right now the sitting President wished that Franklin still had his old job. The whole world might pay a terrible cost for any mistakes made here today.

There were others, seemingly better qualified, that he could have picked, Harrison mused, but I was from the West and could corral our own New Isolationists, and maybe take a little wind out of the sails of the Western Republicans. Someone from Pennsylvania, Ohio, or Missouri just would not have fit the bill. And so here he was.

Fifteen minutes past three. Forty-five minutes late. It was deliberate of course, but annoying for all that. Before long he would have to take official notice.

To distract himself, and because it stirred a memory of another clock and another mantel, Harrison stood up and examined the clock over this one. Lincoln had his log cabin, he thought, and I my sod hut on the prairie. His campaign managers had made much of that during the '44 campaign: the farmer's son versus the slick New York City lawyer. It had played very well, and rather remarkably it was all true.

This mantel clock reminded him of his mother's precious memento of her elegant life back East, one of the few heirlooms that had survived the journey to northwestern Nebraska. She had kept the brass frame of that clock polished to a shine that rivaled burnished gold, and it stood out like a diamond in their earth-walled hut. As a child he had stood before it, watching the hands trace their endless course, carrying with them a mystery of time and memory, and all the promise and pain that such mysteries held.

Before he was fully grown it had held other memories as well, of its chiming the midnight hour while tuberculosis took her from them, his father holding his hand as she slipped into the night. He could remember its chiming the next day as he and his father made her coffin and together lifted it into the wagon to take her up the knoll to the family resting place, where two sisters now had their mother back again.

That clock, so ornate and out of place with its gaudy Victorian styling, held the place of honor on the fireplace mantel in the Oval Office. He smiled at the thought. The weekly ritual of winding it always brought to him the hint of a memory of a childhood caress from a mother now fifty years at rest beneath the Nebraska sod. For those few moments it was as if she were still watching over him and demanding excellence in her stern yet gentle way. He had wound it before coming here; it would still be marking its course and his when he returned.

A door opened. Resisting a momentary impulse to behave like an ordinary mortal, Harrison deliberately kept his back turned. After several seconds a throat cleared impatiently. The President of the United States remained motionless — then finally turned and stared unwaveringly into the eyes of Adolf Hitler.

He had met him yesterday, but that was mere ritual. Even after the press had been shepherded out, there were still all the staffers, the military liaisons, the aides, and the routine of sitting at the long table exchanging genial platitudes. Now they were alone and it was for real.

He studied his enemy closely. He had aged a great deal since the accident, but his were still the cold remorseless eyes of a shark on its unceasing search for prey. His shoulders were hunched, the left side of his face bore a blaze of scars from the plane crash that had almost killed him on December 6, 1941, the day before Pearl Harbor.

Neither Harrison nor the rest of the world could say for certain how different it all might have been if that plane crash had never happened. But Hitler knew. And Roosevelt had guessed about it, often speculating that if Hitler had been in charge during those crucial weeks in December of 1941 Germany might well have declared war on the United States. When Roosevelt spoke of it, it was in an almost wistful tone, as if he had actually wanted a two-front war. The thought of such a fight made Harrison shudder, but then again, things would have been settled now, one way or the other. Much as he may have wanted it, Roosevelt had not even attempted to get Congress to declare war against Germany. Congress had demanded blood in the Pacific, but thought that one war at a time was quite enough.

The plane crash had dashed Roosevelt's hope that Hitler would take care of the problem for him. Hitler had spent several weeks in a coma, during which time a triumvirate composed of Göring, Goebbels, and Halder had taken charge. Realizing that they were on the edge of disaster in Russia, far from declaring war on the USA, the three immediately declared an end to unrestricted submarine warfare in the Atlantic, thereby blocking Roosevelt's hope for a final provocation. Next they had pulled off a masterful strategic withdrawal along the entire Russia front, falling back before the offensive of the Russian Siberian divisions.

Had the German army followed the dark romanticism of Hitler's vision and never relinquished an inch of conquered territory, it was generally agreed, the *Wehrmacht* would have pretty much ceased to exist in the East. Instead, the Russians wound up exhausted and overextended, and the Nazi offensive was renewed in the spring. Meanwhile America, Russia's only real hope, had become fully committed in the Pacific. Before Hitler had recovered enough to resume power, the ruling triumvirate had managed to ameliorate and block the worst of Himmler's SS atrocities as well, committing the Reich to a quasi-independent Ukraine. Result: thirty-nine divisions of Ukrainian and anti-Communist Russians in the Nazi ranks. It did not matter that after the war the SS gained back its power in the eastern occupied lands. The war by then was already won. The result was inevitable. In '43 Russia threw in the towel, the Churchill government collapsed, and shortly thereafter England agreed to a remarkably lenient armistice.

A happy Congress breathed a sigh of relief and congratulated itself for steadfastly ignoring Roosevelt's urgent suggestion after Pearl Harbor to move more forcefully to the aid of England—to say nothing of aiding the Communists. The military, of course, was pleased with the result as well, since they could concentrate fully on the Japanese. This was especially true for the Navy; the total conquest and absolute submission of the Japanese was a personal thing for every American sailor from King and Nimitz on down.

So now it is I who must deal with this man.

"How do you come to speak such fluent German?" Hitler finally asked, in heavily accented English.

"I studied at Heidelberg before the First War," Harrison replied. "Given world events, it seemed a good idea to maintain fluency."

"Good! My English is terrible," Hitler responded in his own language. Apparently now satisfied with Harrison's linguistic abilities, Hitler nodded a curt dismissal to the uniformed aide who had entered with him.

Harrison motioned to the small round table by the fire. Hitler preceded him to it and sat down.

"So. Did you like Heidelberg?" Hitler asked.

"It was one of the happier times of my life. I stayed in touch with several of my professors after the war, until they were arrested in '34."

"Student days," Hitler said with a sigh, ignoring the hint of anger. "I never had them. My school was the trenches of Verdun and the Somme."

"I was in those trenches too," Harrison replied coolly. "Perhaps we . . . saw one another."

"No, no, I never saw an American unit." He waved his hand dismissively. "So what did you learn of us Germans? At school, I mean."

"I learned that the German passion for organized efficiency is the most intense of any people on the planet."

Hitler smiled. "That includes military efficiency."

"Yes. For good or ill, Germans are very efficient."

"You studied history, didn't you?"

"Yes. I specialized in 19th-century Germany, as it happens."

Could it be that Hitler had not immersed himself in the personal history of the American president he was about to meet? On reflection Harrison decided it was *not* possible. So what was he trying to accomplish with this? Soften him up with kindness and attention after the initial insult of being forty-five minutes late? God knew that tyrants had underestimated America and its leaders before, but this was ridiculous.

"Why are you not then a professor?"

"Oh, I was years from my doctorate, not even sure I wanted one. An opportunity for foreign study had come up and I took it, is all. Then came the war. Like you, I was gassed and spent nearly a year in the hospital. By the time I came home I had become more focused on practical things. I completed my Bachelor's and that was that."

The President laughed inwardly. What harm in letting Hitler think he was cozened? It was plausible enough. Other world leaders had fallen for the Hitlerian charm, and Americans were notorious suckers for pretended empathy.

At that moment, however, Hitler again changed tack. "If you know our history, then you know *why* we must be efficient at war. We have no natural boundaries. Only the strength of our army stands between us and the East. As it was in Frederick's time, so it remains today. We are the guardians of the West. The world should not forget that.

"As to the land we took, it was being used haphazardly; we have already doubled prewar crop production in Poland and will do far better in Russia. It was our destiny to control those lands."

"Are you presenting a justification for your conquests?"

Hitler smiled. "I don't need to justify an accomplished fact, any more than you Americans need to justify to me your treatment of your Indians. We control Russia to the Volga, except for the pocket we permitted Stalin around Moscow and back through Gorky. In the west our natural border has been restored and the French are now our allies. On both frontiers we have accomplished what I set out to do."

"Africa?"

"What concern is Africa to either you or me? It's a land of barbarian *Untermenschen*. Let the French and the Italians control it. It suits them."

"If it is of no interest, then why did you take Southwest

Africa and Tanganyika as part of the armistice agreement with England?"

"It was the final stain of Versailles. It had to be rectified."

Harrison hesitated to show too much concern about that region. Whenever the Germans became fully aware of the value of the Belgian Congo's uranium deposits, the richest in the world, that would be soon enough. No need to help them along. "Let's not take our time rehashing the past. I'm more concerned with the future, particularly the future of our two countries."

Hitler stood up and walked over to the giant map that lined the far side of the room.

Such a strange map. Germany was a red smear reaching across the Vistula to engulf what had once been Poland and Lithuania. Latvia and Estonia were marked with the orange of allies as was Occupied Russia and the new puppet state of the Ukraine.

Yugoslavia had disappeared. Slovenia and Dalmatia had been thrown to Italy, while the other provinces had been divided into small independent states ruled from Berlin. Hungary, Bulgaria, and Rumania had also taken small pieces of the former Yugoslavia from their master's table.

In the West, Belgium, Holland, Luxembourg and Denmark were now states within the greater Reich. France had been rewarded for its complaisance with continued existence — as a lapdog whose coastal harbors and airfields from Brest to Dunkirk were occupied by German forces. In all of Europe west of the Urals, only Spain, Portugal, Switzerland and Sweden had some semblance of true independence — and all four knew that they existed now only because the man who stood before the map willed it so. Sure, it would take eighty divisions to conquer the Swiss, but what were eighty divisions to Hitler in a world at "peace"?

But still there was England, marked in green, pugnaciously defiant off the coast. "I don't like this talk of Churchill coming back as Prime Minister," Hitler said, his eyes locked on the one aspect of this new map of Europe that displeased him.

Harrison shrugged, said nothing.

"He caused the last crisis, you know."

"Oh? I thought it was your invasion of Poland."

"Poland was needed for living space and as preparation against Russia. We had no quarrel with England, and wanted none. It was that damnable Churchill who pushed it even after I carefully allowed his army to escape and offered him peace after Dunkirk. Now the stupid British want him back again!"

"And what do you propose to do about it if his party wins the election?"

"Rather, I should ask what you would do," Hitler replied.

Harrison was blunt. "If you attack England we will declare war on you—and this time we won't be diverted by affairs in the Pacific."

Hitler laughed. "Your Congress is tired of war, and your people are too. You Americans have your peace and want to keep it. I don't think your war mongering would garner much support."

"And I think it will," Harrison replied, even though he and the man facing him both knew it was a lie. If America had one lasting tradition, it was that of immediately demobilizing after a war. The Navy had already seen its vessels reduced by nearly half, and the Army had gone from thirty-five divisions to twelve—eight of which were still on occupation duty in the Pacific, or holding positions along the China coast to support the Nationalists. In the first flush of both electoral and military victory Harrison had not resisted demobilization very much. He now was coming to understand the enormity of his error. Half a navy and four ready divisions to face the Beast that crouched over Europe.

"May I recite to you what your current operational levels are?" Hitler said in a voice so cordial as to constitute mockery. The man's intuitive grasp of his interlocutor's mental processes filled Harrison with sour admiration. It was as if he did indeed have the ability to read an opponent's mind. Harrison recalled vaguely that breeding for telepathic ability was a principal tenet of the demented Nazi ideology. Could all that have happened to the world be a direct result of this man mistaking his own intuitive genius for *telepathy*?

"But there's no need of this," Hitler continued, his voice again shifting to a "genuinely" friendly tone. "Our interests are, in fact, the same. As to our points of disagreement, they are minor."

"And those interests are?"

"Peace. I want peace the same as you. Nowhere on this Earth"—he pointed back toward the map—"is there any geopolitical crisis point between us. Our interests don't extend beyond Europe. Yours are defined by the Monroe Doctrine, which we are willing to respect."

"Though you lend material support to Argentine Fascists, and are making strong efforts in Mexico, while the French are building up their base in Martinique." As aviation advanced, airfields on islands such as Martinique and Grenada would pose a greater and greater threat to Latin America and the Panama Canal.

"Friendly diplomacy," Hitler replied, "nothing more—and as for Martinique, quarrel with the French, not with me. And you Americans are not without sin. Only last month we caught one of your OSS spies in the Ukraine. We shot him of course."

"I know nothing about that," Andrew lied. The man had been their key contact into the Jewish underground and was instrumental in gathering evidence on what the Jewish community had begun calling the Holocaust. The agent had managed to get out several hundred photos and four and a half minutes of grainy eight-millimeter film showing a death factory near Kiev. The film, with its nightmare images of mounds of bodies, black smoke, and roaring crematoriums, had run counter to everything he had ever thought he knew about a culture that could produce Goethe, Beethoven and Schiller.

"What I do know something about is this," Harrison said coldly. He reached into his briefcase, pulled out a folder of photographs, and tossed them onto the table. Hitler walked over and looked down at them with an attitude of polite curiosity. When he recognized them for what they were, he waved his hand disdainfully and turned back to the map.

"Cheap Jewish and Communist propaganda. Staged and passed to that agent you know nothing about. Shocking that they would kill so many people for the sake of verisimilitude, don't you think?"

"There's hundreds more like these, and thousands of pages of testimony as to what your SS is doing in Russia and the Ukraine."

Hitler turned, looked straight at Harrison, and smiled. "I know nothing about that."

"But we *do*!" Harrison slammed his fist on the table.

Hitler, for one brief second, seemed shocked by Harrison's reaction. Then he came back to the table and leaned against it, bracing his balled fists on its edge. "Do you want to have a war over these lies?" With a rude brush of his hand he swept the photos off the table. "I doubt, President Harrison, that you'd get more than a hundred votes in your Congress, most of them already in the pockets of New York Jewish financiers, who are the true enemies. And you do not have the power to declare war on your own." He laughed softly at that absurd weakness.

"I am going to make this information public."

"Go ahead. A fair number of your people will applaud."

Harrison sat back in his chair, physically sickened, by the photographs, the reality that underlay them, and most of all by the almost playful nondenial. Perhaps that explained his next, ill-advised words.

"You have no idea of the character of Americans," he

said in an almost conversational tone. "You have no idea of what we are, or what we stand for. We might not be able to stop what you're doing inside the land you control, not yet, but by God we won't let it spread."

"You—*you?*—threaten the *Reich?*" Hitler swelled like a venomous reptile. His rages were legendary. "Do you think we fear your mongrel nation? I hope you intended to start a war here today, because that is what you have done!" His fist too slammed the table. Louder, harder. He turned to leave.

Harrison watched as he stalked toward the oak door at the far side of the room. He knew it was histrionics, part of the famous act. He also knew that Hitler would back up those histrionics with all the power of what was at this moment the world's greatest military machine. As for him, his administration was barely ten months old, and he was less than popular. The Isolationists and others who smelled a chance at last to undo all that Roosevelt had accomplished would surely accuse him of creating a new crisis as a diversion. As for his own party, they still looked to FDR as their leader, and might well accuse his successor of triggering an incident out of lack of experience or, worse yet, simple stupidity. Support for war in the military was nonexistent; given the current state of military preparedness they knew too well what odds they would face.

Harrison stood and uttered a single word, thereby performing the most difficult act of his life.

"Wait."

Hitler turned, even as his hand touched the door.

"Did you say something?"

"Let us continue with our discussion."

"Why? You have made your intentions clear."

"I don't want a war. The purpose of this meeting was to ensure that we don't have one."

Hitler nodded slowly, as if his better, more statesmanlike self were coming to the fore. "That was my intention as well," he finally said, and walked halfway back to the table. "How then shall we have peace?"

Harrison drew a long slow breath. "We need to find common ground. First you must understand that England's continued independent existence is a vital interest of the United States. I promise you that you will find my congressional support not so flimsy after all, if England is attacked."

"That at least I can understand." Hitler paused theatrically. "Very well then," he continued grandly, as if offering a major concession: "England may live—and keep her tottering Empire too. But they, and you, must cease all interference with the Reich's internal concerns. That is *our* vital interest."

"There are also matters to be discussed regarding Africa, Argentina and Mexico, and the right of refugees to leave Europe."

"Details. But your OSS's clandestine support of terrorists, and your pressure against our French allies, must stop."

"Yes . . . our staffs can deal with such things later," Harrison replied, suddenly very weary. He wanted to sit again, but would not while Hitler stood before him.

"Then we are agreed in principle," Hitler announced. "There are grounds for mutual understanding between us."

"Yes." Harrison had known from the beginning that something like this was about the best he could have hoped for. Still, he had the nagging feeling that Franklin would have done a better job, and not left Hitler in a mood to gloat.

"Good. After dinner we'll talk again and our staffs can start their work."

"Very well."

"Your German is excellent," Hitler said, as if they were now close friends again. "Our universities are still the best. In fact—do you know Speer?"

"I know of him."

"My Minister of Strategic Planning and Industry. Like you, he is a Heidelberg graduate. He heard me speak there, back in the early days, and joined the party. Your university has provided some of my best planners. Since they took over in '42 Speer and his staff have worked wonders."

"I'm sure they have," Harrison replied.

In fact some of those wonders they had produced were now the American President's chief concern; new German superweapons were beginning to pose a severe threat to nearly every aspect of American military technology, especially in rocketry and the secret weapons of the Luftwaffe.

"You will meet Speer tonight. You can catch up on old times."

"He was there after I was. I don't think we'll have much in common," Harrison replied coolly, struggling to regain some semblance of control of the flow of events.

"This evening, then," Hitler replied curtly over his shoulder, as if issuing an order as he turned and stalked out of the room.

Harrison turned and went out the opposite door and stepped into the antechamber where his staff was gathered. "Gentlemen," he announced coldly, "before long we're going to have to fight that son of a bitch, and we'd better be ready."

Hitler stormed into the suite where his inner circle waited. As those waiting for him came to their feet he snarled, "We return to Germany tomorrow. Operation Arminius goes forward."

CHAPTER THREE

November 10
FBI "Safe House," Manassas, Virginia

He seemed to be floating several feet above the floor of a medieval torture chamber, hovering weightless over a scene of Boschian horror. Below him, damned souls incarnate writhed in agony, screamed in anguish . . . but there was no sound. As he drifted through the chamber he could see victims stretched out on racks while dark demons capered about them, mocking and laughing. Other victims ran hopelessly about, trailing fire as other devils pursued them, howling in silent delight.

He floated to the door — was it by an act of will? He wasn't sure — and it creaked open — sound — there was sound now; from the next room he heard screams. Now he was afraid. Terror like a gnawing rat ripped into his soul, but he could not turn back; invisible hands pulled him into the lower pits of darkness.

Here the demons were of a different breed, more humanlike, clothed in black, their faces pale slashes in the night. Their tools of torment were far more modern than those of the level above: electric sparks crackled around their howling victims, glistening needles filled with evil plunged into writhing forms strapped to stainless-steel gurneys; naked humanity in endless procession stumbled forward to their appointed doom, curling whips and snarling dogs driving them into brightly lit tiled rooms. Iron doors slammed shut. A hissing whisper like the threat-warning of a venomous snake issued from the next room, to be instantly drowned out by gasping hysterical screams. Through a filth-smeared porthole he could see the distorted face of one of the damned, clawing at the glass with bloody fingers, scratching frantically, digging for air, for life, even as its features rotted into yellow corruption. A guard by the door looked up. His open-mouthed leer revealed a red, gaping emptiness.

"Room for one more. . . ."

Floating above the door like a lost soul he screamed in terror and anguish for all that was lost, for the death of all, for himself.

"MARTEL!"

James Martel reached up with a cry, grasping hold of the hand at his shoulder.

"Come on, Martel, wake up."

Reality started to take hold. The man standing over his cot looking down at him with such cool disdain was Special Agent Brubaker. His eyes were red rimmed from too many cigarettes, too much coffee, and too little sleep. He'd obviously been working hard for a long time.

"Sweet dreams, Martel?"

Jim struggled for composure. He had held out against this man and his tag-team partner for weeks, and he felt a stab of shame for breaking, even a little, even in a dream. "Bathroom," Martel whispered, shrugging his interrogator's hand off his shoulder.

"Sure."

Martel stood on shaky legs and half-staggered the ten feet to the bathroom portal. There was no door, and though he had lived for several years on board naval ships the lack of privacy under these circumstances bothered him. Having given his permission, Special Agent Brubaker, who had been with him since Berlin, stood in the middle of the room, watching boredly as Jim relieved himself and then splashed cold water on his face. He looked into the rather large mirror set directly into the wall. His face, illuminated by the harsh glare of a single bare bulb, was drawn and pale. A week's stubble gave him the look of a wandering vagrant rather than that of a lieutenant commander in the United States Navy. His mouth was gummy and foul tasting. He ran his tongue against the back of his teeth and looked back at Brubaker. He longed for the common decency of a toothbrush, but would be damned if he'd ask.

He stepped back out into the room. He wanted to know the time of day, but was damned if he'd ask for that either. Without waiting for the inevitable instruction, Martel turned toward the table at the far side of the room, and was surprised to see a second person on the other side of it, obscured by the glare of the lamp that was aimed at the chair on the near side. Apparently the new interrogator had come in after Martel had collapsed into exhausted sleep.

Then he recognized him.

"Grierson."

Grierson nodded. Reaching into the pocket of his double-breasted jacket, he produced a pack of Lucky Strikes and held them out.

Forgetting to hide his eagerness, Jim took the proffered pack, put a cigarette in his mouth and inhaled deeply when Grierson lit it with his Zippo, which was embossed with the emblem of the FBI.

"I just want to run over a few questions with you, Martel."

"Your boys tell you I'm ready to break and it's time to come in and get all the credit?" Jim asked, trying to sound calm and invulnerable, knowing he was doing a poor job of it.

"You know the game, Martel. We don't like doing this."

"I just bet you don't." Jim nodded toward Brubaker. "Too bad the Constitution holds back your thug over there from doing a really good job. I can think of at least one country that he'd love to work for."

Brubaker started to reach angrily over the table to grab Martel but desisted at a peremptory wave from Grierson.

Martel smiled coldly at his frustrated tormentor. The

man had stayed at least arguably within the letter of the law at all times, but Martel knew that Brubaker would love to be unleashed.

"You're the expert on the Nazis, Martel," Brubaker said.

"Right. I'm the expert. They'd recruit you in a minute."

Martel's gaze shifted back on Grierson. "You know I'm clean. You've had me down here now a month at least, including this last week of nonstop interrogation. And what have you got to show for it? I'm willing to bet the heat's on to clean this thing up, to pin something on me and get me out of the way. But I'm just not cooperating, am I? And if you can't prove I did it, the leak must have happened back here in the States, and that would mean you guys screwed up."

A glance passed between Grierson and his helper. "We're just doing our job, Martel. Nothing personal. There've been leaks, serious ones, and all the little arrows point to you." Grierson paused for a moment, as if mastering impatience. "Aren't you getting tired of this game, Martel? Why don't you just come clean? Admit what you did and I'll see you get off light." He smoothed his features into something like friendly neutrality. "Martel — maybe we've been taking the wrong tack here. Maybe you just overheard something by accident and passed it on without thinking. We could go to bat for you, Martel. There's this place out in Nevada for people who have heard things they shouldn't have. You could spend the next couple of years there, then be on your way. You'd be comfortable, plenty of good food, women even! It's a real nice place, more like a resort than anything else, very pleasant. You could be there in a couple of days, getting fat and tanned. How about it, Martel? Just give us what we need. Medal of Honor winner like you, we could get you that good life easy. After a year or two you'd be free as a bird."

"It was a Navy Cross."

"What?"

"I didn't do anything to deserve a Medal of Honor. But I earned my Navy Cross."

For a moment Brubaker looked confused, then shook his head impatiently. "Look, stop changing the subject, Martel."

"I didn't do it. And you know it."

"We have all the time in the world, Martel."

Jim sighed and lowered his head.

"On May seventh you met with Wilhelm von Metz and gave him design specifications for the new Midway-class carrier, in particular details related to the armored decking and below-the-waterline armor belting."

"We've gone through this a hundred times already, and you *know* it's a crock. My initial contact report clearly shows I was ordered to do so through Naval Intelligence to justify von Metz's contact with me to his superiors. The information had been compromised here in the States. My guess is through a construction worker." He paused. "You guys must have messed up."

Grierson ignored the dig. "What about the tracking specifications for the Mark 23 acoustical torpedo?"

"Nothing. I've told you that a hundred times!" Martel didn't add that some years ago for an entirely different application he had invented and his father had patented the basic feedback mechanism without which the device would not be practicable.

"The meeting with von Metz on June nineteenth, the fusing systems on the same torpedo?"

"We never met on June nineteenth."

"Are you certain? My records say you did."

"Bullshit."

"I heard you say it, Martel," Brubaker interjected. "June nineteenth."

"You're wrong—hell no, you're not wrong; you're lying. We never met on June nineteenth, and I never said we met on June nineteenth."

"Cut the crap, Martel."

Suddenly some internal gauge in Martel redlined.

"Maybe you sons of bitches would like to know where I was on December fifteenth, 1943. I was fifteen thousand feet over Leyte Gulf. A Zero slipped onto my six and put three rounds into my engine and one into my seat-back. I flew that aircraft back two hundred miles with seven rivets in my back and the oil pressure dropping every minute. That's what *I* was doing, you son of a bitch, and it's a goddamned good thing that the crash boat was there because even if my back hadn't cracked on impact, I'd lost too much blood to climb out of the cockpit. *Where were you* that *day, you slinking stay-at-home bastards?*" He glared at Grierson. "Making time with your secretary?" He shifted his burning gaze to Brubaker. "Trying to make a date with Rosie the Riveter so you could trick her into saying the wrong thing in bed and toss her in the slammer? Where were you, you lying shits, while I was out taking bullets for my country?" Martel slumped back in his chair, eyeing his enemies with wary contempt.

For a moment there was silence. Grierson's face was a study in outrage overlaid with amazement. Brubaker was the first to speak. "Nobody's saying you didn't fight Japs pretty good, Martel. But what about your buddies, the Germans? Hell, as far as I'm concerned, you *are* a German. Are they paying you, Martel, or are you doing it out of pure patriotism?"

This time it was Lieutenant Commander James Mannheim Martel who lunged from his chair, and it was a measure of the effect of six weeks' sleep deprivation on his fighter-pilot reflexes that Brubaker managed to lurch an involuntary step backward before Martel's fist passed through the space his face had occupied a split second before.

Curiously, Grierson shoved himself between the pair not as a fellow cop, but with the attitude of someone separating arguing peers who had passed over the edge of violence. Martel just stood there panting. Brubaker had the look of a junkyard dog being baited from beyond a fence.

"Enough!" Grierson shouted. "Martel, Bru, ease off, will you?"

"Chief, *please* let me squeeze him. He'll talk."

"Maybe later, Bru. Not now." Then, speaking low so that Martel couldn't hear, he added, *"We aren't authorized."* He turned back to Martel, who spoke before Grierson could.

"Know one thing, Grierson. Now or later, if you have one of your thugs lay a hand on me, you better kill me, because by God I'll take it personal, and I won't be down forever. Ever been in combat, Grierson? I've killed thirty men or more." He nodded at Grierson's shoulder holster. "Ever had that thing out in the heat? Ever aim it at anybody for real? Think about it, Grierson. You and your girlfriend there."

Brubaker looked like he was about to explode. Without bothering to look in his direction, Grierson waved him back down again disgustedly. "Martel—"

Jim cut him off. "Not another word. I want a lawyer. Now."

"Think about it, Martel. As long as you haven't been charged we can still handle this administratively. Stay at that country club for a year or two. If we go to court it's twenty-to-life, hard."

"Screw you."

"Closing in on your lies, are we?" Brubaker asked with a vicious smile. "You blew it about the nineteenth and now you can't cover it up. You're nothing but a damn traitor."

"Kiss my ass." Martel shifted his gaze back to Grierson. "Charge me or get the hell out."

"Just a couple more questions, Martel."

"Kiss off." Stubbing out his cigarette he reached over to the pack that was still on the table and fished out another one. He suddenly realized that he didn't have a light and glared at Grierson, who produced his lighter.

"I'll make you a deal, Martel. I won't ask you anything I've asked before, and you answer what I ask. All right?"

Jim started to tell him where to shove his questions, then

thought about it. He had nothing to hide, and didn't want to seem as if he did. Hell, he supposed he even wanted them to get to the bottom of this. He just wasn't going to be screwed with anymore.

"Sure. Why not? New questions only. No repeats. You ask, I'll answer. But start using your psywar tricks on me again, and not another word."

"Okay. Deal. You're from North Carolina, aren't you, Martel?"

"Yeah. So what?"

"Ever been to Manhattan?"

"Sure I have."

"Like the place?"

"It's all right."

"Ever talk about Manhattan with any of your friends?"

"You mean Willi?"

Grierson nodded.

"How the hell can I remember that . . . yeah . . . sure, we must have. Most Germans are curious about Hollywood and New York."

Grierson stared at him intently.

"Ever been to Oak Ridge?"

"What?"

"You heard me."

Jim sat absorbed in thought for a moment. This must have a point, but he couldn't figure it out.

"There's an Oak Ridge at Gettysburg. It's where they built the Peace Monument. Is that what you mean?"

"What about 238th Street in Manhattan, or Apartment U?"

"What the hell are you getting at?"

Grierson remained silent.

"Look, if what you've asked me means something, I haven't got a clue."

"What about the stadium at the University of Chicago?"

"We never played there when I was in the Academy, if that's what you mean."

Grierson took a cigarette from the dwindling pack and

lit it. He continued to stare at Martel, his features expressionless.

"Care to discuss any of it?"

"Discuss what?"

"What we've just been talking about."

"Look, it might mean something to you but it sure as hell doesn't mean a damn thing to me. Manhattan. Apartment U or V. You've got another security leak? Somebody blow your codes?"

Grierson stubbed his cigarette out and stood up. He started to pocket his pack of smokes and then pushed them across the table to Martel.

"So is that it?" Jim asked coldly as the agent headed for the door. "You want to hang that on me as well?"

"We'll be in touch, Martel." A guard on the other side opened the door, and the FBI man was gone. The lock snapped shut behind him.

Martel took another pull on his cigarette and looked over at Brubaker.

"I bet you'd love to call in a couple of your friends to help you kick the crap out of me right now."

"Jesus, I hope they decide to go all the way on you," Brubaker replied wistfully.

Suddenly, for no particular reason, Martel's attention fixed on the bathroom mirror. He waved.

"Crap," Grierson snarled as he turned away from the other side of it, stepped past the cameraman and back out into the main corridor. He hated it when prisoners pretended they could see him.

Damn him. He looked back at the camera crew that had been filming the interrogation, wondering why Hoover was going to so much trouble over this. It bothered him that Martel might know something important that the number-three — all right, number-four — man in the FBI wasn't privy to. And whatever this Manhattan project was, it was surely important.

Grierson stepped out into the early evening chill. The

film would be analyzed for any subtle gestures on Martel's part, but Grierson already knew that nothing new would be discovered. That was a problem; the Navy was breathing hard down Hoover's neck on this. Clearly Martel had some friends in high places, and without clear evidence of Martel's guilt, the case would soon be dropped. If that happened, Hoover would focus back in on alleged leaks within FBI counterintelligence and several of the defense plants that Grierson was responsible for.

Even the hint of a screw-up was enough to put someone on Hoover's blacklist.

Grierson climbed into his car and started back for the ugly confrontation he knew awaited him at FBI headquarters. He was learning to hate James Martel.

CHAPTER FOUR

November 15
Berchtesgaden, Germany

The room clattered with scraping chairs and clicking heels as the Führer entered the palatial conference room with its open-walled view of the Alpine countryside. As he moved to the end of the long marble conference table he felt again the quickening, the narcotic thrill unknown since the last days of the Russian campaign. Both the victories won at the negotiating table and the triumphs earned in dictating to an empire paled to insignificance when compared to that greatest of all human endeavors, war — this time against the United States of America. In a way, he would regret it when this last and foremost opponent ceased to exist, but then he had always been a sentimentalist.

To his left stood Field Marshal von Manstein, his chief of staff for the army. Next to Manstein was Doenitz of the Navy, and then Air Marshal Kesselring, Chief of Air Operations. To his right, down the other side of the table waited Himmler, Göring, Kaltenbrunner, who headed intelligence, the ever-present Bormann, and Albert Speer, head of industrial production and economic strategic planning.

Hitler's gaze fixed on General Kaltenbrunner. "The updated report you turned in yesterday. Do you vouch for it ?"

"The reports are most reliable, my Führer. They come straight from the President's own Chief of Staff. Further-more, what he's saying dovetails with reports from other sources."

"Then it is all too clear," Hitler announced. "They will

try to lull us with hackneyed platitudes about peace—until this wonder weapon is ready. Then watch how their song changes. If they have this bomb first, that farmer and his fat degenerate friend in London will dictate to us."

He paused and looked around the room.

"To us!"

Hitler's gaze returned to his intelligence officer. "Is the estimated date we have for completion as reliable as the rest?"

"Such things are never certain, of course, but Harrison's Chief of Staff believes it to be accurate. The Russians too believe the Americans will achieve their target date. A couple of the American and British scientists, Communist sympathizers, are leaking information to Stalin, and they believe the dates." Kaltenbrunner carefully did not discuss his own pipeline into the Kremlin.

"*Gott im Himmel!*" Hitler roared. "The idiot Americans will give this bomb to the Russians—Stalin will be at our throats!"

"In a way we are fortunate," the intelligence officer continued when Hitler had calmed himself. "Had they maintained their initial pace they would have the bomb right now. Luckily, they slowed down their atomic research after Pearl Harbor so that they could devote all their resources to dealing with Japan. Alas, once the war was over, Roosevelt managed to get the project's priority upgraded again, under the code name 'Manhattan.'

"We already have two intelligence teams in place to survey the main manufacturing site for the bomb." Kaltenbrunner paused and pointed at the map of the United States that covered the wall behind Hitler. "There, in Tennessee. They've concentrated all their production of radioactive material at one site. They're planning to build a second site in the state of Washington but it will be two years before that's completed. Our sources don't know yet at what rate they are producing the crucial elements in Tennessee so we must assume the worst, that they will complete work within eighteen months, just as Harrison's Chief of Staff boasted."

Hitler stirred. "Early 1947."

"Yes, my Führer."

Hitler shifted his gaze to Speer.

"And our bomb?"

"Late 1947 at the earliest, and that only if everything goes perfectly, which it will not. As I have said previously, the British sabotaged some key research sites, and beyond that it will take us at least twelve months to build the massive facilities required to refine bomb-grade uranium in the sort of quantities that will be required. Like the Americans, we will need a factory area where nearly a hundred thousand workers can labor undisturbed."

"Then why not move now?" Hitler demanded. "We are already running rehearsals and training exercises. This conference merely confirms what I already knew. We could be ready in four weeks, six at most."

With one or two exceptions the entire group froze with almost the same look of nervous dismay. This had all been hashed out weeks ago, but Hitler had been known to change his mind. It would be very bad if this was one of those times.

"Because, my Führer," Speer replied quickly, "as we already discussed, we have another generation of weapons just coming on line, but it will be four to six months before we are up to full-scale production. When we have them in sufficient quantity, the new jets, television-guided rocket bombs, hydrogen-powered submarines and improved rockets will give us a tremendous edge. But we need time to develop sufficient reserves. Four months would give us another thousand of the new Gotha fighters and eight hundred more Arado bombers. As for the television-guided rocket bombs, we have only two hundred and fifty; in four months we will have a thousand, enough to send every single American carrier to the bottom.

"What we showed off at the parade looked glorious—and was!—but that display comprised nearly every plane we own of those designs. We will need these new weapons if we are to destroy the American fleet. During their Pacific War the

Americans made tremendous advances in naval warfare. Their fleet is formidable. Our best plan is to keep a close watch on their Manhattan Project—and move just before they have the final design. For the next six months, time is our ally, and with our marvelous new asset in their White House, we will know their every move; if there is some breakthrough we can act earlier if need be. Please, my Führer, let us wait just a little. Come spring, we will be ready."

Hitler lowered his head as if calculating the odds once again. He finally raised his head. One by one, his gaze speared the commanders of the three military branches. "No later than April."

Those gathered around the table visibly relaxed.

"Now, let us consider England. The American Manhattan Project is the *reason* we must fight, but the assault on Oak Ridge is just part of this operation, and a minor one in terms of men and materiel. Gentlemen, I expect to be in Buckingham Palace within forty-five days of the commencement of hostilities. Furthermore, I expect you to arrange matters in such fashion that England's death throes act as a lure to bring the American fleet within range of the Luftwaffe.

"This will not be a repeat of 1940," Hitler said meaningfully, looking straight over at Göring. "Thanks to *Speer*, control of the air will be achieved using our Me-262s and the new Gotha 229s, which are superior to anything the British have. With drop-tanks these fighters will be able to supply cover over all of England, thus eliminating our greatest problem in the previous war: protecting our bombers. This time, in all the British Isles there will be no single place of refuge. As for the invasion itself" — Hitler paused to look over at Manstein — "I've reviewed your proposals." He fell silent for a moment, then, theatrically, "I approve. I will help you refine them, of course, but in general, I approve of your implementation of my original plan."

Manstein smiled and nodded his thanks.

"Full operational details for the invasion to be on my desk within thirty days. Training schedules in Russia are to be doubled immediately."

Hitler looked back at Göring.

"For the Luftwaffe the task is twofold. First you must gain air superiority both in the Midlands and the North, so that the invasion is not hindered by the RAF and the Royal Navy. Next you must destroy the American fleet. Do not doubt that they will come to you. The Americans will not stand idly by and watch England fall. Harrison made that clear to me at Reykjavik.

"According to our naval planners"—he nodded toward Doenitz—"the Americans will be able to marshal a fleet of at least twenty carriers at several ports along their east coast and perhaps even recall elements from as far as Pearl Harbor. They also have available four active divisions, three in the United States—one infantry, one airborne, and one Marine Corps—plus one Canadian infantry, which we can expect will be loaded aboard transports. This fleet should be ready to sortie to England's relief by day twenty-five and will take ten days more to make the crossing."

"The American fleet will be pounded from the time it leaves port until it reaches English waters," Göring puffed. "I have developed plans for Luftwaffe ground units to seize airstrips in Iceland and Greenland. The Americans will have my planes overhead from the beginning to the end of their voyage. And I do mean the end," he said with a laugh as he leaned forward in his seat to look directly across at Doenitz. "Of course, Admiral, your U-boats will be there to pick off what's left," the Air Marshal added with poisonous condescension.

"Just provide decent reconnaissance this time," the man in charge of the German navy replied icily, "and we will harvest our share."

Hitler slapped the table and the two fell silent.

"We need two years to complete our own bomb. To ensure that we have those two years, England must be eliminated once and for all, so that it can no longer serve as a base for air attacks. Furthermore, our holdings in Africa must be pushed clear into the Congo to secure the uranium mines, and to prevent the Americans from building air bases there. But, above all, their fleet must be destroyed, because without their navy the Americans are simply not a threat. To that end, I expect full cooperation between all branches of service." He scanned the room, pausing thoughtfully on Doenitz and Göring. "Full cooperation. Those who do not cooperate will be replaced."

"My Führer, I believe it is my duty to you to raise some concerns," Doenitz said after a moment's silence. All eyes turned to Doenitz, and then toward Hitler to gauge his reaction.

"Go on then," Hitler finally said, apparently all affability.

"My Führer, this American fleet survived attacks from over six thousand Japanese suicide planes during the 1944 campaign. They lost only fifty-six ships, only two of which were carriers, *light* carriers. Only one fleet carrier was lost, not in the battle but as it was being towed back to Pearl Harbor. They will not be an easy nut to crack."

"And our own carriers, which you pressed so hard for?"

"In an open engagement against twenty American carriers they would be quickly sunk," Doenitz replied simply. "We must keep them out of that engagement so that they can continue to support the invasion of England, and later, if they survive, help take the islands in the South Atlantic."

Hitler glared at him. "Then why did you press so hard to have them built, if they can do nothing when the so-terrible Americans come? Why? We ceased production of the current generation of fighters so that you could have your *verdammt* carriers!"

This was not precisely true. Hitler himself had concluded that after England had stood down there would be no need for prop-driven fighters before they were made obsolete by jets, which were scheduled to be in full production by 1946. Better the financial resources go to weapons that would still be useful well into the 1950s, when it might be time to deal with the Americans. Besides, the folk needed butter as well as guns. Or so he had thought before the Manhattan Project. Now — "If it weren't for your *pointless* demands we would have twenty thousand fighters and fighter bombers! The American fleet would be sailing into a—into a furnace!"

"We won't need his carriers," Göring interjected. "Sinking that fleet is a job for the Luftwaffe. And, trust me mein Führer, even with only one thousand jet aircraft, we have the means to accomplish that mission."

In one of his volatile mood shifts, Hitler nodded calmly to Göring. "Go on, explain it to them."

The rotund head of the Luftwaffe stood up and went over to the map.

"For one thing, this time their fleet won't be facing pilots drunk on saki, and flying bamboo planes." He laughed expansively. After glancing at Hitler, the group joined in.

"For another," Göring continued, "the Americans must drive straight for the Channel, since by this stage the invasion will already be in progress and their only hope for saving England will be to defeat us immediately. Our third Air Fleet, which will have just completed its task of destroying the RAF, will now turn to face the Americans as they move into the channel. The American carriers will have some of their new Phantom jet fighters, perhaps a hundred of them. They will be overwhelmed by our thousand Gotha 229s. The rest will be prop planes, Bearcats and Corsairs. Our Me-262s will annihilate them.

"As for the carriers themselves, we will have over one thousand of the new television-guided Henschel 300 rocket bombs, which have double the range of our preliminary 294 version and can strike from a maximum range of nearly forty kilometers." Hitler nodded appreciatively. He was thoroughly briefed on this particular superweapon, and approved of it heartily.

Beaming with delight, Göring continued. "They will be air launched from specially equipped Ju-288s that will move under fighter protection to within thirty kilometers of the carriers before doing so. Six or seven hits from these bombs, diving vertically, each loaded with half a ton of high explosives, will sink even their newest Midway class carriers. Simultaneous torpedo strikes will be carried out on carriers and other war vessels using Arado 234s. Transports and lighter ships will receive the attentions of rocket-firing Me-510s. As soon as the fighting vessels have been disposed of, any transports that have survived will be invited to surrender. If they do not—well, they cannot be allowed to reach England, of course."

Göring paused for breath and triumph, then continued. "When my boys are done with them, your precious carriers will be safe enough, Doenitz. Maybe even the French fleet will finally sortie out to do battle with the American lifeboats that will cover the sea."

Hitler too looked around the room triumphantly, as if Göring's promises had already guaranteed victory for the Reich.

"With England denied to them as a forward base and their fleet smashed, the Americans will have no means of striking at us for a year or more. By then two things will have happened. First, we will be within months of developing our own atomic bomb. Second, yet another generation of wonder weapons will be in the hands of our military. New York and Washington will be at our mercy, and if they continue to fight they will soon be facing atomic bombs delivered by rocket. *That* will destroy their will to resist. If it does not, they will simply die."

Hitler's gaze slowly swept the room and each in turn nodded approval, even Doenitz. "This meeting is concluded," he announced. "You know your duties. Get to them."

As the men who ran the Reich filed out, they noticed a towering SS officer waiting in the antechamber. All were curious, those who recognized him even more so than the others. Almost before the last of the group had exited, an aide gestured the tall SS officer into the presence. As the door closed behind him, Colonel Otto Skorzeny snapped to attention and heiled Hitler.

Hitler smiled and motioned for Skorzeny to join him at the conference table. This time Hitler's affability was not assumed. Otto Skorzeny was his kind of soldier. "Sit down, my dear Otto. You are well? Your leg—does it still trouble you? That was a magnificent achievement—and on one leg!" Hitler laughed admiringly.

As he sat, Skorzeny laughed modestly in response. "Compared to your achievements in the Great War, my Führer, mine are pale. And what is a broken leg compared to a year in hospital from poison gas?"

"Otto, Otto, you deserve your glory. As for me, I was an enlisted man, a runner. How can that compare?" Hitler was enjoying their little gavotte. Here was praise from a man whose praise had meaning.

"You were one of the few, the very few, enlisted men ever to win the *E.K. Ein*, the Iron Cross First Class, my Führer."

"Kind of you to say so, Otto, very kind." Hitler basked for a moment, then turned the conversation to the matter at hand. "Perhaps you are wondering why I have asked you here today. It *has* been a while since I have enjoyed the presence of your company in private."

"I must confess, my Führer, to a certain curiosity," Skorzeny said as dryly as he thought wise.

"You are to plan for a mission, the most difficult of your career."

Skorzeny said nothing, but within him joy began to kindle.

"America and Germany will soon be at war."

At last. Skorzeny allowed a flicker of that joy to shine through. Hitler nodded approvingly.

"This shall be the final struggle. All that we risked is as nothing compared to that which we now embark upon; truly this is the culmination of *Mein Kampf*. And you, Otto

Skorzeny, shall strike the first blow." Hitler looked him in the eye, man to man. "To one such as you I will not belabor the personal advantages that will accompany success. But do consider this: your success or failure will determine whether the Reich survives or is destroyed. In your hands rests the future of Germany."

Both Skorzeny and, despite himself, Hitler, were caught in the moment. It was as if some higher power, the German race itself perhaps, were reaching through them to grasp the future in its fist.

After a time, Hitler motioned for Skorzeny to follow him to the far wall, where the map of the United States waited. Hitler extended his pale hand. "Here"—jab—"is the target you must destroy. This is not a job that the Luftwaffe can do alone, though Göring has pleaded otherwise. With my background I realized immediately that it required a combined effort by air and ground assault forces led by someone with consummate special skills."

Skorzeny nodded his thanks at the praise.

Hitler proceeded to explain the situation in detail, concluding with, "The full resources of the Reich will be at your disposal. You will answer directly to me and to no other. If you have problems with anyone, report them directly to me. Before you leave talk to Speer and Kaltenbrunner. They will provide you with briefings on the target. I expect you to develop a full strike plan and deliver it to me within the week."

Grinning like a starved wolf that has finally scented blood, Skorzeny leaned forward to study the target for just a moment more. This would be a very difficult assignment. His joy was complete.

CHAPTER FIVE

December 12
Drop Zone "Alpha"

Colonel Otto Skorzeny leaned out into the roaring slipstream and craned forward to catch a glimpse of the target. Only six or seven kilometers away now, it was a hell of explosions and fireballs. The ground itself spasmed under the assault. The sense of the demonic was further enhanced by streamers of the new jellied gasoline smearing across the landscape in long arcs of white-hot annihilation.

He pulled back in and checked his watch. The last of the bombers should be clearing their runs by now. . . . A final string of debris-spewing explosions walked across the target, audible even above the shrieking wind and the howl of engines.

Skorzeny reveled. Again the world was as it should be. The sky was illuminated with fire, blanketed by shadows and smoke. The air stank of half-burned oil and gasoline, gunpowder residue, leather and sweat tinged with the scent of fear. War was a dream that burned in his soul, and that strange passion was awakening. Once again there would be the thrill of the hunt, and of the kill. He smiled a smile of cold delight. Like his master, in the absence of a better reason Skorzeny would start a war for the pleasure of it.

Suddenly the plane banked over sharply, nearly hurling him out the door. A bomber shot past off their starboard side not twenty meters away, exiting the target area by going straight into the stream of transports. Skorzeny turned and looked back at his adjutant.

"Karl, I want the name of that pilot!"

Major Karl Radl nodded. The pale dueling scar on his right cheek stood out in the firelight reflected into the transport.

A yellow light snapped on by the side of the door. Skorzeny took hold of his static line and gave it a tug to make sure it was firmly hooked up. He looked back at the fifty men in double line behind him.

They were his best, which meant that they were the best: Headquarters Platoon of the *Friedenthaler Jagdverbande*, the elite special-operations team of the SS. Survivors of Malta and two long years in Russia, they were all, save for a few young probationers, part of his family, closer every one than any brother of blood could be, unless he too was a brother in arms. It was with these men that he had reached the previous apex of his career with the drop behind enemy lines to capture Marshal Koniev in the final days of the Leningrad campaign. Even Hitler had been impressed by that.

The yellow light started to blink.

"Ten seconds!"

He turned back and leaned out the door, hands braced on both sides.

The Me-264E transport, coming in at treetop level, went into a steep climb as it reached the edge of the compound, now clearly illuminated by the burning buildings.

The green light flashed on.

"Go!"

He flung himself out the door and into the blast from the transport's six engines.

His static line snapped and he felt the gut-jarring blow of his harness as the canopy popped open. He looked up to check the lines.

Full deployment, good.

For a moment he was over Leningrad, experiencing again that cold moment of fear as he struggled to cut away the collapsed chute and deploy his backup with only seconds to go before crashing down into the square behind the Hermitage. In spite of the broken leg he'd still completed his mission, taking Koniev alive and then spiriting him out in a *Fiezler Storch*.

But that was then. Now—the ground raced up and he hit hard, rolling over with a grunt. For several seconds he lay stunned, then rose and tested his leg. It was holding up.

Skorzeny got up and hit the chest-release on his harness and peeled out of the gear. Others were doing the same as the rest thumped down.

Already Karl was by his side.

"Your leg all right?" Karl shouted, worrying as always.

"Fine! Get them moving!"

Karl unhooked the flare gun strapped to his side, raised it straight up and fired. The yellow star shell detonated overhead, marking the rally-point for the headquarters team.

Another transport soared overhead, its belly and the stick of paratroopers streaming out illuminated by the ground fires. The night-drop chutes came down like a rain of black flowers, spreading out in a line across the open field of the compound. But . . . the drop was taking too long. The last man of the stick descended straight into a burning building, his screams almost immediately drowned out by the staccato roar of his igniting ammunition.

One of the new gunships came in a thousand feet high at nearly a right angle to the approach of the transports, barely missing a stick of paratroopers. The aircraft seemed to explode as the battery of automatic cannon in its belly began to rake a line of buildings.

The six guns were fixed to fire downward at a 45° angle. A heavy bomber would rip its wings off if it attempted to pull up from an attack like a fighter strafing targets on the ground. By mounting guns on the underside of the fuselage at a forward slant, an aircraft with a bomber's range and payload could fly straight and level while supporting troops with concentrated gunfire.

That gunfire was devastating. Each of the four revolver-breech MG 151/20s spat out over a thousand rounds a minute. Their tracers cut solid lines through the night. The sleet of 20-mm shells tore roofs and cinder-block walls to splinters in a dust cloud.

The pair of 30-mm MK 103s were slow-firing by any standards; lucky bomber pilots had managed to fly between successive rounds from an attacking German fighter's guns. Where the 20-mm rounds chewed their target, though, whole buildings exploded at the touch of one of the lazy green balls spitting from the MK 103s.

The gunship stopped firing as it reached the end of the line of buildings. The pilot banked right, exiting the target area to the north according to plan. A cloud of powder smoke, slowly dissipating in the light of the flames below, marked the firing pass.

Skorzeny hadn't noticed the noise until it stopped. This close, the muzzle blasts of the automatic cannon had overwhelmed all other sound. Now that he could hear again, he shouted impatiently to his second-in-command for data.

"Second Company reporting in," Karl announced over his shoulder as he consulted the headquarters radio operator. "They're moving on objectives now. Third Company reporting . . . they've dropped at least two kilometers wide of its target."

God in Heaven, what a zoo! "All right then. Let's go."

Karl hesitated. "Sir, we missed our drop zone too. We should have been placed in the next field over. We'll have to go straight through the target area for the gunships."

"*Scheisse!* Tell them to hold back while we get in position! Let's go! We have got to keep on schedule!"

The team spread out into a wide skirmish line and started to race toward the burning buildings. As they swept past, several of the men slowed momentarily to throw thermite grenades into the open windows of structures that had not been hit by the bombers or gunships, then sprinted to regain position. The skirmish line, having done its worst, loped into the next field, on the other side of which was their primary target.

Skorzeny looked back over his shoulder and saw a gunship come out of the darkness, aimed directly at them. Karl was frantically shouting into the radio. A platoon sergeant stood and fired a white signal flare straight at the plane. Like a demon raptor deprived of its prey, the gunship pulled up and disappeared into the night.

The headquarters platoon swept across the field on the run. Straight ahead a heavy machine gun opened up from the doorway of a concrete bunker. The lead points of his team swept to either side of the building and closed in for the kill. The high-pitched stutter of a *Schmeisser* cut short the deeper rattle of the heavy machine gun.

Skorzeny sprinted up to the bunker and kicked open the back door. Several bodies were sprawled in grotesque postures around a fifty-caliber Browning machine gun. Puddles of blood oozed from under the olive-drab uniforms. In the corner of the bunker a phonograph was monotonously repeating "Pardon me, boys, is that the Chattanoo—" *skip*. Skorzeny kicked the phonograph over and stepped back outside.

The edge of the field they had just crossed abutted a car-lined street. He rushed up to one of the vehicles for cover, crouching down by its front hood. It was a Ford . . . or was it a Studebaker? Hard to tell. There was a street sign to his left. He pulled out a pocket flashlight and snapped it on. Main and Georgia.

"Our target is one block up!" he shouted as he sprinted up the street, his men fanning out beside him.

More firefights were flaring up. To his right he saw several people darting out of a barracks, attempting to flee. Civilians. None survived the attempt.

Up and down the street men from the third platoon of the first company were already smashing the driver-side windows of the cars parked along the street, leaping in and tearing open the ignition switches to hot-wire the vehicles.

A building to his right flared up in a fireball as an assault team barely made it outside. Off to his left a gunship came roaring in low across the field he had just crossed, hammering the burning buildings with incendiary bullets.

In the glare of the fires he finally saw his objective—the Administrative Records Building. He led the way in a sprinting crouch, his team pelting along behind him. Suddenly bursts of semiautomatic fire came from the building. His platoon, crouched behind the parked cars on the near side of the street, returned fire.

"Smoke grenades!" He raced for the main door. One of his men lunged ahead of him and slammed into the main door with such force that it burst off its hinges. There was an answering burst of fire and the man spun around screaming and collapsed. Cursing, Skorzeny leveled his Schmeisser and let off a burst into the darkened interior as the rest of his team stormed into the building, racing down the main corridor and into the side rooms.

"In here!"

Skorzeny followed the voice into one of those side rooms. In the glare of a flashlight he saw that several large safes lined one wall. A few seconds later the safe-cracking team had pushed past the assault unit and began placing their explosives. In less than a minute the team hurried back out into the main corridor and crouched down. A concussion shook the building. The team went back in through the smoke and started to pry the doors open while Karl, radio operator in tow, called for the intelligence and photography squad.

From across the street, men burdened with heavy leather bags rushed into the building. Part of the team set up their portable lights and tables while others went into the safes and started to tear open the file cabinets inside, looking for scraps of paper that could decide the fate of empires.

Karl came up to Skorzeny's side and waited.

"Twenty-one minutes since drop!" Skorzeny snarled. "Too long!"

"Only six minutes behind our goal."

"Too long! Everything is off schedule. The jumps were in the wrong zones. What if there had been serious resistance?"

Karl nodded, knowing it was best not to reply.

"Second and Third Companies?" Skorzeny asked.

"Second is starting to move, but it will be another twenty minutes before Third is ready to hit their objective."

Skorzeny walked back down the smoke-filled corridor and out into the night. The vast compound area was ablaze, echoing with the steady drone of bombers, gunships, and transports rumbling overhead. Out on the street, several dozen cars and six trucks were waiting for the evacuation to the landing strip.

"Our air support?"

"Ten bombers and all the gunships are circling in position. Our air coordinator is calling in the strikes."

"Pick-up field?"

"Secured."

"This is ridiculous. We screw up left and right and still it's easy."

The night rumbled with the sound of another gunship dropping into position to fire. It took Skorzeny a fraction of a second to realize what was wrong.

"Joachim! Down!" he shouted as he threw himself on the ground. "Everybody down!"

"*Scheisskopf!*" Karl cried. "He's coming from the north! We'll be in his—"

A second gunship, this one on the proper course, was approaching the target as well. Both pilots were concentrating on keeping their aircraft level despite the updrafts from fires in the target area. The copilots acted as gunners. Bent over their offset sights, they saw nothing whatever outside the glass frame and the buildings on the ground which slid toward their cross hairs.

Only when the gunships began firing did the muzzle flashes alert the crews to one another's presence. Both pilots banked to starboard, but by then it was far too late.

One wing of the eastern aircraft sliced through the fuselage of the idiot who'd confused his approach. High-octane avgas and thousands of rounds of cannon shells exploded an instant later in a fireball.

The shock wave flattened, then fanned, the flames of the burning houses. Sprayed fuel enveloped not only the target but several closer paratroopers. *Their mothers will get closed caskets full of sand,* Skorzeny thought. The gasoline explosion slapped his face like a hot towel reeking of burned flesh.

Most of the second gunship crashed a quarter mile away and began to burn. The outer thirty feet of the port wing cartwheeled into the trees at the edge of the field where Skorzeny lay.

"Stop the exercise!" he snarled to Karl. He stood up, then flung his helmet to the ground. "Idiots!"

A siren sounded in the distance, whistles echoed across the compound as floodlights snapped on, illuminating the former concentration camp located on the Polish border.

Skorzeny turned around and looked at the man who had been "killed" crashing through the doorway. The paratrooper was standing up, laughing with the man who had "shot" him, pointing at the fake blood on the "American's" jacket. Both of them suddenly realized that they were being stared at, who was doing the staring, and snapped to attention.

"Very dramatic. Perhaps you would rather be an actor than a soldier of the Reich?"

"No, Herr Colonel," the frightened paratrooper replied nervously.

"Been in combat before?"

"No, Herr Colonel."

"Get out of my sight."

The boy turned and fled into the building, the suddenly resurrected "American" at his heels.

Karl quietly came up to Skorzeny's side and pointed.

A Mercedes limo had turned at Main and Georgia, and was slowly moving up the street, followed by a half-dozen staff cars. Paratroopers lining the street snapped to attention as the cavalcade neared.

"Now what?" Skorzeny muttered. Retrieving his helmet he set it back in place and went down to the curb. As the vehicle eased to a stop Skorzeny too came to attention, as protocol demanded.

Ignoring Skorzeny, a Luftwaffe colonel hurriedly exited from the front passenger side and opened the back door, thereby revealing the rotund form of Hermann Göring, gorgeous in his medal-bedecked, sky-blue uniform. Emerging, with only a few stifled grunts to mark the effort, he too ignored Skorzeny as he took a moment to observe the burning wreckage of the two planes. Only then did he slowly turn back and barely acknowledge Skorzeny's long-held salute with a twitch of his Marshal's baton. Skorzeny found it passing strange that this fat residue of a man had once been a first-rate fighter pilot, an ace several times over and heir to von Richthoven's Flying Circus.

"Two of my latest planes were destroyed in this asinine exercise," Göring said without preamble.

Skorzeny did not respond.

"This whole scheme of yours is madness. I told the Führer that when I first heard of it, and will tell him again tomorrow: You're taking this training too far. Killing soldiers is one thing; destroying my aircraft is quite another!"

"Hard training, easy mission," Skorzeny quoted quietly. "Easy training, hard mission."

Göring started to reply with a string of curses, but was drowned out by the siren of a passing rescue truck.

When relative silence returned Skorzeny replied, with a formal deference that was not quite satiric, "May I point something out, *Herr Reichsmarschal*?"

"Go on," the fat man snapped.

"The first gunship broke the pattern. All aircraft were ordered to orbit the target clockwise at three thousand feet. They were to break the pattern for a run into the target only when called for by the ground teams. Once they cleared the target they were to break back into a clockwise turn out of the strike zone. The pilot of the first plane did the opposite, and turned straight into the second plane. In addition, one of the bombers broke out of the target area one hundred and eighty degrees from the flight plan and nearly took a wing off my transport. There were indeed mistakes made here. All of them by your people. Every miscue had its start not in my plan but your pilots, and that I must state in *my* report to the Führer."

Göring stared at him coldly for a moment, and then the thinnest of smiles creased his fat face. He motioned for Skorzeny to follow him across the street and out to the edge of the field where the two gunships were still smoldering.

"I don't like this plan of yours. It's too ambitious," Göring said when they had arrived.

"Yes, I'm well aware you think so," Skorzeny replied. Certainly Göring had made no secret of his opinion. And yet neither he nor anyone else had come up with a better. Thus his plan remained the only option to complete a job that had to be done. The Führer had called him in personally and ordered him to find a way to destroy the American atomic bomb program. In the joy of the moment — war again at last! — he had assured Adolf Hitler that he could do the job. Now the full weight of his promise, and the consequences of failure, pressed down upon him.

Suddenly the air was alive with exploding ordnance from somewhere in the middle of the field. Faster than thought Skorzeny dove for the tarmac, concluding on the way down that some part of one of the gunships must have survived intact and was now cooking off. Göring following with a pained "*whoof*" a half-second later.

When the detonations finally settled down, several men

littered the field. The two stood, Göring filled with pained annoyance, Skorzeny happy and a little surprised to be alive. After a moment's consideration he decided that none of his men were to blame, and that matters were well in hand. He returned to the subject at hand.

"One month ago our Führer personally directed me to come up with a plan to destroy the American atomic facilities at Oak Ridge. Even given what little detail we have, it is clear that the place is simply too big for an air strike alone. We must follow up and hit it on the ground. We have to make sure the key buildings are destroyed."

He vaguely pointed to the rows of buildings, now illuminated by floodlights, as if the abandoned concentration camp was in fact on American soil.

"Your bombers tonight weren't even carrying bombs, the explosions were nothing more than placed charges on the ground. In reality I don't think they would have been anywhere near as accurate. The only planes carrying live ammunition were the gunships and they damn near killed me and my entire headquarters team." He didn't bother mentioning the casualties who were now being borne from the field, nor where the blame lay.

"I still think," Göring replied, "that my bombers alone can do the job. If Speer comes through as promised with his new production schedule, by next spring we'll have over four hundred Messerschmitt 264Es. Why make it complex beyond anyone's ability to manage with this insane paratrooper drop?"

Skorzeny shook his head imperceptibly. Being a prophet of air power was one thing, but Göring the Great War fighter ace was sometimes quite blinded to mission requirements by his passion.

"We have discussed this before, and the Führer agrees with me," Skorzeny said tiredly. "Given the range-to-target, even your 264Es would be able to deliver only five thousand kilograms each. Furthermore the strike has to hit at night. Less than half the bombs will land within five kilometers of the target area. The facilities at Oak Ridge are spread across dozens of square kilometers. Whole sections would be missed completely. Only by the miracle of a direct hit would specially hardened targets be destroyed.

"Also remember that the overall target comprises not just the buildings and labs; but includes the people of Oak Ridge as well. We need to put a battalion on the ground to make sure that the job is done properly. Otherwise in a matter of weeks, or at most months, they will be moving ahead full speed again.

"The British bombed Peenemünde repeatedly in the last months of the war and it barely dented the rocket research being done there. But imagine what would have happened if the British had been able to drop a battalion of commandos into the lab area and living quarters. They would have annihilated our rocket scientists and engineers, and that would have annihilated the program. If they could have killed a mere hundred key personnel — which is to say, von Braun and his team — the rocket program would have been crippled. It is the same here. In fact a primary goal of that bombing mission was exactly that; they tried to do it by air, and failed. Perhaps that point was insufficiently emphasized during our staff meeting."

Göring nodded slowly. "I still don't like it, what you're proposing to do once you land," he finally said. "These aren't Russians, you know."

Actually, the orders he would issue once on the ground were known only to himself and to Hitler. Skorzeny considered for a moment. He had to have this man's active cooperation. Göring had to understand that bombers alone could not do the job.

"You mean the scientists? They're enemies of the Reich, more so than any soldier in the field. We must kill them. Kill every scientist at this Oak Ridge and we kill their atomic program. That is why the Führer is willing to go to war to stop the Americans before they beat us to this truly ultimate weapon."

Göring turned away to look back at the fire. "Still, this exercise was a shambles. Whoever was at fault, the fact remains that you yourself landed more than half a kilometer from your target, and I am told that your Third Company was more than two kilometers away. Bombers, these new gunships, and transports—all mixed in together. When the time comes for the real thing—it will be chaos."

This was more like it. He was coming around. Patiently Skorzeny continued his persuasion. "That's why the Führer has given us six months to prepare. Not only will it mean that the new longer-range planes will be available in sufficient numbers, it means that my men and yours will be specially trained for the operation as well."

Skorzeny paused for a moment.

"Herr Reichsmarschal, we can't succeed at this without your help. Only you can force the necessary rigor and quality of training, as well as the unstinting allocation of resources that will be required for us to succeed with this one decisive blow. Without your support this mission will fail, and I don't think I need to add that the Führer will want explanations for that failure. If we are successful, I know the Führer will be lavish in his praise for the guidance you will have provided."

Göring stood silent for a moment, visibly weighing the pros and cons of intransigence and cooperation. If Hitler were as committed as Skorzeny claimed, and Göring had no reason to think he was not, there would be no changing his mind—and defiance was unthinkable. Finally he spoke. "Very well. I will cooperate . . . fully. How shall we proceed?"

"I can see already some things will have to be changed," Skorzeny said quietly, carefully masking his triumph.

"Such as?"

"We are going to need more time on the ground. Two, perhaps even three hours. I want to destroy every building, eliminate every middle- and upper-level technician. That means heavy equipment, especially antitank weapons to secure the roads so we can block any counterattacks. We'll also need to hold a secured perimeter around our pickup point. That means light and medium mortars, and antitank guns there as well. We'll need better command control and coordination. The planes will have to hit their drop areas with pinpoint accuracy. The only way to ensure that is to strike from treetop level, which in turn will require intensive low-level night training. I'll want more of the bombers—"

"Quite a mess you have here tonight Skorzeny," a new voice broke in from the surrounding darkness.

Skorzeny turned and stiffened as from out of the flickering shadows emerged SS Colonel Hoffbrauer, Himmler's personal secretary and informer. Hoffbrauer surveyed the entire scene with obvious disdain, and then turned back to Skorzeny, who barely acknowledged his presence.

"I have a suggestion," Hoffbrauer finally said, breaking the silence.

"And that is?" Skorzeny said grudgingly.

"Your men need blooding."

"I lost half a dozen here tonight," Skorzeny replied coldly.

"Oh no, I don't mean in that way. They need to be reminded of what it is to kill. All this foolishness of running around in the dark, firing blanks at each other: it's like playing at 'Cowboys and Indians.' I could get you several hundred residents of one of our camps. You could dress them up as you desire, American, British, soldiers, civilians . . . even some women and children to add verisimilitude. Give your men live ammunition and get the real feel of a kill. I assure you, it would work wonders for their training. We do it all the time with some of our special units."

"Get the hell off this exercise field," Skorzeny growled.

Taken aback, Hoffbrauer said nothing.

"Get out of here before I break your neck. You make me want to vomit."

Göring chuckled softly as the SS officer bowed stiffly

and withdrew with a look of haughty disdain, trying his best to mask his entirely justifiable fear that Skorzeny might follow word with deed.

"You made another enemy tonight."

"An enemy like that is a badge of honor. I am a soldier, not a butcher. I will do my assignment as the Führer orders. The *Totenkopf* units can play their murderous games; my men don't need it. They are professionals, not murdering thugs."

"Yet you are training to cold-bloodedly kill at the very least hundreds of American civilians. I can certainly conceive of no other way to be sure you have eliminated all key personnel."

"Civilian or not, they are not harmless victims. They are a threat to the Reich, to its very existence. What that scum's talking about is chaining up Russians and Jews for my men to shoot like so many goats. I can't stop his kind from pursuing their pleasures—but I'll be damned if I let them contaminate my men. And always remember, any moral issue aside, lingering over fallen prey is operationally inefficient!"

To Skorzeny that was clearly the worst crime of all.

Göring chuckled. "The truth is you are getting soft," he said, pretending not to believe that for the tall SS commando efficiency would outweigh any questions of morality every time.

Since Skorzeny had absolutely no doubts about his ruthlessness when ruthlessness was called for, the blow fell on air. "I'm a soldier. Killing in combat is my job. I'm good at it, and in fact I enjoy it." The witchfire that burned in his eyes as he spoke made the fat Reichsmarschal unconsciously take a half step back.

"But cold-blooded murder for little more than the pleasure of it is something else."

"I never thought you to be interested in such fine moral distinctions. Remember, Himmler is also under the orders of our Führer."

Skorzeny said nothing. Indeed that fact rather troubled

him when he thought about it. For him the hunt, the fight, the climax of the kill, was life itself. But he had no truck with the sort of scum who thought that killing helpless prisoners was a manly thing. He could do it at need, of course, but he rated it somewhere below shooting caged rabbits on his personal scale of enjoyment. Alas, with the coming of peace those who enjoyed shooting caged rabbits had become the majority. Well, with war looming on the horizon, real soldiers would again enter into their own.

That thought having much improved his mood, he looked at Göring and smiled. There were several changes he was already considering. The key one that he had this moment decided on he wouldn't bring up just now; it was to take the raid away from Göring's Luftwaffe and put it under a newly created division of the SS: planes, pilots, everything. Cooperative or not Göring would interfere too much in the months to come and probably find some way to botch the job. Still, he would have to be careful. He had to gain complete control without alienating Göring. The man was simply too close to the Führer to let him become an enemy. Perhaps it should be Hitler's idea. . . . "There's one point to the plan I've been considering," Skorzeny finally said, diverting the conversation to less potentially explosive terrain.

"Yes."

"I had suspected as much before we started, but now it is obvious: I must be on the ground when the strike comes in."

"What?"

"It simply took too long to get my command organized, and even with practice it will still take too long. Furthermore the entire run-in is blind except for the navigator in the lead plane — and once he leads them into the area everything depends on the individual pilots, especially the transport pilots, being able to successfully identify their particular targets. And for that matter we are not even sure we have actually targeted all the sites; our intelligence promises it will get the information but I can't count on that. Infinitely better if the strike commander examines them up close just before the strike."

"How?" Göring asked curiously. "The moment you drop, the alert will be on."

"I won't drop. I plan to infiltrate into America a full week before the assault on Oak Ridge starts, and then travel as a civilian to the target area."

Göring's eyes widened incredulously.

"Think about it, Herr Air Marshal. The Americans have no concept of proper travel control. No permits needed, and everyone minds his own business compulsively, as if it were a virtue to ignore state-security needs. And now think about this: If I direct the attack from the target area, we will win."

CHAPTER SIX

February 22, 1946
A Training Camp,
Somewhere in Germany

Standing before these men, Otto Skorzeny was as nearly happy as a man like him could be when not in combat. To his right stood his second in command, Karl Radl. Across the map table from him stood the five company commanders of his strike team: Captains Holzer and Ulrich, who had both been with him for the raid on Leningrad; one-eyed Muhler who had come up through the ranks and was an expert with demolitions; Richer and Lenz who had both studied in America, and thus had the special skills he now needed. Behind them stood the rest of his staff and the second in command for each company.

Covering the table between them was a highly detailed surveyor's map. An easel covered with an apparently made-to-order map that covered an area that included the United States, the Atlantic south to the Equator, and Western Europe stood to his left.

"This morning I met with our Führer and received his final approval. The attack date is scheduled for April twenty-first, fifty-eight days from today. You've been training hard for the last two and a half months. Now it is time that you learn what you are training for."

He gestured at the table map. "This is Oak Ridge, in the state of Tennessee."

Openly consumed with curiosity, his staff leaned over the brightly lit table, the men behind craning for a look.

"I've traveled through that region," Richer murmured,

breaking the ensuing silence. "In fact, there was this girl in Nashville. . . ." He hesitated, then smiled with a boyish grin that his comrades found a bit chilling. Richer had the reputation of being absolutely pitiless, especially when it came to women. "Anyway," he continued after an uncomfortable moment, "I've never heard of Oak Ridge."

Skorzeny nodded. "Officially, this facility doesn't exist. You won't find it on any road map, in any phone book, or city directory. Oak Ridge is one of the best kept secrets in America."

"Not that well kept, if we are looking at an Army Corps of Engineers map of the place," Richer replied.

"No, not anymore," Skorzeny said grimly, "but we lost some of our best agents acquiring the information in front of you. Once we learned of its existence and purpose, a special division was set up to reveal in as much detail as possible precisely what's going on there. The operation was given the highest classification, was organized outside the usual channels, and made answerable only to the Führer. Right now we have three operatives inside, one with a middle-level American security clearance, and a half dozen more in the Knoxville area. We also have an operative running a small airstrip forty miles from the base. Obviously that information does not leave this room," he added dryly.

"Do we have any close-in aerial shots?" Lenz asked.

"No. I've asked for them but nothing has come through," Skorzeny replied. "We'll worry about that later." He was pleased that no one seemed daunted by the location within the continental United States. During the training the men knew that they were practicing against an American base, but it could have been anywhere. Now they knew.

"So what does go on there?" Muhler asked.

"It is the main American facility for the manufacture of atomic bombs." Skorzeny studied the men across from him. As he'd expected, his reply had made no particular impact. They merely looked at him, waiting for further enlightenment.

"One atomic bomb will have an explosive force equal to a thousand-plane raid by British Lancaster bombers in which by magic all the bombs exploded simultaneously. Three or four atomic bombs would annihilate Berlin. Most cities would be destroyed by a single one. The Führer learned early last year that the Americans were engaged in making this new weapon. Alas, our planners had previously decided it was technically impossible to make such a bomb within a meaningful time frame. They were wrong, it seems. Now we are racing to catch up, but a stern chase is a long one, and this is a very stern chase indeed. If the Americans get it first, you can well imagine what such a catastrophe will mean for the Reich."

Now he had their attention.

"Our mission is to destroy Oak Ridge. Gentlemen, mark me: Only if we succeed can the Reich possibly have this weapon before the Americans. Thus the survival of the Third Reich is in our hands. I do not exaggerate." He paused for a moment, then added, "Our mission will be coordinated with a full-scale attack on England, and the timing of that attack is based on our mission requirements. More than that, the Führer assures me that if it were not for the necessity of our mission there would *be* no attack upon England.

"Consider also that if we fail, it will be worse, far worse, than had we not tried. If we fail, the Fatherland will be faced with an enraged America in sole possession of this ultimate weapon. If we fail, the Reich fails.

"We must not fail."

He paused to glare at his now-rapt audience.

"We will not fail!"

Relaxing slightly, Skorzeny nodded to the room's lone civilian, gesturing him over to the table. The man who came to stand beside Skorzeny was thin and bespectacled. He had receding hair, his double-breasted suit was several years out of date, and his vest was speckled with cigarette ash.

"Gentlemen, I introduce to you *Herr Doktor Professor* Friedrich von Schiller. He's here to brief us on our target. He's been in on the planning of this mission from the beginning and understands what needs to be accomplished at Oak Ridge better than anyone else, so pay attention."

Smiling with the genial contempt natural for such men toward academics, the company officers looked at Schiller as if he were a professor who had wandered into the wrong lecture hall. But their attitude subtly changed when he leaned over the table and returned stare for stare. Clearly he had no doubts as to the rightness of his presence here— while they were a group of students in grave danger of failing a surprise examination. Perhaps he had seen combat in the Great War. Certainly these human wolves did not make him the least bit nervous, which fact probably played a role in his selection as their instructor.

He began to speak. "Listen closely. This will be difficult enough to understand even if you do." The remaining smiles faded and disappeared as he continued without further preamble: "In late 1941 President Roosevelt was informed by a group of physicists that it was possible to make an atomic bomb. Research and development on this weapon was begun shortly thereafter, but given only a moderately high priority from 1942 to 1944 because of their war with Japan, a war that they knew would be over before the bomb could be produced. With the coming of peace, however, and with the new administration, this project, code-named 'Manhattan,' has been made a crash program.

"The Americans currently have two sites for this project. One is in New Mexico, where the assembly team is currently developing the actual bomb mechanism. The second site is here"—he gestured at the map with a metal pointer rather like a swagger stick—"at Oak Ridge. A third site is under construction in the state of Washington, but will not be completed for another twelve to eighteen months."

"How do we know this?" Richer asked.

The professor looked at him blankly.

"That is none of your affair," Skorzeny interjected. "Now be silent and listen."

Schiller nodded acknowledgment to Skorzeny and then continued. "You have been training for the destruction of Oak Ridge and the three key industrial sites around that city." He leaned further over the table and tapped the sites with his pointer as he lectured. "The workers, of whom there are nearly seventy-five thousand, live in the town proper. Most of them are security forces and unskilled or low-skilled labor, but at least six to eight thousand are technicians, engineers, scientists of various levels, and project managers. These other three sites, located to the west and south of the city in separate security areas, are code-named Y-12"—tap —"K-25"—tap—"and X-10"—tap.

"The purpose of these three sites is to manufacture enriched uranium isotope-235 and plutonium, which are the explosive materials for the bomb. Though the process of manufacture is on a very large scale indeed, the actual quantities of material are small. You could hold the amount of plutonium or uranium needed to destroy a medium-sized city such as Stuttgart in one hand."

Schiller pointed to the K-25 site. "This building, which ironically enough is U-shaped, is nearly a half mile long from one end to the other. The facilities housed within it extract from uranium ore the almost infinitesimal portion that is uranium of a special kind, isotope U-235, by a chemical process known as 'gaseous diffusion.' The Y-12 site, just a mile south of the residential area, also extracts isotope U-235, but using an entirely different technique, called 'magnetic separation.'

"Apparently the Americans were not sure which — if either — process would work, so designed and built the facilities in parallel. As it turns out, both methods work. Finally, the X-10 site is an atomic reactor of a particular kind, a 'breeder,' which can turn the more common form of uranium, U-238, into the element plutonium, which we think but are not positive is as useful as U-235 for the fabrication of explosive devices."

The professor noticed that he was losing his audience. They were trying to stay with him, but they were — soldiers. "Never mind that now. You'll understand what you need to know by the time you need to know it. That's my job, to teach you enough to know who and what it is vital to destroy when you are on the ground in Oak Ridge." His audience began to look more comfortable. Killing people and breaking things was something they understood very well.

Having comforted his victims, he continued. "Those of you assigned to strike the industrial plants will have one of my assistants by your side throughout the mission to direct you as to which instruments and papers are to be taken rather than merely destroyed, and to assist in demolitions. Let me add here that while uranium and especially plutonium are not particularly dangerous — you can hold them in your hand safely enough — some of the materials necessarily present in the extraction of U-235 and the transmutation of U-238 into plutonium can quickly kill you. Primarily by inhalation of poison gases in the first case, and contamination by dust that emanates deadly rays in the latter. So listen carefully to your advisors' instructions as to exactly how to proceed with the demo—"

"That information is not to be shared with the men," Skorzeny suddenly interrupted in his command voice. "I repeat: for now, no hint of that information is to go beyond this room. I will decide later what exactly the men are to know, and when they are to know it. Until such time as I have informed you, say nothing at all on this subject. Please continue, Herr Professor."

Though over his initial startlement at the harsh interruption, the professor still needed a moment to regain his train of thought. Schiller was a brave man, but Skorzeny was . . . Skorzeny.

After that brief moment spent composing his thoughts

Schiller redonned his professorial persona. But his excitement grew as he continued. "Success with this mission will result not only in the destruction of the facilities but will also poison the entire area so that it will require months, perhaps years before it can be used again. It will cripple the American program. It will give Germany a lead in atomic development that I promise you will forever end war, leaving the Fatherland the sole and final victor. Truly, as foretold by our Leader, our Reich will last a thousand years!"

Skorzeny shared the pride and repressed excitement that vibrated in Schiller's voice. He had toured the German facilities hidden near the Polish-Ukrainian border and saw the frenzied level of activity there as they desperately raced to catch up. No one in that project, other than Schiller and five of his assistants, knew that in less than two months it would be the Americans who were desperate to even stay in the race.

"Thank you, Professor Schiller," Skorzeny broke in, resuming control of the meeting. "The Herr Doktor Professor will brief each of you later as to the details of the target to which you are assigned, and team you with your specialist assistants—who will train with you from now on. You are to defer to the judgment of your assistants as to what is to be destroyed, photographed, and, if possible, taken once on the ground. You are also to do your utmost to keep them from killing themselves during training.

"Now as to the actual plan of attack," he continued, "our total force will consist of one hundred and seventy of the new Me-264E bombers. One hundred and forty of them will be configured as standard bombers. The others will serve as transports, tankers, and gunships.

"It's the new stretched 264E that makes the raid possible," Skorzeny continued, "and even with it, to attempt a raid straight from Europe would so limit our load capability as to make the raid pointless. Therefore we will use the French-held island of Martinique"—he gestured toward the map on the easel just behind him — "as a staging area. Of course it was originally intended as a dagger aimed at their Panama Canal, to be used or not as the Führer chose, but it will serve our purposes very nicely. Wasn't it nice of our allies the French to build it for us?" The group chuckled along with Skorzeny. "As they land, the planes will be immediately refueled and take off again. Thirty additional 264s will accompany us but not be part of our mission, and that is all you need to know about them."

Skorzeny picked up a pointer and traced out their route. "We will penetrate the United States at low level along the Gulf Coast, *here*, and fly directly inland for four hundred and fifty miles. From there we will proceed in single-line formation to the city of Knoxville, thirty miles south of Oak Ridge. That will be our navigational fix for the final approach. Once over Knoxville, we will break into our separate attack formations and make the final run into the target area, pick up the Clinch River and follow it into the target area. At this time the 264s that are actually configured as bombers will separate into four attack groups.

"The first group of thirty bombers will strike the main building at K-25. The second group of thirty will strike Y-12, and the third group of sixty will strike the town of Oak Ridge, aiming at the security headquarters, and the residential area most likely to contain the top personnel. The fourth bomber group of twenty planes will be a reserve force and loiter over the target area to supply additional treatment as needed. In addition, there will be twenty Me-264s, converted to gunship configuration flying with the transport group. Ten will strike secondary targets in Oak Ridge and ten will be held in reserve."

Skorzeny looked up and smiled. "Now comes our job. Our assault team will be aboard ten transport-configured bombers, forty men and their equipment per plane. Holzer, your two transports will join up with the bomber group assigned to K-25. Ulrich, your two will join the Y-12 group."

Skorzeny nodded to his oldest, most trusted friend. "Karl, you and your eighty men are assigned to X-10, the one with the atomic reactor. Muhler, you will be Karl's second-in-command. Because of its nature, the reactor is constructed in such fashion that it might as well have been intentionally fortified; an initial bomber assault might leave it intact but so buried in debris as to be made unapproachable given the time constraints that will be imposed upon us by the US military."

Skorzeny paused indulgently while his commanders dutifully chuckled at his little joke, then continued. "Because an initial softening up might do more harm than good, yours will be the one group not to be preceded by a bomber attack. Instead you will arrive five minutes before the rest of the strike. If all goes well, that should give you total surprise and negligible opposition—an important consideration, since it is vital that the reactor be well and truly destroyed. Since your job is so crucial, Dr. Schiller himself will be your specialist-advisor, and in addition will brief you at length on what you must look for and the exact procedure to be followed, insofar as we can specify an exact procedure without having actually having seen the reactor."

So Schiller would be with them on the sharp end. The men looked at the graying professor with new respect. Nearly middle-aged and obviously of great value as a scientist he could clearly have avoided this duty. "We will work especially hard to keep you alive, Herr Professor," Muhler said with a friendly laugh that Skorzeny and the others joined.

"Please do. I am very valuable, and quite fragile," the professor deadpanned to renewed laughter.

Still smiling, Skorzeny returned them to the matter at hand.

"On your departure from the area you will call in the reserve planes to apply the finishing touches to your work. I've planned the ground strikes so that if we lose a plane going in, half the team should still be able to carry out the mission. If we should lose both planes assigned to a given target, we will divert one from one of the other strikes. In your case, Karl, if we lose even one of your planes another will be assigned to either you or Muhler, whichever of you is still alive."

Again Skorzeny paused momentarily, this time with an inward expression quite unsuited to him. "The remaining hundred and sixty men, commanded by Richer and Lenz, will drop into the town." Skorzeny looked at the men in question. "Your men will be dressed as American military police. Their job will be to kill as many of the technicians and scientists as possible. You will receive blowups of this map on which every single building is marked. The houses marked as E and F units, which are clustered primarily toward the center of the town, are the ones for the top personnel. I expect each and every one of those homes to receive a visit. No one is to be left alive."

"Including children?" Lenz asked quietly.

Skorzeny hesitated.

"If they get in the way you are not to hesitate. The Führer has ordered that we are to be successful no matter how difficult the task."

Lenz nodded slowly.

"As for myself, I will be there, directing the attack as it comes in."

The men around the table looked over at Skorzeny in surprise.

Skorzeny smiled.

"A week before the strike I will be in the vicinity of Oak Ridge with my personal team to do a final recon on the target. Our information flow out of Oak Ridge is too slow and something vital could change. A last minute delay would be a disaster, it cannot be postponed no matter what. This attack is but one part of a far greater plan. Even if visibility over the target is zero still we must strike. That means someone has to be there beforehand."

"And I'm not going with you?" Karl asked.

"Karl, you will be in command of the strike force until we link up." Skorzeny nodded toward the white-haired officer with the mashed-in face. "Hans is going with me, along with eight other men. If something happens to me Hans will take over the group until you land, at which time he will place himself under your orders."

Karl barely turned to acknowledge Hans, as if the man had won a coveted prize. Hans grinned broadly, his battered features lighting up with open delight at having been chosen.

Skorzeny realized that Karl's acceptance of his role was an important factor in the mission's overall likelihood of success. Besides, he knew just how his friend must feel right now. "Karl, I need you with the strike group to ensure that the reactor is destroyed. Furthermore, if something should happen to me only you could make sure the assault takes place just as it would if I were still giving the orders."

Skorzeny paused again, looked at each of his men in turn. "This will be our only chance. A day after this war starts they'll have a thousand fighters covering this facility, and penetration will be impossible. This attack will be like the Leningrad extraction and the surprise we were planning for Stalin. The mission will go on regardless of weather, or even detection by the Americans.

"Over the next couple of days I'll review with each of you the various contingency plans. If all goes according to schedule, I'll be over the base in a light plane as close to the administrative area as possible. Our pickup point will be this new airstrip"—he outlined the area with his pointer— "southeast of the administrative area. It will be taken over by a platoon from Lenz's team supported by two gunships. Once the airstrip is secured the same transports that dropped us will land to take us out.

"When you have completed your missions, you will commandeer vehicles and assemble at the rendezvous point for pickup. If there's time we'll continue to hit the town, eliminating as many surviving personnel as possible.

We'll drop antitank weapons with Lenz to secure the main approaches into our pickup area.

"Holzer, you'll be the farthest out from the pickup, over fifteen kilometers. Richer and Lenz, your men will have the most territory to cover between the administrative buildings and the residential area. Nearly a thousand homes will have to be serviced."

"Is there any possibility that their security is strong enough to block us?" Richer asked.

"They are relatively few, and their focus is espionage and sabotage. The worst they have contemplated is a small team going for the reactor. The combination of gunships and antitank teams will be more than adequate."

Skorzeny paused for a moment. "Of course we all know that nothing is certain in an operation such as this. But even if the Americans turn out to be supermen, or by bizarre coincidence an armored unit is conducting exercises nearby, consider this: the ten support bombers working as backup will each be carrying five thousand kilograms of jellied gasoline. One strike from such a plane can turn an area half a kilometer on a side into an inferno. If there are any troop concentrations building up, these planes will be diverted to handle it."

"What about resistance from the civilians?" Karl asked. "I understand that most Americans own guns and know how to use them."

Skorzeny shook his head and laughed. "Maybe in other parts of the country, but Oak Ridge is special. The Federal government runs the facility and in a typically brilliant display of bureaucratic wisdom has decreed that no one living in Oak Ridge may own a firearm. If it wasn't for that our job would be a lot more difficult."

Richer laughed softly. "I can't wait to meet some of those arrogant Southern 'good old boys.' Disarmed, they'll be like rabbits waiting to be slaughtered." Richer being Richer, Skorzeny wondered if perhaps he hadn't had an unpleasant experience with some good old boys already. *There was this girl in Nashville. . . .*

Outwardly he simply nodded in agreement and continued. "Richer, Lenz. A fair portion of your target should already be flattened and on fire. Your job is simply to make sure no one who could possibly be a scientist, technician, engineer, or project manager survives."

"There is such a thing as female scientists," Richer said mildly. "Young female scientists."

Skorzeny spoke as to a child. "Yes, Richer, there are young female scientists. And you are to shoot anyone who might *be* a young, female, scientist. But do not *linger* over them, and do not prefer them to old, fat, males, who are very much more likely to be important targets."

"Of course not, Herr Colonel," Richer replied innocently.

"To continue. Dropping into the target area dressed as American military police will enable you to maximize the confusion. Unless there is an opportunity to herd a group together and draw out lurkers, simply shoot everyone you see. We'll have the names of some of the people we want to make sure are taken out. Try to find them and then eliminate them."

"It seems like they'll have all the fun," Muhler interjected.

"There'll be plenty to amuse you at the three industrial sites," Skorzeny promised. "Those facilities are running twenty-four hours a day, seven days a week. The two major plants will have thousands of personnel in them when the air strike begins. Besides making sure that the plants are destroyed, eliminate any survivors you might find.

"Muhler, I know what you consider to be fun," Skorzeny added. "Just make sure you blow the reactor. Do that right and you'll sow a thousand times more destruction than you ever dreamed of."

"Even better than the bridges at Leningrad?"

"Far better," Skorzeny replied, and Muhler finally

smiled. He was not, unlike Richer, simply a sadistic killer who preferred young girls: it was destruction that he craved. Killing was all very nice, but nothing could compare to the joy of gazing over the smoldering ruins of a dead city, dead because of you.

"What about the range on our planes?" Karl asked. "Even staging from Martinique this is one hell of a long strike, to say nothing of the return to base."

"The Me-264Es have a maximum range of fifteen thousand kilometers. That will get us from Martinique to Oak Ridge and from there back to Germany. As for the bombers, they'll be carrying heavier loads, which will cut their range. Therefore the bomber stream will exit the target area heading east, then make for Bermuda, which will be in our hands by the time they arrive. Not the entire island, of course, but the airfield and its environs. The planes will touch down and refuel. If the capture of Bermuda fails, the bomber crews will bail out and be picked up by pre-positioned U-boats."

"What does Göring say about that?" Karl asked with a laugh.

"He wasn't happy. If Bermuda is not taken we lose nearly half of the new long-distance bomber fleet on the first day of the war. Too bad if it happens but the target is worth any number of 264s."

"What about us?" Richer interjected. "What's the exit plan? The commandeered airfield is too short."

"The transports will be fitted with Rocket-Assisted-Take-Off pods. Assuming we survive the take-off, we'll fly low—very low—over the mountains and then run for the coast at treetop level. Fighter bases from Washington, D.C. to Florida will be on the alert but they'll be after the bombers if we stay lucky. Once clear of the coast we'll pop up to higher altitude and rendezvous over the Atlantic with tanker planes. If we miss them, or if they run into trouble we can make it without the in-air refueling," Skorzeny added carefully, "but we'll land on vapors."

"Or land in the drink," Karl said quietly. "These are long odds. I would have thought we were planning something closer in—Greenland for example."

Skorzeny laughed. "Of course the odds are long; if they weren't, they'd have given this job to someone else. Remember when I first proposed snatching Koniev out of Leningrad? They told us that was a suicide mission. As for the plan to kill Stalin, we all knew that would most likely be a one-way trip. This mission is much more important than killing Stalin would have been. Regardless of the odds, we will do it, we will succeed, and we will be greeted by the Führer as heroes when we return. If we return. If any of you think the Reich isn't worth the risk, tell me now. You have my word no one outside this room will know. You will simply be assigned out because you weren't right for the mission, which will give you a lifetime to live with your choice."

Skorzeny looked around the room. "Come, come! Which will it be? Long life or glory?"

No one said a word, though a discerning observer might have noticed a glint of humor beneath Karl's shamefaced demeanor.

CHAPTER SEVEN

March 10
Washington, D.C.

Walking across the Pentagon parking lot from his old pre-war Studebaker convertible, James Martel paused to inhale the crisp air. It was the sort of day that made spring his favorite season, a day that refreshes body and soul, and . . . try as he might he could not shake a winter-long depression.

The weeks spent under arrest still haunted him.

The vindication, when at last it came, had been almost anti-climatic: A naval lawyer he didn't know informed him that the FBI had decided that he had not after all done whatever it was they had thought he had done, and that was that. The lawyer, however, had proved unable to tell him to which office he should apply to get his reputation back. Neither could he have his old job: "Too risky," the lawyer had said.

"For me or for the United States?" he'd asked quietly.

"Perhaps for both," was the studied reply.

The new assignment was a limbo, not hell, but most certainly not heaven either. Striding through the main doors of the Pentagon, part of the morning crowd, Martel briefly brandished his identification card for the security guard, then made his way down a series of broad corridors, turning at last into the cramped little suite that housed a subdivision of a subdivision supporting operations in China. His area of responsibility lay in tracking down undelivered requisitions.

Nodding politely to the civilian secretary who worked for him and four others, he picked up his mail, went into his office, and struggled yet again with the urge to slam the door hard enough to shatter the glass.

Settling in behind his desk, he looked around at the four bare walls. The FBI had admitted they had no case but they would be damned before they would admit they were wrong. Since a renewal of his security clearances was out of the question for the present the Navy didn't know what to do with him, so they had dumped him into a job that a trained monkey armed with a rubber stamp could perform adequately.

He knew that his best course was to follow his father's advice and do nothing—but for how long? This could go on forever. A little note tagged into his fitness report would dead-end him for as long as he chose to stay in the Navy, while six more months — six more weeks — of manning a forgotten desk in a forgotten corridor of the Pentagon would drive him insane. Quitting was looking more and more like the best option.

Wayne Mason had come back from Berlin in January and was now on the next floor up. His job was a lot more interesting than Jim's, if you liked studying grainy photos of German aircraft and personnel, but he had talked to Jim more than once about resigning and heading back to the Pacific and starting up a charter seaplane line. Mason had fought to stay in the service after the war, but discovered that if he wasn't allowed to be a pilot—well, he'd rather be a pilot out, than a bureaucrat in.

Jim flicked through the stack of mail, most of it complaints from the Far East about shipments that should have turned up six months ago.

Maybe Jennifer was right, he thought wistfully. Their marriage was something he had not allowed himself to think about, but in this enforced idleness, especially with Betty seemingly lost to him, it was hard to keep old memories at bay. It had been a mistake from the start, but a wonderful one for a while. It had barely survived the two and a half years he spent in the Pacific, but mostly at sea, and when he announced his posting to Berlin, wife not included, that had been the end of it. The romance of being married to a flyer had not, for her, matched up with the reality. The ironic part of it was that she wound up marrying another flyer.

Suddenly out of nowhere Jim realized that he wasn't *feeling* anything as he contemplated his ex-wife's new marital adventure. The night he'd first learned of it he'd downed most of a bottle of vodka in his room. As a matter of fact, it had been Betty's warm solicitude the next day for his alcohol- and self-pity-reeking self that had first made him aware that she was looking at him as more than someone whose schedule she had to keep straightened out. Jim smiled at the recollection. Only someone who truly cared could have overlooked his repulsiveness that day.

For his part, up until then he had thought of her as a beautiful young woman whose talents were being wasted in leading him and Acres and Mason and a few others around by the hand. She should have had a high-profile job, like maybe a —

He had sifted his way to the end of the pile, and there on the bottom was a plain cream-colored envelope with no return address.

He looked at it closely. The stamp featured a portrait of Hans Christian Andersen, postmarked Copenhagen, February 26th, twelve days ago.

If he had needed proof that the FBI was not paying serious attention to him anymore, the pristine condition of the envelope would have done nicely. . . . He looked more closely still. No sign of tampering . . . he tore it open and spread the single sheet it contained flat on his desk. He instantly recognized the handwriting, which was not surprising, since Willi had been not only his cousin but his intelligence assignment.

He read and reread the letter and then, turning to the typewriter by his desk, translated it into English.

Just a quick note, old friend. Winter here has
been dreary, the nights long and cold. The northern
lights filled the sky the other night. With spring
coming, maybe the lights of the old Norse Gods will
be more active than ever. Let me know when you
see them over where you live. I've developed an in-
terest in such things of late and I think you will too
when you see them.

Tell your father I asked for him. Perhaps come
spring you and he could come to England where
my friends and I might meet you, or perhaps we
might get to Manhattan like I've always dreamed.

He tore the translation out of the typewriter and pored
over it yet again.

No doubt about it. The mysterious operation was going
forward. Look for it "in the spring." But in Manhattan? A
bomber raid on Manhattan? What the hell? "Don't be
stupid," he whispered to himself.

Manhattan. Why did that word keep coming up? He
sifted through his memory, coming up blank. He studied
the letter, reading it again and again as if it were a Zen
conundrum. It had to be a war warning, but when and
where?

Jim quickly typed out two more copies of the letter, one
in the original German and another in English. The copy in
German went into his desk. The original and the first
translation he tucked into one breast pocket, the second
translation into the other. Time to go.

"Commander Martel, don't forget your meeting with
Captain Broderick this morning at ten."

Jim smiled meaninglessly at the secretary as he closed
his door. To hell with Broderick!

Moving quickly down the hallway, he reached a broad
ramp and started down. Four ramps down, two floors

beneath ground level, was the main office of Army
Intelligence.

When he finally arrived there, he paused for a moment
to gather his thoughts, looked at his hazy reflection on the
glass door, straightened his tie and stepped in.

A military policeman at the entryway looked up at him.

"Can I help you, sir?"

"I want to see General Acres."

"Do you have an appointment, sir?"

"No. Just tell him that Lieutenant Commander Martel
wishes to see him."

The sergeant seemed to hesitate. Martel knew the man
had no idea who he was, but he felt a twinge of paranoia
nevertheless.

"Listen, Sergeant, just do it, and tell him it's urgent."

The sergeant picked up a phone, spoke softly, finally
nodded and put the receiver down.

"Someone will be with you in a minute, sir," and the
sergeant motioned for him to be seated.

Sitting, however, was not something Martel found
congenial just then. He paced back and forth in the small
area between the sergeant's desk and the door trying not to
appear nervous.

"Commander Martel?"

Jim turned and saw a young second lieutenant standing
at the doorway to the back offices.

Jim nodded.

"May I see your ID please?"

Jim fished out his ID card and passed it over. Everyone
who walked Pentagon hallways on a daily basis carried one
just like it. The lieutenant studied his face and the card
intently before handing it back.

"Come with me please."

Jim followed the young man down a long corridor lined
with doors all closed on whatever secrets they concealed,
several of them with heavy padlocks. The lieutenant
stopped at the final door at the end of the corridor and

knocked. After a moment the lieutenant pushed it open and stepped aside, motioning for Jim to enter.

As he came into the room, Martel felt a certain coolness from Acres that he had never known before. In Berlin they had been friends, with an element of mentor-protégé to their relationship. None of that now: Acres was standing behind his desk, and though he offered his hand, there was no warmth in it.

After a perfunctory greeting he said without further niceties, "If you're here to give me crap about your situation, there's nothing I can do."

Jim reached into his pocket, pulled out von Metz's letter and tossed it on the desk.

Acres's eyebrows rose. "What's this? Your resignation? A denouncement?"

"Just read it, sir."

Acres picked up the envelope, opened it up, and slowly studied the note. Finally, he looked up.

"You know, Martel, when somebody has shit thrown on him, even after it washes off, the aroma lingers for a while. I just want you to know that, before we go any further."

"I know that, sir. That's one reason I haven't looked you up before now."

"Some of that stink clings to me too. I didn't exactly volunteer to return stateside."

"Are you blaming me for that, sir?" Jim asked coldly.

A pause. "No. Now, tell me about this note."

"It's from von Metz and it came in this morning's mail. Wilhelm and I worked out a private code and he reminded me of it just before I was pulled. He said that if he ever mentioned my father in a letter that would be the signal that the balloon was about to go up."

Acres blew out noisily and leaned back in his chair.

"Coffee?"

"Sure. Thank you, sir."

The general came out from behind his desk, opened his door and barked out a command. Less than a minute later, the young lieutenant came in bearing two steaming mugs and quickly withdrew. Acres opened his desk, pulled out a bottle of brandy and poured a small amount into his mug, then offered a shot to Jim, who refused.

While sipping his caffeinated booze, Acres studied the letter and Jim's translation.

"Explain what's in here."

"I lived with von Metz for nearly a year, and I can tell you he doesn't give a damn about astronomy. He lives for baroque music, the way his older brother did, and skiing. Then it hit me. In Norse mythology the Northern Lights appeared when a warrior had died and the Valkyries came down from the Hall of the Gods to gather up the slain. They're going to be busy this spring."

Jim picked up the English version of the letter from Acres's desk and read slowly, "'With spring coming, maybe the lights of the old Norse Gods will be more active than ever.'"

"War in the spring. That's very soon," Acres said quietly.

Jim nodded and then continued to read. "'Let me know when you see them over where you live,' that means it's coming straight at us."

"What about the rest?"

"'Tell your father I asked for him.' That's the tip off code. 'Perhaps, come spring, you and he could come to England or even here for a family reunion, or perhaps I might get to Manhattan like I've always dreamed.'"

Jim put the letter back down.

"He says 'spring' a second time just to reinforce the point. As for our going to England, he knows Dad can't travel since the heart attack. England is involved in this, whatever-it-is as well."

"And Manhattan?" Acres asked softly.

"I don't know. Maybe they're going to strike at something in New York. The 'E' variant of their Me-264 bomber is code named Manhattan, though I don't think Willi knows I know that."

"Not much of military value there other than the docks and Brooklyn Navy Yard. Psywar strike perhaps? Hit us hard on our own soil to throw us off balance?"

"Not likely sir, especially for a first blow. Their whole military doctrine is toward focus, hitting the point of attack with overwhelming strength. The Brits might go screwing around with psychological attacks, but not the Germans—especially at the beginning of something. Besides, they know enough from the way we went after Japan to realize that the psychological effect would not be a desirable one from their point of view—it would be the same as after Pearl."

Jim hesitated . . . *Manhattan*. Of course! The code screw-up that had had Grierson so exited. But he had a strong feeling he ought not mention that, not even to Acres. "A code name then?"

Acres looked at him closely, saying nothing.

"Anyhow, sir, this is a clear undeniable warning from the best source we've got." He paused for a moment. "If I might be so bold, sir, may I ask what you're going to do about this?"

"Kick it up the ladder."

"Kick it up the ladder," Jim repeated softly. "Given it started with me, you know what will happen."

Acres shrugged. "Like I said before, son, you still stink."

Jim looked at him, incredulous.

"And that's it?"

"That's it, Martel. Unless you have something else you need to talk about?" Acres inquired dismissively.

Since Acres had never been one for salutes in private, Jim simply stood and headed for the door. Clearly there was no point and considerable risk in continuing to prod this man who not long before he had thought of as a friend.

"Martel."

Jim turned back.

"There's no sense in drawing attention to yourself over this. One theory that was kicking around was that you'd get fed some disinformation, that you might even know it was disinformation. If there's going to be a war, all the signs are that the Russians will be getting another dose. Why go out on a thin limb? Cover yourself. Just let it drop."

Jim suddenly realized that Acres's crap about supporting him had been just that — crap. Whoever had gone to bat for him, it hadn't been General Acres. General Acres, it seemed, while he might be brave enough in a fight, was a moral coward. As he closed the door carefully, finally, behind him, Jim felt the original copy of the letter inside his breast pocket. Well, at least he'd tried channels. He strode off briskly towards his future.

After a while he stopped in front of a bank of phones and looked back up the corridor. No one was following. He stepped into a booth and closed the door. He felt a trickle of perspiration going down the back of his neck and half opened the door as if to step back out.

No, damn it, or he'd be no better than his erstwhile "mentor." The note was nearly two weeks old. In another two weeks it would be officially spring. If he didn't do something personally, this whatever-it-was would be over before anyone realized it was coming. He reclosed the door.

He was tempted to call his old man, but he already knew what his answer would be: There were times when a man had to lay his life on the line, and that meant not just his physical life — most servicemen understood and accepted the probability that from time to time they must step in harm's way — but his career as well, which far too many were afraid to risk. It was something he and his dad had often talked about, that men who would not shrink from death itself trembled at the thought of the disapproval of the herd.

Opening a phone book, he looked up the number he wanted, picked up the phone, dropped his nickel in and dialed.

"Capitol Hill, House of Representatives."

"The office of Congressman Brian McDonnell please," he said quietly.

✧   ✧   ✧

Two hours later Jim was poking nervously at the ice in
his drink as he looked around at the customers who filled a
restaurant several blocks away from the Capitol Building
on Pennsylvania Avenue. Scanning the crowd, some of
whom were in uniform, he felt fortunate that he didn't
recognize anyone. The rest of the clientele seemed to be
mostly congressional staffers. The radio was playing Glenn
Miller's newest release, "Persuasion." As he half listened to
the tune, he saw McDonnell come through the door and
look around.

The congressman walked slowly through the
smoke-filled outer room, nodded a couple of hellos, and
then stepped into the dining area in the back. Coming up
to Jim's table, he took off his coat and draped it over his
chair before sitting down.

"Hello, Jim. Long time."

"Yes sir, a very long time." The last time he had spoken
with the congressman he had been a middie, home for
vacation.

"Ever eaten here before?"

"No, sir."

"Well, let's order what they're known for."

When Martel nodded an assent, McDonnell turned in
his chair to motion toward a waitress. When she got to
them he ordered up crab cakes and a round of beers.

"How's your dad? I haven't seen him since the heart
attack."

"Hanging in there. He's working on his boat and talking
about getting it in shape for the season. He wants to sail it
up to New England this summer." Jim couldn't keep a
certain sadness from his voice.

"Not well, is he?"

Jim sighed. "The doctors say one more like the last will
be the last."

"The boat will keep him busy and, who knows? He's a

tough old bird. He might outlive us both. Damn, I wish I could break free and go for a sail with him. I served under your dad in the Great War. I was a spoiled know-nothing reserve officer when I joined your dad's staff. He helped me do one hell of a lot of growing up. I didn't love him for it then. I do now."

"I'll be sure to tell him that, sir."

McDonnell laughed softly and shook his head. "Now let's get to the point. What's bothering you?"

"It's got nothing to do with my situation, I want to make that clear."

"That thought hadn't even occurred to me, Jim," McDonnell said gently, but seemed to relax a bit. "Maybe you ought to know that even though you didn't ask, maybe because you didn't ask, I did look into it a little. Since I'm on the Armed Services Committee"—he had just become its chairman—"I have some contacts. The way they told it, you seemed to be caught in a turf fight between the FBI and the Navy and there was precious little I could do. I should add that your dad did give me a call."

Jim smiled and shook his head. "I told him to stay out of it."

"You can't blame him. But by then I'd already looked into the situation. I explained to him that I couldn't push it, that it might have gotten you a better assignment for now, but later on they'd have nailed you. Even though you were as innocent as a driven lamb, a couple of admirals had their noses bent over this flap, and as far as they were concerned you were guilty of bad luck and be damned to you for embarrassing them." McDonnell paused to grin. "Right now they're just grumpy, but any political pushiness might have put you on their permanent shit list. You've most likely been told to let things simmer down a bit. The advice is good. I hear Broderick is okay and he'll give you a good fitrep at the end of the year. And a word or two *has* been dropped here and there. Keep a low profile for a while and we'll get things straightened out."

Jim thought about how he had stood Broderick up this

morning. "Maybe before today he would have. Not now—but that doesn't matter. What matters is this," he said, patting his breast pocket. "This can't wait. I tried to go through channels with it—and ran into a brick wall. That's why I stepped outside the loop."

Jim reached into his breast pocket and pulled out a copy of von Metz's letter and handed it over, explaining as he did so his relationship with Willi, and what the letter meant.

Suddenly, in the midst of Martel's explanation, McDonnell's demeanor subtly changed. "What else do you know?"

Martel looked at him blankly for a moment, then shrugged. "Nothing, I guess. Except that it's genuine. And you know as well as I do that all the talk about them going after Russia again is a crock. Some others will claim that von Metz probably was fed false information to throw us and the Russians off or, worse yet, that the Gestapo already had him, and the letter is a phony. I *know* Wilhelm von Metz. Willi's not just my cousin, he's like a brother to me. I know how he feels about those maniac swine who have taken over his country. He lost two brothers in Russia. If he had been compromised, we had contingency codes. A mention of my mother, for instance, rather than Dad would have told me he was under immediate duress—and failing to call me 'Old Friend' would have done the same. As for where he got the information, it comes straight from Canaris, head of *Abwehr*."

"You shouldn't have told me all that," McDonnell said quietly.

"Who should I have told? You're part of the committee as well as an old family friend. If I can't trust you, then who the hell can I trust in this damn town?"

McDonnell smiled. "Very few, very damn few. But don't disclose your sources."

Jim still thought that this time the risk was justified. McDonnell had to be convinced. "Anyhow, that's it. This thing is too vital to get lost in channels."

"What are you saying, Jim?"

"I'm saying that I want you to put it on the President's desk."

"That's a lot to ask."

Jim shrugged. "You're an old friend of his. Cut the tape."

"With your name attached?"

"Yes . . ." Jim hesitated a fraction of a second and added, "if need be."

"You know the blow-back it might cause?"

Jim shrugged. "So I'll become a civilian and go teach German and aeronautics in some cow-town college. I'm telling you sir, this is real and it's coming straight at us — and very damned soon."

McDonnell nodded, looked down at the letter, and then back again.

"What do you think the reference to Manhattan is about?" he asked offhandedly.

There was something about the way McDonnell asked the question. He felt as if beneath that one innocuous word there was a dark and bottomless pit . . . "I don't know a thing about 'Manhattan,' whatever it is, but I've been asked that question before."

"By whom?"

"Grierson. The FBI agent who was interrogating me." Jim paused, noticing how intently McDonnell was staring at him. "He asked me if I ever discussed Manhattan with anyone."

"What else did he ask?"

Jim fished back through his memory. "I think there was something about an apartment U on 238th street. Also something about Oak Hill—Oak Ridge, I mean."

McDonnell continued to stare at him.

"Is that it?" Somehow McDonnell no longer seemed the old family friend.

"I think so, sir."

For several seconds McDonnell gazed grimly at Jim. Then he seemed to come to some decision. Taking both copies of the letter, he folded them up and put them in his pocket. "You're not to say a word to anyone about any of this."

He looked around, visibly regretting the public venue. "Listen. This meeting never took place. And if somehow it gets out that we did meet, it was strictly so you could cry on my shoulder."

"Yes, sir."

"Do you have any more copies of this letter?"

"I made one before coming to see you this evening."

"Where is it?"

"I left it in my office."

"When you go back to your office you are to burn it. No one else is to see it. Do you understand me?"

Jim nodded.

"Has anyone else seen it?"

"I did try through channels like I said."

"Who?"

"General Acres, Army Intelligence Office at the Pentagon."

"Christ. Do you think he's shown it to anybody else yet?"

"I doubt it. He won't pass anything up the line with my name on it."

"Thank God for small favors. What do you think of Acres? Is he okay?"

For a moment Martel was at a loss for words, then said, "Yes. He's . . . okay."

McDonnell looked at him perceptively. "Well, someone will have a talk with him. You might get a call within the next day or so yourself. Just listen to what your caller tells you, and do it. I'm not going to tell you to relax. You've just put your butt into a fire, but you knew it when you did it—and I know I can count on you."

"You mean you believe this is for real?"

"I just wish I didn't."

Jim felt as if he were going to collapse from the sudden release of tension.

McDonnell finished his beer, stood up and fished out a five-dollar bill. "Enjoy my crap cakes," he joked as he tossed the bill on the table and strode out.

"Bad day, Lover?"

John Mayhew took the drink Erica proffered, but said nothing.

Playfully, she kissed him lightly on his neck. He turned away.

"What is it?" she asked. "Little Wifey asking questions again?"

He went over to the window and pulled the curtains back so as to look out, then carefully closed them again.

"It's over," he said quietly.

"What do you mean?" Was there a note of real feeling in her voice? How . . . odd.

He turned back at her, looking hungrily at what he was about to dismiss from his life. His wife was a bore, the children were bores, it was all emptiness. Erika had changed all that. She had granted him eighteen months of paradise—a fool's paradise.

"You heard me. We're finished. Now, tonight."

"*Is* it your wife? Have you decided that her family's political connections matter more than me?"

He nodded.

She looked at him closely. Her face became still, expressionless. "You're lying."

He said nothing, staring at a point on the wall just past her left shoulder.

"It's something else, isn't it?"

"I don't want to discuss it. It's over with. You can keep the apartment, I'll pay the rent until you make other arrangements."

"I don't want other arrangements. I want you." Fiercely, she grabbed hold of him and forced him to look into her eyes. "You're afraid of something."

"I don't want to talk about it."

"You must," she said quietly, "I insist. *What happened today?*"

He shook his head. "I'm not going to . . . " With a crashing blow she slapped him across the face.

"*What happened?*"

"The Secret Service," he replied automatically before regaining control of himself. *Christ!* that had hurt. She really knew how to hurt a guy. . . .

"What about the Secret Service?"

Seeing the look on her face, for a moment he was actually afraid of her, and again found it easier to answer than maintain silence.

"The head of the Secret Service visited my office this afternoon. Officially, since I'm Chief of Staff to the President, he was conferring with me, briefing me on a suspected security leak . . . I was being checked out."

"Were you followed here?" she hissed, forgetting to mask the fear from her voice.

When he heard that fear his suspicion was replaced with certainty. Suddenly, he knew—and knew too the answer to his dilemma. Regrettable perhaps, but at least this course offered a clear resolution to a difficult situation.

"No," he replied after a long pause spent in reflection. "I was careful about that. I went to a bar I know that has a back exit. I left by the alley and caught a taxi on the next street. You're . . . safe. No one followed me."

She relaxed slightly. "Good. But as for it being over for us, for you, the answer is no."

"What?"

"Just that. No. Spell it out: N-E-I-N. Now do you understand?"

His head rocked back as if she had hit him again.

She smiled at him with a certain sympathy.

"You bitch! You think I'm under your thumb, don't you?"

She smiled and, leaning up, kissed him lightly on the cheek, affectionately. "Yes, lover, I do. You will never be free of me. And to think that when we started I was little more than a throw-away container for your lust. How we have progressed since then." Despite the words, her smile remained soft, almost loving. Much as it had always been.

"You're the leak. Everything I've told you. I started to

suspect it months ago! You're a spy for the Nazis!" His voice filled with hysterical menace as he nerved himself for the next act in their little drama.

"It took you long enough," she chuckled throatily, nuzzled his neck, nipped very gently.

He pushed her roughly away, then began to advance on her, death in his eyes.

Still smiling, she slowly backed away.

"Ah, so you would be a murderer as well as a traitor? *Such* a piece of work you are, my—darling!"

He suddenly realized that it wasn't a sudden decision after all; he had come here to kill her. Even if they couldn't actually prove anything in a court of law, if the FBI and Secret Service ever found out about her it would be the end of everything. The power, the knowing, the surge of exultation every time he walked into the White House. All gone. And in its place? He shuddered. Loathing, humiliation, unending darkness. His very name would enter the national lexicon as an insult.

From the side table he picked up a heavy chrome-plated ashtray, all sharp corners, hefted it, moved to block the door. Still she just stood there, smiling gently, knowingly. Would she smile till the end? he wondered. He moved slowly toward her.

A blow to the back of his neck sent him crashing to the floor. The kicks that followed caused no pain. After a brief time a distant voice, Erika's, snapped out a command and the kicks stopped.

Rough hands rolled him over and through a cloudy haze he looked up into a roughly chiseled face filled with savage contempt, and a curiously personal hatred.

Unfortunately the haze was beginning to lift. Pain and awareness returned as one. Sickened, John closed his eyes and rolled fetally on his side, struggling, failing to hold back the tears of rage and humiliation. Had they never been alone?

After a few moments he felt a warm hand taking his and a coolness on his forehead. He opened his eyes to see Erika kneeling on the floor beside him, gently stroking his forehead with a moistened towel. His tormentor was gone, or at least behind a door that did not look like a door.

"So, now you know."

He could only jerk his head, unable to speak.

"John . . . we could keep things as they have been."

He shook his head.

"No, truly. You can still keep everything: your reputation, your wife's wealth, your job, your power, your reflected glory." She hesitated a moment. "You can even keep me."

John still didn't speak, but some of the tension was leaving him.

She pounced. "Of course I will expect a full weekly report on your White House affairs."

"Go to hell," he whispered.

She laughed softly. "I know where I'm going." There was almost a note of sadness in her voice. "They got me a long time ago. Just as I now have you. What can you do but cooperate? You can't expose me; if you did, you'd lose it all. And what is more, you would disappear into some dark little cell where you'd grow old."

She gazed tenderly at his convulsing form still curled in a fetal ball, gently wiped the tears from his cheek with her finger. "John, we mustn't let that happen to you. You are too good a person to suffer so for such a simple, human mistake."

For a while she silently stroked him. When his breathing slowed she returned to the job at hand. "But there will be new rules. First, I expect you to continue as you are. Tomorrow you'll go back to your office, do your job, soak up all the information you can. Please don't try to hold back or to lie to me. You are not our only . . . friend in Washington. If you try to cheat us I will learn of it. The first time I would be forced to give you to Joachim, he who so enjoyed kicking you. The second time we would simply expose you in such a way that you would wish that you were dead."

She gently brushed the damp hair from his forehead. "Do we understand each other?"

Though he did not answer directly his sobbing became audible. Kindly, she took that for assent. Explicit submission to her will could wait until he had composed himself. She was, after all, rather fond of him, and genuinely looked forward to further "games" in the context of their new relationship.

"Come, *Schatzi,* my little treasure." Carefully she helped him to his feet and guided him into her bedroom, laid him down. A minute later she returned with a glass of bourbon, slightly watered, three ice cubes. Just the way he liked it.

"Take this; you need to sleep for a while." When fretfully he made as if to refuse the glass, she said to him slowly, "John, from now on you must do exactly as I say."

Like a child, he followed her directions. After downing the drink he rolled over and faced the wall, silent now.

Turning off the lights, she closed the door behind her and walked back to the kitchen where Joachim too was having a glass of bourbon.

"You didn't have to kick him like that."

"I was just having a little fun." Joachim smirked. "It was all to the kidneys. There'll be pain, lots of pain, but no bruises."

"You hate him, don't you?"

"He is scum. In Germany he would have been found out and shot long ago."

She settled herself at the kitchen table and lit a cigarette. As she poured herself a drink she looked at him from under lowered lids and said softly, "But such useful scum. We have dealt with others as low. Why him?"

"All right. I don't like what you do with him, having to listen."

"That is all you do, listen?"

"Except for when taking the photographs, yes. Listen. That is all."

"It doesn't . . . excite you? I but do my duty to the Reich, you know."

"Yes, of course it excites me. That's what I hate! You. With him. *Scheisse im Himmel!*"

"Is it so different with us . . . Lover?"

"He is a traitor. Filth."

"Yet you do share certain tastes . . . I can tell, though you try to pretend otherwise."

Joachim refused the bait. "Sometimes I indulge you. That's not the point. *Ach!* There is no point! Him. You. It disgusts me.

"Do you think they know about the leaks?" he asked, changing the subject.

After a moment lost in thought Erika replied, "Nothing lasts forever."

"Too true. Me, I think they're on to him. Let's just kill him and get the hell out."

She shook her head in angry disbelief. The Chief of Staff of the President of the United States? "Without orders? You must be mad. Besides, now I can interrogate him, rather than having to be satisfied with bits and pieces, always worrying about my cover." She stared contemplatively at her drink. "Also, we have to find out more about 'Manhattan.' Now we can send him back to get the information we need."

"You're protecting him."

She looked up and smiled. "He's like a child who has been disciplined too harshly. I feel sorry for him."

"At the first hint of pressure he'll spill his guts to the Secret Service. Then they either pick us up or start feeding us false information."

"You were right when you called him a coward," Erika replied. "We need merely keep him more frightened of us than of them. Between us, we will not find that a difficult task. Remember, while as far as you and I know he's our only top-level source, he doesn't know that. He'll continue to feed us straight information including whether he thinks the Secret Service is closing on him."

"And you'll continue to play with him, won't you?"

"Only when I'm not with you," Erika said coolly. "Now go, but stay close by. When he wakes up, I want to give him a little motivation before sending him on his way."

CHAPTER EIGHT

March 29
A Training Camp in Germany

Otto Skorzeny leaned back in his chair and laughed. After the mind-numbing training schedule of the last few weeks they were finally getting to blow off some steam. The scent of beer and roast sausage mingled in the heavy smoke-laden air with other less savory odors faintly emanating from the rear of the establishment. A rather pale Richer staggered past on his way to where the bad smells came from.

"He looks like such a mama's boy," Karl slurred drunkenly. "I still remember how he cut up that whore in Smolensk. Turned my stomach. Takes a lot to do that to me." Coming from Otto Skorzeny's Number Two, that last was something of an understatement.

Skorzeny, who hadn't been there, only shrugged in reply. Richer was a weapon; many weapons did more harm than was strictly necessary for the completion of a mission. If there were a weapon more precisely tailored to the job Skorzeny would use it, but what counted was that the weapons used do the job. As he drained his tankard he saw Richer come staggering back. Two of Richer's NCOs jumped up from the table they shared with their commander to prop him up and half-carry him back.

"Despite present appearances they are in near-perfect form," Karl said. "So sharp and ready that much more training would start to take the edge off. They needed this break."

"Just remember, there won't be a second chance, and we *must not fail.*" Skorzeny slammed the table with his fist.

Karl looked at his boss. Skorzeny wasn't drunk, not as a

German soldier would understand the term, but his inner concerns were rather more visible than he normally allowed them to be; even old Joy-Through-Strength Skorzeny was not completely immune to responsibility-overload. To change the subject, Karl asked, "What about the models of the targets? When will they be ready? From the little you told me it is hard to believe people could have such fun while contributing so much to the war effort."

Skorzeny smiled. "You think they are having more fun than us?"

Karl laughed in return. This was more the Otto he knew. He continued to look inquiringly, wanting to keep his friend's mind on the new topic, and actually curious about these genius grown-ups playing with doll houses.

Skorzeny took the hint and continued. "They're finishing up right now. It really is rather marvelous. The entire facility, accurate right down to the different types of houses, is laid out on an indoor drill court near Potsdam. Leni Riefenstahl is in charge. You remember her: she directed *Triumph of the Will.* The Führer loved it. She has her very best camera people working on it now. They run cameras over the model at speeds that simulate an actual approach from two hundred meters up, with the only illumination coming from inside the models and from the miniature streetlights. Happily, we need not assume blackout conditions for this job. The pilots of all the planes will train with the films starting next week.

"Just before the strike, when security requirements no longer disallow it, all the officers and NCOs will be taken out to look at the model as well."

"Ach, what will they think of next," Karl said wonderingly. "But I'm still concerned about the weather, Otto. Only a fifty percent chance of clear skies, a one in four chance of rain and the distinct possibility of heavy gusting at ground level." Having spoken, with careful deliberation Karl opened and refilled his tankard.

"Karl, old friend, I am not the least bit concerned about the weather."

Karl looked at him quizzically.

"Why am I not worried?" Skorzeny asked. He paused for a moment and the humor dropped from his face like a mask. "Because it doesn't matter. You go in no matter what. No. Matter. What. In the middle of a hurricane in the face of massed enemy fire, you and the men drop."

He clapped Karl on the shoulder. "On the other hand, you will know what you are dropping into. The Americans love to hear about their weather. Their radio stations will supply you with updates all the way in. Plus, the navigational planes with each group, as well as all the transports, will be equipped with the new ground-targeting radar. Getting a fix on the targets will be dead easy. So stop worrying!"

"You gave me the job of worrying—while you and that dumb ox go to America and have all the fun."

"Hans could not take over the operation if I fell. You know that, Karl. But he is a radio expert and the best barehanded fighter in my command. If you wanted to grow up to be a cowboy you should have pretended not to understand strategy. As it is, I need someone I can trust to lead the attack, and that is you."

"Thanks for the compliment, Otto, and the ulcers that go with it."

Skorzeny laughed. "Don't worry about your ulcers. Before they have had a chance to get really bad, we'll both be long dead."

Karl smiled one-sidedly at his boyhood friend. "When do you leave?"

"Right after morning inspection. We catch our ship at Bordeaux tomorrow night. It should dock in Charleston by April thirteen. You will get daily updates throughout. If we are captured, the Americans will think we are just part of an espionage team. Not that it matters from your point of view. Whatever happens, you go in as planned."

"Just you be careful over there in America. Your English still needs some work, you know. With that ugly face and your accent, open your mouth and they'll be on you like flies on . . . honey."

"Mine English not so bad is," Otto replied slowly. Richer, over at the next table, turned and laughed.

"Like I said, you just be careful. Don't speak unless you must."

Otto smiled and nodded. "Yes, Mother. I will be a good little citizen of Poland." Slapping his friend on the shoulder he added, "Ach, I have always come back before. I will this time too."

March 30
Antietam Battlefield Park

Jim Martel got out of his '40 Studebaker, slammed the door and drew a deep breath of the icy wind whipping in from the west. A scattering of flurries promised worse to come. He walked hurriedly to the stone tower that stood alone and forlorn in the middle of an open field. Stopping at the entryway he turned and looked back the way he had come. There was only one other car parked beside the tower, and no one was in sight.

Turning again, he walked through the tower's open portal and started briskly up the stairs. Each time he passed one of the slit windows that were set at regular intervals on the stairway he caught glimpses of South Mountain to the east and Antietam Creek to the west. Reaching the top landing, he saw a broad-shouldered form leaning over the side of the observation deck, looking at the fields below. He walked over to him and came to attention.

"You're late." The man spoke without moving.

"Sorry, sir. I took the wrong turn back at Boonsboro."

The man turned and smiled.

Jim recognized him immediately. He had imagined a lot of possibilities. After all, the voice on the phone never identified himself, had simply arranged the meeting, given the directions, and then hung up. The fact that OSS chief Bill Donovan, "Wild Bill" as his friends called him, had driven an hour out of Washington to meet him loomed very large in his consciousness just now.

Jim stayed at attention, not sure if Donovan was still officially in the military. Donovan smiled and motioned for him to stand at ease both literally and figuratively. "Cut the crap and have a drink. Damn, it's cold up here."

Uncorking a thermos bottle, he pulled an extra cup out of his pocket and poured out a cup of black coffee, handing it to Jim. Grateful for the warmth, Jim took a long sip. The coffee was laden with sugar and what Jim suspected was an excellent whiskey, and doubtless as Irish as Donovan's seemingly open visage.

"You know, having this meeting was really just an excuse for me to come out here." Donovan nodded toward the open fields. "It's one of my favorite places. It's rich land here, rich with the blood of patriots from North and South.

"Did you know I was Colonel of the old 69th New York in the last war? There was more than one man in that unit whose daddy or granddad had fought with the original 69th, back when they were part of the Irish Brigade of the Army of the Potomac."

Donovan leaned over and pointed down at the sunken lane that ran at a right angle out from the base of the tower and snaked up to a low crest several hundred yards away.

"This ground here, from that sunken road down below us up to the Miller cornfield"—he pointed to the north—"is the bloodiest square mile in America. The rebs were packed in that road down there in a battle-line three and four deep. It was a natural trench. The Bloody Lane it's called now. Before the battle it had no name at all. The old 69th came charging in from over there." Donovan pointed off to the right. "By the time they'd gotten to within a hundred yards of Bloody Lane the fire was so fierce that the charge ground to a halt. Then Colonel Meagher, the brigade commander, stood up in his stirrups, screamed for the boys to charge, and galloped forward without looking to see if he was followed. Those glorious boys charged into a storm of bullets, screaming, '*Erin go bragh*, Erin go bragh . . ." Donovan said the words as if calling out to the ghosts in the field below. "Erin go bragh. . . ."

"They say half of the 88th New York, our sister regiment, went down with the first volley, the dead and dying laid out in a long straight line. Meagher's horse was shot in full gallop, and Meagher went down, knocked unconscious. The brigade was melting like ice tossed into boiling water. Finally the boys went to ground, keeping up a hot fire, and hung on till a relief column went over them and pressed the charge the rest of the way home."

Donovan fell silent for a moment as he looked out across the field, the icy snow hissing down around them.

"The survivors were pulled back from the line then, fewer than five hundred of the thousand or more who went in. And I'll tell you, James Martel, they formed up in columns of four, under fire, and marched from the field. They might not have taken that road, but they left like soldiers. Like *soldiers*."

Smiling self deprecatingly at his display of emotion, Donovan uncorked the thermos and poured them both some more Irish coffee. He raised his cup in a toast to the fallen and downed it. Under the spell, Jim followed suit.

"This was the bloodiest day in American history," Donovan said. "Worse than anything in the Argonne, and Christ knows it takes something for me to say that, because I was there. It was worse than Pearl, Iwo, or the day those thousand kamikazes hit the fleet off Tokyo, and I know you took part in that one. Twenty-three thousand American boys were killed or wounded on these fields in less than ten hours." He paused for a moment. "I'm afraid we'll see worse than that in the days to come."

For a moment Donovan stood lost in thought. Then, suddenly all business, he turned and looked at Jim. "So tell me about yourself."

"Where shall I start, sir?"

"At the beginning. You. Your parents. Actually I'm quite interested in your upbringing. If you begin to bore me, I'll let you know."

Jim started back from before he was born. He talked briefly about the Mannheims and the Martels, then went on to the conflict between his parents after the war.

"That must have been very painful for you."

"I loved my mother. I used to pretend that I was her knight-errant, ready to protect her. You see, during the War Dad was gone for two years. I was not quite four when he left. Anti-German feelings were running high and Mom, well, Mom reached the point of refusing to speak English. Former friends shunned her like she had the plague."

"I'm not proud of how some things were handled back then," Donovan commented quietly.

"I used to get taunted and picked on a lot at school. That's when I learned to be a scrapper. When word came of the Armistice, and Grandda's suicide, she just locked herself away for weeks. Suddenly everyone else acted like it was time to forgive and forget, but Mom couldn't."

"Why did she marry your father, then?"

"Oh, about what you would expect. He was dashing, exciting. Her father had a fit over it, I'm told, though he offered no actual objections. Anyhow, recall that feelings toward Germany back before the war were actually rather positive, and the two of them never imagined there'd be a war to divide them like that." Martel mused for a moment, briefly shook his head, and continued.

"When Dad came home it was never the same. I realize now that Mom had withdrawn into something not very different from a situational psychosis with a good touch of paranoia. The fights were nearly constant until she died from diphtheria when I was seven."

"How did you handle that?"

"For a long time I blamed Dad for it. But as I got older I realized he loved her as much as I did. Maybe more. He never remarried, you know."

"I suppose all this explains your fascination with your mother's country, its culture and language."

"I guess so. It was rather a defiance, hanging on to something that was uniquely hers, though Dad never objected. To a degree I suspect that my clinging to her heritage kept her closer for him as well. Maybe that's why he encouraged my year in Germany and living with my mother's sister, Wilhelm's mother."

"And then home to Annapolis. Why the Navy?"

Jim shrugged. "Tradition. A Martel captained a ship in Napoleon's navy at Trafalgar. When the Emperor fell he fled to America and settled in North Carolina with some other French refugees, down on the Cape Fear River. His son, Dad's grandfather, was an officer in the Confederate Navy. My grandfather and dad were both Annapolis graduates. It was simply assumed that I wanted to continue the tradition. And I did. Since my German grandfather was a navy man too, an added benefit was that it was a way of carrying on family traditions from both sides. In most ways they pulled against each other. In this, though, they were one."

"I've seen your naval record. Admirable. Navy Cross, twenty-three kills, three tours of duty. America's Number-Seven Ace. How did you feel about combat, the killing?"

"I won't deny there was a thrill," Jim said quietly, "The thrill of the hunt, the triumph when you broke away and saw the other guy's plane going down in flames. Knowing it was one-on-one, and you were alive and the other guy wasn't. Do you have a problem with that, sir?"

"Wild Bill" ignored the question. "Did you hate them?"

"After Pearl, right up to Midway, I hated their guts. I couldn't wait to get them in my sights. But the night after Midway, it hit me. Or maybe the night after Midway I let it hit me, since after that there was no way we could lose."

Jim looked back out over the battlefield.

"I was escort for Wade McCloskey's flight of dive bombers. The Zeroes had no choice but to come after us if their fleet was going to live. I took down three that day. . . . Anyhow, that night all I could remember was seeing that third fighter explode. I'd never seen anything quite like it. Not from up close. It just lit up, not fifty yards in front of me. The pilot got out, but he was on fire. He kept slapping at the flames. His mouth was open in a scream I couldn't hear, except later in the nightmares. The only difference I could see between us was that he was a human torch falling three screaming miles to the sea and I was on my way back to base."

Martel paused for a moment. "They had to be stopped, stopped dead in their tracks, but hate is pointless. If you let hate get in the way, it will tear you up inside. At least that was how it was for me."

"And if we fight the Germans? Your cousin Wilhelm, half your family, your mother's blood will be on the other side."

"Willi would want me to win, even if it meant his own death."

"Could you kill him if you had to?"

"Knowing who he was? I doubt it. Don't ever ask that of me," Jim said quietly. "I would have no problem in a fight with the German military. Soldiers understand each other, and the necessities of war. As for the Nazis, especially the SS, I'd love to help bring them down. They have ruined my mother's beloved Fatherland. The world now sees the people who gave us Beethoven, Kant, and Goethe as a nation of monsters. As for Willi, I think he'd regard a victorious America as Germany's liberator."

"Your father and I both fought that other Germany."

Jim nodded. "You and Dad were soldiers, as was my grandfather." He pointed out across the fields of Antietam, "It was just like with the boys who lay out there. Their job was to kill the other side, but they'd share the last drinks out of their canteens with the men they'd shot only minutes before. That's the paradox of war, especially for Americans. And I think as well it's a reflection of what's best in us, that we fight when we have to but we—most of us—never get to quite that intensity of hate where we can't still feel compassion for a fallen enemy."

Martel snarled unconsciously. "With the SS it's different. Most who chose SS over regular Wehrmacht service would pour water on the ground where some poor dying son of a bitch couldn't quite reach it—and then cut his throat as he stretched."

Donovan nodded, his features grim, as Jim continued.

"Hitler and his scum, they're evil incarnate. Theirs is an empire of darkness. The people of Germany have made a Faustian bargain. Somehow, to some degree, they must go through the fire to be redeemed. There's no way they can be saved without having first experienced some of what they have done to others."

Martel gestured toward the long-deserted battlefield. "Lincoln said we were the last best hope of mankind. Paradoxically that's why those boys on both sides fought so well. Now we are all that stands between the world and Hitler. Sooner or later there's going to be a showdown." After a moment he added in a different tone, "I think it will be sooner."

"I saw the letter," Donovan said. "I believe it's a true warning."

"Thank God you do."

"I'm not the only one. McDonnell was in the President's office a half hour after he left you. I was there a half hour after that."

Jim could barely contain his surprise that events had moved so fast. "What did the President say?"

Donovan smiled. "We'll discuss that some other time, when I know you better. After the three of us had chewed over the letter McDonnell asked me to check into your case. Since the President didn't object, I did so."

"And?"

"You got royally screwed. It was an FBI snafu. The information about the radar and torpedoes was leaked here, Stateside. The FBI just wouldn't admit it when the cards started to fall into place. You were the one other possible source and, since your defection wouldn't reflect on them, the FBI concentrated on that line instead. You caused some embarrassment with the military, since Hoover was breathing down their necks, so even after you got cleared, you were a pariah. It was that simple." Donovan laughed ruefully. "Right now along with everything else the President is trying to figure out how to make sure that the FBI doesn't let things happen just for the sake of covering its butt." Donovan paused and looked Martel squarely in the eye. "But that's not our concern. The bottom line for you is that for me and the President and whoever else needs to know, you're in the clear."

"So the President knows I'm okay, and you do, and McDonnell—but I'm to remain dipped in shit to the rest of the world," Jim said quietly.

"Why do you say that?" Donovan asked cautiously, as if what Martel thought were somehow important to him.

"Better the Gestapo continue to think that they screwed me good. That's why I will remain buried at the Pentagon and told to keep my mouth shut."

"Very good, *very* good," Donovan said softly.

"There *is* one other person," Martel began. "She —"

"No exceptions, Jim," Donovan said simply. After a pause he added, "You could still work on it though."

Martel lifted an eyebrow. Somehow he knew the stakes for him personally had become very high, and in the manner of fighter pilots that fact had made him dead calm.

"By joining my team. A lot of people with the OSS are on leave of absence from the military."

"Damn."

"I take it 'damn' means 'yes.' You just hang tight while paper gets routed We don't want to draw attention by going outside channels."

"Hell, I could put in for immediate administrative leave. That would probably come through in a few days."

Donovan thought about that for a moment. Both of them knew that time was very short. "Do it."

Martel didn't know if the relief he felt had more to do with personal vindication or the fact that at last he had the go-ahead to get to work thwarting a conspiracy against his country. What he did know was that the world had come back to life.

Donovan turned back to the parapet and gazed over the field once again. It was almost as if he were praying, and somehow Jim was not surprised when he lowered his head and made the sign of the cross.

"It's sacred ground," Donovan said, as if he needed to explain himself.

He led the way back down from the tower and headed to where their cars were parked side by side. As he reached for the door he paused and said, "One more point. You're a very curious guy, Martel, and that's all right. You've got to have the curiosity of a cat to be good at this job. But kill that curiosity regarding 'Manhattan.' You got that?"

"Yes, sir. Absolutely."

Donovan unlocked his car and got in.

At the last moment Jim added, "Thank you, sir."

Donovan waved his hand as he drove off.

As the sound of Donovan's car faded and disappeared, Jim turned and walked down the sunken road, alone with the icy snow that swirled around him like hovering ghosts.

March 31
The Oval Office

As he did every week at this time, Andrew Harrison opened the face of the clock that rested on the mantel over the fireplace in the Oval Office and wound it. Ritual completed, he stood before the crackling fire for a moment, then turned and walked to the bay windows set in the opposite wall. The snow outside was swirling around in thick heavy flakes. He found it a comforting reminder of his long-ago home, where blizzards would come roaring in across the open prairie.

"You like snow, John?"

John Mayhew looked up in surprise from the sofa where he was reviewing the next day's appointments. "Sir?"

"Something wrong, John?" Andrew asked.

"Ah, n-no, sir, nothing wrong at all. I was just concentrating, that's all."

"You've seemed out of sorts the last few days."

"Just a lot going on, sir, same as always, really."

Andrew looked at him closely. Something *was* wrong, but he wasn't sure what. Probably some family thing.

"How are the kids?"

"Just fine, sir. It looks like Harvard for Robert come fall."

Andrew smiled politely as his mind shifted tracks. He really had nothing to say since he was not about to vent his opinions regarding East Coast snobbery and intellectual hauteur. Strange the things that sometimes mark us out to fate.

He knew that his antipathy for the East Coast Elite—he'd graduated from a land-grant school himself—was in large part the reason FDR had chosen him as his successor. In 1944 the Democratic Party was beginning to split along regional lines, and a Western nominee would help to hold the coalition together. The East Coast crowd would have to play along, Roosevelt knew, since for them it was the only game in town.

Now though, with Franklin gone from the scene, the Easterners might be able to start their own game. Already there were indications of coming fractures in the midterm elections. The liberals were pushing hard for a continuation of the New Deal and a more aggressive stance toward Nazi Germany. At the same time isolationism was reasserting itself on his own home turf; some of his old party friends were even saying he had sold out. The picture was not looking all that great for '48. For the President's part, were it not for Hitler and his crew, isolationism would look pretty good. As things were, he had to run with the internationalist crowd.

But at the moment he had more immediate worries.

Andrew settled down behind his desk, the same desk Lincoln had once used and looked back at the clock. Two minutes after five. Even as he took note of the time the scrambler phone on his desk rang.

"Harrison."

"M-M-Mr. President. How are you?" The gravelly voice on the other end was one that nearly every American would recognize, though the stutter would surprise them. In public address the speaker used a sort of singing delivery that both avoided that problem and added a certain majesty to his utterances.

"Fine, Winston, how are *you*?"

"Very well, Andrew. I cannot say so much for England, I fear."

Andrew looked up at John and gestured dismissal. The Chief of Staff started to gather up his papers. His mind seemed far away.

"Winston, what do you think of that letter I sent over yesterday?"

"M-My people think it's real. I see no c-cause to doubt them."

Mayhew started to walk toward the door, but stopped to re-gather his documents when his folder somehow slipped from his grasp, spilling the papers out across the floor.

"Damn, I was hoping you could tell me it's a fake," the President replied. "That 'Manhattan' reference has us worried."

"Do you think they would dare to try something on your side of the Atlantic?"

"I don't know. I've got Donovan working on it. General Groves and his man in charge of security down there think some more spies might have been infiltrated into the area.

We've already nailed several over the last year, though thank God none of them had penetrated to the real secret. Still, the Germans may know enough to be considering some kind of sabotage. Or maybe a team of assassins. They could cripple us if they get the right dozen men, and, as it happens, all the top Los Alamos people will be there during Easter Week, finalizing the next phase of the project. George Marshall will be there as well, to review the schedule. Or all that could simply be coincidence, and the mention of Manhattan the merest red herring added for the amusement of our source's own counter-intel. God knows it's amused us enough."

John Mayhew picked up the last renegade piece of paper and quietly left the room.

Harrison laughed without humor. "Remember last fall, when I told you about that crossword puzzle in the *New York Times*? The one that mentioned Manhattan, uranium and Oak Ridge within a couple of lines of each other? Hoover almost had a baby over that."

"Andrew, this came from a turned German intelligence officer, not a *New York Times* crossword puzzle."

"Yes, I know, but it is so vaguely phrased—how can we tell what it means? At any rate I'm not willing to do anything pre-emptive based on what we have so far."

"Well, I have more information for you," Winston said gruffly. "And it is not at all vague."

Andrew felt a knot start to tighten in his stomach.

"Go on."

"Ultra has been shut down."

Andrew closed his eyes and leaned back in his chair. "That is very bad."

"It happened at midnight, Berlin time. At first we thought they'd changed the settings, usual routine. By noon we knew it was much worse."

"Tell me."

"The old system was five-letter coded word groups. Now it's nine-letter word groups. They couldn't have done that with Enigmas. That means they've replaced the old coding machines with a whole new system. New machines, new code systems, everything."

"Do you think they learned we'd broken the old one?"

For a moment static overwhelmed the call, then Churchill's voice came through again. "I think they have. Perhaps it was a leak. Perhaps we acted one too many times on information gained from having broken it. Maybe they planted false data and we acted on it. Who can say? Andrew, is it p-p-possible th-that . . . ?"

"Is it possible that the leak, if there was one, was on this side? I don't see how. Only myself and one or two others are aware of exactly why your intelligence is sometimes so uncannily accurate. Or 'was,' perhaps I should say. . . . Well, let's never mind that now. How soon can you crack it?"

"It took us years to crack the old machines, even though we had one. We don't even know what cryptographic system they've implemented. I told our wizards they had to crack it within a week. They replied that it would take six months just to learn how the machinery is constructed. They did say that if we could get access to that new 'computer' your army has it might speed things up. Indeed, that request is on the agenda for this call."

"Consider it done. I'll have Marshall clear things for you. Just get a team out here."

"They are already en route. I t-took that liberty."

Harrison smiled. That was just like Winston—and it was also exactly what he ought to have done. "Not a liberty, quick thinking."

"Mr. President, I want you to consider something else: the timing of this. If they are planning an offensive for the spring, this is precisely when they would change their coding systems. Monty said he'd have done it thirty to forty-five days prior to a general attack, because that's how long it would take the orders to start to filter down into the corps and division command structure. Andrew, we have a clear signal, and we disregard it at our terrible peril."

"It could still mean Russia, though. The Germans know we'd tip them off."

"Russia!" Winston said scornfully. "You know as well as I do that it will be years if ever before the Germans need worry about Russia again. Why should they bother with them now? The most likely — by far the most likely — explanation of all this is that the Nahsties," Andrew smiled at Winston's deliberate mispronunciation, "learned about your bomb. They're going to strike first, as best they may. Assassination and sabotage for you, an all-out assault against us. They must deny you access to a base of operations against Europe, to say nothing of the not-entirely-insignificant military force of which we still dispose. And all that aside, we have irrefutable proof that those amphibious maneuvers on the shore of the Black Sea are a rehearsal exercise a-aimed d-d-directly at England."

Suddenly Harrison felt he was too close to agreeing with the English leader. "Winston, let's not get ourselves too far out on a limb here. I simply can't commit significant resources on the basis of what little we have. It's hard enough keeping the appropriations for the Army and Navy up as it is. The budget is just starting to get laid out for next year. It's at a very vulnerable point, and if we holler 'wolf' at this particular time a hell of a lot of people will accuse me of faking it just to jack up military funding. It doesn't even matter if they believe what they're saying. They'll use it as an excuse for *cutting* spending. For that matter, just keeping the money flowing to Manhattan is going to be hard enough."

"Andrew, apparently this letter is having a more profound effect on us than on you, the intended recipients," Winston said calmly. "For my part, I've ordered a secret alert for the Royal Air Force, starting at midnight. Also, the army will move its spring maneuver schedule up so as to increase troop strengths throughout England. I'm also going to make a speech before the House next week accusing Hitler of preparing to launch an attack against us."

"Winston, I wish you wouldn't do that."

"Why?"

"Because the 'America First' crowd will go to town on you, that's why. They'd claim it was part of an on-going plot to drag us into yet another European conflict. They'll say it was a repeat of what you and Roosevelt tried to do in '40 and '41. They'll say you're deliberately trying to provoke Hitler, that you came back to office intending to do just that, to finally drag us into a showdown with Germany. If you make that speech I won't be able to back you up."

A cold, static-laden silence was the only response.

"Even Roosevelt didn't start to move openly until after the '40 elections, you know," Andrew continued after a moment's pause. "You also know I agreed with him a hundred percent. I could see the threat as far back as the denouncement of Versailles and the move into the Rhineland. I knew then and I know now that the maniac son of a bitch would never stop on his own, and that nothing short of a full scale war with the United States could stop him. We should have been in it back in '41; if it hadn't been for that damned accident he'd have declared war on us after Pearl Harbor — he all but told me that himself. In '41 we'd have won easily. Now, he's ten times more dangerous."

"And yet you don't think he's about to strike us now?"

"No, I don't. He doesn't want a two-front war, and he suspects that Russia would turn on him while he's busy with us. At the same time he knows our two democracies are politically incapable of a pre-emptive attack while his forces are otherwise engaged. He'll finish Russia off, and then turn on us. Furthermore the balance continues to tilt in his direction."

"That analysis doesn't hold water, Andrew. It is obvious that Stalin will simply sit it out if Hitler goes against England and America. Both he and Hitler know perfectly well that once Hitler turns west it will be a very long time before he turns east again. And as for the balance of military power—Andrew, they know about Manhattan."

Harrison ignored this. "Winston, you mustn't go public. This country has just finished one war and still has two hundred thousand troops in China committed to a cause nobody outside of government feels is worth dying over. I'm losing more and more support in Congress every day on that. The last thing the American public wants is another fight, and if they don't see the cause for it just as clear as clear can be, they'll turn you down flat."

"The American people are tougher than you think. They will fight."

Andrew felt the sting of the rebuke and spoke more personally than he otherwise might have. "Winston, your mother is from the American upper crust, and for an Englishman that may give you some special insight into *my* people, but I'm telling you that without a clear enemy we will not fight."

"There is no clearer enemy than Hitler."

"We both know that. The Lord knows we do. But some of the characters up on the Hill will play this for their own political gain and the hell with what's best for this country, to say nothing of what's best for England. They'll wring their hands and talk about the coffins coming home from overseas adventures, and how England dragged us into the first war and almost got us into a two-front war back in '41. If you give them the ammunition, I will lose my majority. Consider what that would mean for England. Wait, Winston, wait for '47. We've got a lot of young fellows, veterans who know what it's all about, running for office. They will recognize the nature of the threat."

"By then, Andrew, all of us on this side will know, in the most intimate way, the nature of the threat."

Harrison winced, but his voice was clear and firm. "Maybe so, Winston, but I can't do my job on a 'maybe.' so I'm asking you not to rock the boat. Get your air force on alert, move up your maneuver schedule if you think you must, but don't make that speech."

There was a long pause. The crackling static rose and fell like waves.

"All right, Andrew, I'll hold back. But one more piece of evidence and—"

"We'll cross that when and if we come to it, Winston," Andrew replied quietly.

"Andrew, we will cross it sooner than you think."

"I think you are right on the facts, but not on the timing. We've got to play a close hand until there's a smoking gun."

"Must we await another Pearl Harbor?"

Andrew slowly turned his chair around to look out at the snow which was now falling thick and heavy. "If need be, yes," he whispered, "though anything on that scale would have to be aimed at you, not us."

"I'm aware of that," the war leader of the English replied. "Though I doubt the Germans shall find us so unprepared as the Japanese found you."

"Not with our example to guide you. Keep your guard up, Winston."

"And you yours, Andrew, and you yours."

Both men were certain they were prepared for whatever might come to pass. Both were in for a surprise.

CHAPTER NINE

April 13
Charleston Harbor

"America," Otto Skorzeny said quietly, nodding toward the lights of Charleston on the horizon.

Hans said nothing, spitting over the railing, suppressing yet another urge to vomit.

"We'll be landing soon, Hans."

"For Christ's sake, next time throw me out of a plane without a parachute," Hans moaned. Leaning over the railing, he dry-heaved once more.

Skorzeny struggled not to emulate him. The ocean was still rough, with seas at eight to ten feet, but it was a blessing compared to what they had endured for most of the crossing. Seasickness was the last thing he had ever worried about in his life and, as a paratrooper, the mere thought of it somehow implied a certain weakness. The fact that he had spent a fair part of the crossing either in the head or on his cot had filled him with self-loathing. His men knew better than to dream of saying anything, yet he could sense their amusement, even though half of them had suffered as much as he had. Well, he supposed that once back on dry land he might regain a sense of humor about it himself.

Right now, however . . . struggling with dizziness, he looked over at Hans.

If he would have no mercy with himself, that was reason enough not to spare anyone else. Besides, they had no time to coddle each other. "Remember the briefing, Hans. If anything happens to me, it's your job to take over."

Hans nodded. "Why the concern, Colonel?"

"Remember. We know General Marshall will be at the target along with a number of their top scientists from Los Alamos. Richer has the information as well. Regardless of that, he might get lost coming in. I want Marshall and those people hit. Do you understand me? You are to take care of it personally."

"Sir."

Skorzeny turned as the captain of the freighter approached him. He, along with the rest of the crew, was hand picked from the French Fascist Party, but it still made Skorzeny nervous that the captain knew his identity.

"My crew has been sent belowdecks," the captain reported. "Your pickup boat is coming alongside."

Skorzeny nodded acknowledgment.

"Get the men up, Hans."

Hans started to salute and then let his hand drop. Turning, he slowly weaved his way across the deck, the captain watching him with the mock sympathy that all sailors have for those who have recently sacrificed to the sea gods.

As Hans went below, Skorzeny joined the captain at the railing where he was peering into the fog and spray that hung low over the water.

"Anything on radar?"

"Some traffic, nothing suspicious. The Coast Guard has a cutter chasing down a small boat in distress about ten miles south of here. I think you'll have a clear run in." The captain laughed softly. "It's an open sieve, this country. You could run the *Tirpitz* right into the harbor and open fire before they woke up."

Otto said nothing. Unknown to the captain, the small boat the cutter was looking for was part of the plan. But even so, he'd not relax until they were ashore.

He heard the low muffled rumble of a diesel engine. From out of the wisps of fog and spray a fishing trawler emerged. Their pickup. Skorzeny looked back over his shoulder and saw his men coming up from below decks, each of them taking a deep gasp of fresh air as he finally emerged from the dank hold where they had stayed throughout the crossing.

Skorzeny studied them for a moment, then turned back to his third in command. "Gear check, Gunther." Punctiliously they went down the list: radios, navigation beacons, signal flares, civilian clothing, personal weapons. . . . As they did so, Gunther Rothmann slapped the boxes that they had brought up from below.

At last, "Everything secured." Gunther knew that Skorzeny would have been shocked beyond measure to discover that a single item of equipment was missing or out of place; he also knew that unlike many officers Skorzeny would insist on this personal checkoff until the day he died, a day that might come much later, thanks to his careful habits.

As they were going over the equipment, the trawler had sidled up along the freighter's leeward side, matching speed as her crew tossed fenders over the railing. With surprising delicacy, considering the chop of the sea and the masses involved, it brushed up against the side of the freighter, rebounded, touched again. The captain gestured for some of the commandos to help him manhandle a rope ladder over the side. Down on the trawler two of the crew grabbed the dangling end as it jerked back and forth.

While he and Hans were going over the list, the men had been busy hooking lines to the boxes. Now they began gingerly lowering them over the side. Skorzeny watched the operation nervously, breathed a sigh of relief as each one thumped the deck below and was hustled off to concealment by the trawler crew. Everything had been packed so that if a box were lost or damaged there was back-up equipment in the other boxes, but he did not want to lose any of that reserve.

When the last of the boxes had been lowered, Skorzeny ordered the group to line up for a final inspection. As they did so he asked, "You have all double-checked yourselves and then checked each other before coming up?"

They nodded in unison.

"All clothing is American? No personal identification on any of you? Not even a photo? You're all clean?"

More nods.

He walked down the line of seven men, looking over each in turn. Even though they were dressed as laborers, it was obvious from their conditioning that they were professionals. That was his one concern: their simple physical perfection would not bear the examination of a knowing eye. Had there been time he would have *de*conditioned them, forcing them to sit around swilling beer and eating great masses of greasy food while their comrades labored like demons. Perhaps had them constantly arm-wrestle each other, but only with their right arms to make them unbalanced, more like laborers. . . . A soldier's paradise, and how they would have loathed it. In a rare moment of humor that even overcame his seasickness he grinned at the thought.

Except for their remarkable physical fitness he had no fear for their ability to blend into the local population. Each spoke perfect American, and each had assumed and practiced a false identity for months in preparation for this mission. As for himself and Hans, they would pose as Polish refugees; few Americans could tell the one accent from the other. It was not a perfect solution, but it would serve, or so he hoped.

"Let's go," he said quietly as he swung himself over the side and started down the ladder. The dizziness from the twelve days of battling seasickness troubled him and he moved cautiously, gauging the relative motions of himself and the boat below, which was bobbing up and down on the eight-foot swells. He waited for the boat to start coming back up and—at not quite the right instant he let go of the rope ladder and jumped down, striking the deck hard. Almost before he had his breath back he became aware of the new, more emphatic, motions of the small boat; within seconds he was leaning over the side, cursing his weakness.

Emptied now, gasping for breath, he turned and straightened to watch his men, one after the other, come down. Even though they were all trained paratroopers, this type of landing was different from what they were used to, and for a seasick landsman, just as treacherous as parachuting into gusty winds.

When the rest had all landed successfully, Hans finally eased himself over the freighter's railing and started down. He hesitated for a moment, obviously in the throes of yet another spasm. Gunther muttered a curse when he was hit by some of the spume. The men around him chuckled softly.

Skorzeny lost patience. "Move it, Hans!"

His friend looked down at him, nodded bleakly, and continued his descent. At the final rung he stopped again, waited, and then stepped off the ladder, releasing his hold as he did so. Had he been more alert he might have detected the particularly heavy swell that raised the trawler up on a crest and simultaneously pushed it away from the side of the freighter. In that case he would have turned the step into a leap, or perhaps managed to snatch the ladder again. Instead, an aborted grab at the ladder caused the heel still on the rung to catch, and he slammed transversely along the trawler's gunnel.

Stunned, he began to slide headfirst toward the sea, but as he did so Gunther, lunging from several feet away, snagged an ankle, and Hans managed a shallow one-handed grab onto the gunnel's edge. Still all might have been well, but then the trawler dropped into the trough, Hans's grip gave way, and he recommenced his slide, Gunther still clinging to his foot. Cursing, Otto staggered across the heaving deck to Gunther's side, reached out, and—the trawler surged back.

The sound of two ships slapping against each other was muffled by the human body between them. "Hang on to him!" Otto roared over Hans's screams as he leaned over and tried to add his grip to Gunther's. Hans continued to scream as the trawler scraped its way up the side of the freighter. Gunther, still clinging to his doomed comrade, was being dragged over as well.

Otto could see he was about to lose another man. He gave up on Hans to grab Gunther around the waist and pull him back aboard. As he did so, Gunther finally lost his grip on Hans's ankle. The sound of two hulls scraping ceased to be muffled by intervening flesh.

"We've got to get the body!" Skorzeny roared over at the trawler captain, who of course had been observing all of this. The captain, still at the wheel, shouted for his crew to cast loose from the ladder. Backing the trawler away from the freighter, his crew positioned themselves with boat hooks as Otto and his men lined the sides, straining to catch sight of Hans.

"I couldn't hold him," Gunther said quietly, coming to Skorzeny's side. "I'm sorry."

"It wasn't your fault," Skorzeny replied in a dead voice, knowing too well whose fault it was. He continued to scan the dark waters.

"Do you want some light?" the captain asked. After a pause he added, "Even with lights we'll never spot him on a night like this."

Skorzeny balanced the dangers in his mind. Hans was dead—that he had known from the moment his friend had stopped screaming—and there was precious little chance of spotting his floating body, if it floated, in the failing light. Contrariwise, every minute they spent here would increase their chances of being spotted. Any one of the ships currently in the harbor or approaching the channel could be a Coast Guard vessel, and floodlights trained on the water's surface would certainly draw attention. "His rib cage must have been crushed; with his lungs collapsed maybe he went straight down," Skorzeny finally said. "Just get us out of here."

The captain, obviously relieved, swung the trawler around and throttled the engine up.

Skorzeny looked over at his men, who stood silent, dejected.

"Listen. Probably our comrade is sinking toward the bottom as we speak. But even if he washes up, the chance of anyone linking him to our operation is almost non-existent. As for his dying, well, we all knew this operation would be the riskiest we'd ever done, Hans included. So now we carry on."

"But to die like that," Gunther replied sadly, "falling off a stinking fishing boat."

"Nonsense, Gunther. Even for us, death seldom comes before some stupid accident has rendered us vulnerable to the enemy. This was no different, and Hans would know that too." But it *was* different; in this little grotesquerie there had been no enemy.

With Hans gone, Gunther would have to be their primary radio operator. But Gunther wasn't Hans, a man who had been with him from the beginning. And Gunther was right: Hans had survived all the missions into Russia only to die senselessly because of being seasick and losing his footing. A sad, bad way to go.

The trawler turned into the main channel of Charleston Harbor, clearing Moultrie and Morris islands. Directly ahead, the lights of the city were now clearly in view, and in the middle of the harbor the dark foreboding bulk of Fort Sumter was silhouetted by the glare of the city.

The trawler turned out of the main channel, heading in behind Morris Island. Skorzeny watched intently as it weaved its way through the maze of channel markers and headed toward a labyrinth of broken-down wharves. He went back to join the captain.

"Should we get below?"

"No one's there. We bought the marina a couple of years back. Our rents tended to be a little too high and the maintenance a little too sloppy, so folks moved elsewhere. It's nice and private now."

"You've run other teams in?"

Perhaps realizing that he had been overly talkative, the captain looked at him coldly. "Look. I don't ask your business and you don't ask mine. Do we understand each other?"

Smiling inwardly, Skorzeny nodded solemnly at the rebuke.

Breaking off the conversation, the captain slowed the boat and weaved his way through the final needle-thin inlet, and cut the engine as the trawler drifted up to bump gently into its slip. As it did so the crew, waiting poised on the gunnel, leaped to the wharf and tied the boat off.

"You've got a truck waiting for you at the end of the wharf. You'd best get your men and gear the hell out of here."

"Thank you, Captain."

The man simply nodded and turned to bark orders at his crew. Skorzeny wanted to suggest that a slightly reduced crispness might constitute better tradecraft, but resisted the temptation, and instead motioned for his men to grab their gear. A gangplank was thrown across the railing and the men started off.

The captain turned back to Otto.

"I don't normally pass out free advice, but you should let someone else—anyone else—do the talking."

"Thanks for the free advice," Skorzeny replied with a grin. "I was planning to."

"Good luck."

Skorzeny shook the captain's hand, and then turned to follow his men to the waiting truck. As he did so, to his immense delight he realized that he was no longer seasick.

It was a joy to be alive.

April 14
Bergen, Norway

As the He-177 transport plane drifted to a stop, the door swung open and the strains of *Deutschland Über Alles* entered along with the crisp northern air. To Field Marshal Erwin Rommel such ceremonies were one of the more annoying aspects of high command: No matter where he went, the local commander had to put on a show, and Rommel in turn had to pretend appreciation of the tinny band and the troops drawn up in review.

"It's not every day that our old commander, hero of North Africa, comes to visit us," Major General Hans Bayerling commented in response to Rommel's muttered complaint as they walked along the front rank, pretending to inspect it.

Yes, there had to be the brass band and its tinny music, and yes, there had to be the honor guard. But the inspection? That was gratuitous. Having at last reached the end of the interminable rank of soldiers, Rommel nodded curtly and stepped into the waiting black Mercedes, first having motioned for one of his aides to replace the driver. Once seated he beckoned for the man who had been one of his staff officers and later a divisional commander to join him.

When they were both settled, Rommel unbent a little. "It is good to see you again, Hans."

Bayerling smiled. "Nearly two years now since you left Africa. A long time, my friend."

In response, Rommel looked over to his Afrika Korps comrade and patted him on the shoulder.

Americans would be startled to discover the degree of camaraderie that existed not just between different ranks within the German officer corps, but between officers and rankers. Though the practice had its roots in the mutinous conditions prevalent in the German military at the end of the Great War, perhaps Germans could afford the informality because German society was so thoroughly status conscious —whereas Americans, so unready to grant superiority to anybody, needed the outward manifestations of rank because otherwise they would lose track of who issued orders and who took them. Whatever it said about the intrinsic merit of the two cultures, certainly the resulting increased unit cohesion, unanticipated side benefit or not, was a major advantage for the German side. . . .

"Those were great days." Rommel laughed, breaking his own train of thought. "'Fun in the sun,' as the Americans might say. How have your men acclimated to this very different climate? Are they fit?"

After a silent moment spent contemplating the incongruity of that "fun" appellation as applied to the experience, Bayerling replied: "We are fit enough. And eager to go home. You know, that is where we thought we were headed when they pulled us out of the line in North Africa. Instead, they sent us up to this icebox to freeze our stones off. We fought the Brits in Africa for three years, then we spent eighteen months on the armistice line—and now here. Do I sound bitter? I promise you the men are bitter."

Bayerling shook his head, then continued. "It just doesn't add up. My men gave good service in Africa—and then they get shipped from that hellhole to this god-forsaken place. Morale is at rock bottom, and I don't blame the men for that one bit."

"Perhaps there was a reason for sending you here."

"Punishment is all I can think of. But what could it have been? We were the best. I keep coming back to that. It must have been sheer bad luck."

Rommel smiled. "No my friend, it wasn't luck, good or bad, and it wasn't because you or your men screwed up in some special way."

"Why then?"

"Because you *are* the best. And because you are mine."

His major general looked at him incredulously, too sure Rommel was leading up to something to be angry at his drollery.

"Don't you like it here?" Rommel asked innocently, exacting a small revenge for the pointless ceremonials.

"Like it here? We fought the Brits for three years on a shoestring. If we'd gotten just ten percent of what they were pouring into Russia we would have been on the Suez. But we didn't get piss, and we didn't get Suez. So the Heroes of Russia are cycled back home and we get sent off to this ice cube as . . . as what? Honorary Italians? Now I find out you did it, and you ask me if I like it here! Would you mind telling—"

Rommel held up his hand. "Because I wanted a unit in this location that I knew I could depend on absolutely."

"Depend on for what? In two weeks we go home!" A flicker of doubt passed over Bayerling's face.

Sure enough, Rommel's next words were, "Not directly home. You have a little side trip first."

"Where to, Madagascar?"

"No. Scotland."

Bayerling looked speechlessly at his old commander.

"Last fall the Führer decided to knock England out once and for all. This time we won't be playing games out on the flanks. It will be a drive straight into their island. Your division will be part of the landing force that strikes near Edinburgh. That's why I wanted you and the men conditioned to this abominable climate and, more importantly, positioned for the strike without drawing notice."

Rommel ordered his driver to pull the car over to the side of the road. When it had stopped he got out and his once and present division commander perforce followed. Though it was late afternoon, below them the city and its harbor basked in the light reflected from the high mountains to the west.

"Your men will load onto their transports as planned.

The ships, however, are to be combat-loaded — and I expect all equipment to be operational."

Bayerling nodded phlegmatically. One of the reasons Rommel had chosen him and his division was that he could be sure that however bitter they might be, as a killing machine they would be in perfect working order.

"With the exception of your own staff, with whom you may discuss matters on the eve of embarkation, you will brief no one, *no one*, until the fleet clears the harbor on the nineteenth. The 6th Mountain Division will ship out of Trondheim the day before and rendezvous with your flotilla. Together you'll proceed down the coast as if heading for Hamburg. On the evening of the twentieth, just after dusk, the fleet will turn and make a high-speed run across the North Sea to arrive off Edinburgh at dawn. The 196th out of Oslo will come in as the second wave behind us."

"Three divisions? That's it?"

"Five more will be sealifted over the following two weeks."

Bayerling looked dubious. "They promised us the same thing in Africa. All we ever got was a trickle. I hope they do better this time. Once this show starts the Brits will come pouring out of Scapa Flow like wolves."

"Doenitz will commit everything we have to blocking them. There'll be a cordon of U-boats and destroyers securing our sea lane, backed up by the fleet's three carriers and the *Tirpitz*. We'll have air-lift capacity as well. Also, the 1st Airborne will drop as we land. The 22nd will follow up on the second and third days."

Bayerling kicked at the dirty snow bank lining the side of the road. "And the Luftwaffe?"

"—has a previous engagement."

Bayerling grunted and asked no further questions. Even German military informality had limits. "Our mission objectives?"

"Two-fold. Our first priority is to secure a line from Edinburgh to Glasgow by the end of the second day, and landing fields for the 5th *Luft Flotte*, which will be made up of ground support Fw-190s and Ju-88s, a limited number of He-277s configured as medium bombers, and for air superiority, Me-262s and Do-335s, all of which will be under my operational control.

"On the second and third days of the operation, elements of the 3rd Airborne will secure several airfields within range of Scapa Flow, their main naval base. Unfortunately the constraints imposed by other operations make it impossible to achieve complete surprise by performing all the drops simultaneously. Over the following week the 6th Mountain will swing north to relieve them. As soon as we have secured the bases, we will proceed to make Scapa Flow untenable."

"By the time we do that, they'll have every division from the Midlands north on us."

"That's part of the intent," Rommel replied. "We want to draw them north. After securing the Glasgow-Edinburgh line, our next wave, another division and two regiments of the 10th SS Panzer, will have arrived from Hamburg."

"What the hell do we need those SS bastards for?"

"Their presence is intended to convince the British that we are the main invasion. We are to advance to a line from Newcastle-on-Tyne to South Shields, as a move to threaten the industrial Midlands. At the end of the second week we'll have six divisions on a line moving south. They'll commit to stop us—they must or we'll just keep on going—and then the main invasion will hit on the south coast."

"So we are just a diversion then?"

"The British navy will not think so. But as to the second part of our mission, yes."

Bayerling shook his head.

"And your plans?"

"If we should happen to take Liverpool and York, I won't mind."

"That might happen—if we get the support we need."

"This won't be North Africa," Rommel said confidently.

For a while his old staff officer said nothing as he looked back out to the harbor below. Then, "No. Of course not. But again we are to be the sideshow."

April 14
The Pentagon

Admiral William "Bull" Halsey's face turned to stone as he recognized the other person awaiting him in the Office of the Army Chief of Staff. When he'd been summoned from half a world away to attend this meeting with George Marshall, he hadn't dreamed he would on arrival be facing his old adversary, General Douglas MacArthur.

MacArthur stood with the regal air of an earl who had decided to be polite to a baron. Smiling, he extended his hand. "Good to see you, Halsey."

Halsey suffered the handshake in silence. Unlike MacArthur, he was not one to put on silly airs, nor to pretend for decorum's sake that things were other than they were. Both men had nurtured a deep and abiding hatred of each other ever since the bitter debates in the first year of the war on how best to close in on Japan. Over Halsey's strenuous objections, MacArthur had successfully argued for first retaking the Philippines rather than going straight for Okinawa and Formosa. As far as Halsey was concerned that avenue had had absolutely nothing to recommend it other than soothing the MacArthur ego by punishing those who had had the temerity to kick the MacArthur butt—and Halsey had not been shy in sharing his analysis. Wasted men, wasted ships; the Philippines would have fallen like rotten fruit after the Home Islands surrendered.

"How was your flight, Admiral Halsey?" George Marshall asked, gesturing him to the other chair arranged on the carpet directly before his desk. MacArthur, noblesse oblige accomplished, had already resumed his.

"Other than the fact I haven't slept in over a day, no complaints."

"Sorry to drag you in here like this, Admiral," Marshall "but it was imperative that the three of us sit down together. Now, gentlemen, before we go any further, I want both of you to understand something: I tolerated a great deal from both of you last time out. This time I will not.

MacArthur started to interject.

"General MacArthur, please just sit quietly until I'm finished."

MacArthur, his smile barely flickering, leaned back in his chair.

"We might be talking about nothing here. This whole thing could blow over, but if it doesn't, I expect both of you to follow my orders and those of the President to the letter or, by heavens, I'll fire either or both of you on the spot, publicly, in utter, career-blasting humiliation. Is that understood? And my first order is that the two of you cooperate with each other like fellow officers. I will tolerate nothing less."

Halsey looked over at MacArthur. He agreed with Marshall that the pair of them were a marriage made in Hell, and he was tempted to ask why the devil they were being teamed in the first place. There were other admirals, other generals. The look on Marshall's face warned him to reconsider. He remained silent.

"What's the problem then, General?" MacArthur finally asked. "Germany?"

"I met with the President three days ago. There have been some disturbing indications from that direction, and he asked me to bring the two of you into the picture."

"You mean the Brits and their alert?" MacArthur asked.

Marshall nodded. "That, and other things. The President still believes that the blow will fall on Russia, and a lot of our intelligence points in that direction. But he also wants us to quietly start preparations."

"Using the Black Seven plan?" Halsey asked dubiously.

"General Marshall, I can tell you right now that plan is worthless," MacArthur interjected.

Halsey nodded.

Marshall looked at Halsey. "Admiral, you agree with him for once?"

Halsey felt a flicker of resentment, as if he'd just been cast as MacArthur's front man. "Sir, you must know that plan is obsolete. The last full review of Black Seven was just after the British agreed to terms. They were in arms and we were at full mobilization against Japan. We had over eight million men in uniform. Part of Black Seven called for keeping at least four active divisions in reserve in the States as a reaction force if Germany should try to invade England, along with a light-carrier task force to provide support. Roosevelt made it clear to the Germans that he wouldn't tolerate an invasion of England. He meant it, and they knew he meant it. Since England had gotten the upper hand in the submarine war, within days of a German attempt on England we could have shipped those divisions out of their depots and started moving them across. Not one of those assumptions holds true now."

MacArthur nodded in agreement.

"On the other hand, we won't be committed on two fronts," Marshall replied.

"In a way we still are," Halsey said. "We've got thirty-eight carriers. But of that number ten are committed in the Pacific, four are stationed off China supporting the Nationalists, fifteen are in mothballs, and the others are in varied states of readiness. Is the President willing to pass down an order right now mobilizing the reserve fleet to active status and pull the mothballed carriers out?"

Marshall shook his head in negation.

"May I ask why not, sir?" MacArthur said quietly.

"The President feels that would be overreacting. Germany has no reason at this time to renew the conflict. It's still trying to digest all that it swallowed in the last war.

Maybe three or four years from now the picture will be different, but the President believes that if Germany has a concern at this time, it's over Russian rearmament."

"And do you believe that?"

"That's neither here nor there. My job is to carry out the orders of the President of the United States. Your job is to carry out mine."

MacArthur smiled to himself at Marshall's forceful dodge. "But things have changed, sir. Last year's budget gutted us. The boys I'm getting out in China now are confused children, brand-new draftees who hardly know which end of an M1 to point downrange. It will take nine months to a year to restore our forces to wartime levels. We are not ready to face Germany."

"Next year must take care of itself, General. For now, think about the next forty-five days.

"Do you have hard information on that?" Halsey asked.

"Just unconnected warnings, but too many of them."

"We should have been more worried a year ago," MacArthur commented as he tamped tobacco into his trademark corncob.

"Perhaps true. But that's in the past," Marshall said grimly. "We have to deal with the present, with the resources we have available in the present." He paused for a moment, as if going down a list. "What we have, fully operational, is the 1st Infantry, the 3rd Marine, the 82nd Airborne, and the 3rd Armored. Additionally, the Canadians have undertaken to supply an infantry division."

"It's getting them there—wherever 'there' is—with the capacity to fight that's the real problem," Halsey said.

"That's what I want you two to look at."

"And the plan itself," MacArthur interjected. "It's not just that it assumes nonexistent resources. That's obvious enough for anybody to see." Halsey bristled, but Mac-Arthur didn't look his way. "Black Seven is obsolete conceptually. It's just plain wrong."

"Regarding what?" Clearly Marshall did not disagree; he was prodding for more information. Just exactly how much could he depend on these men for understanding?

"The main thing was the landing areas, disembarking our troops at Plymouth, Bristol and Liverpool. If the Germans have air superiority it will be a slaughter, and I doubt the Navy could hold them back."

"The Navy will do its job," Halsey said sternly.

MacArthur shook his head. "You just said you doubt you'll be able to mobilize the carriers in time."

Halsey looked over at MacArthur, exasperated. "Maybe I spoke too soon. I'll get them there, but I want room to maneuver; I'll be damned if I'm going to put them inside that bathtub of an Irish Sea the way the plan says. I still prefer the variant on the old plan, Plan Black Five: go straight up the Channel, charge right in, meet them head on."

MacArthur look at him sidelong. "'Hey-diddle-diddle, straight up the middle.' Just like in the Pacific, huh? Listen, even *with* carrier support—"

Marshall's hand slapped the table. After a long moment of stony silence he finally said, "Gentlemen, perhaps I did not make myself sufficiently clear. The President of the United States wants his two victors from the Pacific War available to bring him victory in the North Atlantic if Germany does indeed try something. That is why you're both here. But the President has also made it clear that at the slightest sign of insubordination — and that is exactly how I will view any absence of comity—I can rid myself of one or both of you. And that is just what I will do." Marshall paused for a moment to let either of them reply. Neither chose to do so.

In the silence, Halsey realized as he calculated the consequences of defiance that he'd never actually seen George Marshall angry before. For him, normally a man of the most extraordinary formality and politeness, the foregoing had been the equivalent of a small volcanic eruption that might or might not presage a Vesuvian eruption.

Marshall continued: "Now gentlemen. Can you work together? Will you work together?"

Neither Halsey nor MacArthur met his gaze. After a moment they simultaneously looked at each other and nodded an understanding. Both would let bygones be bygones, or at least try to.

"Yeah, we can work together, right . . . Doug?"

"Sure, Bill," MacArthur said with friendly ease. "No sense in giving up a leading role in the biggest dust-up in human history over an old spat."

Both men pasted sincere-looking smiles on their faces.

Marshall sighed. As long as they took this attitude he had no choice but to keep them—and MacArthur, for all his glamour, was a very fine general. "All right. The first thing I want from you is consensus-reviews of Black Five *and* Black Seven. Get them to me within the next ten days, complete with mutually agreed-on modifications to bring them up to date."

Halsey looked over at MacArthur and the pair nodded.

Marshall leaned back in his chair for a moment, then said, "General MacArthur, please supply me with a review of what troops we can get moving within ten days of a full alert. We can airbridge the 82nd, maybe even elements of the 1st, if the Brits can keep their airfields open. But the heavy equipment, including at least one armored division, has to go by sea. I want them ready for embarkation."

"I'll need logistical staff support."

"You've worked with General Eisenhower before. Right now he's my adjutant. I'll assign him to you. Nobody better for this kind of work."

"Ike's a good man. How's he doing?"

"General Eisenhower is doing very well. He is still unhappy that he didn't have a command last time, of course."

MacArthur chuckled. "Too skilled a paper pusher for his own good."

Marshall unbent enough to make a wry face of sympathy for his adjutant, then turned to look at Halsey.

"Admiral, from you I would like a complete and detailed review of our fleet situation on the East Coast. I also want you to see to it that our active carriers on the East Coast are made ready for action immediately. And we can at least get started on the ones in mothballs—concentrate on the ones that can be made seaworthy relatively soon. But do it quietly. Cover it as 'training exercises' and so forth."

Halsey nodded. "I'll see what we can do."

"Fine. Now let's think about our Pacific resources. Task Force 43 is currently off the China coast, scheduled to head back for Pearl on May 15th."

Halsey nodded.

Marshall paused to look at the calendar on his desk.

"You're giving them early leave for Easter. Pull them out and move them back to Pearl at top speed. Now. If we keep Task Force 56 at Pearl—you could say something's wrong again with the engines on *Yorktown*—that will give us eight carriers at Pearl ready to steam for the Canal at a moment's notice."

"Chiang will throw a fit," MacArthur said. "He was counting on that air support for the spring offensive in the north."

Marshall shrugged indifferently.

"What about Mountbatten in Indochina?" MacArthur added. "I promised him a carrier for air support against the Viet Minh."

"Thanks for informing me of that," Halsey snapped angrily, forgetting his earlier resolve.

MacArthur merely looked contemplative as Marshall glared at them.

"Let him complain to Churchill," Marshall finally said. "Why, in this day and age, the British are attempting to snatch a former French colony is beyond me. It is also beyond me why you want to help them."

MacArthur maintained his studious silence.

Marshall leaned back in his chair. "Let us hope that all this is a smoke screen for action to the east. In that case, who knows? Maybe they've put enough of a scare into us that when it is our turn, we'll be ready."

MacArthur smiled as he puffed on his corncob. "Bill, we'd best get to work."

April 14
OSS Headquarters
Washington, D.C.

Bill Donovan smiled as he contemplated how Hoover would howl were he to discover the conduit from the Bureau to OSS. Actually there were several, all of them reporting directly to Donovan. Official channels were just fine for all the usual routine, but they weren't nearly as much fun and not nearly so reliable.

Take the report in front of him right now. It would never have wended its way to him via normal channels — yet something about it touched a nerve, even though the Bureau didn't think it worth pursuing.

Who to send down on it? After a moment's thought, the answer was obvious. He picked up the phone, drummed his desk impatiently while waiting for the Pentagon switchboard to route his call through.

"Martel? Time to get to work."

CHAPTER TEN

April 15
Charleston, South Carolina

Though it was still early spring, Charleston was already so hot that James Martel actually breathed a sigh of relief as the cool, formaldehyde-laden air swirled around him. The room he was in appeared empty, but he knew that the wall to his right was lined with roll-out trays on which lay the customers of this establishment.

"Mr. Martel—over here."

Martel followed the voice to a side alcove. When he turned the corner he was confronted by the body of an obese elderly man split from sternum to groin. The way the thick flaps of skin were pulled back brought to his mind the image of a butterfly pinned to a wall. The top of the skull was gone. The cranial cavity gaped empty.

Though embarrassed at his own weakness, Martel found himself turning away. He'd thought himself inured to death, but he realized now that his exposure had been a limited one, nicely packaged in metal or from a distance, and none of his affair. Facing what he had just turned from required a different sort of nerve. After a short pause to find it, he summoned it forth.

"Care for some coffee?"

Martel looked back and saw the coroner step over to a side table where a pot was kept hot by a barely lit Bunsen burner. The heavyset medico pulled off his heavy rubber gloves, which glistened with half-congealed blood, and threw them into the sink. Taking off his rubber apron, the coroner draped it over the sink as well, and then poured out a cup of coffee. He came over to Martel, extending his hand.

"Harry Weiss, and I assume you're Martel."

Jim took the doctor's hand, knowing that the offer to shake it was more a test of nerve than a friendly gesture.

Weiss looked into Martel's eyes and smiled.

"Ever seen a dead man before?"

Jim nodded.

"Just not up close?"

Again the sudden image of the Japanese pilot falling in flames . . . "Something like that."

Weiss nodded and walked over to the line of steel locker doors. "Number eleven, this is him." The coroner pulled the door open and the steel tray, body atop it, rolled out. Martel had seen swollen, drowned bodies during the Pacific War, but he was not prepared for the stink. He choked back a gag.

Weiss smiled.

"Can I get a full copy of your report before I leave today?" Martel asked, after a moment.

"Can't you just get the copy the FBI took?"

"No. That would take too much time."

Weiss laughed softly. "And obviously this is troubling somebody to the point that they can't wait. Is that it?"

"You certainly enjoy asking questions in response to my questions," Martel snarled. "Look, pal, I don't know or care what your story is, but either you start answering me straight up, or let's go get your boss, so he can talk to *my* boss, which I promise you your boss will not enjoy one little bit. You get me?"

"Hey, no need to get testy. That's my job, asking questions." Weiss nodded placatingly down at the body. "He doesn't talk, but he's got plenty of answers if you know where to look."

"That's better. Keep going."

"Six foot two, Caucasian, blond hair, gray eyes," Weiss began. "Cause of death, drowning. He'd have died of his injuries within minutes, but he never got the chance." Weiss traced his finger down the man's side. "Ruptured

spleen, four broken ribs—one punctured the left lung—
ruptured kidneys, crushed pelvis, broken back: he was a
mess, but the proximate cause of death was drowning."

"Was he beaten?"

"Nobody hits hard enough to do what was done to this
man. It could have been a boom falling, or cargo shifting."
He paused thoughtfully. "Whatever happened, he was in
the ocean within a couple of seconds, a minute at most,
following the event. He washed up off Morris Island, and
from the way the tide was running at the time I suspect he
floated in from the main channel. So it happened on a ship
off the coast."

"Murder?"

Weiss shrugged. "Maybe. But no reason to think so.
Much easier to simply club him and throw him overboard.
Same result for less effort."

"Who found him?"

"A local ship, of course. But he's been dead two and a
half days now. If it was local, like a fishing boat, we'd have
had a 'missing' report. Nothing's come in."

"If it wasn't murder, why hasn't someone reported him
lost?"

"Maybe the ship was from a distant port. Maybe they
didn't notice him gone for a while. In that case there would
be no good reason to report immediately, and plenty of
reason not to. Reporting a man missing means tying up the
ship for a day or two and answering a lot of questions.
Believe me, there's more than one ship coming in here that
can do without that, even the legit ones—and every day a
ship sits doing nothing costs the owners a great deal of
money. So they keep on going and when they get back
home, or wherever it is they're heading, they report him
lost then. But I still can't figure what could have done all
that to him, *and* knocked him overboard without
somebody noticing. It's almost as if he was caught between
two hulls. . . . But what would two boats be doing that close
to each other?"

While Weiss was holding forth, intent on showing off his deductive skills now that he had finished with being a general pain in the butt, Martel looked down at the body, examining the face. The eyelids, lips, and part of the nose were gone, as if he had been attacked by rats.

Weiss followed Jim's gaze.

"Ever since I got into this job I can't eat fish anymore. I always find myself wondering about their last meal."

There was something about the face that Martel found vaguely familiar. It was like a memory that tickled at the back of his mind that he somehow should know this man but simply couldn't place him.

"You've given me the general information. Now give me your gut feeling, your hunches, the kind of thing that doesn't wind up in a typed report."

Weiss looked down at the body and smiled. "Well, for one thing, he's not a manual laborer."

"How can you tell that?"

"Even after days in the water you can still see that every muscle on this man's body is toned. Manual laborers tend to develop some muscles more than others. Sometimes I can look at a dead man and tell you just what he did for a living, but not this one. I can tell you a lot of things he doesn't do—things like construction work and even fishing leave lifelong marks on your hands—but not what he does. And he's no mere gymnasium habitué; he's had a couple of injuries. Look: his right leg was broken several years back, a compound fracture." Weiss pointed to the scar. "And whoever patched him up did a hurried job of it." As he spoke he traced out the long white scar. "My guess is it's from a gunshot wound."

"How can you tell that?" Martel asked quietly. He pulled out a small notepad, started to write.

"This man isn't somebody from the backwoods. He's a sleek, well-oiled machine who must have received first-rate medical treatment. The stitch job was either done by an amateur or by a doctor who had fifty or a hundred other cases to deal with. That usually means a battlefield."

The coroner moved back to the other end of the table, tapped the body's front teeth. "He's also had three teeth knocked out, and his nose was broken several times. Plus he has a deviated septum of the type typically seen on prize fighters."

Martel, nodding, continued to write, and then paused for a second.

"Something I say hit you?"

"I'm not sure."

"Anyhow, he's European, not American."

"From his clothes?"

"All his clothes were made in the USA, and that in itself is interesting. They were brand new, not even any lint in his pockets. For that matter, he had nothing in his pockets, no cigarettes, wallet, matches, even loose change. He was totally clean. You usually find that with someone who doesn't want anyone to know who he is."

"So why European?"

Weiss casually pointed down to the dead man's privates. "Most Americans are circumcised. In Europe, only the Jews, those who are still alive. Obviously, our dearly departed here never had the experience." Weiss paused for a moment, as if remembering. "It's one of the ways the SS does a quick check: forces a suspected Jew to lower his pants. Nothing definitive, of course. But this one's pristine condition does increase the odds he started life in Europe." Weiss returned his attention to the corpse's mouth, which was open in a death-grimace, and pointed inside it.

"His dental work seems European, too: three fillings, all of them gold."

"I have a gold filling myself," Martel commented.

"And probably one or two that are not. But there are other little pointers. Even though he's well built, some bone structuring indicates that for a couple of years in early childhood he didn't eat well. In fact, he barely ate at all, say around 1918 and 1919." Weiss paused to assess the effect he was having. "I could go on but I think you want the punch line."

"Something like that."

Weiss gestured at the cadaver with a slight flourish: "The specimen was a German soldier from an elite unit. He was up to no good."

"Did you tell that to the FBI?"

"Of course I did."

"And?"

"They said they'd get back to me, but I could tell they thought I was crazy."

Without otherwise responding, Martel looked back down at the body.

"So why German?"

"Because his last meal, what little there was of it — I think he may have been seasick not long before his end — was sausages and sauerkraut."

"What the hell does that mean? He could be a Pole for that matter," Martel snapped, suddenly remembering his own childhood and the taunting he had endured at school over the "foreign" smells coming from his house.

Weiss shrugged again. "That was his last meal, and it's not the usual thing you're going to find being served up and down the waterfront of this town. Call me a racist, but this guy has 'Teutonic Superman Thug' written all over him. No offense, but guys like this," he nodded down at the body, "give me the creeps."

"Why?"

"Because I'm a Jew. I got out in '28, when the signs were getting obvious but getting out was still possible."

"Your English is perfect."

"Assimilate, don't stand out," the doctor replied coolly.

"You probably think I'm a little too Teutonic-looking, for that matter."

Weiss nodded. "I try not to equate body type and personality, but you would fit in real well over there, in what used to be my country. Sorry if I've let my feelings show."

"Where were you raised?"

"Berlin. It used to be home, but now it's my family's graveyard."

"Berlin," Martel said quietly, and the realization came at last.

April 15
Asheville, North Carolina

Half dozing, Otto Skorzeny was startled by a quick shove to his ribs. The driver nodded toward his side-view mirror. "Police car behind us."

"Where are we?"

"Just west of Asheville."

"How long has he been following us?"

"He passed us going the other way a couple of miles back and now he's on our tail."

Skorzeny leaned forward to get a glimpse out of the mirror on his side of the van that was transporting them to Knoxville. All he could see were the headlights.

"How do you know it's the police?" Skorzeny started to ask and even as he did so he heard the thin wail of the siren.

"Pull over," Skorzeny said as he reached forward to press the alarm button, signaling the men hidden in the back of the truck to remain silent.

The driver edged the vehicle over to the side of the road, pulling up hard on the parking brake.

Lighting a cigarette, the driver looked over at Skorzeny, who nodded.

Skorzeny heard the crunching of boots on pavement and felt the shifting of the vehicle's weight as the policeman stepped up onto the driver's-side running board.

"Open up and come on down."

The driver gently swung the door open and stepped down onto the pavement.

Skorzeny looked back in his mirror and saw a second officer silhouetted by the patrol car's headlights.

"Anything wrong, officer?" the driver asked.

"You've got a taillight out for one thing."

"Damn, I thought the boys back at the shop took care of that. Thanks, officer."

"Let me see your license and registration."

"Sure, officer, just a second," and the driver climbed back into the cab.

"It's all right," the driver whispered, looking over at Skorzeny.

"You say something?"

"Just talking to my buddy up here. He was asleep when you pulled us over and wanted to know what was going on."

"Tell him to come down, too."

Skorzeny sighed. Good help was *so* hard to find . . . he slid across the seat and alighted next to the driver. The cop, who was nearly a foot shorter than Skorzeny, backed up slightly and looked up at him. From the look on his face, this short little police officer disliked tall men.

"Okay, buddy, let's see your license, too," the cop snapped, shining his light straight into Skorzeny's eyes.

The heavy Carolina accent threw Skorzeny for a second and he hesitated.

"Your license, buddy. Get it out now!"

"Stanz," the driver said slowly, "your driving license."

Playing dumb, Skorzeny grinned stupidly. "The license, yes," he said slowly, "I have it here."

Reaching into his back pocket, he pulled his wallet out and deliberately fumbled for a second as if nervous in the presence of authority. He then handed the card over.

"Baltimore, Maryland? What the hell are you doing driving a truck with South Carolina tags?"

"He wasn't driving. He's my brother-in-law," the driver said for him. "He married my sister and just moved down here. Stanz here's a *Polack*. Used to work on the docks up in Baltimore. I got him a job with the company."

"He should have a South Carolina license then."

"He's got thirty days and besides he's along just to help me unload, not to drive."

"How do I know that?" the cop snapped.

"Sir, even if he did drive, it's legal," the driver replied slowly and Skorzeny silently cursed the man. Never attempt to argue the law with the authorities.

"I'm sorry, sir, I didn't mean trouble," Skorzeny said with his head lowered. "My brother here asked me to help."

"Listen, buddy," the cop snapped, "you stay out of this."

Skorzeny fell silent and lowered his head.

The bantam-sized police officer continued to shine his light on Skorzeny's face and stood silently.

"Where'd you get them scars on your face?"

Again, the accent threw him and he looked over at his companion.

"Your face, Stanz."

"Oh. Cut in fight. Against Germans when they invade."

The reaction wasn't what he expected. Rather than manifest a sudden show of sympathy for a "gallant Pole," the cop laughed contemptuously.

"Ran away, did you? I was in the army, and I saw a lot of big dumb oxes like you. Most of them were cowards."

"Hey, Charlie, any trouble up there?"

Skorzeny looked to his left and saw the second officer appear.

"I dunno. Something's not right with these boys."

The cop stood silently for several seconds and then smiled. "I think we should see what you boys got in your truck."

"It's just furniture sir," the driver said.

"Fine, then let's get a look at it. We've had some boys like you trying to run a little shine through here, and untaxed cigarettes. So let's take a look."

The driver shrugged as if only mildly pained by the needless work. He reached up into the cab, pulled the keys out of the ignition, and went around to the back of the truck. He looked over at the first cop, who stood with feet apart, his right hand resting lightly on his revolver butt.

"Go on, boy, open it up."

The driver unlocked the door and swung it open.

"Like I said, furniture," and he pointed up at the sofa, mattress, and bed springs piled up high.

"Come on, Charlie, they're okay," the second cop said mildly.

Charlie looked back over at his companion and shook his head.

"Hal, you know they could simply have something hidden further inside. I think Stanz here should start unloading."

"Sir," the driver pleaded, "if we don't keep our schedule there'll be hell to pay with my boss."

"There'll be hell to pay with me if you don't get your Polack friend into that truck right now."

Skorzeny looked over at the driver inquiringly.

"Unload it, Stanz."

Skorzeny stepped up into the truck and, untying the ropes that bound the sofa in place, he grabbed it and lowered it down. He looked over at the cop.

"Keep going, boy."

"Hey, Charlie, c'mon. We have our own schedule, you know," the second cop said.

"That dumb Polack can't even speak English and yet he runs over here and gets a job when there's more'n one ex-GI looking for work. I'm sick of these damned refugees."

Faced with such irrefutable logic, the other policeman resigned himself to the process that was unfolding.

Skorzeny moved the mattress and bed springs down. Behind those there was a stack of boxes . . . and behind the boxes was the compartment containing his team and their equipment.

He looked back down at the cop.

"Keep going, boy, and let's see what's in those boxes."

Skorzeny looked over at his driver. The man casually reached into his pocket and pulled out a fifty-dollar bill, folding it over. He walked up to the short cop and, leaning over, whispered something while extending his hand.

The cop looked over at him, smiled and took the bribe.

"Boy, I think you just put yourself into a whole lot of trouble," the short cop said with a cold grin. "Now you get up there too and help your friend unload."

The driver looked back at Skorzeny, waiting for orders.

"Hal, this boy here just tried to bribe me and it wasn't enough by a long shot," the short cop said, backing up slightly and unclipping the safety strap on his revolver.

"Now both of you start unloading and let's see what you got in there."

The second cop, now interested, moved up beside Charlie. The silence was broken by a lone car passing them. The road behind was black, empty.

Skorzeny picked up a box and, turning, stepped down from the truck and started to put it down, looking up the road in the opposite direction. The car that had just passed them disappeared around the bend.

Instead of releasing the box, he swung around with it like a discus thrower, flinging it into the second officer's face, knocking him to the ground. In the follow-up to that swing his foot flashed into his tormentor's groin, who doubled over, clenched on himself. When he'd turned back to him, the other cop was halfway up, fumbling his revolver out of its holster. Skzorzeny broke the man's neck with a single blow just below his left ear. Swinging around again, he relaxed slightly as he saw that his driver had already kicked the gun out of Charlie's hand. The police officer, gasping in pain, began to rise.

Skorzeny came up behind Charlie, slammed him back down.

"I'm not a big dumb Polack," Skorzeny chuckled into his ear. "I'm a big smart *German*." With a quick pull, he snapped the man's neck.

Standing up, breathing hard, he looked back up and down the road. There were still no lights, but from a distance he could hear the whisper of an approaching car.

"Throw them in the car. Move it!" Seconds later Skorzeny had helped the driver throw Charlie and his partner into the back seat and slammed the door shut.

"How long to Knoxville?"

"Another three hours."

"We can't leave them here. The alert will be out within the hour and the driver of the last car might remember something. You drive the police car and I'll follow until you find a place that's safe to ditch them. I'll pick you up then."

"Suppose I get stopped?"

Skorzeny shrugged. "Then keep your mouth shut or you're dead."

"Why not put them in the truck?"

"Because we might get stopped again. Once you pull out of here, there's no longer a link between the dead policeman and us."

"You don't know the way to our drop-off."

"I know the address and I'll find it if need be. We don't have time to argue. Give me the keys to the truck!"

The driver reached into his pocket and handed them over. Pushing aside the sofa lying on the ground, he reached up and swung the doors shut, locking them. The car they had heard finally came around the bend and roared past. Skorzeny climbed into the cab and slammed the truck into gear as the police car pulled out in front of him.

April 16
Washington, D.C.

Major Wayne Mason, cursing roundly, finally opened the door.

"Jesus Christ, Jim, you know what time it is?"

"Somewhere around oh-three-hundred. Now be a pal and get me a cup of coffee." Jim stepped into Wayne's apartment. Down the hallway to the back bedroom he saw a wisp of curly blond hair framing a remarkably attractive face that was peeking out from behind a half-closed door. Jim smiled and waved. The door slammed shut.

"Jim," Wayne said sadly, "couldn't this have waited until morning?"

"No."

Various items of clothing formed a trail from the living room to the recently slammed door. That evidence, when combined with an empty champagne bottle and a couple of long-stemmed glasses lying on the floor, didn't leave much room for further speculation.

"We've been friends a long time, but this is pushing it, pal," Wayne said bitterly. "Six months, *six months* we've been thinking about it—well, I've been thinking about it—and you come gallumphing in just when—"

"That can wait. This can't."

"Bullshit. This has got to be some kind of spooky government bullshit, and there is nothing of that kind that can't wait for oh-seven-hundred. Now, if you will *excuse* me . . . ?" Wayne made as if to rise and see Jim to the door.

Jim just sat there. "I'm not going anywhere, not for a few minutes, anyway." He was a little startled at Wayne's attitude—his friend wasn't the sort to make such a big deal of love's labor's lost . . . so maybe it *was* love . . . not that right at the moment he cared very much.

Even Wayne's sunny disposition was starting to fray under the humorless assault. "Jim—out. Talk to me in the morning. You've had your dramatic little surprise. Now, out." Wayne pause for a moment, clearly torn between friendship and love. "Please," he added.

As if the "please" had been a request to do so, Jim opened his briefcase, extracted a photograph, and placed it carefully on the coffee table.

Wayne, curiosity overcoming exasperation, leaned intently over the photo. Exasperation gave way to disgust. "What is *that*?"

"A dead man."

"No shit. Makes me want to puke just looking at him. But why am I looking at him, rather than—"

"Because I want you to tell me who he is."

Wayne sat back on his sofa, picked up the picture and studied it closely, then looked over at Jim. "You're back in the game. How'd you get cleared?"

"You know who this guy is?"

"Yeah. So do you. You met him back in Berlin."

"I knew it! I only saw him the one time, so I wasn't sure. What was his name?"

"Hans Fretter or Freiter. Something like that. He's Otto Skorzeny's right-hand man, almost like a personal bodyguard. One tough bastard, an SS major. He was with Skorzeny at the parade, the day you got your ass in the wringer."

"Yeah, that's where I recognized him from. Look. Can you get me copies of the photos you took that day? Quietly?"

"It'd take a little doing but . . . yeah, I think I can arrange it."

"Do it. I'll have somebody drop by your office and pick them up."

"Long as he's cleared," Mason said absently. "Where did old Hans turn up? Looks like the rats got to him."

"Let's just say someplace unexpected."

Wayne gave Martel a conspiratorial smile. "Couldn't let me in on it, could you? I'd love to know how this guy got his. I'd have called him damned near unkillable."

"Sorry, Wayne. You didn't even see the picture, let alone me. Now, I need to use your phone."

Wayne pointed to it on its little stand to the side of the sofa.

"Isn't it time for you to go in there and soothe somebody's feelings?"

"Yeah, okay. I can take a hint."

"I'll let myself out," Jim said. "And thanks."

After the door to the bedroom opened and closed, Jim smiled at the muffled protests and his friend's softly soothing rejoinders. Judging from the rapidly decreasing volume, the rejoinders were apparently having the desired effect.

Out of nowhere he suddenly wondered how Betty was doing, and if she still thought of him sometimes, and what it was she thought. He shook his head and picked up the phone. Resolutely ignoring the muffled coos and giggles that had replaced the more strident sounds of a moment before, he dialed the number and waited. Finally someone answered.

"Sir, it's Martel. Sorry to wake you up like this, but I think the show is about to start."

CHAPTER ELEVEN

April 16
The Oval Office

"Mr. President, this man is a member of an elite SS commando team, code named Friedenthaler Jagdverbande."

"The Hunting Club," Harrison said quietly, picking up a photograph of Hans Freiter. The photograph, supplied by Mason, had been taken by him during the Victory Day parade in Berlin.

"He floated up three days ago, just outside Charleston Harbor." Donovan dropped another photo on Harrison's desk, this one less glamorous. The President studied the morgue photograph intently for several seconds, then glanced back and forth several times between it and the one showing Freiter in SS regalia.

"How did you come to have this?" Harrison asked. "I'd have thought that Hoover would have been the one to bring this in."

"Remember Martel, that young naval officer McDonnell had an interest in? I sent him down to check out the report on this body. Charleston's the closest port to Oak Ridge and we had just had that mention of Manhattan. I wanted one of my people to take a look, and by sheer luck Martel recognized him."

"Does Hoover know about this yet?"

"No. A negative report from his investigative team will probably surface on one of his assistants' desks in a couple weeks. It will talk about crazy Jewish refugee coroners who see Nazis behind every lamp post."

Harrison smiled. "He'll crap when he realizes you beat him to the punch."

"That's why I thought it best that you tell him rather than me."

"So the boss can rub it in a bit, is that it?"

Donovan shrugged.

"That's twice I've seen the Bureau screw up recently," the President mused. "First on Martel, and now this. Maybe they're getting too involved with their own damned infighting."

Donovan maintained a beatific silence. There would be some sore butts in Bureau-land, after Hoover recovered from his own personal humiliation.

Harrison turned his attention back to the photo. "You think they've infiltrated a commando team into this country?"

"They wouldn't have sent this Freiter character in alone. He's part of a strike team."

"Target?"

"Oak Ridge. Charleston Harbor. Has to be."

"You think this has to do with the 'Manhattan letter'?" Harrison asked reluctantly. Clearly he did not want to go where this conversation was leading.

"Undoubtedly, sir. This 'Hunting Club' is run by an SS colonel named Skorzeny. He's the best they've got for special ops. Furthermore, he's the type who leads from the front if at all possible. I'd bet he's in this country right now."

"'Skorzeny.' Where did I hear that name before?"

"He snatched Marshal Koniev out of Leningrad."

Harrison leaned back in his chair for a moment, fingers massaging the bridge of his nose. "And now he's here. Him and his team. Why?"

"Industrial-grade espionage at the very least. Likely combined with sabotage. It can't be just recon. One thing the letter shows is that they know in a general way what's going on down there: if the letter's legit, they know. If the letter is disinformation, they know; elsewise how could they have inserted it? Either way, they know."

"How many men do you think they have, Bill?"

"I can't say yet. No fewer than three or four. No more than . . . twenty. I'm guessing twelve."

"Why twelve, precisely?" the President asked curiously.

Donovan shrugged. "Monte Carlo odds. A guess, but a gambler's guess, better than nothing. Skorzeny had to have made some kind of compromise between effectiveness on the job and the chances of detection. I'm plunking down in the middle of that range. . . . And anyway, that's the number I'd have gone with."

"That's one hell of a big place down there. Even the full twenty couldn't do all that much."

"Oak Ridge has several dozen miles of perimeter to patrol. A team could slip in, do some recon, pick their moment, do their damage — I don't know enough about the place to say precisely what kind of damage, but ten pounds of Composition-C will seriously dent most anything—and then get the hell out of Dodge."

"I don't think Hitler would authorize that."

"Why not?"

"An act of war on American soil would unify this country like nothing since Pearl Harbor. Especially if there were civilian casualties."

"Well, sir, haven't we been getting signals in that direction?"

"Winston certainly believes so. But you saw the information coming in from your own people over the last several days. Reports from Istanbul, the embassy in Kiev, Helsinki — they all indicate German feelers regarding renewed action in Russia. Yesterday the Brits ran a plane out of Iran up into the Caspian Sea. A lot of shipping has been assembled on the western shore and several new divisions are moving into Astrakhan. Hell of a lot of action to be a ploy."

"So you're sticking with that?"

"Not entirely. But I can't let Winston slip his leash and cry 'Havoc!' " the President misquoted. "If things do flare up between England and Germany, I've got to make certain-sure that Hitler looks like the one-hundred-percent villain that he is.

"Sometimes Winston is his own worst enemy," Harrison added. "This would be one of those times if I let him."

"Mr. President, are you sure this isn't a time for simple truth?" Donovan asked quietly.

Harrison looked at the OSS chief in surprise. "That from my Master of Spies? Your game has been the playing field of liars since the Trojan Wars."

"I'll feed the enemy anything I can if it helps to beat him. Your field is different."

"Do I sense a rebuke here, Bill?" Harrison asked in a tone of polite inquiry.

Donovan sighed. "No sir, just an observation. You're the boss."

"Bill, I'll tell you what I told Winston: in a situation like this 'might' just isn't enough. Winston might be right, and he might not. If he isn't, we don't need the saber rattling; it might even get Hitler going. And if he is right, I want him to look pure as a virgin, not like someone who went into a bad neighborhood looking for trouble. If we go to war with the Nazis, it's going to take years of maximum effort, and there must be no doubt in anyone's mind that we had no choice but to fight." He half-rose. "Otherwise, the country will tear itself apart and we will lose. Lose to those monsters. Would you like to see *Hitler* sitting in this chair?"

Harrison paused and visibly calmed himself as he resumed his seat. "Plus there is the political side: I don't want anyone up on the Hill able to credibly say that England is trying to lure us into another fight with Germany. Roosevelt faced that back in '40 and '41 and it, well, paralyzed him. We have to take the long view here, Bill, and so must Winston."

"And Oak Ridge, sir?"

"Spying, definitely. The Nazis are on to our secret. We have a leak somewhere and, by damn, it'll be plugged. They've picked up on something and are sending in their best people to check it out. You've been trying to do the same with that reported site in Poland for the last year and a half and have yet to get within a hundred miles of it."

"Their system's a little different than ours. By the nature of our society, we are always more vulnerable than an aroused tyranny."

"Are you certain it's Oak Ridge?"

"As certain as can be, sir. And on my way over here I was handed something that will convince even — convince anyone." Donovan reached into his briefcase and pulled out a newspaper clipping. "Just look at this, sir. Two cops were found dead outside of Asheville early this morning. Their necks were broken."

"And?"

"A military-professional job. No weapons, just open-handed kills. Whoever did it was damn good. I expect Hoover will be calling you shortly."

"He already has," Harrison said with a smile. "He's had a flop or two lately, but don't think he's gone entirely soft. The cops pulled over a moving-van. Some furniture was found lying by the side of the road about five miles from where the cops were found. The FBI thinks the police officers had started to search the vehicle and were jumped. The killers threw the bodies into the patrol car and then ran the car into a ditch farther up the road."

"And the cops were found in the direction of Knoxville, relative to where the van was first pulled over?"

Harrison nodded.

"It was Skorzeny. No doubt. Any lead on the van?"

"Nothing."

"Then they're in Knoxville by now."

"That's what Hoover thinks," the President replied.

"May I ask what you intend to do, sir?"

"Plenty. First, Hoover's moving a special detachment down to Knoxville right now to beef up the FBI team already there. Also, I've informed General Groves of the situation; additional military security is being assigned to

Oak Ridge as we speak. On top of that, the local police have been alerted, and you know how they feel about cop killers. They'll put every available trooper they have on it. By the way, I want you to pass a copy of your file on Skorzeny over to Hoover."

Donovan nodded.

"Maybe with this break we'll can nab this son of a bitch before he can do any harm."

"I don't think it'll be that easy."

"How come?"

"Like I said before, he's the best they have. He once operated for nearly two weeks behind Russian lines disguised as a Soviet infantryman, and finished up by wiping out a Guards headquarters. He did the Leningrad job, and he's crazy enough that they supposedly were planning to drop straight into the Kremlin to kill Stalin. He's already in Knoxville, maybe even inside Oak Ridge. He'll have gone to ground. Unfindable until he moves, and he won't move until he strikes."

The President was quizzical. "You sound like you think he's some sort of superman."

"He is, and I want some of my people in on this."

Harrison sighed.

"Internal security is for the FBI. You're asking for a precedent that I'm not comfortable with, using the OSS for work inside this country."

"My job includes intelligence and counterintelligence against nations hostile to the United States. We cased Skorzeny several years back and know how he operates. I'm just asking you to allow a team to set up in Knoxville. We'll stay out of the FBI's hair. If we stumble on anything, they can do the kill. Damn it, sir, we're talking about *Manhattan* here, our ace in the hole against the Nazis. We can't afford any mistakes."

Harrison finally nodded.

"You have my permission, but not my directive. Furthermore you are sending your team down there strictly to advise on security for Oak Ridge. If they get involved in anything more, the FBI will roust them, on my authority."

"Fine, sir."

When the President nodded dismissal, Donovan closed his briefcase, stood up, and then hesitated. "One final thing."

"Go on."

"The leak. I hope Hoover is running a full check on that."

"He's working on it right now. Absolutely anyone who might have had access to the code name 'Manhattan' and the purpose of the project is getting a full review. It'll take time, though. There are several hundred possible sources when you count people directly in the know and their assistants—in other words, people who might have access to reports. Several people involved with the project have Communist ties and were already under suspicion for feeding information to the Russians. One theory is that the Germans picked up on it through their operatives inside the Politburo. It's going to take time to track it down."

"I'd like to put some of my resources into this one. It'll take several weeks to set it up but maybe we can trap this bastard."

"Again, that's not your territory."

Donovan said nothing and continued to stare straight at the President.

"I never authorized it, is that clear?"

Donovan smiled. "Take care of yourself, sir. Frankly, you're starting to look run-down."

Harrison laughed and shook his head.

"I feel just like a one-armed juggler at the moment. Stay on top of things, Bill, and, on your way out, have Mayhew set you up a daily briefing with me over the next few weeks." Harrison thought for a moment. "And tell him that after he's done that I'd like to see him."

Harrison closed his eyes as the door shut behind

Donovan. Was he making the right move? Maybe Winston was right. Maybe the thing to do was blow it right out into the open. Call Hitler's bluff, tell him to put up or shut up, fight—or back the hell off. He stood and walked over to the window to look out across the South Lawn. The tulips in the garden were in full bloom, the day outside warm and balmy. Spring had finally won. *With spring coming, maybe the lights of the old Norse Gods will be more active than ever. . . . Perhaps we might get to Manhattan. . . .*

"If they mean to start a war, let it be here and now." So they had said at Lexington Green, and so, he finally realized, his heart was advising him this fateful day: confront the beast now, before it grows any stronger, and one day simply comes to devour us. Yet the beast was already so strong. . . .

A knock interrupted his thoughts and he turned to the door.

"Come in."

John Mayhew stuck his head through the door. "You wanted me, sir?"

"Sit down, John."

Mayhew came into the office and sat down across from the President's desk.

"I want some schedule changes worked out over the next couple of weeks. I think we might have a situation developing."

"Germany?" Mayhew asked quietly.

"I'm not sure, but if so I want us to be ready, and I need to start pulling some people in. I don't want anything to look out of the ordinary yet, but we need to get cracking on it. If the Germans are up to something, it would be much better if they don't realize we're onto them. I'm depending on you to keep a low profile while still getting things done."

Mayhew opened the President's schedule book and started to write.

April 16
Oak Ridge, Tennessee

Amazing! Intellectually Otto Skorzeny was fully aware of the lax nature of American security procedures, but actually experiencing them was something else. He found himself almost tempted to descend from the truck and berate the white-helmeted MP who had just waved them on—with not a word, and barely a glance at the proffered ID. Instead, having retrieved the card, he rolled his window up as the truck started rolling forward. Gunther, who was sitting between him and the driver, smiled.

"We are now on the Oak Ridge Turnpike," Louis announced. Louis was their contact in Knoxville. To Skorzeny's immense gratification and mild disbelief, the trucker had delivered them to Louis with zero additional complications.

Skorzeny took it all in, trying to suppress any display of surprise as they rolled down the hill from the security gate and crept along through the tangle of traffic.

Coming straight into the base was a deviation from their plan, but the cop-killing had left him uneasy. Rather than going to ground on arrival at their base of operations, a small airfield forty miles northeast of Knoxville, he'd decided to immediately grab a quick look around before any disturbance they had caused could possibly result in enhanced security. Louis, to Skorzeny's surprise, had not objected to the delay in delivering them to their final destination, nor to leaving the rest of the team hidden at his warehouse in Knoxville, and had suggested he come on the afternoon delivery run to the food market inside the compound.

Louis's cover was that of a produce trucker, a most convenient one for this operation. Skorzeny much preferred him to be the person who knew their final destination, as opposed to the idiot who had somehow managed to get them to Knoxville. A good German, Louis. He hoped their final contact would be as competent.

"This is the main east-west road running through the reservation," Louis announced. "The main residential areas are on our right, going up along the slope of the hills."

"Those are type-D cemesto houses — that's 'cement' plus 'asbestos,'" Gunther said, pointing out the small single-story homes that were lined up, row after row. "The E and F model homes are in toward the administrative area."

Skorzeny scanned the mass confusion around him. Oak Ridge had the feel of a frontier town, or one of those new fortified settlement towns in Occupied Russia. Everywhere there was traffic, cars, trucks, and buses; and everywhere there was mud. The main road was paved, but most of the side streets were merely graveled. They rolled past a mud-spattered traffic cop, and several soldiers leaning against a storefront that stood behind the wooden sidewalk. The men were obviously enjoying the view as an endless stream of women walked past them.

"Are those typical security?" Skorzeny asked, nodding toward the soldiers.

"Pretty much," Louis replied. "You've read my reports, so you know there are about a thousand of them, and that they are primarily concerned with the thirty-mile perimeter and the internal checkpoints. They're spread thin."

Nor, in Skorzeny's estimation, did they seem very concerned with the difficulty of their mission. He grinned to himself. Amazing the false sense of security three or four thousand miles of ocean could give people. Soon they would learn the hard way that times had changed since an envious Bismarck had complained that "God protects fools, drunkards and the United States of America."

"What about plainclothes?"

That was a different story. "They're everywhere. We work on the assumption that anyone we talk to is a member of either the military or the FBI. We lost three people to them last year, but since we operate under a cell structure, they couldn't use their initial success to roll us up. As for the rest of the security here, there are several thousand private guards, hired by the various companies involved in the operation. Most of them are no better than you might suppose, but we assume there might be FBI in their ranks as well."

As they crossed through a heavily traveled intersection, Louis nodded to the left. "Y-12 is two kilometers down that road — just on the other side of that line of hills. Travel another two kilometers past Y-12 and turn right, and you come to X-10 another ten kilometers to the west."

Skorzeny nodded encouragingly. He knew this area like the back of his hand from maps and models, but the map was not the territory: it was still necessary to scope out the actual ground. Continuing with that line of thought, he asked, "Have you had a look at the facilities? Could we?"

"Not a chance. We'd have had to go overland, dodging patrols all the way. They've got different ID badges for each part of this base. The badges we have now are for outsiders coming in to make deliveries. If they catch us even a hundred meters past where we are supposed to go, we'll be in the security guardhouse. Viktor has been doing custodial work in K-25. You'll meet him tonight after he comes off shift. I also had a man in Y-12, but he was one of the three picked up."

As Louis talked, most of Skorzeny's attention was focused on the visual data that came streaming in. The buildings were flimsy temporary structures, nothing more than plywood and studding. Even light-caliber bullets would exit the far side of most of them. That plus the extreme population density meant that for virtually every piece of ordnance dropped into the area there would be a significant kill ratio. After the bombing, though, the streets would be packed with panic-stricken survivors and wreckage; forcing vehicles through the confusion might prove problematic. Well, a little terror shooting would go a long way toward clearing the streets again, one way and another.

"That last turnoff led to the airstrip?" Skorzeny asked, making sure.

"Right. They just started working on it. It's not even paved yet but it's good enough for C-47s and C-54s."

"But is it long enough for our 264Es?" Gunther asked.

"We were told it was a thousand meters," Skorzeny said. "I couldn't tell you."

"Then where did that datum come from? Who vouched for it?" Probably it was somebody's damned "estimate" masquerading as a fact. It wouldn't be the first time an operation had failed because of such an idiot misunderstanding. "Well, then, I'll have to check it out."

Louis said nothing, but Skorzeny could sense his discomfort. The man was undoubtedly a capable spy, he had, after all, been active inside the United States for nearly four years, two of them in and around this hypersensitive site. But by the very nature of his job he preferred to operate alone, not drawing attention, moving with caution. It was a method that would no longer apply in these final days of the operation.

"Here's our delivery." Louis turned the truck off the main road, pulled in behind a food market, and backed the truck up against the unloading platform. Climbing out, he motioned for Gunther and Skorzeny to follow. After unlocking the back of the truck, he went into the bay.

"Hey, Albert!"

A florid-faced rotund grocer emerged.

"I got fifty crates of lettuce, ten of oranges, ten bananas and ten tomatoes."

"I ordered twenty oranges."

"Say, don't blame me, buddy. Ten's what's on the invoice, ten's what I got for you."

"I ordered twenty."

"You want the ten? I should take 'em back?"

"No, I'll take 'em. Of course I'll take 'em! But I ordered twenty."

"Up to you, pal." Louis looked back at Skorzeny and Gunther. "Let's give the man his produce."

Albert pulled a half-smoked cigar out of his pocket and lit it, watching intently as they moved the crates from the truck to where the store manager pointed.

"Well, I tell ya. Don't ever get yourself tangled with running a store where the military is in charge. It's enough to drive a guy crazy. Check this, explain that, sign this paper here," and he waved his hands about. "I should have stayed in Cleveland."

Albert paused and looked over at Skorzeny and Gunther. "Say, who are these guys?"

"I screwed up my back. The doc said lifting's out for a while. I put them on the payroll last week. Besides, I'm thinking of expanding. They're gonna take over this run once I get another truck. This way I get them cleared to come in here and learn the ropes, *and* I save my back."

After finishing the job, Skorzeny and Gunther paused and looked inquiringly at Louis, who nodded a dismissal. Jumping down from the loading dock, Skorzeny went up to the front of the truck, casually lit a cigarette, and looked around. After a moment Gunther followed.

"It's almost too easy," Gunther whispered.

"Don't worry. Something is bound to go wrong. We've already experienced that with Hans, and then the police." Skorzeny, with his hands in his pockets, casually strolled away from the truck and back to the main street.

Traffic inched by, the buses packed with passengers heading out to the west where the K-25 plant was. He yearned to board one, but the card clipped to his shirt pocket wouldn't even get him on the bus. Still, the viewing was good right where he was. The administration building was plainly visible not two hundred meters away, as was the security building, though it was some distance away. Across the street and a hundred meters up the hill, the housing projects started. Turning and looking to the south he could see wisps of smoke coming up from the other side of the ridge —Y-12. Two MPs strolled by, not even slowing as they passed their *raison d'être*.

April 16
Knoxville, Tennessee

"So where's our pickup?" Wayne Mason asked as he looked around the Knoxville Air Terminal.

"Beats me," Jim Martel replied laconically.

"So what do we do now?"

"Wait. What else?"

"What else. How about I go back to D.C.? Do you know how long it took me to get things going with Sarah? Then you come along and drag me off on this wild Nazi chase."

"C'mon, Wayne. You were born wild. This way Sarah will get a chance to know what she's buying into when she buys into Wayne Mason. Besides, now that you 'have things going' the days of the relationship are numbered anyway. Am I right?" Jim really couldn't decide whether to feel guilty or amused at what he had arranged to have happen to his friend. He settled on both. "Besides, I thought you'd enjoy getting out of the Pentagon."

"Well, first off, it's different with Sarah."

"Yeah. It's always different."

"This time it is—"

"Oh, stow your guff. You know you wanted to—"

"Damn, it's that weasel Harriman," Wayne announced softly, as he pointed at a figure approaching them.

Jim turned. It was indeed the OSS spook from the Berlin embassy walking briskly toward them.

Harriman came up to the two and gave a little nod. "Gentlemen, our friend said I should pick you up. My car is out this way."

"How the hell did you wind up here?" Mason asked as they followed dutifully.

Harriman looked at him with raised eyebrows. "Didn't Martel fill you in?"

Jim smiled. "Wayne spent so much of the trip down bellyaching that there wasn't time."

Harriman laughed. "We all have one thing in common besides being stationed in Berlin. We've all met our quarry. Donovan felt that qualified us as much as anything else. And Major, you actually had dinner with him and several members of his team once, which is what got you dragged into this in the first place."

"And here I thought it was all your idea," Wayne said in an aside to Jim.

"Heh. So did I. I guess my boss thinks for himself sometimes. I wonder if he has any other surprises lined up for me."

"I hope so," Mason responded dryly.

"As for myself," Harriman continued, "I guess you could say I'm your boss here." He paused to look at them. "I expect neither one of you thinks he has any particular reason to like me, and that's fine, though Martel, you might want to know that my personal report to Donovan said I thought you were clean. The point is, just as long as you listen to what I have to say and follow through on it, we'll get along okay."

"Oh, Donovan set me straight on that. You did what you were supposed to do and even made the right call about me being a fall guy. I have no complaints. I did then, because you didn't seem to give a rat's ass one way or the other—but hey, that's baseball."

"Okay, Harriman, me too," Wayne added.

"Call me Trevor."

"All right, Trevor, you're an okay guy. So now what?"

Harriman smiled. "I've booked us a room in town. Rooms are okay, restaurant is better than you might expect. We've got two appointments tomorrow: one with Groves and one with the head of FBI operations here. So our mission tonight is to book in, eat, and get a good night's sleep."

Harriman looked at Jim and spoke in the flat, affectless way that in some men denotes absolute sincerity. "I'm glad you got cleared. Now's your chance to dish some back, right to the source."

CHAPTER TWELVE

April 17
Abbeville, France

Adolf Galland walked down the line of Me-262 and Gotha 229 fighters. The pilots stood before their planes at rigid attention. That at least had stayed the same in this new jet age, he thought. Such changes in a mere —what? —six years? Even the smells were different. No more the warm, familiar scent of petrol and oil; now it was all jet fuel and hydraulic fluid. Still, though he missed what had passed, or at least was passing, away, Galland had to admit that the sharklike silhouette of the 262 looked far more deadly than that of the old 109s, while the batwinged 229s embodied stealthy death. The pilots standing in front of their planes looked fit and eager. Though they had not been briefed yet as to the mission, all could sense that something was in the air, that the hunt was about to begin.

"If only we had these fighters back in '40," Colonel Kleiber, his intelligence officer and second-in-command, who had been standing silently at his side, said wistfully. "We'd have crushed them in a week."

Galland was impatient with this particular brand of fantasizing. "You might as well wish that we'd had them in 1919. Keep in mind that we are not going up against Spitfires and Hurricanes this time. The British haven't been standing still. Their upgraded Meteor IV is said to be a match for the 262, and on top of that they'll still have the advantage of defense. If we lose a plane we also lose the pilot. If their pilot gets out, he's in the air again the next day."

"But our jets outnumber theirs almost four to one," Kleiber replied. "Those are formidable odds."

"We outnumbered them in 1940 too," Galland replied. "And we were as sure of ourselves then as now." Galland turned and looked back down the line of fighters. He could sense the ghosts hovering about him. It was from this same airfield that he had led the attacks against the British back in August of 1940, when victory had seemed a foregone conclusion. Instead of the sleek new jets, he saw in his mind's eye the line of 109s. Instead of the whine of jets, he heard the coughing rumble of piston engines turning over, revving up, and pointing to the west for take-off. And then, like now, victory was supposedly in the bag before the fight began.

Well, this time maybe so. If the initial onslaught caught the RAF on the ground, certainly so. Even if it did not, the Luftwaffe could wear the RAF down; they had the numbers to do it this time, unless the Americans intervened. But what *about* the Americans? Would they not fight for their British cousins? If not out of sentiment then because England and only England allowed the Americans something like strategic parity with the Reich? And once the Americans arrived on the scene, the strategic situation changed drastically. The US Navy was an air force unto itself, and when it came to logistics, the Americans were demons.

Well, the answer to that was simple enough: batter the English into submission before the American carriers arrived, before they started ferrying fighters across the Atlantic. That meant that not only the assault against England must go like clockwork, but the operations against Iceland and Greenland as well. He wondered how close to zero were the odds of every single factor clicking together like that.

He looked back over at Kleiber, who stood saddened and disturbed at his commander's sudden fit of doubt. Suddenly he was ashamed of himself. He might be tired of war but he still had his duty. It was wrong to project such feelings, especially now. They needed to believe. Belief itself was a vital component of victory. He forced a smile. "When we return wreathed in glory from that first strike, chances are I'll say you were right after all."

April 17
Near Oak Ridge

Otto Skorzeny lifted the camera out of its carrying case and locked it into the brace mounted over the instrument panel of the Piper Cub.

"Just keep it steady."

"I'll only be able to hold this path for a couple of minutes. We are right on the edge of the restricted air space." The pilot, Friedrich Bachman, owned and operated a small private airport that had become their base of operations; he was their ultimate contact. From the moment Louis had delivered them to him, he hadn't seemed entirely happy with his new and more active role.

"That's all it will take," Skorzeny lied as he leaned over the camera and played with the focus. Oak Ridge, ten miles ahead, stood out with crystal clarity in the early morning light, and a beautiful sight it was.

The trees below were showing their spring colors. The apple orchards in the hollows were a happy riot of pink and white. The leaves on the early-blooming maples and beeches on the southern slopes of the hills stood out in pale lacy green against brown. Below them, the valley of the Clinch River, which formed a sweeping bow around three sides of the base, was blanketed with a soft morning fog. A few puffy clouds completed the picture.

Skorzeny aimed the lens straight at the town of Oak Ridge, swung it slightly to the south until he picked out the airstrip, and started to snap off shots. Several C-47s were parked along the airport apron, a perfect measuring reference for the length of the strip, which as reported ran on an exact east-west axis. Finishing a roll of film, he popped it out and quickly loaded another.

"Take it in a bit closer."

"We are getting warned off."

"Do it. Now." Bachman would probably have leapt from the plane had Skorzeny told him to do so in that tone while wearing that expression.

"Sir! P-51s!" Bachman need hardly have spoken, because at that moment the wash of two Mustangs, one after the other, buffeted the little Piper.

"*Scheisse!* They must have been loitering in the neighborhood — what better place to practice patrolling? — and were vectored in using the cumulus to give the Piper a surprise. Well, they hadn't shot him down, which the technical rules would have permitted. They were probably taking this as a chance to teach local student pilots a serious lesson about how the neighborhood of Oak Ridge wasn't a good place to lose track of location. Plus maybe have a little fun.

As Skorzeny contemplated the possibilities, the P-51s began to execute what had to be Immelmans. They were a ways off now, but they would be looping over and diving back soon, probably with the intention of closing in and forcibly escorting the Piper to their own field.

Skorzeny grinned. Well, every mission has some bad luck. . . . and now he'd have some fun of his own. "Get down!" he shouted to Bachman. "I'm taking control!"

"What?"

"Maybe they didn't see you! Get down now!" Looking like he would have preferred to be ordered to bail out, Bachman did as bid.

Taking the stick, Skorzeny yanked it back and over, slamming in left rudder as he did so. The Piper Cub rolled up, flipped over and was suddenly pointing straight down. He pulled the throttle back to idle as the Cub went to meet Mother Earth. The P-51s passed straight over and high. After a few moments they both went into split-Ss as well, but physics dictated that their speed carry them well past the little plane they were pursuing.

Behind him Bachman was cursing wildly, fighting with the stick, trying to pull it back, but Skorzeny kept control. The Cub continued its straight-downward trajectory. As the airspeed indicator redlined, Skorzeny at last began to pull back, pushing in a little left aileron as he did so, turning the plane just enough to enable him by looking back over his shoulder to view the P-51s. They were out of their diving turns, lining up on him—but from well astern.

As the hills to either side came level with his wing tips, the Cub at last stopped shedding altitude and began skimming down a narrow valley just south of the Clinch at treetop level. The P-51s were still on him.

When they had closed to less than half a mile, he pulled the stick back and turned, racing up the side of the valley, barely clearing the trees along the crest line. The fog-shrouded Clinch was below and just ahead. The P-51s streaked past behind him and started to pull back up.

He dived down toward the river and seconds later was into the fog.

"You're going to kill us!" Bachman screamed.

Not bothering to respond, Skorzeny dropped the plane down lower, hoping that the man behind him had set the altimeter as carefully as a good German should. There was a break in the fog, and less than twenty feet below he saw the river. He gave the plane a touch of right aileron, watching carefully. He couldn't quite see the bank that he felt looming up to his right; it was more of a pale green glow.

Skorzeny slammed in left aileron and rudder, banking the plane over sharply.

He had to concede that the little plane handled very nearly as well as a Storch, as the Cub executed a full 180-degree turn within the width of the river. Heading east now, he edged back over to the north bank of the river. What fun, he thought, it would be to pop back up and run north for a kilometer or two and pull a treetop run over the atomic reactor. The fighter pilots would go out of their minds! Now that his blood was up he was almost crazy enough to do it. . . . But no, the odds of surviving such a stunt were little better than fifty-fifty. The mission had to come first.

With wheels nearly skimming the water he continued eastward, weaving along the almost-visible shadow of the riverbank, following it as the river turned north.

"Bridge!" his companion shrieked.

What the pursuing fighter pilots had seen could possibly be attributed to a combination of panic and beginner's luck. Negotiating the damned bridge was a job for an expert. Absolutely no possibility of popping over . . . for a moment he contemplated simply slamming into it, but concluded the mission's chances would be harmed more by his absence than by news of an acrobat pilot nosing around the outskirts of Oak Ridge. He pushed the nose down slightly, brought the wings to about fifteen degrees from horizontal so the plane could slide underneath the span like a key fitting into a lock. One wing *tcked* against a slanted support strut, the other had at least a centimeter of clearance. As he emerged from the other side, Skorzeny faked a stall, let one wingtip drift almost to the water, "recovered," and continued up the river for a while with wings now aligned about twenty degrees from horizontal, then "overcompensated" and wound up ten degrees off in the opposite direction. That would at least give some credence to the idea of a lucky beginner who wanted nothing but to get the hell out of town.

"They've lost us. They're calling in a probable crash," Bachman announced in a shaky voice. "A very under-standable error, in my opinion."

"Well, let's just follow the river a little farther, then weave our way home."

"You are a madman."

"This was a lark," Skorzeny replied. "You don't know

what madness is." As he spoke he unmounted the camera from its brace and stashed it in its case. There had never been a second in which to do that until now. He hoped no one had noticed it.

April 17
Oak Ridge

Major General Leslie Groves, overall commander of the Manhattan Project throughout the United States, tossed the photographs of Skorzeny back across the conference table toward Harriman.

"You're sure?"

"I'd give it ninety percent at a minimum, sir. Martel here identified the body of one of his closest henchmen." Harriman pulled another photo out of a folder and slid it over to Groves.

"Little the worse for wear, isn't he?" Groves quipped to Colonel Charles Soratkin, head of security for Oak Ridge, as he slid that photo over to him as well.

"This man, Hans Freiter," Harriman said, "washed up in Charleston Harbor four days ago. He was Skorzeny's personal bodyguard and batman. If he was bobbing around in Charleston Harbor, that means that Skorzeny was with him, and is therefore now in the United States."

"Why?"

"Sir, aside from the fact that Freiter was his personal aide, Skorzeny tends to keep operational control firmly in his own hands. While operating behind Russian lines he once walked right through the middle of Baku, dressed as a Soviet officer, for no other reason than to thumb his nose at Russian security and prove he could do it."

Soratkin stirred angrily. "If that bastard shows his face within ten miles of this facility, he's a dead man. Every one of my people has his photograph as of this morning. They'll nail him."

"Sir," Martel said quietly, "I think he's already been in here. Our guess is that he made Knoxville by the morning of April 16th. He most likely assumed that we were starting to get a tail on him and, given the way he operates, we think he would have decided to do a personal recon."

Harriman looked over at Mason and nodded.

"General, I did a profile study on this man just after the war with Russia ended. He's courageous to the point of being suicidal. He leads from the front, always. He never sends his men into something; they follow him in. Nor is he the type to sit back and just wear his medals. He's constantly seeking an ever-bigger challenge. If you examine his missions, you'll see that every single one was more spectacular and risky than the one before. He's compelled to push beyond the edge of what is thought possible. In other words, he's a lunatic, but a very functional lunatic."

"You'll notice the facial scars," Harriman added.

"Prussian dueling scars?" Groves asked.

"Yes, sir. He later said that when he got the first one he was thrilled because it didn't hurt as much as he expected and, more importantly, he didn't flinch. No matter what we do, this man will not flinch. Die, yes; he's only human. But flinch? Never. Trying to scare him would be pointless."

"So what the hell are you suggesting?"

"Nothing, sir," Harriman replied calmly. "I'm just trying to give you the background, that's all. You and your people are the security experts here, not us."

"So who exactly are you people?" Soratkin asked pointedly. "You said the White House sent you, but where are you from? OSS? And who exactly sent you?"

"I never actually said who sent us," Harriman said. "But you know as well as I do that there is only one place that can issue our boss orders, and that's the White House."

"But you *are* OSS?"

"Our boss is William Donovan. Let's just leave it at that."

"A little outside your territory, aren't you?"

"Look, we're all on the same team here," Martel

interjected, ignoring Soratkin and looking over at Groves.

Groves held his hand up. "Enough of that, for now. Let's get back to our Aryan superspy. You say this character has already been in and out of the project area."

"What we are trying to say is that he's penetrated behind Russian lines on a number of occasions—behind the lines of a police state engaged in war. By the very nature of their system they can secure themselves in ways that we wouldn't dream of, even if we were at war. He beat them consistently. Frankly, penetrating here, before his photograph was distributed, would have been child's play. Not the plants, maybe, but the city."

"We also think he might have been behind that flight early this morning," Mason added.

"We've had student pilots off course before," Soratkin said reasonably, "Why not this time?"

"The same pilot was so unskilled a navigator he couldn't keep on course—and so skilled an aerobat he could evade fighter planes with flying circus maneuvers and fly under bridges?" Mason asked dryly.

"We're checking on it," Soratkin replied. "If there's anything behind it, the FBI will get whoever did it. You don't work here day to day, I do. If I got worked up every time a plane went off course I'd have been dead years ago. I could show you a stack of reports five feet high regarding planes off course over this area and usually they're some damn stupid pilot who couldn't piss north after you show him Polaris. The FBI is checking every airfield within a hundred and fifty miles, and if they get a lead, they'll haul the idiot in.

"As for the fighter report on the acrobatics, well, they lost him, didn't they? Of course they'd say he was superman in a plane. Chances are he was some kid thinking he was a navy pilot." Soratkin stared straight at Martel and smiled. "And as for Skorzeny, he hasn't beat us yet. We've already been briefed by the FBI on this, and I should add that they've been working with us since this project started. We've yet to have a serious security breach and I intend to make sure that record stands.

"Now, answer my question: Just what the hell are you people doing here?"

"As I told General Groves, we've had dealings with Skorzeny before," Harriman said calmly. "Mason here has met Skorzeny and several men of his team. Martel's met him as well, though only briefly. We just wanted to put ourselves in a position to offer our assistance. We're the only people working for an American security agency with the experience of personal contact. After all, our job is intelligence and counterintelligence, and that falls under what must surely be part of Skorzeny's mission."

"Until we hear otherwise directly from the President or General Marshall internal security remains the sole responsibility of the FBI and the Army as far as this project is concerned," Soratkin replied. "We can handle this Skorzeny from here. Maybe he was able to pull off his games on the damned Russians, but he's up against another team here, Mr. Harriman, and that bastard is in for a rude awakening."

At that moment an aide appeared at the door.

Groves glanced at the lieutenant and asked, "Yes, what is it?"

"Phone call for Mr. Harriman, sir. From a Mr. Donovan. He says it's urgent."

Groves turned to Harriman. "You can take it in my office."

Harriman nodded his thanks and followed the lieutenant.

Groves, lighting a cigar, looked at Soratkin, started to say something and checked himself, and instead turned to Martel. "Commander, it was you who first put two and two together on this. Maybe you got four, and maybe you came up with five. For argument's sake let's say it was four. So what do you think is the real game here? Just what is your super commando up to?"

Jim paused for a moment in thought. "Sir, I just don't

know. It's like a mouse attacking an elephant. No matter how evil its intentions, it doesn't have the means. But just because I can't figure out what he's up to doesn't mean he isn't up to something. In my opinion the weight of evidence has become incontrovertible. I think, sir, that within a week the United States will be at war with Germany. I also think that the war will start right here at Oak Ridge, Tennessee."

Soratkin snorted derisively, but a sharp look from Groves silenced him.

"Go on, Commander. Why here, why now?"

"You're building an atomic bomb."

"Just what the hell makes you think that?" Soratkin shouted.

"It was felt essential that we should know," Harriman, who had just reappeared, interjected. "The clearance came straight from the White House, sir."

"The Germans know about this project," Jim continued, "and for Hitler that is reason enough. Hitler wants to fight us before we have an unbeatable weapon. To achieve that end he must cripple this project. He knows what he would do with such a weapon as you are building here, and assumes the same of us. I suspect the notion of having it and not using it isn't even within his mental universe."

"Not a bad thought at times," Groves muttered. "It'd be a pleasure to test drop it on that bastard's resort while he's there."

"Given the points I've just outlined," Martel said, fixing Groves with his gaze, "I believe that Otto Skorzeny is not here just to spy or support a spy effort. He's here for sabotage. Furthermore, this action could only be contemplated as part of an overall surprise attack on the United States."

Finally Groves crushed out his cigar and took overt control of the meeting. "You're the third briefing I've received today on this subject," he said. "First, before my damned breakfast, a call from the President's Chief of Staff.

Then the FBI tells me there's a spy loose. And now you.

"Son, I've been on this project for four years. I've lived, eaten and slept with it. I've looked at every angle and so has Soratkin. We've got layers of security on this place you wouldn't even dream of. You're talking about at most twenty commandos running around with this Teutonic superman. Oh, they might be able to penetrate the outer barrier, but we'd have their asses in the wringer before ever they closed on the inner circle. Furthermore, if they've scoped this place out, they know we'll nail them."

Groves's tone turned sardonic. "However, in view of your concerns, which you have so dutifully shared with the President, and he through his chief of staff with me, I've arranged for further measures. I'm bringing in two companies of Rangers. They will be posted inside the key facilities on a twenty-four-hour watch for point defense, and on the perimeter in hunter-ambush teams. If Skorzeny's their best, he'll meet some of our best — and when they're done with him we'll send his scalp back to Adolf as a souvenir of the visit. Does that make you happy?"

"Yes sir. Thank you, sir," Harriman said, snapping his briefcase shut and standing.

Martel looked over at Harriman, wanting to say more but fully understanding that Trevor wanted to end the interview.

"Gentlemen, thank you for your input," Groves said.

"Sir, just one request," Harriman asked.

"Go ahead."

"Our boss expects us to be here and to be available to supply you with advice when and as needed. Those are his orders, sir. Can we at least get security badges to come here, to the administrative area of this base, and a room at the hotel here on base? We just want to be available. I know our boss would view it as a personal favor on your part, and he'd be glad to send our security clearances over to you."

Groves nodded. "For the administrative area and hotel only. Step one foot beyond the permitted area and my people will lock you up so deep it'll be winter before Donovan can dig you out. Is that clear?"

"Thank you, sir," Harriman said with a smile, "perfectly clear."

"Soratkin will assign someone to set you up. I've got other things to attend to. Good day, gentlemen."

On their way out Harriman told them, "My call was from our boss. He had a tip for us."

Both Jim and Wayne were suddenly attentive.

"The tip comes from Europe. You guys are to check out every airfield in a pie slice due east to east-northeast from Oak Ridge outward as far as it takes, up to one hundred and fifty miles. If you get past the fifty-mile point I'll see about getting you a plane, but you can start out by car."

"Why are we going to do that?" Wayne asked.

"Because, according to Mr. Donovan's informant, at some airfield within that range you will find Otto Skorzeny and his merry men."

"Aren't you going to tell Groves about this?" Jim asked.

"Of course," Harriman replied. "But not while he can decide to detain you two so you can't 'muddy the waters.'"

April 17
Fort Knox, Kentucky
Headquarters, 3rd Armored Division

"George, this is MacArthur, how are you?"

MacArthur's voice was distinctive, and easily imitated. For a moment Major General George Patton was tempted to bark an obscenity and slam the receiver down, but at the last instant something stayed him.

"Doug?"

MacArthur chuckled softly, something that both caused Patton's blood pressure to go up a notch and confirmed the identity of his caller. One of the many things Patton disliked was being caught by surprise, even in conversation.

"George, are you alone?"

"Yes, sir."

"Good. We need to talk."

"Is this about China, sir?"

"No, George, I'm out of the China business."

Damn! There was no glory in China, but still it was action. Cursing silently, he leaned back in his chair. The last war had been a bust as far as armored operations went. He had been allowed a brief stint as an observer with Montgomery during the last six months of the African campaign. He'd witnessed the Second Battle of El Alamein, where Monty had stopped Rommel's '43 offensive, but that was as close as he ever got to commanding armored formations in battle. There had been the promise of an armored corps command for Operation Overlord, but then the damned Japanese surrendered. That had been the greatest and most secret disappointment of his life.

"What can I do for you, sir?" Patton asked, trying to not let his disappointment show in his voice.

"George, I'm in Washington right now. I need a man who knows armor. My thoughts naturally turned to you."

Patton smiled sardonically at the flattery, of which he was almost as masterful a practitioner as MacArthur.

"Go on, sir. What's the problem?"

"George, the Germans are on the move again. The betting money here is still that they're going to finish off Russia."

"But some think they're going to do the Brits — and maybe us too."

"Precisely."

"What I've been saying for years, sir. That paperhanging son of a bitch won't be happy until he owns the whole shop and sooner or later we're going to have to have a showdown. Well I say—"

"We're in agreement on that, George. Let's get to the particulars."

Something else Patton did not much care for was being cut off in mid-sentence, but this time he found it easy enough to take, given the topic under discussion.

"What can I do?"

"Nothing official yet, just some preparatory moves. Now, just how combat ready are you?"

"One hundred percent, sir. And I'm the only armored commander on this continent who can say that."

"George, I know the numbers game as well as you do. With that in mind, I repeat: just how ready are you?"

"Sir. My manpower is just over ninety percent at ten thousand men. I have two battalions of Pershing tanks at full strength. The third battalion is just now getting to full operational capacity with the new Pershing-105 upgrade. My battalions of armored infantry, artillery, and engineering are on-line. The recon battalion is still saddled with Shermans, but that is neither here nor there in terms of operational readiness, just effectiveness. They're ready. We're all ready. Look at our latest efficiency report."

"I have it in front of me, but I know that game as well. I have a simple question for you, and I want an absolutely straight answer. No games. Don't play with me."

"Yes, sir. No games."

"If you were thrown into an action against a couple of German armored divisions with what you have right now, today, could you hold your own?"

"I'd kick their asses right off the map. Their King Tigers are too heavy and slow, their Panthers are pretty good, but not as good as our new stuff. We've continued improving our designs over the last couple of years while they've been locked into mass production of the models they have. That's been our one break. We weren't forced into mass-producing a stopgap machine like the horrible old Sherman. We could afford to take the time to move ahead. Get us on dry land and we'll tear them a new asshole. Sir."

MacArthur laughed softly. "George, I want you to — quietly—get all your people back to base. Don't make a big deal of it. Say it's part of a drill. I also want you to start preparing your gear for ocean shipment."

"Everything, sir? We have nearly three thousand vehicles."

"Everything, George."

"What about the trains? We'll need over a hundred."

"We'll make the arrangements up here. Rolling stock will start arriving within the next two days. As quickly as you fill a train it will get moved to a siding in Louisville and you will start loading another one. Mind you, we need absolute discretion on this. No public announcements, and if the press does get wind, let it 'slip' you're heading to Texas for war games, and at the same time leak that we're moving the 3rd to China to finish off Mao. They'll dismiss the Texas story, and fall for China."

"It's England, isn't it?"

"Why England?"

"If they're going to come after us they'd be fools not to take England out in the first blow. From our perspective, England is nothing but a giant unsinkable aircraft carrier anchored within range of Berlin. It will also provide a staging area just twenty miles off the French coast when it comes time to invade. They can't let us keep it, and we can't let them take it."

"George, your personal opinion is now Top Secret. You keep it to yourself, you hear?"

Patton knew he had hit the mark.

"We're hoping that the blow is going in the opposite direction. If it is, we don't want it to be obvious that we were in the middle of a war mobilization."

"Personally I hope that it is coming our way, sir. We're going to have to fight Hitler sooner or later, so let's get it over with — while Congress has still left us something to fight with."

There was a moment of silence on the other end of the

line. "George, if this threat is real, we will suffer at least a million casualties, and may very well wind up fighting street-to-street in our own cities. Have you ever seen the films of Stalingrad? I pray to God that this is nothing more than a false alarm, and I hope you will do the same."

"Of course I will, sir," Patton lied.

"Good. But while we're hoping, we'll also be getting ready. I'll be calling you daily from now on. Let's get it done, and get it done right."

The line went dead. George Patton sat in delighted contemplation of his unexpected good fortune. He knew it was a character flaw, but how he would love a good war. . . .

CHAPTER THIRTEEN

April 18
Norris, Tennessee
(Forty miles east-northeast of Oak Ridge)

"They're gone."

Stretching, Otto Skorzeny climbed out of the secured basement, dug in under the hangar floor, the rest of the team climbing out after him.

Bachman stared nervously down the access road in the direction they had gone, as if afraid the government car would suddenly reappear.

"It was the FBI. They were looking for you."

"Of course they were looking for me," Skorzeny replied calmly, staring straight into Friedrich's eyes. His pupils were dilated.

"They showed me your picture and asked if I'd seen you."

"And you said?"

"Nothing, of course."

Skorzeny looked over at the four Piper Cubs located outside the hangar.

"Did they check the planes?"

"They went over them, but I pointed out there must be a hundred planes just like them in this part of the state."

"Anything else?"

Friedrich looked around nervously. "My cover is good. I've lived with it safely for twelve years. I was born in this country. No one knows of my membership in the *Bund*."

"Perhaps too safely," Gunther interjected calmly.

"What?"

"He thinks you're scared," Skorzeny explained, "and scared men are dangerous."

Friedrich hesitated for a moment.

"I know nothing about what you're doing here. I've done as ordered since setting up my flying school three years ago. I've done the photographs asked of me and kept my cover story intact."

"Yeah, great photos," Gunther sneered. "Taken from twenty kilometers out. My blind grandmother could have done better than that. Why? Because she has more courage. You didn't give us a damn thing till we got here."

"Maybe I haven't been as aggressive as you think I should be — but I haven't kicked up a hornets' nest like you have, either. They shoot people like me. You know that, don't you?"

"Oh, no! Not with real bullets!" Gunther laughed softly. "You would have loved it in Russia."

"Listen! I'm doing my duty for the Fatherland the same as you. It's just that my job works differently, and being careful is the first rule. You were on the radio for nearly fifteen minutes last night. Don't you think they have equipment to triangulate that?"

"We had to get the updates."

"Updates for what?"

Skorzeny held up his hand for the two to be silent.

"Friedrich, you're doing a fine job. It's just that my men and I are tense. We were down in that hole for nearly an hour. Let's just go about our business and forget about this. Don't worry, Albert's down watching the access road. If someone comes back, he'll give plenty of warning."

Friedrich looked around nervously and then, with a nod of his head, turned and walked away.

"Do you think the FBI picked anything up from their little visit?" Gunther asked.

"We have to assume so. It must have been evident to them that he was hiding something. Chances are they'll do a follow-up visit a couple of days from now. They might stake out an observation post as well. May already have done so." Skorzeny nodded to the hills surrounding the small valley containing the airport. "We'll stay in the hangar from now on. No one steps outside."

"I think little 'Fred' will crack if they talk to him again."

"For now, we need him. He owns this place. Locals know him and expect to see him. But that's becoming less important minute by minute of course; if you think he's getting erratic, you can kill him."

Gunther brightened.

Skorzeny added thoughtfully, "But not just because you don't like him. In my estimation he is still marginally more useful than dangerous to us." He grinned. "And remember: if you do kill him you will have to do all his work."

April 18
London

Winston Churchill and several of his aides, who with one exception were clustered well off to either side, looked down sourly from the balcony at the situation table set up in his old headquarters beneath Whitehall. The map, which covered a rectangle defined by Greenland to the north and west, the Ural Mountains to the east, and North Africa to the south, was covered with small chips. Most of them were black, and represented known Nazi military assets.

From Archangel in the north to Baku in the south, the Russian front showed an estimated one hundred Nazi divisions in place, but most of the intelligence data from that quarter was days, even weeks, old and had not been very reliable in the first place, being provided by contacts within Russian intelligence. But there were certain key factors that were revealing nevertheless, the most interesting being that the Germans had added only forty divisions in the last two months. Hardly what they would have done were they truly planning to invade. There was signal traffic for another hundred, but all evidence indicated that the traffic was smoke with no fire.

What was even more significant was the latest photo intel, just arrived by jet courier from Iraq: without exception, the ships in the Caspian were riding high in the water; not one of them had been loaded. Furthermore, the vehicles photographed nearby were sufficient for not much more than a single division of motorized infantry—a far cry from the three divisions of *panzer grenadier* and three divisions of armor that the signal intelligence seemed to show was in place for a cross-Caspian offensive.

And there was the other intelligence out of Russia as well — a report from Kiev concerning the transfer of the 5th SS and 7th Armor, moving by rail at night — not east but west. There was a similar report for the 23rd Panzer as it moved through Smolensk.

There were clear warnings on other fronts as well. In Tunisia and Libya the 15th and 21st Panzer had gone out on "maneuvers" with the 164th Light Division. They were currently reported just a hundred and fifty miles from the Egyptian armistice line. They could be on the El Alamein front within a day.

But threatening as all the rest of it might be, the key concern was for Europe and the North Atlantic. Churchill slowly paced his way around the balcony that looked down on the situation board. Even as he watched, black chips were being nudged westward. Without Enigma, the intelligence seemed horribly spotty and shallow, but it all pointed in the same direction: west.

A report had come in just hours ago from an agent working aboard a Finnish liner that the tank regiment and antitank battalion of the 10th SS were in Hamburg, and had been partially loaded on board four transport ships. Other reports indicated movement of half a dozen more divisions toward Hamburg as well. There also seemed to be a great deal of positioning of military units along rail and Autobahn routes leading into France, and there were reports of massive buildups of aviation-fuel stocks along the French and Belgian coasts. A train had derailed near Caen the night before loaded with V-1 bombs. Night train traffic throughout France was up several hundred percent, all of it moving west under heavy guard and returning east empty. A dock worker reported that the sub pens of l'Orient were empty, too.

There were also hundreds of anecdotal reports — a drunken Luftwaffe officer boasting about what he would personally do to the RAF this time, a French prostitute who had an offer to set up in London once the war was over, a deserter in Norway who couldn't face combat again. . . .

Standing unobtrusively with Churchill was a man who by his rank of captain ought not to have been there at all, or only in a menial capacity. Instead, and unlike the others, he stood close enough to the great man to communicate *sotto voce,* giving his opinions as requested. While his attitude was certainly deferential and attentive, it was neither strained nor marked by any particular tension.

"Well, Basil," asked the War Leader of the Britons, "what do you suppose your precious Belisarius would have done in these circumstances?" He gestured disgustedly at the map below.

Accurately judging this as no time for the informality that generally characterized their relationship, military teacher, historian, and theoretician Sir Basil Liddell Hart spoke gravely and to the point. "Prime Minister, I do not know. I can tell you, though, that he would never willingly have allowed himself to have arrived in such a situation in the first place."

Churchill raised an imperial eyebrow at the implied criticism.

"Which is not," Liddell Hart continued, "to say that the emperor Constantine might not have placed him in an analogous and equally bad one. Just as, I think, President Harrison has done to you."

Churchill glanced to left and right. "Well, yes, perhaps so. But keep your voice down."

"Three months ago we might have amused our German friends with veiled feints in North Africa, forward placement of bombers that could strike into their oil fields, tempted them in other ways to misallocate their resources. Now? It is hard to be subtle with a knife at your throat."

"Hmm. I thought you might say something like that. You damned policy boffins are all alike. Filled with grand theories, but sterile when it comes to cases." Churchill knew he was being both unfair and unkind, but then he knew that Liddell Hart knew it too, and would make allowances.

Liddell Hart smiled lopsidedly, then continued. "Since our prospective ally has seen fit to pin us in place while our enemy maneuvers around us, at this late moment there is little we can do but endure the onslaught. Nor do I think we have much chance of surviving it."

Churchill glowered at the confidant he had chosen to protect him from his own penchant for military follies such as the Dardanelles, while at the same time not limiting him to the dull plodding that was a sure recipe for doom on the part of a military underdog. "What? Defeatism? From you? Have you nothing better to offer? Then why—"

"I misspoke, sir," Liddell Hart broke in quickly. "I should have said rather, 'we have not much chance of surviving it alone.' Therefore our every move should be predicated on the arrival of the Americans in the nick of time and ensuring that they do so arrive. For example, it is imperative that their President be informed instantly of any threat to their Canal. Conversely, while any other first strike against the Americans should also be thwarted, it would be better for us if that thwarting occurred after such a strike were irrevocably launched."

Churchill glanced about him again. "Hrmph. Keep such opinions to yourself, sir. But I take your point."

"I would add that when the Americans arrive it may be

that they do so in desperate straits, so to speak. In such a case an American carrier might be worth more to us than a British city."

"Yes, yes. It follows that if we cannot survive without the Americans then we must see to it that the Americans survive at any cost to ourselves. Any cost at all."

Liddell Hart nodded. His point had indeed been taken.

Churchill turned to Rear Admiral Rushbrooke, his head of naval intelligence. Rushbrooke moved to stand directly next to him as Liddell Hart faded unobtrusively into the background. "What's the latest on the U-boats?"

"Not much, I'm afraid. Both their new Type 17 Walter hydrogen-peroxide engine boats and the Type 21 electro-submarines are fitted out with snorkels, and that makes them the bloody deuce to find even in transit. And once in place they simply don't surface. Also, it's a certain bet they have radar detection mounted on their snorkels. When they detect an aircraft, they just slip even the snorkel below the surface and pop it back up after the danger has passed."

Churchill had been growing visibly impatient during this. "I didn't ask for excuses! It's answers I want. Give me answers! Tell me what you know!" Though he played the public as if it were a musical instrument and he its master, he was not always so inclined in private. When crossed Winston Churchill could be hard to bear.

Wordlessly the admiral picked up a long pointer. Leaning over the balcony, he tapped four black markers at the edge of the near end of the table. "Starting with these, we've had four contact reports in the last day. It could be one sub, it could be a pack of them. Actually, they're probably off this board now; they were running on a course taking them toward the Bahamas. We have another contact, off the board as well, a hundred and eighty miles east-northeast of Bermuda. We've had another contact here"—he indicated a point on the map fifty miles off the point of Greenland—"and one moving toward Labrador.

They were picked up on the surface by a Canadian B-24." The admiral drew a deep breath. "Within the last two days we've had twenty-seven contacts with subs exiting their bases at Bordeaux, l'Orient, Cherbourg. Again, we could be catching only a small part of the movement, or most of the contacts could be multiple, so numbers are vague at best."

"But it could be a wolf pack."

Rushbrooke nodded. "Oh, yes."

Churchill looked back down at the map and pointed toward Norway. "Is that their 6th Mountain Division?"

"It sailed from Trondheim this morning, sir. The 90th Light Division is slated to pull out tomorrow. The Luftwaffe ground division, scattered in airfields along the northern coast of Norway, has nearly five hundred transport planes and is supposed to airlift back to Germany starting Easter Sunday."

He looked past the admiral to the head of MI-6, British intelligence. "Why back to Germany, 'C'? One might think it better positioned where it is." By convention, the name of the head of international espionage was never spoken.

"C" shrugged. "I can't say, sir. Unless they calculate they won't need to defend their northerly approaches after what they are about to do."

"Are all their sub yards empty?"

"We think so, sir."

Rushbrooke nodded in agreement.

"Frankly, sir," Liddell Hart added, "the Germans know they haven't a hope of keeping such massive movements secret. What they are trying, I think, is both to keep us in the dark as to tactical particulars, and maintain deniability with the Americans until the last possible instant. As long as their noses aren't rubbed in it, the Yanks really don't want to know."

Churchill nodded. He knew too well the truth of that.

The head of MI-6 went on. "I've been flooded these last two days with contact reports from nearly every one of our

European agents, and their reports all point to one conclusion. Either Jerry is coming at us again, or he wants very badly for us to think that he is. A few hours ago the most telling report so far came in: one of their printing offices has ditched its current run of commemorative stamps for the fifth anniversary of the invasion of Russia in favor of petrol-rationing stamps — to be issued on May first."

Churchill shook his head. "The idiots. You think this is it, then?"

"Definitely, sir. Sometimes they're simply too organized. I've also received reports on orders for military headstones, blackout curtains getting shipped, even an increase in production of penicillin and bandages."

Churchill lit yet another cigar. "Yes, this is it." His gaze shifted to Air Marshal Leigh-Mallory, head of the Royal Air Force

"And what have you to contribute to our joy?"

That worthy coughed and cleared his throat. "Last night a photo-recon Mosquito equipped with a high-power strobe made low-level runs over two airfields near Dieppe." He reached into his briefcase and pulled out several photos, passing them over to Churchill.

"You'll see, sir, that the fields are packed. You're looking at Me-262s and 229s, Dornier 335s, and Me-510s. You'll see circled on the second photo an angled shot into a warehouse that's packed with munitions, while the rail line running just next to the airfield has nearly sixty tanker cars that we must assume are filled with av fuel and jet fuel. Contrariwise, the airfields we photographed near Baku and along the Caspian coast are stripped, just a light force of obsolete Fw-190s and Ju-88s. I'm willing to bet Jerry has very nearly every one of his modern fighters within strike range of us. . . . We also have a report of nearly two hundred of their new Me-264E long-range bombers engaging in some sort of low-level night maneuvers in eastern Germany, near the Polish border."

"Low-level?"

"Strange, sir, I know."

Involuntarily Churchill glanced back at Liddell Hart, who moved forward to his side and followed him to the balustrade, where again they stood alone.

"What are they doing, Basil?"

"Perhaps we can reason it out, sir. Two hundred is a very large number, after all, very nearly their entire long-range bomber force. . . . Therefore whatever they are rehearsing for is not small. Furthermore, they must anticipate surprising their target."

Churchill raised an inquiring eyebrow.

Hart shrugged. "Such large and lumbering aircraft could not survive low-level runs in the face of significant antiaircraft defenses."

Churchill nodded his understanding.

Hart went on. "They certainly don't think they can surprise *us*—"

Churchill broke in. "So who then? The Americans?"

"Who else? We have already discounted the possibility of a renewed assault on the Soviets for good and sufficient reason."

"Yes, yes. The Americans. It must be they who are the target. But what about range? Surely even Adolf is not prepared to launch a suicide run at this early stage."

"Yes, that is the problem: there would not seem to be a valuable enough target within range of those planes. Unless . . ."

"Unless what?" Churchill prompted.

"Can the Germans have developed some method of in-air refueling?"

"By God! That must be it!"

There had been numerous intelligence reports of German work in this area. Supposedly it was still all very experimental, but it wouldn't be the first time Jerry had surprised them with the speed of some military development, not by a long shot.

Churchill switched his attention to Rushbrooke, who

stood a short distance away. "Is there anything else going on here we know that the Americans do not? If so, we must inform them instantly, and with the greatest possible frankness." Churchill paused in thought. "No. We must do more than that. Andrew will surely discount any bald reports of these exercises. We must 'discover' information pointing to an attack — even if we must invent it. If the Americans do not want to believe the simple truth, we must help them along. And we must ensure that they defend that canal!"

Without bothering to wait for a reply from the admiral, Churchill turned back to Liddell Hart. "What shall we tell him?" he asked quietly. "Remember that it must be dramatic and plausible, but that it need not pass a long-term muster. Next week it will be a small matter that I grew overenthusiastic today."

Hart shrugged. "In that case, why invent anything? Unimpeachable source. Our single most valuable asset. You have sworn never to speak his name. Of course you might have to give your word that what you say is true."

Churchill stared bleakly at the other for a moment, then nodded dismissal. The others, sensing his wishes, maintained their distance. Once again he gazed thoughtfully down at the vast table map with its clustered assets. Soon he would talk to Harrison, but for now he would concentrate on what was before him.

War was coming within a matter of days. But what was the German plan? Where should he put England's chips on the map below? He shook his head, glowered. One major error on his part and England would fall. And even if he did everything right, still survival depended on the American response. How should he advise them? He was sure Harrison would react if his Congress let him — but would it? Churchill had begun to suspect that nothing would bring the Americans in quickly enough to matter except an attack upon American soil.

Churchill smiled in sardonic despair. Had it come to this?

Was England's one hope that Germany attack America as well? Even Churchill could not quite bring himself to understand that the assault on England was merely an inevitable consequence of the assault on America.

He looked back down at the plot table. A Wren, pushing a shuffleboardlike stick, placed another U-boat identification marker off the Bermuda coast. Well, it was time to act.

He walked back over to the knot of commanders who waited on his word. "As of noon tomorrow I'm ordering a full alert and mobilization of all our forces." He hesitated for a moment and then looked over at Leigh-Mallory. "Draw up plans for a pre-emptive strike on German airfields located in the French occupied zone."

His staff looked at him incredulously.

"No, I haven't gone mad, not yet at least. But if we have an incident, just one incident, those airfields are to be smashed instantly."

"If we do that we'll lose any hope of support from the Americans," the RAF commander said.

"I know that. Harrison wants us to be as pure and pathetic as a virgin about to receive her rapist. Well, gentlemen, if virgin sacrifice we must be," Churchill growled, "then at least we shall deball the bastard on the first stroke."

Turning, he walked into the small glass-enclosed office reserved for him and reached for the red phone. How similar this felt to the dark days of 1940 when he would talk to Roosevelt while overhead the dull concussion of the bombs stalked across London. But he knew that what was to come would not be like the summer and fall of 1940. It would be worse, far worse. Not only must it be assumed that Hitler and Göring had learned from their mistakes; simple technological progress had given the Luftwaffe the range to sweep Britain from one end to the other. . . . *and a new broom sweeps clean.* Also there were nearly four hundred U-boats now, half of them of the latest designs, compared to the sixty at the start of the last go-round. And those sixty old-fashioned subs had come close to strangling England. Along with more and better subs, fighters and bombers, the Germans now possessed massive quantities of landing craft, a huge airlift capacity, and an army that had fought and beaten the world, excepting only America, without even breathing hard. . . .

And what of England? The RAF was more competent and nearly as up-to-date as the Luftwaffe—but too small, too small. There was the secret buildup over the last six months of a reserve force of four hundred additional Meteors based in Wales, Northern Ireland, and Scotland, but that still wasn't enough. The navy was weak, and the army weaker, with but ten divisions capable of being mobilized for immediate home defense. Aside from the vital North African garrison, the remainder were trapped in that foolish—he realized it now, how he realized it — venture in Indochina, and in trying to hold India, badge of empire. What of India when there was no England? What of the jewel in the crown, when there was no crown?

He picked up the phone.

"Get me Harrison," he said calmly while lighting another in the endless stream of cigars.

April 19
Norris, Tennessee

"I'm getting sick of looking at flea-bitten flight schools," Mason announced as they turned off the gravel road that had rattled their teeth for the last three miles onto the deeply rutted dirt road that covered the last few hundred yards to Harry's Crop Dusting Service and Flight School. Finally the place was in sight, as cheap and weather-beaten in appearance as the sign that had announced its existence three miles back.

Having heard this song several times too many already, Jim ignored his friend as he negotiated the car over a rickety wooden bridge and then out to the edge of a grass-strip runway.

Suddenly Wayne's mood changed. "On the other hand, I first learned to fly at a place just like this. I was sixteen at the time. A wonder I didn't kill myself. But I tell you one thing: if you learn to land on something like this you can land anywhere."

"Try a carrier at night in a force-five blow," Jim laughed in reply.

"You damn Navy pilots. You weren't out in the jungle the way we were. Air-conditioning, good food, no malaria. What a life."

"Yeah, well we earned it every time we came down on that damned jerking postage stamp of a deck. . . . Or near it," he added as he became aware that the jouncing he had just been through had awakened old wounds. "You Army Air pukes think zooming around is all that pilots have to do; you don't know what flying is about."

Seeing the sardonic humor replaced by a look of pain on his friend's face, Mason forbore to reply in kind. For both of them this whole thing was getting damned tedious and frustrating. They had spent yesterday and today on what was looking more and more like a fruitless endeavor, visiting every airport and airfield within one hundred and fifty miles of Oak Ridge. Had Harriman sent them on this wild-goose chase just to get them out of the way? They were both beginning to suspect as much.

They pulled up to the side of a dilapidated hangar, its tin siding streaked with rust. "Guess that's the owner," Wayne said as he nodded toward the pudgy, balding man standing in the open door of a wooden hut behind the hangar. The figure under discussion stepped forth, rubbing his hands on his greasy coveralls, and slowly walked over.

"How you doing?" Jim called, getting out of his car and walking to meet the other. Wayne followed more slowly.

"What do you fellas want?"

Jim extended his hand. "Jim Foster. This is my partner, Wayne Anderson."

The owner slowly took Jim's hand, shook it quickly, let it drop like something a little too hot.

"I'm Fred Bachman."

"Where's Harry?"

"Harry sold this place to me. I never bothered to change the name. Now what do you fellas want? I'm kind of busy today."

Jim turned and started to walk over to the hangar. Bachman quickly moved to his side.

"Wayne and I are starting up a little business down in Knoxville," Jim announced. "Tell me, you ever heard of Levittown?"

"No."

"Whole new idea in housing. Make homes the same way you do cars, do it like an assembly line, but right on the site. We've picked Knoxville for our project, and we thought you might be able to help us out."

"How's that?"

Jim put his hand on Bachman's shoulder, turning him slightly, away from the hangar and casually holding him in place.

"I guess you know there's one hell of a housing shortage around these parts. A lot of government workers and all, and they need places to live. Whoever builds the right kind of housing for these people is going to clean up big time. Now we've got half a dozen possible sites we're interested in buying but we want to get a look from above. You know, fly over them, take some pictures, that kind of thing.

"Tell me, do you have any experience with aerial photography?"

As he spoke, Wayne moved behind the two and went up to the hangar door. The overhead casters of the door squealed loudly.

Bachman pulled away from Jim and turned around.

"Hey, what are you doing there?"

Wayne stood marveling before the now-open hangar door. "Damn, you know? I learned to fly in one of those babies!" Wayne announced excitedly as he stepped into the hangar's gloom.

"Get outta there!"

Oblivious, Wayne kept walking. Bachman followed distractedly.

"Yeah, back before the war. Piper Cub, what a plane."

"I said get out of there!"

Jim watched Bachman closely. There was a nervous tension that was almost palpable. At the other fields they had visited, the owners, ever on the lookout for a quick job, had been eagerly forthcoming, and more than ready to trade war stories with Wayne.

Bachman pushed his way in front of Wayne.

"Leave the hangar."

"Ah, come on. I haven't flown since I got shot up over Bougainville. Say, where were you in the war?"

"Right here."

"How come? The army was desperate for pilots."

"I flunked my physical. Now get out of here."

"Say, you hiding some sort of military secret?" Wayne asked, as if cracking a joke. Moving past Bachman, he quickly walked down the line of Cubs, looking each of them over.

"I'm not hiding anything," Bachman shouted after him excitedly.

"So what's your beef? Come on, I'd like to rent one of these Cubs and take a spin. I haven't flown since the Japs shot me up. I'd love to get back up again, even if I have to have someone flying behind me."

"I don't have the time."

"What about arranging for that photo flight we need?" Jim interjected quickly, forcing Bachman to turn back around.

Bachman nervously rubbed his hands on the sides of his pants.

"I'm booked up. Dusting."

"This time of year?" Jim asked with mock incredulity, still smiling.

"Yeah. Orchards."

"What are you using?"

"DDT." Bachman looked back at Wayne, who was walking around one of the Cubs and leaning over to peer into the cockpit.

"That's why I don't want you guys in here," Bachman announced. "Some people get sick from that stuff if they breathe too much."

"No sweat, buddy. I got hosed down with it all the time out in the Pacific. Ain't nothing dangerous about a whiff of that juice." Wayne pulled the door of the Cub open and looked inside. "Say, what's this rig up here in the cockpit? Damn . . . *nice* radio gear you got in here."

Bachman quickly moved over and slammed the plane door so vigorously that Wayne had to lean back to avoid being hit.

"Got it surplus. Now *leave the hangar!* I don't have time for you two. If you need a photo flight try Benson's down at the Knoxville Airport. He does that sort of thing."

Bachman walked over to the hangar door and, turning, looked back at the two coldly.

"Okay, buddy," Wayne said. "You're losing some good business with us. Too bad for you."

The two walked back out into the sunlight and started toward their car. Bachman remained by the hangar door. Jim suddenly turned.

"Hey, just one question."

"Yeah, what?"

"Just what is it that they're doing over there at Oak Ridge?"

"What do you mean?" Bachman said, his voice barely a whisper.

"You know, that government project over there. Nobody wants to tell us."

"I don't know."

"I understand it's pretty big."

"I guess so."

"Well, you must fly near it a lot, so what's it look like?"

Bachman hesitated.

"It's restricted airspace."

"Yeah, that's what the guy at the airport we were at this morning told us," Wayne interjected.

"You've been to another airport?" Bachman whispered.

"Sure, just comparing prices," Jim replied. "Anyhow, I heard they were fooling around with atoms and stuff."

Bachman looked at him, wide eyed.

Wayne turned and slowly walked back toward Bachman. "Anything you want to tell us, buddy?" he asked softly.

Bachman looked back and forth at the two.

"I know nothing. Nothing!"

"Relax, buddy," Wayne said softly. "We aren't giving you the third degree. I guess this is all secret type of stuff. If you knew anything the FBI would be down your throat, is that it?"

"I know nothing."

"'Course not." Wayne grinned a conspiratorial grin. "I heard they lock people up around here if they find out anything about what's going on over there, even if they don't do it on purpose. I also heard they can get pretty rough on people they suspect of being a little too curious. You know what I mean?"

Bachman said nothing as he again wiped his hands on his trousers.

"Yeah, like the cops who pulled us over. They were looking for those cop killers," Wayne continued. "Said if they ever get the bastards who did it, they'll shoot them first and worry about the trial later. Hah! You shoulda heard where they're gonna shoot 'em. Buncha comedians, these Southern cops."

"Get out of here," Bachman shouted. "You're wasting my time."

"Sure thing," Wayne replied. "Didn't mean to get you riled." He stepped back and looked around.

"Yeah, you sure do look busy."

Wayne slowly walked back toward Jim.

"Come on. I guess the man doesn't want our business." They walked back to the car. When they had crossed the bridge and started down the dirt road, Wayne finally broke the pregnant silence.

"They're here."

"Yep. Sure as shit."

Jim pulled out onto the gravel road and drove for a while, then pulled the car over and turned the engine off. "What'd you see in the hangar?"

"Like I said, nice radio. I got the frequency number it was set to: a military channel. And that guy was seriously rattled, scared to death. Skorzeny's there and little fat boy's petrified. He was most likely running a nice cushy operation more for the money than anything else. Do an occasional fly-by, get a few photos, and send them out. No one suspects, no risk, and plenty of pay getting socked away, and then old Otto shows up and starts kicking up dust. So in comes the FBI sniffing around, and now he's ready to crack."

Jim nodded. At all the other fields they'd checked, a recent visit from the FBI had been a feature of the conversation, and most of them had already heard through the grapevine enough to know all about the illegal flight. The one common refrain was that nobody who could fly like that was idiot enough to get where that plane had been by accident.

That certainly jibed with the earlier conversation they'd had with the P-51 pilots. They had been in no doubt whatsoever that the man they had been chasing was a professional. A student pilot would have killed himself trying a split-S with a pullout at fifty feet and then going into the fog. As for going under a country bridge with less than six feet of clearance, that was a barnstormer's trick. "Frankly," one of them had said, "I was too filled with admiration to be properly humiliated."

"Time to talk to Harriman," Jim finally said.

"Then what?"

"Have the FBI come down and rip this place apart."

"And suppose they won't?"

Martel knew that wasn't as ridiculous as it sounded. Damn the not-invented-here syndrome, anyway! Jim pointed south toward a ridge looking down on the runway. "I think, old friend, that up there would be a good spot for you to hang out and keep an eye on things."

"Me? Why not you?"

"Like you were moaning about before, you lived out in the boonies during the war; you're used to it. I, on the other hand, am of effete naval-pilot aristocratic lineage. Also, Major Mason, I am the boss on our little expedition," Jim added with just enough of a smile to show that he didn't want to have to *really* pull rank.

By now they had crested the ridge. Jim pulled the car over as Mason cursed under his breath. While Jim pulled a backpack and portable radio out of the trunk, Mason reached under his seat, pulled out a forty-five semiautomatic and slipped it into his pocket.

"If it rains I'll sort of have to shoot you when this is over, pal."

"The weather's beautiful. Find a good vantage point, set up and keep in touch. I'm Black Knight, you're White." Martel opened up the back door of the car and pulled back the blanket concealing the portable transceiver that they had wired into the car's antenna.

"If anything jumps, holler. Otherwise check in every two hours during the night. I'll wait here till you get set up and we make sure the radios check out."

"Great, just great. I'll freeze my tail off out here when I could have been back in a warm bed with Sarah."

"You could not love her half so much," Jim quoted with what pretended to be a mock-serious look.

"What if the FBI won't play?"

"Then we'll get Donovan to loan us some people and do it ourselves. I'd love to be in on nailing Skorzeny. He's starting to get under my skin."

Wayne lit a cigarette and slowly exhaled. "I'd wager that we're starting to get under his, too."

Wayne was more right than he knew. Lurking in the stairway leading down to the secret basement, Skorzeny had recognized both of them while they were giving Bachman the pseudo-friendly third degree.

April 20, Midnight
Somewhere in Germany
(April 19, 6:00 P.M. in Oak Ridge)

Shifting his shoulders under his backpack, Karl Radl walked slowly down the line of men, making one final check. Earlier he had watched the enlisted men carefully for signs of dismay as they were finally briefed as to where the target was, and the reason behind the strike. No need to have worried: the months of training, the months of speculation, were finally over for them, and they were eager to begin.

The forty men of his platoon were bent forward under the weight of their gear—parachute and backup, first-aid kit, gas mask, machine pistol, two hundred rounds of ammunition, two hundred rounds for their squad's heavy MG-42 machine gun, six fragmentation and three thermite grenades, two signal flares, knife, pistol and twenty-four rounds, two mortar rounds or one antitank round, four kilograms of plastic explosive already prepacked into steel rods for insertion into the reactor, flashlight, target maps, compass, two canteens and three days of rations. In addition, some of the men were carrying radio equipment and backups. In some cases the gear very nearly outweighed the men carrying it.

Underneath each of the stretched long-distance Me-264Es were three drop-containers that would be jettisoned at the same time the first man went out the door.

The containers held additional ammunition, two hundred kilograms of plastic explosives, a mortar, three heavy machine guns, and a specially designed 47-mm antitank gun which could be assembled in under five minutes. It could be pulled by two men, or simply hooked onto the bumper of nearly any commandeered automobile.

In the glare of the brightly lit airfield Radl saw a *Kübelwagen* coming down the taxiway. He turned to his men and barked, "Attention!"

They did their best to comply.

The Kübelwagen pulled up and Radl snapped off a salute as Herman Göring climbed out of the vehicle. Grinning broadly, the Reichsmarschal returned the salute with his baton, and then came up to slap Radl on the shoulder.

"All set, are we?"

"Yes, Herr Reichsmarschal."

"Good, good. The Führer sends his personal greetings to all of you. His eyes and mine will be upon you and your men. The Reich is counting on you for its salvation. If you are victorious, our nation will survive. But if you fail, Radl, the Americans will rain down atomic destruction on our cities. Germany will be destroyed."

"My men understand that, sir. We've trained more than half a year for this moment. We will not fail." Privately Radl thought that Otto had expressed the same thoughts much more effectively. The knowledge that both men were merely passing on the words of Adolf Hitler would have left him speechless.

Göring grinned again, and again slapped Radl on the back. Turning, he went down the line of men, patting some on the shoulder, shaking hands, and wishing them well. Down at the end of the taxiway, the engines of the first of the 264s in line started to cough, a sound soon joined by the whine of its two jets. One after another, the others joined the chorus.

After an inquiring glance at Göring, Radl nodded to the

platoon commander at the head of the line. The man started up the steps into the aircraft, the rest of the section laboriously following. Ground crews waited at the door to help hoist the overloaded soldiers in. Once aboard the plane they would not leave it for the next twenty-eight hours.

Göring stood by Radl's side as the line filed aboard. As they did so, Göring nodded to an aide, who came forward and handed Radl a sealed manila envelope.

"The final briefings, weather reports, and intelligence from Skorzeny," Göring explained.

Radl looked down at the envelope curiously. "Is everything all right?"

"They had a bit of a scare from the FBI late yesterday but it doesn't look serious. Weather is projected to be good over the target tomorrow night."

"And the rest of the plan?" Radl asked, unable to contain his curiosity.

Göring smiled. "Let me worry about the big picture. Now get aboard, Radl, and good luck. There's a Knight's Cross waiting for you when you get back."

Radl stepped back and snapped off the Nazi salute. Göring answered with his baton, then warmly shook his hand, and Radl turned and started for the plane. Reaching the ladder, he gladly accepted the help of two ground crew, one pulling him up, while the other pushed from behind. Going through the door, he took a deep breath. No more drills. This was finally it. The men inside the cavernous transport broke into cheers at the sight of him. He waved good-naturedly.

Unclasping his parachute harness, he lowered it down on the floor and then sat down and unsnapped the quick-release for his combat pack. Sighing with relief, he stood back up, placed his Schmeisser into the gun rack lining the bulkhead, and then shoved his pack and parachute into their holding bin and strapped them in tight.

Standing up, he went forward, checking to make sure his men were settled into their bucket seats up forward. The distribution of the men and gear was crucial since the transport was at maximum weight. In fact, the men would have to remain in their seats not just for take-off but for several hours while fuel burned off.

After confirming that all was as it should be, Radl went through the forward door and climbed up into the cockpit, where the crew was intently running through final checkout. When he became aware of Radl's entrance the chief engineer looked back and smiled a welcome. "It's going to be one hell of a take-off, sir."

Radl nodded mock-ruefully and climbed into a pop-down seat behind the copilot and strapped himself in. He plugged in a headset to listen to the control tower as it directed the fleet of transports. Five planes were already out of their stands taxiing down to the end of the runway. One after another, the remaining transports took position until finally their plane, with all six engines howling, pivoted out onto the taxiway and turned east.

The engineer tapped Radl on the shoulder and pointed up.

Discernable from their running lights, a stream of bombers was passing overhead at five thousand feet, going into a broad banking turn. The bombers had been taking off for the last half hour from airfields to the south. Soon they all would rendezvous and begin the main leg of their journey.

The tower cleared the first transport down at the end of the runway. It turned out, lined up, and started lumbering slowly, painfully down the runway. Fifteen seconds later the next plane came into position and started forward; fifteen seconds later the third. . . . One after the other the line of transports moved slowly forward. The fourth, fifth and sixth planes turned out. They were next. . . .

Radl saw a brief glimpse of Göring, standing in his Kübelwagen, waving excitedly. The pilot snapped off a quick salute. The tower gave their plane final clearance. The pilot and copilot leaned into the throttles and the mixed howl and growl of the jet and prop engines became a unitary roar. They quickly scanned their instruments one last time even as they swung out onto the runway. The plane started to labor forward. This was Radl's first take-off in a 264E under full combat load. The plane moved forward as if its wheels were mired in mud to the axles.

Looking over the copilot's shoulder, he saw the airspeed indicator slowly click up to twenty and then thirty kilometers per hour. Far down at the end of the runway he saw planes lifting off. The needle on the airspeed indicator slowly continued its climb to sixty then seventy then eighty kilometers per hour. The plane ahead started to tilt back. Its wheels lifted off slightly, touched down, came back up. Airspeed was now over a hundred and twenty kilometers . . . a hundred and forty. The end of the runway was less than two hundred meters away. Radl watched its approach, mesmerized.

Then the view tilted back, and suddenly the bouncing stopped. They were airborne. The copilot quickly reached up to the toggle switches overhead to raise the landing gear. Airspeed went past one hundred and eighty kilometers and the pilot reached down to click the flaps in to ten degrees and then finally to neutral. The man looked back over his shoulder with a shaky smile; Radl suddenly realized that the take-off had been every bit as tricky and potentially catastrophic an operation as it had seemed to his amateur's eye.

Well, in the event, they had all made it. The stream of transports ahead started to wheel into a wide and shallow turn, while those further back in the line banked in steeper to cut across and thus come up alongside to form up into two flights of five. Overhead, the bombers and gunships made one final orbit as well, waiting for the transports to climb into formation. Radl listened as the group leaders reported in. Only one bomber had aborted so far, because of an overheating engine, and all the transports and gunships were still in the formation.

They were on their way. Strange that he didn't feel better about that. Of course much could yet go wrong. The weather could turn against them, forcing them to jump into the middle of a storm, too many planes could fall out for mechanical problems, or the Americans might figure out what was going on. But that wasn't it . . . nor was it the feeling of impending doom that bothered him. That feeling was an old friend by now, with him at the start of every mission. Perversely, he would be made fearful by its absence.

No, he was bothered by the mission itself. Not one of his men fully understood that if they were still there when the reactor core was breached, a most unpleasant death would come for all of them within a matter of hours.

He leaned over slightly to look back down at the airfield as they continued to go through their wide banking turn. There was really nothing to leave down there. He had no life, he realized, other than the unit, other than wherever it was that Otto would take him to next in their career of destruction. He understood that relationship as well. Otto most likely agreed with him that the two were each the other's closest friend, yet Radl knew Skorzeny would not think twice about sacrificing him for the sake of a mission, any mission.

Is this all that I am? Radl wondered. A cog in a machine created for the greater glory of Otto Skorzeny? All the propaganda about the future, about those generations yet unborn who would view them as heroes out of an epic age —what good was it? Fatuous nonsense.

And as for the Americans . . . he felt nothing, for or against them. It was easy to hate the Russians. With them, it would be much the same whoever won, the main variable being who was on the receiving end. The Americans, though, were something different. Strange they were, almost amusing in their innocence. Would they use that new bomb of theirs the way Germany would, without hesitation?

Radl thought about it. Doubtful. Anything the world had that the Americans wanted badly enough they would simply buy. We Germans have been taught to see this as a wolf age of struggle between ethnic nations; the Americans simply didn't care about such notions, could hardly comprehend them. Oh they were willing enough to fight when forced, and after their Great Pacific War it had to be acknowledged that either the Japanese hadn't been as tough as they'd looked, or the Americans were much tougher than a bunch of free-enterprise degenerates had any right to be.

And look at the current aftermath of that war: the fallen enemy was being *coddled*, and carefully converted to a civic philosophy designed to make future war between the two nations nearly impossible. What a difference if the Home Islands had fallen to the Reich. Radl pictured the endless convoys carrying all the wealth of Japan home to Germany. . . . No, the Americans would not use this bomb of theirs, not as long as its frightfulness was enough to stop others. To stop us. When it came to world conquest, Americans just didn't get it. How could one feel passionate hatred for a people like that? What point?

And finally, what did he care *for* anymore? Except for Otto, his friends were all buried in Russia on land that fat party members now scrambled for like medieval barons. Our blood, our sweat, he thought. Their profit.

Karl Radl suddenly realized that he was finished. Out of boredom as much as anything he had thrown himself into this mission and its intricate planning as if it were nothing more than an intellectual exercise to while away the long boring days of peace. But if peace was burdensome, war no longer held the promise it once had of honor and glory. He chuckled softly. As if it had ever actually contained those things, rather than a mere mirage of them that obscured war's single reality: death and misery in all their guises.

Perhaps after tomorrow the questions would be moot, he thought. The Party will have of me what it wants, and I shall have what it seems I want. Karl Radl sat back in his chair and closed his eyes. The flight turned southwest, chasing the night that receded before them.

April 19, 10:00 P.M.
Harry's Crop Dusting Service & Flight School

"Bury him in the woods."

Skorzeny looked down at the body of Friedrich Bachman, whose head lolled obscenely to one side, victim of the trademark Skorzeny neck-break. A thin, dying stream of blood trickled from the nostrils.

Silently, two of his team picked up the corpse and disappeared into the darkness.

Skorzeny looked over at Gunther, who seemed a little bemused by the quickness of it all. "He was panicked. If someone from the government were to have returned he'd have started talking for certain. We can't take the risk, not now."

Gunther nodded in agreement. His surprise was strictly a matter of Otto's earlier words. Nothing had changed since then—except Otto's opinion, and that change had led to swift and violent action. Well, Skorzeny was like that.

"So, I guess you're Bachman's hired hand," Skorzeny announced. "If anyone shows up, say that he took off to visit some friends down in Georgia for the weekend."

Skorzeny patted Gunther on the shoulder. "Can you pull off this American southern accent?"

"Ah reck'n Ah kin, if Ah put mah mand to it," Gunther replied with a smile.

CHAPTER FOURTEEN

Andrew Harrison looked up from his desk, where he had been sitting for the last sixty minutes. When it came to getting up in the morning, the American President remained a Nebraska farm boy. His mother would have approved.

"Mr. President." It was Mayhew, standing just inside the door. "Mr. Donovan is here to see you sir, as scheduled."

"Send him in, John."

"Thank you for seeing me at such short notice, sir," Donovan said as he walked toward the President.

"That's all right, Bill. I'm sure it's important or you wouldn't have asked."

The head of the OSS started to take a seat before the President's desk, but Harrison rose and motioned to the overstuffed furniture and the fire.

"I have some updates, sir," Donovan said quietly, as they settled themselves.

"Go on."

"Though we still don't have a clue regarding the new German coding system, we can at least tell that they've taken to rescrambling every four hours. They haven't done that since the armistice with England. And then there's this Oak Ridge situation."

"What about it? Have they caught that damned superspy yet?"

"We might have a lead on him. I sent three people down there, including Martel. You remember him, the one who—"

"Yes, yes. The letter. Go on."

"They were checking out some possible leads and Martel believes they've found Skorzeny and his team. They're holed up at an airstrip about forty miles east of Oak Ridge."

"Does Hoover know about this?"

"My head of operations informed his FBI counterpart last night. They claim they already checked out the location and it came up cold. They're focusing on another airstrip."

"And you think Martel's pick is hot?"

"Martel's been right more often than anybody else, sir. His partner is staking out the airstrip right now. They'll keep an eye on it until they get some support."

"Well, I don't want to overrule Hoover, but . . . send some of your own people down as backup. If we have a war coming on, the last thing we need is damage at Oak Ridge."

"That is just what I was going to suggest, sir."

"And is that all, Bill?"

"Yes, sir, it is. I didn't realize you would anticipate and grant my request this way. I wanted to be sure I had a chance to make the case in favor of the . . . irregularity."

Harrison nodded. "Oh, I'm with you on this one, Bill. There's just something too strange about what's going on down there, and the FBI has been consistently wrong on everything to do with it." The President paused, shook his head in irritation. "I can sympathize with them though; it is confusing. What do the Germans have to gain from all this? I can't understand what it is they think they're doing."

"That troubles me too, sir. There's something not right about all of this. Skorzeny is their top man, and they're wasting him. Leading from the front the way he does, there is very little damn chance he gets out of this country alive once he initiates an op. And there's nothing they can do to Oak Ridge that's worth losing him over. Hell, there's nothing they can do to Oak Ridge that's worth making us mad!"

"And so?" the President prodded.

Donovan looked at him with angry frustration. "I don't

know, sir. All I know is that we have to be missing something."

Harrison, who had leaned back in his chair and wearily closed his eyes, stirred and looked at Donovan. "Well, if all you have is a feeling, I can sympathize with the Bureau not taking the whole thing too seriously."

Donovan winced at the rebuke. "All I can tell you sir, and vague as it may sound this is a professional judgment, is that Skorzeny knows something we don't. Something important." Donovan winced again, as unhappy with the useless "advice" he offered as the recipient obviously was. This really wasn't the way he'd pictured this interview going.

He tried again. "Let's try to think it through. Why Skorzeny? He's not the spy type, not even the sabotage type. His forte is the sort of special ops for which large numbers of men are required. Maybe somehow he's gotten more people in here than we think."

"According to Groves, ten times as many as we think he has wouldn't be more than an annoyance," Harrison replied. "You don't think he could have salted away *hundreds* of agents, do you?"

"No sir, I don't. No way more than fifty, tops. Absolute tops."

"Then . . . ?"

"This is where we came in, sir. Skorzeny knows something we don't."

Harrison apparently changed the subject. "I was speaking with Winston a little while ago."

"Sir?"

"He thought he had an answer."

Donovan said nothing, politely.

"In-air refueling. He says the Germans are much farther along than we thought. He tied it in to some sort of low-level bomber exercise his intel has dredged up."

"Nothing doing, sir," Donovan said instantly. "We are on top of that area, as well we might be. Obviously it's of much more interest to us than to the English, since when the Germans perfect it their Luftwaffe will have intercontinental range. We have operatives all over that particular project, good German-American operatives. Maybe twenty or thirty planes could be serviced as of now, no more. Enough for a demonstration, and a bloody obvious demonstration at that. Dead ducks before they got past Iceland, once we had picket ships out. Hell, the carriers could deal with them without leaving port."

Harrison smiled. "Well, that's that, then. Exactly what LeMay told me. Just thought I'd check. To keep Winnie happy I've put the Canal on special alert, not that they need it. I should also hint that his special agent of influence has either been doubled or led a very long way down the garden path."

Donovan smiled back. "Curtis is right. We'd clobber 'em good if they tried it. When they have in-air refueling for fighters, then we'll worry."

"Or when their bombers carry A-bombs?"

"Yes, there is that, of course," Donovan admitted. "But sufficient unto the day, sir, and that's not a problem we have to deal with right now."

Harrison nodded, eyes unfocused, as if looking into the future. "No, not today." After a lost moment, Harrison shook himself and looked at Donovan again. "I guess that's about it?"

"Yes sir, that's about it. Thank you, sir."

April 20, 2:00 P.M.
Martinique

Karl Radl half-stood behind the copilot to catch a glimpse of the still-exploding wreckage less than fifty feet below, though now blessedly farther than that behind them.

"What happened?" Radl shouted.

The pilot, intent on holding the plane aloft as they skimmed over the ground, said nothing. Suddenly the ground slid away and they were skimming over the dark blue waters of the Caribbean. The pilot was still struggling to gain altitude. A rogue wave combined with a sudden gust could still kill them all.

A little altitude gained, the plane started to bank and Radl could see, this time from the copilot's side window, a plane come bursting out of the dark oily smoke, cutting swirling eddies as it did so. And at just the worst possible moment the crashed bomber fireballed, and the plane overhead was caught in the blast, its portside wing shearing off and the plane instantly collapsing to that side. When the nose touched the ground the bomber proceeded to cartwheel across the beach, but before it reached the water it exploded, sending enormous sheets and gouts of flaming gasoline out over the ocean. Even for a fully fueled bomber it was an impressive exit. . . . Damn! It was one of the precious tanker planes.

Inevitably, fifteen seconds later yet another plane appeared out of the smoke, this one banking hard to starboard so as to avoid the conflagration. Its right wing looked as if it would tear into the ground. Then it straightened out to skim low over the ocean and slowly gain altitude.

Radl's pilot finally looked back at him. "The first one lost an engine, the tire blew, or—well, we'll never know. As for what happened to the second, that was the natural result of taking off overloaded at fifteen-second intervals."

Radl nodded, saying nothing. At least it hadn't broken up on the runway. The pilot had simply kept on going, right off the end of the concrete strip and into the row of palm trees that fringed the edge of the beach several hundred meters downrange.

He heard the tower calling for the stream of bombers to stop their take-off rolls but the pilots simply kept going, one after the other, every fifteen seconds.

Eight planes lost to the strike now, Radl thought. Six bombers, a precious gunship, and now the equally precious tanker. One had gone down over the Atlantic, three had aborted back in Germany, two more after landing in Martinique and now two more at take-off. They were still within mission parameters, but barely.

Radl wiped the sweat from his face. The plane had been an oven during their four-hour layover while waiting to be refueled. He tapped the copilot on the shoulder.

"All right to go back to my men?"

"Yes. But don't let anybody else move around yet. We're right at maximum."

Radl unbuckled and moved aft, climbed down the ladder into the lower deck area.

"What happened back there, major?" one of his men called. "It sounded like an explosion."

"We lost a couple of planes at take-off."

"Any transports?"

Radl shook his head. "We've still got everyone. How are you boys doing?"

The men grinned, though some of them looked a bit ashen from the hours of sitting in hundred-degree heat without any ventilation. Now, however, the cabin was rapidly cooling as blasts of fresh air washed in.

"Now that we can breathe again, just settle back and try to grab some sleep. In less than eight hours we'll be getting out to stretch our legs a bit."

April 20, 8:00 P.M.
The North Sea

Erwin Rommel stared hard at where the spotter was pointing. The Mosquito was impossible to pick out with the unaided eye, but unless the spotter had gone mad it was definitely there, circling at well over twenty thousand feet. On the horizon he could pick out two more Mosquitoes sweeping across the far end of the convoy, hovering near the *Tirpitz,* which had just reported two British destroyers trailing them as well.

They're onto us.

He turned and looked back to the west. The western horizon was drifting into a dark indigo. According to the plan, it was time for them to turn to the west and start the high-speed run across the North Sea. Churchill had declared before Parliament that movement of German forces in or over the Channel toward Great Britain would be construed as an act of war. Presumably, as soon as they made the turn the British would feel free to start throwing things at them.

He looked back into the bridge. A messenger from the radio room had just come in and was handing a note to the captain. Seconds later the captain came out to join Rommel, silently handing him the note.

The message consisted of one word:

ARMINIUS

Rommel turned to the captain.

"Signal the fleet."

The captain saluted and went back into the bridge. Within seconds the cruiser heeled over as it made a due-west heading.

Rommel braced himself on the bridge as the salt spray stung his face. In North Africa it was so much easier to lose track of who was the aggressor, he thought sadly.

Knoxville, Tennessee
4:30 P.M.

The team disembarking from the C-47 looked quite ordinary, much like a group of construction workers, Martel thought as he followed behind Harriman on his way over to greet them. Having been acknowledged, Harriman started through the ritual of introductions, finishing up with the man who Martel realized must be the leader of the group.

"Jim Martel, this is Fred Johnson. He's going to head up your little adventure."

At just over six feet, Johnson stood nearly as tall as Jim, but was maybe twenty pounds lighter. Jim thought he looked like he'd been a track man or basketball player in school. There was something vaguely familiar about him. . . .

Johnson smiled. "Annapolis, class of '36. Same as you."

Sudden, embarrassingly vague recognition. Jim smiled and shook Johnson's hand. "Johnson! . . . how've you been?"

"Busy. Same as you," Johnson replied with a grin.

They walked over to a line of dark sedans parked along the tarmac. The rest of Johnson's fourteen-man crew opened the trunks and threw in their duffels.

"So what's the job?" Johnson asked.

Jim pulled out a hand-drawn map of the airfield and summarized the situation.

"Do you have surveillance there now?"

"Man in the woods with a Mark-2 radio. He's been checking in every half hour. So far nothing. They haven't stirred from the house or the hangar."

"What about the FBI?"

"They're chasing some lead at another airport. They think we're off the mark. Besides, they're stretched way too thin as is." Jim shrugged.

Johnson smiled. "They didn't find it, so it's not there, huh? Fine, all the more for us. What about the Ranger battalion that's supposed to be moving into Oak Ridge?"

"They've got only one company on site so far," Harriman replied. "Another company is slated for arrival later this evening. Groves won't release any of them to us."

It was Johnson's turn to shrug. "I've got thirteen men with me. Plus you, me and your guy on the ridge, that's sixteen. They've got eight to ten. Easy odds. The game will be over before it's even started. We'll move in fast and take them by surprise. No sweat."

Jim hesitated for a moment, then said, "Skorzeny's the best they've got. Let's not go into this half-cocked."

Johnson looked at him. Suddenly his whole tenor had changed. "Ever done a field op before?"

"No," Jim replied flatly. "I've had a lot of combat kills, but I've never done a field op."

"Well then thanks for the advice, Martel." Johnson took the map from Jim's hand, turned away and motioned for his team to gather round. When they had done so he went on: "There's this bridge at the edge of the property. We'll have to turn onto it, so we won't be going that fast. But by the time we get to the far side of it we'll be going in like gangbusters. With our lights out, they won't know we're coming until we're on top of them."

"What if there's a spotter on the bridge?" Martel asked.

"They might have a spotter out there, but I don't think so. Whether they do or not, our best bet is speed and surprise. We'll give 'em the message before the spotter can." He nodded toward one of his men. "Gary, you drive the first car. If the hangar door is open even a little bit, smash straight in. Otherwise gain entrance as best you can. If there's any resistance at all, that's what Thompsons are for. I'll be driving the second vehicle. We'll pull up by the side of the house opposite the hangar and charge in. Kevin, you drive the third car. Your group holds back in reserve. You'll decide just what to do when you see where the action is. My bet is we'll all converge on the hangar, but we'll see, won't we? Okay, let's go to work." Johnson turned and walked to one of the waiting government cars and climbed in, motioning for Jim to join him.

Jim started to do so, then paused to look quizzically at Harriman.

"Take care of yourself, Martel."

"Not coming along?"

Harriman shrugged his shoulders. "General Marshall is

coming in for the meetings with the Los Alamos crowd. Donovan absolutely requires an OSS presence on site for the duration of his visit. He gave me a direct order to stick with Marshall no matter what. Otherwise . . . otherwise nothing." He smiled painfully. "Besides, if it is Skorzeny you're tagging out there, I think we need someone inside Oak Ridge to rub Groves's nose in it."

Jim nodded in silent commiseration. Donovan was right, but it sure must be painful to be Harriman just now.

Harry's
5:40 P.M.

"Well?" Standing just behind the half-open hangar doors, where he could observe without being observed, Otto Skorzeny had been waiting for Gunther to return.

"We've got a strong radio signal, almost on top of us, I've been monitoring the channel for the last hour. We could have detected it from in here."

Skorzeny led Gunther back into the corner of the hangar where he had set up a portable radio directional finder. "Frequency?"

"Military, one of the channels used by their OSS transmitters. Here, let me set it for you." Gunther matched deed to word and stepped back. "He's been checking in every half hour. It's almost time for him to do it again."

Gunther leaned against the hangar wall as Skorzeny began to work the radio, his right hand on the directional dial. For a while there was only static, but then a transmitter clicked on.

"White Knight reporting. No activity."

"Black Knight, our guests have arrived. Expect us for dinner."

The signal clicked off. Skorzeny turned the dial slightly, centering the directional needle, and then sat back. "The bearing points right down the runway," he said quietly. "He's sitting up on the ridge."

"'Guests for dinner,'" Gunther repeated.

"Yes. I think we ought to expect company before very long." Skorzeny leaned back, contemplating his options. It was still five hours until the strike. If they took off in the Cubs now, whoever was coming would have time to vector in fighters over Oak Ridge. The last thing he wanted to do was arrange for a reception committee. Even a committee of only two or three would play havoc with a stream of unescorted 264s coming in at low level. No, leaving now was out of the question.

"It's almost six o'clock. We're not supposed to leave for another three hours. Let's just wait. If they're going to do anything, they'll contact their man here first. If they've sent a heavy force we can block them, force them to deploy. That will give us time to get out. If it's a small unit . . ." He smiled. "They will serve as an appetizer before the main course."

"How's everything else?" Gunther asked.

"The flight's on schedule. The strike on Los Alamos just turned into Mexican territory as well, and no one's reported it so far."

Skorzeny went to the back of the hangar and looked out assessingly. The grass along the side of the runway was nearly thigh high. Then he moved past some crates to the corner door that led to the cellar and called down.

"Alfred, get up here."

Alfred's head stuck up through the cellar door.

"We've got company," Skorzeny said. "Take a Schmeisser, a silenced Luger, and a hand-held radio. Go out the back door. Use the high grass for concealment. Get inside the woods, then work your way down to the end of the runway. From there, ease up to the ridgeline and acquire our friend. We're pretty sure it's one man. If we're wrong about that, just call in and we'll send a team. Otherwise wait for further orders."

Alfred went back down into the cellar and returned

minutes later wearing a camouflage smock. "Good to get out for some fun." Slipping out the back door of the hangar, he went down low and disappeared into the matted grass.

Nodding to Gunther to stay on the directional finder, Skorzeny joined the rest of his team where they lounged on makeshift cots in the cellar. "We are expecting some visitors shortly," Skorzeny announced as he went over to the far wall and motioned for some help lowering a crate. "All of you get into camouflage and be ready to move."

As he spoke he pulled the lid back on the crate and lifted out a *Panzerschreck*. Looking over at his men he hefted the beast and smiled. "Won't our guests be surprised?"

6:20 P.M.
Just South of Harry's

"Black Knight to White."
There was a click as Mason's transmitter came on line.
"White Knight here."
"Anything?"
"As they say in the movies, it's quiet, too quiet."
Jim looked over at Johnson.
"We go in as planned then," Johnson announced.
Jim shrugged and spoke into the mike. "Dinner in ten minutes. Stay put."
"Roger that," Mason replied.
Johnson leaned out the window of his car, motioned for the two vehicles behind him to get ready, and then looked back at Jim. "Relax. We have them in the bag, and the Pacific ace gets to be a hero all over again."
"Yeah. Right." So Johnson had a problem with that. . . . Speaking of the Great Pacific War, this felt worse than Leyte Gulf.

6:21 P.M.

Gunther looked up from the radio. "'Dinner in ten minutes.'"

Skorzeny grinned, and passed the Panzerschreck he was holding to Gunther, reached back into the wooden case for a second one and tossed it to Kurt. The third he kept for himself.

"Go. You know your positions!" The team ghosted out of the hangar, headed for the ambush site. After watching them go, Skorzeny picked up his short-range radio and clicked it on.

"Albert?"

There were three clicks in reply. That meant that Albert was sitting right on top of his target.

"Kill him!"

6:22 P.M.

Wayne clicked his radio off and raised his binoculars to scan the airfield one last time.

Damn, it had been a long twenty-four hours. Maybe, if they wrapped this up, he could still get back to Sarah by tomorrow night. Sarah—he was a bit nervous about it, but he couldn't wait to see her reaction when she saw what was in the little jeweler's box. He smiled in anticipation. Was it the six months she'd played hard-to-get, or what he'd got when she'd stopped playing? He wasn't sure. He just knew he wanted it for the rest of his life.

Suddenly he was dying for a cigarette. What the hell, in five minutes the game went down anyhow. Even if the bad guys saw a flicker, they wouldn't have time to investigate. It might even provide a distraction. Having properly rationalized what he was going to do, Wayne pulled a Camel out of his breast pocket and reached for his Zippo, opening it as he did so. Usually that was a cool move, with flame leaping the instant the lighter saw daylight. This time, it snagged on his pocket and, already lit, jumped out of his hand and made for the tall grass. Or would have, except that with a fighter pilot's unconscious speed he jerked forward and caught it before it landed.

Crack!

6:35 P.M.

There hadn't been much conversation on the trip in, and there wasn't any now as they turned into the rutted road and approached the little bridge. Had things not been so chilly Martel might have questioned the way their little caravan was bunched up. Well, he supposed, in a surprise raid you got everybody across fast, so that the target would not have time to react—bunching up being the price you paid for speed. He sure hoped their arrival was indeed a surprise, though. The car in front clattered onto the bridge, with the other two close behind.

"What the—shit!" was Johnson's startled comment as he saw a dark figure step in front of the car in front of them and raise some sort of tube.

Following a fighter pilot's instinct, Jim swiveled himself backward to "check six," and saw a second figure step out and point a similar tube at the car behind them. Before he could inform Johnson of that, a round slammed through the windshield of the car ahead and detonated inside.

Johnson had already slammed on the brakes, and while the car skidded on the wooden planks of the bridge slapped the gears into reverse. Just as the car started to accelerate backward, the car behind them, also on the bridge now, exploded in its turn.

"Out! Out!" Johnson screamed as he braked again.

Jim struggled with the door handle, and even as he

jerked it upwards he saw a third round coming almost straight at him. The irrelevant thought passed through his mind that if he'd been in a plane he'd have had a full second to kick in aileron and rudder and maybe dodge the shot. The door was opening, but far too slowly . . . and the rocket-propelled warhead missed the windshield with nearly an inch to spare. Shrieking its frustration, the Panzerschreck round crossed the road obliquely to blow up a tree on the other side. The exhaust vapors that swirled in through the car's open window stank like Hell itself.

The door had opened enough now and Jim dived out, slamming against the wooden side-railing of the bridge. Urged on by the sound of a Schmeisser hammering rounds into the car he had just exited, he tumbled over the side, falling half a dozen feet into the muddy creek below as the Schmeisser continued to search for him.

Looking up, he saw that one of Johnson's men had made it part-way out of the back door but was jerking spasmodically as half a dozen rounds stitched up his body. Another agent made it out of the car in a rolling tumble, but as he gathered himself to run, he took a hit in the shoulder that spun him half around and back to one knee. Before the Schmeisser could find him again he had regained his footing and sprinted around the back of the car and into the woods.

As this was happening, Jim heard a splash on the other side and saw Johnson rising back up out of the water, pulling a forty-five semiautomatic out of its shoulder holster as he did so. Feeling foolish at his omission, Jim fumbled for his own.

Aside from an afternoon's OSS orientation before coming down here, it had been years since he had last fired a handgun. The Thompsons and grenades, for which accuracy was no great requirement and might therefore have given him, with his off-the-charts reflexes, an edge, were half a dozen feet above him in the car they had just vacated. They might as well have been on the Moon.

With a suddenness that was nearly as startling as the impact of the first Panzerschreck, the firing ceased. Shouted commands echoed in the silence . . . in German. *"Friedrich, Wilhelm, take the bridge! Two got out there; they must be hiding in the water. The rest come with me after the two who ran!"*

Jim looked over to where Johnson was crouched under the bridge, pistol raised and waiting, then slid over to cover the other side. . . . What was that smell? Christ! Gasoline was trickling down from the shattered car overhead and spreading out on the water. If they stayed in the water, all it would take to kill both of them was a single match. Jim looked over at Johnson, pointed at the trickle.

Johnson, not lacking in courage, nodded and eased up the side of the embankment and peered over. An instant later he flopped back down into the muddy water. The top of his head was gone.

Jim scurried back under the center of the bridge, clawed his way up the embankment so that his back was pressed up against its wooden planks. Half a dozen feet from him the gasoline continued to spill down. . . . Since Leyte, the prospect of being trapped in a fighter going down in flames with gasoline spewing into the cockpit had been his special dread. A dull plop sounded near to where Johnson lay. What could it be but a grenade?

Covering his face with his hands, Martel waited for the end. But Johnson proved a better shield in death than he had in life. The grenade had fallen so that most of its force and shrapnel were expended on a corpse. What remained of it showered Jim with mud and bits of Johnson. An instant later there was an explosive *whoomf* as the gasoline caught in the backwater under the bridge ignited. The fireball washed around him, stinging the backs of his hands where they protected his face.

He had survived the blast, but unless he did something to change things, in seconds he would still die, and a far worse death it would be than merely being blasted apart. He uncoiled from his fetal crouch and slid down, evading the worst of the rising heat trapped under the bridge. A Schmeisser snarled to his left. He saw someone standing by the side of the bridge, crouching down and firing toward the other side of the creek, where Johnson's tattered body lay.

Jim raised his forty-five and squeezed off a round, catching his man in the leg, spinning him around. The man looked toward him, startled, as if Jim had somehow cheated by not being where he was supposed to be. Jim continued to fire. His next two missed, but the fourth round blew a hole through the German's chest, causing him to collapse into the burning creek.

Just as he started to hope, the flame-covered water began to froth as splinters showered down from above and holes appeared in the wooden planking. Some bastard was shooting through the bridge. Jim aimed straight up . . . no, the car was there . . . he aimed farther back toward the edge of the bridge and fired off his three remaining rounds —the Schmeisser's track went wide in an arcing curve, and then fell silent. Lucky shot. Well, he'd had precious little luck lately.

Sliding through the mud Jim crawled out to the edge of cover offered by the bridge. He had to move *now*, before he succumbed to the fumes . . . scrambling up the side of the embankment, he crouched back down for a brief instant, and by the edge of the bridge he saw his second man—the bullet had caught him in the mouth. Lucky shot, indeed.

From the woods to the north of the bridge loud shrieks suddenly cut through the silence — the words were not comprehensible, though they were English. One more shot, and silence. Then more shots echoed in the woods. Schmeissers. A forty-five answered, but only once. Skorzeny's crew was hunting down the other survivor. Jim fought down the temptation to try to help. It was useless . . . he tried to block out the heart-rending cries of the last OSS agent after the hunters had brought him to bay.

Apparently they were trying to extract a little information before sending him on his way.

Nerving himself, he ran crouching to the car he had ridden in. The radio was smashed. He reached into the back seat, dragging out one Thompson and snatching the clip from the second. No longer at quite such a horrible disadvantage now, he slipped into the woods.

6:45 P.M.

Otto Skorzeny drifted like a phantom from tree to tree. The air was heavy with cordite. The stink of it competed with the smell of resin on the shoulder of his jacket from when he had brushed against a wounded pine. He slipped out of the woods and up onto the road and approached the edge of the bridge. He paused for a second, kneeling down to touch Wilhelm's carotid artery . . . nothing.

He crept up to the side of the burning bridge and peered over . . . Friedrich was floating facedown in the muddy creek, the back of his uniform smoldering from the fire that still flickered across the water.

He moved to the other side of the bridge and saw one of the two Americans half-submerged on the other side.

No, it wasn't him. There had been a moment of recognition when the OSS men got out of the car—one of them was Martel. He scanned the ground by the embankment, and within seconds picked up the trail: muddy tracks and, here and there, a spot of blood. The hunt was still on.

He held up his hand and motioned for one of his team to come forward.

"You were supposed to hit the middle car," Skorzeny hissed. "At that range it should have been impossible to miss."

Kurt nodded, unable to offer any defense for his poor shooting with the Panzerschreck. True, to call them inaccurate weapons was an understatement, but had he aimed lower, not tried for perfection, he couldn't have missed. "We tore the car apart anyhow," Kurt finally whispered.

Skorzeny fixed him with an icy gaze. "Friedrich and Wilhelm are dead because of your disgusting ineptitude. If we both survive I'll not forget this."

Kurt lowered his head.

Skorzeny continued angrily, "By missing, you gave them seconds of warning. Their leader was in that car! That means the radio was in there too. What if they were transmitting at the moment we struck? They could have gotten a signal out. The whole plan was to wipe them out before they could possibly do that. Now, we don't know."

Probably they had not been transmitting, but there was always the chance. A backup team — or for that matter a company of MPs — could be on its way, and they would not be taken unaware. He looked down at his watch. Six-fifty. "Get the rest of the team back to the hangar. Have the planes ready to lift off at the first sign of fresh company."

Skorzeny checked the flare pistol at his belt. "Keep watch. If I set off a flare, get the hell out. If I'm still out there at," he paused again and looked at his watch, "at seven-ten, set off a yellow recall flare. If I don't respond within two minutes that means I'm either dead or pinned down. In that case Gunther will assume command. Gunther, you get yourself and the men the hell out of here."

"You're not coming back with us now sir?"

Skorzeny pointed at the trail leading off into the woods. "There's something I have to take care of first."

"Couldn't *I* do that for you, sir?" Kurt begged.

"No. I want it done right."

The wretched Kurt nodded and turned away.

"Kurt, wait."

Kurt turned back, hoping for some other task of redemption.

Skorzeny motioned toward Friedrich. "Take his weapon and push his body into the creek. That should be within your powers."

Without waiting for a reply, Skorzeny drifted like wind-driven smoke into the woods.

Once clear of the road he slowed, walking softly. The evening dusk was starting to settle down. The light was soft and diffused, the shadows lengthening. He smelled a whiff of smoke, a hint of charred flesh, as he followed the bloody spoor of his foe up to the road running parallel to the airstrip on the far side of the woods—and then he heard a vehicle approaching the bend leading to the bridge. He froze in place, waiting.

A battered pickup truck came into view and slid to a stop. Three men climbed out.

One of the three moved down the lane and approached the remnants of the little caravan. He looked inside the car closest to the road and quickly turned away. Gagging slightly, he told the others, "There's five burned-up fellas in there."

The other two now tentatively approached as the first man slowly moved toward the second vehicle, and then froze. "Fellas, let's get out of here," he hissed.

"Shouldn't we see if somebody's still alive?"

"Man, this car's been shot all to hell. Come on, let's go and get the sheriff, before whoever did it comes back."

Never speak of the devil. . . .

Otto Skorzeny stepped out onto the path. The three froze, gape-mouthed, as he raised his machine pistol and pulled the trigger.

The ripple of gunfire sent Jim Martel diving for the ground. It was behind him, less than a hundred yards away. The targets must have been the occupants of the pickup truck that had just passed by. Then he heard the crack of a branch. Rolling, he aimed his Thompson in the general direction of the noise. A shadow moved and he drew a bead, began squeezing the trigger . . .

He lowered his gun. "Wayne." Jim's voice was barely a whisper.

Wayne Mason froze, and then, recognizing Jim, he crawled over, dragging a German machine pistol.

"You scared the crap out of me," Wayne hissed. His face was covered with blood.

"Hurt bad?"

"Head feels like it's going to explode. His first shot grazed me, damn near knocked me out. The bastard had me. I don't know how the hell he got behind me, but he did. I think my bloody head saved my life. He must have thought I was dead, came up to, I dunno, search me, maybe. That's when I rolled and got him. I may not be smart, but I am fast." Mason laughed. "I guess he didn't know I was a fighter pilot in the Great Pacific War." Then his friend drew his hand away from his side and Jim saw the blood there too. "He got *me* again too, busted a couple ribs. . . . Jim, what the hell is going on?"

"We got wiped. Someone's stalking behind me."

Wayne peered up, silent.

"Where's your radio?"

Mason shook his head. "Shot up. Time for you to hit the road, and get some backup in here. I'll guard your rear. That's all I'm good for right now."

Jim didn't have the energy to be diplomatic. "No. I've got a feeling something's going to happen real soon now—besides, the shape you're in you wouldn't stand a chance if it's Skorzeny out there. Let's take care of this bastard first, and then figure where we go from there."

Wayne nodded. It was hard to discern his expression under the blood, but he seemed relieved. "Whatever you say, pal."

"I'll move to the edge of the road, you stay here. With luck, we'll cross-fire him."

Jim started to crawl away and Wayne reached out, touching him on the shoulder. "Next time, just leave me home with the women."

Jim forced a grin and began to move out to the edge of the woods on the road. He peered out.

The pickup truck was empty. Its doors gaped open.

He looked back into the woods. Darkness was closing in fast.

A shadow moved, crouched low. Jim came up on one knee and raised the Thompson, but the shadow was gone. A few seconds later the tree he was leaning against exploded in a burst of splinters.

Otto Skorzeny saw his target go down, but before he could follow up a pistol cracked behind him. The shots followed him as he dove and rolled for cover, but suddenly, just when he thought he'd run out of luck at last, silence returned. He heard a muffled curse followed by the familiar sequence of someone trying to work a stuck bolt, followed by the sound of the bolt slamming onto an empty chamber.

Never one to miss a cue, Skorzeny leaped up and forward, vaulted a fallen log, and—there he was. The man before him started to scramble backward, then froze against the side of a tree.

"Skorzeny."

Skorzeny looked down quizzically at the man. Beneath the blood, there was something familiar . . . oh, yes. "Too bad, Mason," he said, the slightest note of regret in his voice as he raised his machine pistol.

"Jim, it's Skorze—!" Mason's last word was cut short by Skorzeny's Schmeisser.

"Wayne!" Suddenly Jim was up and charging through the woods, holding his Thompson low and madly firing. Had he not tripped and sprawled just as a burst of fire snapped overhead, he would have died then and there, just as he knew his friend had. As it was, he rolled up against a moss-covered log and slammed another clip into his weapon. He leaned up over the rim of the log, searching for his enemy—and found his friend. The back of his head was gone, but his face was untouched, and oddly serene.

"Skorzeny!"

A taunting laugh, a flicker—

He continued to fire until the clip went empty, then slid back down for cover. He fumbled for another clip, and realized he was out. With that came a return to something like sanity.

He set the Thompson down and pulled out his forty-five.

"Too bad about your friend, Jim."

The voice was still taunting, still drifting through the shadows. "I rather . . . liked him . . . but he should have . . . known better . . . than to come . . . after . . . *me*." The voice steadied to a single location somewhere to Martel's left.

"Of course he had to, for friendship's sake, since I was about to finish you off. It must have been heartwarming to have a friend like that. You will miss him, will you not?"

Jim peered over the log again. He thought he saw movement and snapped off a shot.

"Hmm. Single shot? What happened to the Thompson? Out of ammunition already? Rather amateurish, don't you think?"

"I'll cut your heart out, you son of a bitch!" Jim screamed, meaning just what he said.

"Jim, Jim, we're professionals, you and I. Don't let emotion get in the way. It spoils the game." A low chuckle in the dark. "Don't make it too easy for me."

Suddenly a signal flare arced across the sky. "Well, Jim, you're in luck. I've got other things to attend to. Can you guess what they are? Goodbye for now."

Jim quietly moved back from the log, squeezed himself as low as he could behind another much smaller one. Seconds later a grenade plopped down where he had been. After the detonation he waited, hoping that Skorzeny would check his kill.

Even before the grenade had exploded, Skorzeny was sprinting back over the access road and down to the hangar. When he arrived Gunther was already rolling the doors back. From within the hangar he could hear the sound of the Cubs' engines turning over. He looked around, checking his team as Gunther tossed him the black trousers and shirt of an SS uniform. Skorzeny peeled off his camouflage smock and quickly pulled the uniform on, then hooked on his equipment belt and went over to his plane. Now if captured he could not be shot out of hand as a spy.

"Did you get them?" Gunther asked.

"One for certain. The other might still be out there, but all he has is a forty-five. Still, more help could be arriving at any minute. Time to leave."

"We just got a signal from Radl. They're crossing the coast right now."

Skorzeny looked around at his team. "We'll take off and circle until the bomber stream is within forty-five minutes of the target. Then we move in. Gunther and I will circle the town. Peter, you and Erich take the reactor. Wilhelm, you take K-25. Kurt, you fly with Wilhelm. As cargo. Let's go."

Otto climbed into the front seat of their Cub, and Gunther swung in behind him.

Wilhelm pulled out first, lined up, and pushed his throttle full-forward. Peter and Erich followed him out the hangar doors with the same procedure. Skorzeny, ever the stylist, revved up the engine while still inside. As the Cub lurched forward, he pushed in hard-right rudder to exit the hangar at full throttle.

Jim lay quietly for several long minutes, waiting for Skorzeny to make his next move. The only sound was that of the spring peeper frogs chorusing around him. Then he heard the engines.

Christ! He stood up and raced through the woods to the airstrip. From the hangar, a couple of hundred yards to his right, he saw the shadowy form of a plane emerge, turn so that it faced him head-on, and start accelerating under full throttle.

He ran toward the plane, cursing madly. When he was sure it could not take off before coming close he stopped.

The plane's tail lifted up as it gained speed.

Panting hoarsely, he waited.

The plane drew closer. His breathing slowed. Gripping the pistol with both hands, he crouched slightly, drew careful aim, fired, recovered, fired again until the clip was empty. The plane continued on. When he had given up hope, ever so slowly it nosed over, crashed down into the runway, and ignited.

Now, ammunition gone, he could only watch as the second and then the third plane lifted off. Unlike the second plane, the third stayed low as the pilot pushed in just enough left rudder to cause the plane to crab over to the edge of the grass strip so that it passed by not twenty feet away from where Jim stood. Otto Skorzeny looked down, grinning demonically.

And James Martel finally understood the meaning of hatred.

7:50 P.M.
Tallahassee, Florida

Karl Radl climbed back up into the crew compartment and squatted down between the pilot and copilot. Directly ahead a brilliant glow lit the night sky.

"Tallahassee," the pilot announced. "We're on schedule and on course. We'll pass it twenty miles to the west and then run straight up the border between Georgia and Alabama." The plane banked slightly to the left as the pilot spoke.

Karl looked back at the navigator, who was hunched over his plot board. He finally looked up.

"Two hours to target."

"Any contacts?"

"Military channels are quiet. A civilian airplane reported seeing our stream as it started its approach into Tallahassee Airport. The traffic controller there is running an inquiry."

Radl nodded. "Keep me posted. I'm going aft."

Harry's
7:57 P.M.

Martel had never had occasion to hot-wire a car before, but five minutes ago the principle had seemed simple enough. . . . Cursing, he kept fruitlessly touching the different wires from the ignition switch to each other, one after the other. Then, with a cough, the truck turned over. He eased the choke, giving the Chevy pickup more gas. The engine caught and held. Jim backed up and swung around, gravel spraying out from under the wheels.

After fumbling for the switch he turned on the headlights. The first thing they showed him was three bodies sprawled to the side of the road ahead of him. Then he was racing down the road, through the narrow ravine, and into the next valley. He drove with his foot nearly but not quite to the floor, barely holding the road through the twists and curves, torn between the need for speed and the utter importance of not wrapping himself around some telephone pole or finishing his trip upside down in a ditch. Though a hot pilot, unlike Skorzeny he had never been a racecar driver. Finally he saw a light ahead. A few moments later he pulled into the driveway of a small clapboard shack and leaned on the horn.

A woman came to the door.

"You got a phone?" Martel shouted.

"Hey! That's our truck!"

"Ma'am, do you have a *phone*?"

"You got my old man's truck. What 'ya doin' with it?"

Jim thought for a moment. If ever there was an occasion when pragmatic need ruled, this was it. "He sent me back here to get some help."

She stood beneath the single bare light bulb that illuminated the porch, wiping her hands on her apron.

"Come on in."

He leaped up the steps of the porch and followed her

into the house. Though it was obvious that money was a distant stranger to this home, the tiny living room and kitchen were neatly arranged. She pointed to the old crank phone on the wall. Jim went over to it, picked up the earpiece and turned the crank.

"Say, mister, you're bleeding."

"I'm all right."

While he waited for the operator to pick up, the woman of the house renewed her interrogation.

"Where's my Bill?"

"He's back at the airport."

"I ain't never seen you before. Who are you?"

"I'm with the government, and I borrowed your husband's truck."

She stared at him intently.

"You're lying. Something happened back there. I told him to mind his own business. But he and my brothers just had to go find out."

"He's all right, ma'am."

An operator finally came on.

"Could you connect me to the county sheriff, please?"

"Just a moment."

A voice finally answered.

"I want you to listen carefully," Jim said. "I'm just outside of Harry's Crop Dusting Service on Allison Road. There's been a shooting out here. Federal agents cornered the people involved in the killing of those cops over in Asheville, but they got ambushed on the bridge into the airfield. The bad guys got away. Several people have been . . . hurt." He paused and looked over at the old woman who was peering up at him. "I want you to send some people out here."

"Who the hell are you?" queried the voice on the other end.

"James Martel." He hesitated for a second. "I'm an agent with the . . . FBI. Now listen carefully. I want you to call up the office of General Groves at Oak Ridge. Ask for Trevor Harriman. You got that? Trevor Harriman. Tell him that I called and that Skorzeny is coming by air. Do you have that? Skorzeny by air. Tell Harriman I'll be there within the hour."

"Score zany by air. Got it."

Martel hung up, and then cranked the phone again.

"My husband's been hurt, ain't he?"

Jim wanted to block out the woman and her pain, but couldn't. He looked straight at her. "Yes, ma'am, he has. But you just heard me call for help. Now I have to make another call."

She stood silently as the operator clicked on again.

"I'd like to make a collect call to Washington, D.C."

Jim gave the operator the number and waited for what seemed like an eternity. A distant voice answered at OSS headquarters and accepted the charges.

"General Donovan, please."

"I'm sorry, sir, he isn't in."

"Then get me one of his assistants!"

"Sir, not many people are in at the moment. It's Easter Saturday, you know."

"Locate someone for me. This is an emergency."

"It might take some time."

"All right. Then listen carefully. When you find him, tell him the entire team assigned to Skorzeny was wiped out. *Wiped out.* This is Martel. Except for Harriman at Oak Ridge, I'm the only one left. Skorzeny and his team have taken off in two Piper Cubs. I believe he's headed for Oak Ridge. For God's sake, get that to Donovan now! Tell Donovan I'm returning to Oak Ridge. Do you have all that?"

"Yes, sir. The team assigned to Skorzeny was wiped out. Skorzeny and his team took off in two Piper Cubs. You are Martel. You are on your way back to Oak Ridge. Where is Oak Ridge, sir?"

Christ. "Listen. For one magic moment the future of the country rests on your shoulders. If you don't do this right there could be a disaster. You might even lose your *job*." Jim slammed the phone down and turned to head out the door.

The old woman was standing by the door, still looking at him.

"He's dead, ain't he?"

Jim didn't want to answer. He lowered his eyes and tried to edge his way past. She reached out with a clawlike hand, grabbing his injured arm.

He gasped and the woman, hearing his pain, let go, but persisted in her questioning. "Don't lie to me. He's dead, isn't he?"

Jim slowly nodded.

She closed her eyes, as if praying. He wanted to stay, to do something for her.

"What's your name, ma'am?"

"Dottie Henderson."

He turned back to the phone and picked it up, ringing one more time. The operator came on.

"Ma'am, I'm at Dottie Henderson's house. There's been a tragedy here. Dottie has just found out that her husband is dead. Could you call some of her neighbors and have them come over?"

Without waiting for a reply, he hung up and looked back at her.

"Ma'am, I still need your husband's truck. I'll make sure it gets back to you tomorrow."

"I told him to mind his own business. I told him not to go."

"I'm sorry, ma'am."

He touched her lightly on the shoulder, then opened the door and sprinted back to the truck, climbed inside, and sped out of the driveway.

The Widow Henderson stood watching with empty eyes.

8:17 P.M.

Sheriff Frank Watson hung up the phone and turned to face his guests.

"Boys, I just got the damnedest call."

"We can finish this one hand now, cain't we?" one of his two guests asked with plaintive prescience.

"Game's over, Lloyd."

"Well, wouldn't you just know it." Watson's deputy, Lloyd Yancy, tossed his cards faceup on the checkered oilcloth that covered the Watson kitchen table. Dinner was over, and Mrs. Watson had been sitting in on a more-or-less friendly game of poker. Normally Frank Watson was not the sort of man who left any doubts as to who wore the pants, but when his wife sat in, well, he had to admit about three times as much money stayed at home as would otherwise be the case, and there was no arguing with that logic.

"First time I ever got dealt three aces in my life," Lloyd sighed.

Frank grinned. "Lloyd, you got dealt three aces just last winter. I remember the occasion. . . . Lucky for me that fella called, I guess."

"So what's it about? Better be important since it cost me the whole pot."

"Fella said he was with the FBI. Claims those cop killers from over in North Carolina were out at the airstrip up on Allison Road. Says the FBI caught 'em and there was a shootout. Says the bad guys won."

Lloyd shook his head disgustedly. "And you believed that? Hell, next thing you know the Infernal Revenue is gonna ask Congress to do away with the Income Tax, and make shine legal to boot. . . . I'll bet it's those Lowrie boys again, pulling your leg."

"Should still check it out," the other guest announced, sliding his chair back and coming to his feet. "I'll go with you."

Frank nodded appreciatively. It hadn't sounded like any of the Lowrie boys to him. The voice had been that of someone who had spent time in North Carolina or maybe Virginia, but not in a long while. Upper crust sort of accent too, what was left of it. Definitely not one of the trashy Lowrie boys.

"Alvin, I'd appreciate that a whole lot. When we get there you just stay back a ways and keep an eye out, okay?"

Having Alvin York providing cover was the next-best-thing to being someplace else when the shooting started. After thinking a moment, Frank added, "Hey, we're both sheriffs, but you're way out of jurisdiction. Maybe I should deputize you?"

Alvin York grinned. "Okay, I'm a deputy. Now just toss me one of those deputy badges I know you must have stashed around here someplace. I don't much care for card playing anyhow."

Lloyd snorted disdainfully. "I still say it's them damn Lowrie boys throwing you off some trail they think you're onto. Most likely they'll be running a little shine later tonight. Remember the time they called and said that Widow Guthrey had fallen in the creek and was drowned? We fished that damn river for hours, and then come to find that old lady woke up and a-singin' and a-hollerin' in her own spring house, drunk as a coot."

"Lloyd, I do believe your boss is right on this," Alvin broke in. He nodded at the table. "Those three aces are blinding your judgment."

Frank added, "Even if it was one of them damned Lowrie boys, which it wasn't, Alvin's on the money. We gotta go look. If there ain't nothin' there, we'll cut over by the Lowrie place for a look around. That suit you, Deputy Yancy?"

"Damn them Lowrie boys anyhow," Lloyd muttered.

"Oh, they ain't so bad. They're just doing what their pappy and his before him did. They run shine, and me, well, I chase 'em. . . . Like my pappy did their pappy, now I think on it."

"Well, hell, don't you think I know all that, Frank?" Lloyd answered. "They just cost me the *pot*, is all, plus in general making my job about twice as hard as it needs to be."

"I'm telling you, it ain't them this time," Frank said. "That wasn't no Lowrie boy I was talking to, nor no friend of no Lowrie boy neither."

"When you was on the phone just now I heard you say something about calling some general," Alvin asked.

Frank shook his head. "I said it wasn't no Lowrie boy. I

didn't say I necessarily believed him. Wouldn't I just look like one horse's ass if I called them up at Oak Ridge and none of it was true? We'll go take a look around first."

Alvin looked at his friend dubiously. "You sure about that, Frank?"

"Oh, all right, Alvin, seeing as it's you." Frank turned back to the telephone, cranked it. "Hello? Connect me to Oak Ridge, please. . . . This is Sheriff Frank Watson in Clinton. I need to speak to a Trevor Harriman in General Groves's office. He's with you folks, right? Or maybe he's with the FBI. . . . You can't tell me that? But I'm the sheriff. . . . No, I won't leave a—yes, I will leave a message. The country's being invaded by Germans and we're going out to investigate a firefight. I hope the general has your ass, boy." He slammed the receiver into its cradle.

"Well, Alvin, you can't say I didn't try."

"You might have been a little less short with the boy on the other end of that phone, Frank."

"Well, maybe I might have been at that, but he was just purely annoying. Twenty years old if he was a day, and talking down to me, the sheriff, like I was the village idiot. Damned sojer boys think they're God's own gift. Not like when we was serving." Frank stopped, thought it through. "Look, this is strictly a civilian matter. Unless it's a full-scale national emergency those boys in Oak Ridge can't do a thing in my county until I tell them they can, and I'm not going to tell them they can until I've seen for myself, and maybe not then. So let's stop wasting time and go find out if there's anything to all this in the first place."

Alvin followed his friend out onto the porch, casually snagging his battered Springfield rifle from where it leaned by the door on the way by, and proceeded on to Frank's Ford, which conveyance currently doubled as the county patrol car.

"What kind of message would that be to deliver anyway?" Frank muttered to himself as he shifted into reverse. " 'Score zany by air.' If I'd tried to tell him that he really would have thought I was the village idiot."

As they pulled out of the drive the phone inside the house started to ring. The operator, who had just talked to Dottie Henderson's neighbors, confirmed the terrible truth of what had happened, but there was no way for Mrs. Watson to inform Frank; the radio in his car had been broken for a month, and the county commissioners had yet to get around to buying him a new one.

Just as had happened at Pearl Harbor, a final chance warning was lost in bureaucratic fog.

April 21, Easter Sunday, 2:45 A.M.
London (April 20, 8:45 EST)

Churchill walked back into his office, opened a desk drawer, and pulled out a bottle. He looked up at his head of naval operations.

"Join me?" His voice was thick and raspy after the hours of nonstop smoking.

Rushbrooke nodded and Churchill poured a splash into each of two tumblers, adding a great deal of water to his own, and handed the other one to the admiral. After drinking half of it, he set it down and left his glass-walled office to walk back to the balcony overlooking the plotting table. A redheaded young Wren was leaning over it, edging the markers representing Rommel's fleet farther west. Normally Churchill enjoyed watching young redheaded Wrens leaning over plot boards, but now his eyes saw nothing but the symbols she was manipulating.

"It's coming straight in, somewhere between the Midlands and Edinburgh," Churchill whispered to himself. "We could cut it to ribbons." This delay would cost them ten thousand casualties if it cost them one. Would it cost them England?

He looked back at his office and the red phone sitting on his desk.

April 20, 9:00 P.M.
Oak Ridge

Pounding the steering wheel with frustration, Martel waited in a fury of frustration as the line of cars at the security gate inched forward. Pulling up to the barrier at last, he flashed his OSS identification card and the security badge that gave him clearance to go to the administrative area.

"Sir, would you step out of the car please?"

"Listen, Sergeant, this is an emergency. I need to get to General Groves's office immediately."

The Sergeant looked into the truck and then suddenly stepped back and pulled his pistol out.

"Put your hands on the steering wheel!"

Jim started to open his mouth and the sergeant cocked his pistol.

"Move and I'll blow your head off!" The sergeant's partner yanked the driver's-side door open.

"Now climb out real slow and keep your hands up."

Jim stepped out and someone reached out from beside the truck. He was spun around and his feet knocked out from under him, slamming him down hard on the pavement. A stab of pain exploding from his wounded shoulder nearly caused him to black out as his hands were yanked back behind his back. Handcuffs slipped over his wrists and snapped shut. He gasped with pain as he was yanked back to his feet.

"You stupid son of a bitch, I'm with the OSS," Jim roared, "I need to see General Groves right now!"

The sergeant who had first stopped him said nothing, pistol still pointed at him.

The corporal who had handcuffed him looked at Jim's shoulder.

"Hey Sarge, this man's been shot."

"That's what tipped me off. Now call headquarters."

"You idiot! It's a grenade fragment, and I am Lieutenant

Commander James Martel, USN, on detached duty with the OSS!"

The corporal looked at him, wide eyed.

Jim looked back at the sergeant and took a deep breath. "Listen, soldier, I know you think you're doing your job. Go ahead and call security headquarters. But before you do that, just call Groves's office and ask for Trevor Harriman. Either way, you win. If I'm a bad guy, you're a hero. If I'm not, I swear I'll say you were vigilant for stopping me, and smart for calling. Do it any other way, Sergeant, and by next week you will be a private stationed in the Aleutians."

The sergeant suddenly seemed less sure of himself.

"For Christ's sake! you have me handcuffed! What am I going to do while you make the call? Guide in an air strike? Do it, Sergeant!"

9:00 P.M.
Harry's

Alvin York, rifle in one hand and flashlight in the other, walked back from the still smoldering wreckage of the Piper Cub. "One dead in the plane, Frank."

Watson, features pale, continued to stare at the bodies of Dottie Henderson's brothers and husband.

"Some fight they had here," Alvin added as he looked inside the leading car, and the four charred corpses within. "Automatic weapons tore up that car in the middle of the bridge. The two bracketing it got hit by mortars, or some kind of rocket. There's two bodies down on the creek bed, along with a couple of revolvers and a German machine pistol. Looks like a couple of grenades got tossed as well."

"What the hell was this, some kind of war?" Watson asked softly.

Alvin turned to Frank's deputy. "Lloyd, didn't you say

you have a cousin working at Oak Ridge?"

"Yeah, I do. He said they told him if he ever talked about what goes on there they'd shoot him."

"Well, I don't want to know what they do, just how well the place is guarded."

Lloyd snorted disdainfully. "All they got is a bunch of military police, no better when you come down to it than a bunch of railroad bulls. Guard-duty soldiers, that's all."

The three looked at each other knowingly. All of them had "seen the elephant" up close and personal in the Great War, and all three shared the combat soldier's disdain for anyone who wore the uniform while specializing in something, anything, other than fighting the enemy. Such men might have the potential of becoming soldiers, they might be brave and capable of dying like men, but until they'd stood in harm's way, they weren't *soldiers*.

"That's all they got there, Lloyd? MPs?"

"Hell, they won't even let you have a game rifle there, not even a twenty-two. No guns there at all, 'cept for them MPs at the gates and the guards in the factories."

Alvin shook his head. "Our tax dollars at work." He turned to Frank. "Cousin, I think you better make another call to Oak Ridge. And this time don't take 'no' for an answer. And be sure you tell 'em just what that fella told you to tell 'em, same exact words."

"'Score zany by air,'" Frank muttered. "They're gonna think I'm crazy."

"Frank, maybe it's some kind of code. Maybe it will mean more to them than to us."

"If'n you say so, Alvin. Still sounds crazy to me, though."

"And as soon as you've made that call, we should head into town, stop by that Legion post you got here."

"You know, they was fixing to throw you a dinner tomorrow night. Supposed to be a surprise for you. There ought to be a fair number of people there tonight, both folks working on the dinner party, and folks there just to have a good time."

"Matter of fact," York decided, "let's call down there right after you get off the phone with Oak Ridge. See just how many we can have waiting for us when we get there. If there's twenty there now, maybe each of them can find ten more. Wake up the county. We might have to go hunt ourselves a couple dozen Germans, tough Germans. There ain't nothin' like fellas who fought and beat 'em once already for a job like that."

A few minutes later the three were back in Frank's car, headed for town.

Lloyd sat in the back, looking thoughtful. Then he spoke up. "Uniforms. We oughta be in uniform."

"Well, we're all in sheriff and deputy uniforms, ain't we?" Frank asked.

"Well," Lloyd continued, "I think we ought to tell our people to spend five minutes digging out their old service uniforms, so we'll know each other. Besides, it's fittin'."

"Maybe you got a point there, Lloyd," Frank admitted while Alvin nodded agreeably. "Come to think of it, I can have Mrs. Watson meet us at the Lodge with my two old uniforms." He looked at Alvin. "You won't mind being a corporal again, will you Alvin?"

York laughed.

"As for you Lloyd, well, surely *somebody* at the Lodge can dig up an old sailor suit."

9:30 P.M.
Twenty Miles East of Oak Ridge

Otto Skorzeny looked at his watch. Thirty minutes left.

He looked out his port side; his companions were holding formation nicely. Skorzeny wagged his wings to signal his intent and then went into a sharp climb, pulling up out of the valley they had been circling in for the last two hours. As he cleared the crest line, he could see the glow of Oak Ridge twenty miles ahead. He slammed the throttle up to the wall.

"All right, Gunther, call them in!"

Gunther picked up the mike, double-checking that the radio was set to the correct frequency.

"Valkyrie, Valkyrie, do you read?"

"Valkyrie One, here."

"Position check, please."

"Fifteen kilometers southeast of checkpoint C-A."

Skorzeny, listening in, grinned with delight. The head of the bomber stream was approaching Chattanooga. "We are thirty kilometers northeast of target. We will switch on our directional beacon in five minutes."

Oak Ridge
9:45 P.M.

"Christ, Martel, you look like hell."

Harriman met him at the door and guided him in. The sergeant escorting him started to follow. A captain on Groves's staff stopped him. "Sergeant, you're dismissed."

The sergeant hesitated and Martel looked back. "Don't worry, Sergeant, you did your job. Captain, I have no complaints," he added, not quite able to repress a sullen snarl as he mouthed the words that honor demanded.

"Mason, the others?" Harriman asked.

Jim shook his head. "All dead. They nailed us clean. We never stood a chance."

Harriman turned to Groves's staff officer, who was looking wide-eyed at the blood soaking Jim's left shoulder.

"You better get us Groves right now!"

Now it was the captain's turn to hesitate.

"Then take us to him!" Harriman shouted.

Suddenly presented with a viable alternative, the captain said "Let's go," and led them back out the door and into a waiting jeep.

Abbeville, France
3:55 A.M.

"Clear!"

Adolf Galland looked over to his right where one of his ground crew waited, fire extinguisher poised in case the engine caught on fire.

A tongue of blue flame shot out as the jet engine of the Me-262D pulsed to life. He watched his instruments as power started to climb. He hit the ignition switch for his right engine. It too caught and held.

He revved them up, scanning his instruments.

9:55 P.M.
The Oval Office

President Harrison checked the clock on the mantel. In forty-five minutes it would be dawn over England. He looked at Donovan, who had just hung up the phone. "I just talked to an assistant sheriff near Oak Ridge, Mr. President. He confirms Martel's message. The sheriff was out at the airport. He says there was a slaughter. He's found fifteen people dead on and near the entry road to the airfield."

Harrison looked over at Mayhew, who was on another phone.

"Damn it, John, don't you have Groves yet?"

"Still trying to reach him, sir."

Another phone rang on the desk. Harrison nodded for Donovan to pick it up.

Donovan listened for a moment. Suddenly his jaw clenched tight. He hung up and looked back at the President.

"What is it?" Harrison asked.

"Sir. That was a report from General Warren, head of 8th Tactical Command, based in Atlanta. Civilian airports at Atlanta and Chattanooga report a stream of at least one hundred planes on radar near the Tennessee-Georgia border. These planes have ignored all queries. They're currently approaching Knoxville on a north-northeast heading."

Harrison heard the words but for a moment couldn't quite grasp them. Then, "Oak Ridge. Churchill was right," he whispered, closing his eyes as reality crashed its way through his illusions.

Donovan nodded dumbly. He too was in shock, though for him, unlike Harrison there was a simple answer to internal confusion.

"Mr. President?"

My God, what have I done? I should have seen it. All the signs were there, yet I didn't put them together. Wouldn't *put them together. What have I done?*

"Mr. President."

He opened his eyes. Donovan was leaning over the desk.

"Mr. President, what are your orders, sir?"

Much as he might want to he couldn't let go, Harrison realized. The future of the world rested on his shoulders. He couldn't run, he couldn't hide. He pointed to one of the phones on his desk.

"Call the Pentagon. Marshall's at Oak Ridge, but MacArthur should be over there. Tell MacArthur that until we get Marshall back he's in complete operational control of the US military. I want a full scramble of all aircraft and all naval forces. Any German forces discovered in this hemisphere are to be engaged and destroyed. Anything that tries to run is to be considered German."

He looked over at Mayhew, who stood stock-still, as if struck. Harrison was shocked to see tears in the man's eyes, but didn't have time to deal with the issue. "Snap out of it, Mayhew! Get me Groves. Now!" Even as he spoke, he picked up another phone. The line had been opened hours ago and within seconds he heard a familiar voice on the other end.

"Winston, in about fifteen minutes nearly one hundred German bombers are going to start dumping their loads on Oak Ridge. God forgive me for holding you back. I think you should expect the Second Battle of Britain to start any moment. You must kill all the Germans you can."

4:02 A.M. (10:02 EST)
Whitehall

Winston Churchill stepped onto the balcony, and all in the war room were silent. He looked back down at the plot board. Over the Calais area a Wren slid a symbol representing a Luftwaffe air group into position. Within seconds, more ratings bearing little slips of paper were entering the map room in a steady stream, and more symbols started to appear all along the French coast clear down to Cherbourg.

Churchill turned and addressed his staff. "Gentlemen. President Harrison reports that the United States is under attack by German forces, and he concurs therefore that the German forces assembling off our coast are engaged in an assault on our island. He urges us to seek out and destroy these invaders wherever we may find them. Never doubt that in the long run we must win. But first we must survive the initial onslaught, and for that we must all do our duty flawlessly and unstintingly. England's fate rests in our hands this hour."

After a pause he added more prosaically, "Rommel's forces will be landing by mid-morning a little more chewed up than he would like. And this time the Luftwaffe will not find our air force on the ground."

CHAPTER FIFTEEN

As Harriman emerged with a surly-faced General Groves in tow, Jim caught a glimpse of the smoke-filled room on the other side, illuminated by the glare of an overhead projector. The screen was filled with arcane equations.

"Now what?" Groves snarled. "How much more of my time are you guys going to waste with your damned Chicken Little stories?" He fixed Martel with his icy gaze, then did a double take. "What in hell happened to you?"

"Skorzeny. He was at that airfield, like I said. My entire team was wiped out. We could have used some help."

Groves's features set in stone. "Are you telling me that you and your precious OSS blew it?"

"Sir, we asked for help from the FBI and from your Ranger detachment. You refused," Harriman interjected. "So we went in on our own, undermanned, without local knowledge—and got ambushed."

Groves wheeled on Harriman, but seemed to reconsider. He turned to an aide who had followed him from the conference room. "Get the FBI rep. Move it." The aide duly moved it. Since Groves did not seem willing to continue, the groups paused, waiting for the FBI man to appear. A few seconds later he did. It was Jim's old nemesis.

"*Grierson!*"

Before Grierson could respond, Groves said to both of them, "Let me talk." He then spoke directly to Grierson. "You told me this guy was crazy. Probably a traitor.

Unreliable. Under a cloud. Trouble from the word 'go,' and obnoxious to boot."

Grierson, who had paled on seeing Martel's condition, pulled himself together. "It's all true. He's the —"

"I don't want any more of your input, Grierson," Groves snarled. "Just listen." He turned back to the others, his features relaxing ever so slightly. "Harriman, I was operating on the information I had at the time."

Harriman just looked at him.

His gaze shifted to Martel. "So where's the demented son of a bitch now?"

Martel pointed straight up. "Right about there, sir. He and part of his team escaped in two Piper Cubs."

Groves looked puzzled and a bit relieved. "What can he hope to accomplish with two Cubs? That thing is shielded with seven feet of reinforced concrete. He could kamikaze the reactor with one of those and just bounce off. If he tries to parachute in, well, I've got a platoon of Rangers positioned there as well."

This was a point that had been bothering Martel. He simply figured that Skorzeny had a plan. Whatever it was, he did not expect to like it when he learned its precise nature.

"General Groves."

Groves turned to face an anxious lieutenant standing behind him.

"Sir, the President is on the line."

"Stay right there," Groves flung over his shoulder as he followed the aide briskly down a side corridor. "You too, Grierson," he added, when the ruined FBI man made to follow.

Less than a minute later he was back, running.

"Get General Marshall out here now!" Groves shouted as he headed for the main door.

Jim and Harriman followed the general outside, where he stood on the front steps, looking up at the night sky. For a moment Jim thought the general believed he could somehow make out the Pipers overhead, but then he suddenly extended his hands, gesturing for silence. "Do you hear it?"

Jim, his ears still ringing from the near misses of two grenades and a firefight, cocked his head but heard nothing. Then the door behind him swung open and he was startled to see General of the Army George Marshall standing behind him. Though out of uniform, Jim snapped to attention. Marshall ignored him.

"General Groves, what is going on?"

"Sir," Groves replied shakily, "the President just informed me that a stream of at least one hundred German bombers is approaching Oak Ridge, and will be here momentarily. Listen. You can hear them."

Marshall stood silent, his gaze following Groves's gesture. Suddenly a parachute flare ignited with blinding intensity, followed seconds later by two more.

"Skorzeny!" Martel shouted. "He's guiding the strike in!"

Marshall squinted up at the flares as they gently floated down, followed by several more. "Straight in on top of us," Marshall said, his voice awestruck. "Across the Atlantic, straight in on top of us."

10:04 P.M.
500 Feet Over Oak Ridge

"Yellow!"

Karl Radl watched the light by the open door. Below, just ahead, he could see glints from the moonlight-dappled Clinch River . . . now it was below them . . . they'd crossed it. His hands tensed, grasping the sides of the open bay. The light by the door snapped to green.

"Now!" Radl shouted as he flung himself out the door, sucking in a deep breath as the transport's slipstream blew him astern. From the corner of one eye he glimpsed the tail of the plane slashing by overhead, gone in an instant as his harness gave him a vision-blurring jolt. Now he was floating, not falling. He looked straight up: the canopy was deployed, lines looked good. Other canopies were snapping open above and behind him in a long string.

He saw a flash of light to what had to be the northwest. The first bombs were hitting K-25.

He looked down. Their aim had been almost too good. They were on top of the damned target; the square reactor building was less than fifty yards to his right. He drifted down past a smokestack, fearing for a second that he might tangle in it. He heard a curse, looked up, and saw that the man behind him had indeed caught on the top of the stack. One lost already. Even if he and the stack survived the bombing, he was stuck until the Americans fetched him off.

The ground was coming up, no, it was tarmac. This was going to hurt. . . . He flexed his knees, drew in a deep breath, hit, narrowly missing the hood of a car, and rolled. Ignoring various skinned parts of himself he got to his feet and began dealing with his shroud lines, pulling them in to collapse the canopy. Next he hit the quick-release harness, peeled out of his parachute and dropped the reserve chute as well.

"Hey buddy! What the hell are you doing over there?" An American MP came walking toward him. Then he saw the parachutes drifting down.

"What is this, some sort of drill?"

Radl unclipped his machine pistol from its sling, brought it up and cocked it.

The MP looked at him, wide eyed.

Radl, feeling as if he were committing murder, squeezed the trigger, hammering the man with a three-round burst. He saw two more MPs at the guard post at the end of the parking lot and charged toward them. One of the MPs burst out the back of the shack and started to run. The other fumbled with the clasp to his holster. Radl first shot the MP who showed fight, then the one who ran away.

The plane with the second team was nearly overhead.

Another stick of parachutes streamed forth.

Staccato bursts of machine-gun fire started to echo. Most were Schmeissers, but an increasing number were not. The ground to his right was swept by a deep-throated burst from what must be a Browning. He rolled behind the shack and peered out.

The source of the fire was emplaced on the roof of the reactor cooling-building, which was located a little to the east of the reactor itself. He saw several men run out of the reactor building and start to sprint across the yard toward the cooling-building. Raising his gun he fired off another burst, dropping one of them. The rest made it to safety.

Several shots slammed into the guard shack, inches above his head. He rolled over and apparently just clipped a man charging up the slope from the reactor. The American, though hit, continued forward. Radl shot him again. Still he continued, but now on simple physical momentum, weapon fallen away, to crumple at Radl's side. Radl tried to ignore the fear in that brave man's eyes as his third burst ended his life.

This was a garrison soldier? Then he saw the patch on the American's uniform and understood. They were facing Rangers, fellow commandos who would never admit that, man for man, there were any soldiers in the world who could defeat them. Radl smiled with grim sardonicism. Wouldn't Skorzeny be pleased.

The machine gun opened up again, tracers soaring heavenward, cutting into several of his men as they drifted down on top of the building. Radl pulled out his whistle and gave three short blasts to rally his group for the assault on the reactor.

10:04 P.M.

"Valkyrie One, Valkyrie One, we've just dropped our

flares over the primary target area. Bring your strike in on an east-to-west axis." As he spoke, Skorzeny edged his plane over into a banking turn, circling at two thousand feet. The bomber stream would pass fifteen hundred feet below him.

A flash of light ignited off to the west, followed seconds later by a dozen more. Valkyrie Four, the strike on K-25 had already begun.

He continued to wheel in tight over the administrative area. Traffic still flowed nearly bumper to bumper on the Oak Ridge Turnpike directly below. The streets were brilliantly lit so that the target area was as bright as day, standing out sharply against the dark hills. Then, over the radio, "This is lead marker for Valkyrie One. I am crossing the river now! Stand clear! Stand clear!"

"There he is!" Gunther shouted, pounding Otto on the shoulder and pointing off to their right.

Otto looked where Gunther was pointing and saw a dark shadow come roaring in directly beneath them. As it did so it dropped twenty cylinders containing among them five tons of napalm. A half-mile length of the highway below was suddenly awash in fire, and the Piper Cub was batted heavenward by the explosion of superheated air. As he struggled to steady the small plane, Skorzeny gazed raptly down at the destruction that was starting to walk across Oak Ridge.

10:07 P.M.

"Merciful God," Marshall gasped as the wall of fire swept down the main street, consuming everything in its path. Jim looked up at the general who stood rigid, framed by the doorway. The wave of fire swept past them less than a hundred yards away.

As a burst of heat began to scorch them, Jim grabbed

Marshall and wrestled him to the ground. The general made to rise. "Damn it General, *will* you stay down?" Jim shouted angrily. The general apparently saw the wisdom of Jim's request and the two of them lay there crouched in the doorway, watching in horror as from out of the sea of fire wavering human torches began to emerge, their high keening cries clearly audible between explosions.

Suddenly the double doors behind Marshall swung open and a crowd of men poured out to stand transfixed. The individual detonations had begun to merge into a single drawn-out convulsive roar, a mad cacophony of explosions, shattering glass, the whooshing gasp of exploding napalm and, intermingled, less audible now, the shrieking cries of those caught in the inferno.

To the north of the flames, Jim saw a string of explosions blasting through the main residential area. Seconds later another stick of bombs came down, and then another. Each bomber was dropping eighty fifty-kilogram bombs, "HE," high explosive, intermixed with incendiaries in a stream hundreds of yards long. Well, there was nothing he could do about that.

Jim came to his feet and pointed toward the parking lot. "Get away from the buildings! The buildings are death traps. Stay out of them, crouch behind the cars!" he shouted to all those within hearing. He encouraged Marshall down the steps with an urgent shove, then grabbed one of the scientists standing on the porch and got him moving in the right direction as well.

"Move it! Move your damned asses!"

Suddenly, somehow, Jim's message made it into the collective consciousness of the scientists, and there was something close to a stampede into the parking lot, so enthusiastic that it nearly knocked Jim over. A lone figure, however, remained stock-still.

Jim was about to berate the man, but it was Groves who stood mesmerized, as plane after plane, the swastikas decorating their wings and tail assemblies clearly illuminated by the flames below, swept past. As Groves stood gazing at all that in a very real sense his own intransigence had wrought, it seemed to Jim that here stood a man who did not want to live but knew he must, at least for a while.

The entire hillside residential area north of the line of napalm seemed to be swept with an unending succession of strobe lights as dozens of bombs detonated with every passing second.

Groves looked over at Jim.

"Stay with the scientists and Marshall. Guard them."

"Where are you going, sir?"

"To get some defense organized. You stay with these people!"

Groves turned and started to run toward security headquarters, to save what could be saved. Harriman fell in behind him.

Jim returned to the parking lot, which was filling not only with panic-stricken scientists from the conference center, but with the everyday inhabitants of Oak Ridge who had been on the edge of the first napalm strike. The air filled with the cloying stench of gasoline and burned flesh. Brilliant flashes etched the ridgeline a half mile away to the south. Whatever facilities were hidden in the next valley were getting torn apart as well.

Jim saw General Marshall standing beside a jeep and joined him. Marshall looked at him and said softly, "Don't try knocking me down again son. I'll decide when it's time to leave my feet." Marshall pointed over toward the administration building. "Have you noticed that every single bomber is hitting north of the main road?"

"Sir?"

"They've yet to hit the major administrative buildings. I wonder why."

Suddenly, seeming to give Marshall the lie, a stick of bombs came walking out past them. Even Marshall ducked down low as splinters howled across the parking lot, shattering car windows and cutting down more than one spectator who had dared to stand too soon. Then another stick, and another. But still the main buildings were spared.

Jim crouched low beside Marshall, waiting for the madness to end. Concussion waves snapped over him, slamming the breath out of his lungs, forcing him to hands and knees. The ground beneath him rolled and bounced as if about to be torn apart. He closed his eyes and waited, but somehow death missed both him and America's highest ranking military officer.

10:24 P.M.

"Thor One! Thor One!"

Karl, crouched low against the curb of the reactor parking lot as a burst of fifty-caliber rounds swept the area, shouted into the radio. The entire perimeter of the reactor was a chaos of explosions, gunfire, men screaming and cursing. Worse, the Rangers still held the main building, and atop the cooling-building they had clear fields of fire covering the approaches to the north, south and west. The place was going to have to be hit before his team went in after all.

"Thor One! Thor One!" he repeated.

"Thor One here."

At last. Radl clutched the radio handset, ducked down as another burst of rounds stitched past him.

"This is Siegfried Two. We need fire support!"

"Coming in over your position now, Siegfried Two. Mark your target and perimeter."

"Mark our lines!" Radl shouted to his men, "Red flares!"

Radl looked over to a sergeant and nodded. The man raised himself to one knee, aimed a flare pistol at the cooling-building, and fired. The green target-marking flare arced up over the building. Before the sergeant could crouch back down a bullet knocked him over backward.

"We have the target in sight, Siegfried."

"Pull it in tight," Radl shouted. "We have teams all around the perimeter. Concentrate on the flare and the building due west of the flare."

"Get your heads down. Lining up now."

Radl surveyed his line as squad leaders popped off red flares and threw them forward to mark the perimeter. Above the staccato roar of the firefight he heard the deep, throaty rumble of the gunship wheeling in tight over its target. Then bullets vomited from the gunship. First the top of the cooling-building disappeared in an inferno, then the streak of fire smeared its way across the open courtyard to engulf the reactor building as well. As the gunship turned and wheeled the radio spoke once more.

"We're making another pass, Siegfried. Stay down!"

The 264 lined up again. Again the ground beneath it disappeared in a whirlwind of explosions. A shower of shell casings rained down as it passed overhead.

For a brief moment Radl wondered if the man stranded atop the stack was still alive up there. Perhaps he had found a ladder implanted in the stack and climbed down? Annoyed with himself, he brusquely dismissed the man from his mind as the irrelevancy he was.

Radl stood up, blew a shrieking blast from his whistle, and he and his team swept down the hill. When they came to the chain-link fence that surrounded the reactor area, the men equipped with wire cutters quickly and efficiently sliced their way through. Radl ducked down and through the hole held open for him, then weaved and dodged his way up to the side of the cooling-building. There still awaited a fifty-meter run across a wide-open field of fire to the reactor itself.

"Smoke!" Radl unclipped a smoke grenade, pulled the fuse and threw it. Half a dozen more followed from the men behind him. He moved to the corner of the building, took a deep breath and started to run, hoping that the gunship had suppressed all resistance. Not quite. Halfway across the open area to the reactor one of his men pitched over and skidded as pieces of asphalt sprayed up around him. Radl kept on running, slammed hard against the side of the reactor building when he reached its blessed relative security.

The gunship attack had converted the corrugated steel siding of the building into a ragged steel lace. From inside Radl could hear screaming.

Two men emerged from the smoke to crouch beside him. Radl motioned at the door, and the two pulled out grenades. Radl stood and yanked the door open. The grenades were lobbed in, and the three crouched back down.

From inside Radl heard, "Grenades!" The cry was punctuated by the dual explosion. Crouching low, he pulled the door open again and darted in, emptying a clip as he did so. His two companions entered firing as well. There were more screams, then silence.

Radl stood and slapped in a new clip. The corridor in front of him was a shambles, illuminated only by light filtering in through the hundreds of holes that had been punched into the building from a streetlight that, surreally, was still glowing outside. By its light he could see half a dozen dead in the corridor. Two were Rangers, the rest civilians.

Radl moved to a door on his right and repeated the entrance routine: two grenades; follow the explosions firing in a dive. This time there was no response and cautiously he stood up.

Several emergency lamps glowed dimly through the smoke. The open concrete floor in front of him was littered with a dozen mangled bodies. He craned his neck upward. With twenty-foot walls, the room was like an open warehouse. The ceiling was ripped to shreds. Halfway across the room was a staircase, leading into a booth several meters off the ground. The glass walls of the booth were blown out. A body hung over the side.

In the middle of the room stood the centerpiece: a blocklike structure fifteen yards high. The side that faced him looked rather like a pegboard with dozens of regularly spaced holes from floor level to halfway up the side of it. Each of the holes was marked with arcane symbols. Some of the holes had wires trailing out of them. Others were sealed with what looked like metal plugs.

He approached it slowly, cautiously, as if it were the temple of some dark god who would strike down unbelievers who dared violate its holy self. Suddenly he heard running feet behind him. He spun, ready to fire, but it was four more of his own, part of the second platoon.

"Where's Muhler?"

"He was caught by the gunship," one of them replied bitterly. "Cut in half by friendly fire."

Christ. His demolitions expert was gone.

"What about Hiller?"

"Broken neck. He landed on a car, went through the windshield."

Muhler's backup was gone as well.

Radl pointed at one of his sergeants.

"Find the supply packs dropped by the two planes. I need the plastic explosives in here now." Then he looked at the other: "Get Lieutenant Bruckner with the second platoon to set up the two antitank guns. Tell him I said to place them facing both directions on the road and to set up the mortars for fire support as well. We've stunned them for the moment but they'll be back like hornets. The last time I saw Professor Schiller he was still up in the parking area. Bring him down here. Now go!"

The sergeants saluted and ran out the door.

Radl turned to the two men who had charged with him and survived.

"Get back outside and set up a security perimeter around this building. Pick six men to come in here to help me. Each man is carrying two kilos of plastic; collect it and don't forget to get it off the dead and wounded. I need a hundred kilos in here fast!"

Radl motioned for the men remaining with him to sweep around the sides of the reactor. When that was done, he walked slowly up the stairs and past the shattered door into the control booth. The floor was slippery with blood. Broken glass crunched beneath his feet. The air was thick with the stink of cordite and electrical fires. Sparks sputtered out from behind several instrument panels.

He came to a corner into a back room set against the side of the reactor. A low moan greeted him when he started to edge around it, his machine pistol pointing the way. Four men were sprawled on the floor. Three were obviously dead. The fourth was lying in the corner, fumbling to hold within it the contents of his abdomen. He looked up at Radl.

Radl walked up to him and knelt down by his side.

The man looked at him, wide eyed, staring at his uniform.

"Nazi monster," the man whispered in German.

He started to cough. Radl uncorked his canteen and held it up to the man's lips.

He took a sip, discovered it was cognac, gagged, but nodded for more. "A Jew just drank from your canteen," the man said when he could speak again.

"Yes."

"My luck to take my last drink from an SS canteen." The man reached up and seized Radl's hand, smearing it with blood. "The Americans, they'll build another just like this, you know, give you a taste of the hell you deserve." A groan escaped him. "Finish me. You must be an expert at killing Jews; what's one more to you?"

Radl stood back up and pulling out his Luger he pointed it down at the man's forehead.

The man closed his eyes. "Another glorious victory for the Fatherland?" he whispered.

Radl pulled the trigger and turned away.

He heard footsteps on the stairs leading up to the control booth and turned to see the mission's chief technical consultant arrive, escorted by four of his men.

"Everything's shot to hell in here," Schiller said bitterly.

"How am I to get any information? For all I can tell the reactor's getting ready to go critical on its own!"

"Just do your job. Grab what notes you can, take anything you believe will be of value."

Radl stepped back out into the main control room and saw more men coming in. Several of them dragged boxes loaded with plastic explosives already cut and shaped to be pushed in through one of the reactor openings for the fuel and control rods.

Radl called the physicist over.

"I've lost my demolitions men. Tell me how to blow this thing."

The physicist looked around and then turned and pointed back out into the main room at the pile below.

"That wall is solid concrete. They most likely have a graphite containment wall inside, and then the actual reactor pile. You need to breach right through the concrete and graphite, burst the whole thing wide open. While you are preparing for demolition, I'll start pulling the graphite control rods; that will get the reactor started toward meltdown. If we blow it and melt it at the same time, I promise you they'll never use it or the ground under it again. Never even come near it, except with bulldozers."

"How long will it take?"

"Half hour, perhaps an hour. I'll have to figure out which are the control rods and then pull them."

"The radiation. How dangerous will it be around here?"

"When it blows we want to be a kilometer away and upwind," the physicist replied softly.

A burst of machine-gun fire slammed through the building, sending Radl and then the physicist diving to the floor.

"Just get it done!" Radl shouted, "I'll start placing the explosives."

10:33 P.M.

As the last of the bombers swept across and added to the inferno below, Otto Skorzeny continued to circle the town, observing the results of his handiwork. More than three thousand fifty-kilogram bombs had been dropped on Oak Ridge by now, and fires raged from the turnpike all the way up the side of the hill, several square kilometers in all. In the glare of explosions he could see thousands of antlike figures running panic-stricken in the streets. Over in the next valley the Y-12 plants were ablaze, while off to the west the K-25 facilities were burning as well. There was just one more item. . . .

Skorzeny banked and flew over the main administrative building and toward the airstrip. "Siegfried One, Siegfried One."

"Siegfried One here. We are in position."

"Get ready for your drop. Thor One will strike first. Come straight in behind him. Release on the flares."

10:34 P.M.

Jim Martel stood next to Marshall watching as the bombardment of the town continued to thunder through an agonizing climax of destruction.

And then there was a lull, the echoes of explosions continuing to rumble across the hills.

"General Marshall, sir!" A jeep, driven by Soratkin, squealed to a halt behind them. General Groves leapt out before it had fully stopped, followed by Harriman and Soratkin. Their jeep was followed by two more, both loaded with Rangers.

Ignoring Martel, Groves offered an M1 carbine to Marshall.

Jim suddenly felt naked without a weapon. He walked over to the jeep. The back seat was piled high with weapons. He reached in, grabbed a carbine, then took a pouch containing half a dozen clips, slinging it over his shoulder, indifferent to the pain.

One of the civilians, a gangly individual with thinning hair, came over to join Groves and Marshall. "If they're landing on the reactor that can only mean they intend to blow it."

"Oppie, don't you think I know that?" Groves shouted, "I've sent the remaining company of Rangers down there."

Marshall's attention snapped to Soratkin. "What do we have left in reserve?"

"Just a few security personnel, sir." He glanced at Groves, who didn't speak. "Everything else is going to K-25. We've got a reported paratroop drop there."

"What about Guard units, anything?"

The security man shook his head.

Marshall looked frantic. "Then how do we guard the scientists? Don't you realize they are our greatest asset?"

Soratkin just looked blank. His career had culminated in a job where his entire mission was to guard the physical assets of Oak Ridge. Until this moment the infestation of pointy heads from New Mexico had been nothing but an unpleasantly hectic interruption to the smooth administration of security on the base. Suddenly he paled, seeming to realize that his values had been askew.

Groves broke the tableau. "I'll call them back." He pointed at one of the Ranger Sergeants. "Go with that man to K-25. Bring back Company C. Tell the Company Commander it's a direct order from me, and I *know* what it means!" He turned to an aide and pointed at the jeep. "Use the radiophone to confirm what I just told him. Keep at it until you get through."

Before he had finished speaking to the aide, Soratkin, the sergeant, and his three men were making a high-speed squealing turn out of the lot and were gone.

Meanwhile Jim had continued to look toward the east

and was the first to see several flares ignite and start to drift down over the open fields and parking lots beyond the administrative building. "Everybody down!"

Seconds later the sky seemed to explode as three gunships roared in behind a wall of explosions that swept over the administrative building, across the medical center and bus stations, and into the parking lot where they were standing.

Jim huddled down next to Grove's jeep as the firestorm swept overhead, cars around him exploding, screams echoing, glass and steel spraying down around him.

The storm passed.

Jim waited, then opened his eyes to see Marshall lying prone beside him, his face bleeding from tiny cuts. Several hundred yards to the east, over by the administrative building and the baseball fields to the south of it, dozens of black canopies were swooping down from the sky. "Paratroopers!" Marshall snarled, scrambling up. Jim stood as well. Groves was already up, carbine raised and firing.

The jeep that had held the remaining Rangers had taken a direct hit. Its occupants, who had used it for shelter, were nearly all dead or dying. From the field where the paratroopers had landed Jim saw a skirmish line already sweeping forward, firing as they ran, dropping everyone in their path. To the north, just short of the still-burning wreckage on the main road, another line of canopies were opening and sliding down.

Jim grasped Groves by the arm.

"General, does the main administrative building have a basement?"

The general nodded. "Why?"

"We're cut off. This is an enveloping sweep. We've got to get these scientists to shelter!"

Groves nodded in instant agreement. "Round them up. Let's go!"

Jim looked at Oppenheimer. "Have your people here grab what weapons they can and start moving to the Admin building!"

Oppenheimer nodded and did as he was told.

Arguing, pushing, shoving, and in one case threatening to shoot, Jim guided the mob to the only building that offered a hint of defensibility. Some with particular presence of mind stopped long enough to salvage the dead Rangers' weapons. As they ran toward the building, shots began to snap overhead as the team that had landed to the north started its sweep toward them.

Hoping to momentarily halt the line of skirmishers, Jim stopped to return fire, but it just kept coming. Then he noticed the sound, absurdly out of place after the roar and thunder, of a throttled-back Piper Cub engine sweeping by him to touch down where one of the paratroop teams had landed. Realizing who it might be, he snapped off a shot, but without real hope. The plane disappeared into the darkness.

4:45 A.M. (10:45 P.M. at Oak Ridge)
The North Sea

Plumes of spray swept across the pitching deck as the cruiser heeled over sharply. Rommel ignored the captain's advice that he should go below, that there was no benefit accruing from the risk he was taking. Rommel had never seen a battle at sea.

The forward battery was already in play, joined seconds later by the 37-mm antiaircraft guns just below the bridge. The targets were low on the horizon, coming out of the pre-dawn darkness to the west, almost impossible to see. Suddenly there was a brilliant flash to the south; Rommel turned his binoculars to the brilliant glare. A transport was exploding. A thousand men gone.

The cruiser started to reverse its turn, nearly tumbling him over. Seconds later a geyser erupted a hundred meters off the starboard beam, the force of the explosion vibrating through the soles of his feet. Rommel looked up and saw a British Typhoon fighter bomber breaking out of its dive, skimming low over the water, tracers pursuing it into a low-hanging bank of fog.

Rommel gripped the railing as the cruiser heeled to the other side as another explosion erupted a hundred meters to port. This time the cruiser maintained the turn until it had cut a full circle. While it did so Rommel noted that several ships in the convoy were trailing smoke. A broken-backed light cruiser was swiftly sinking, bow and stern both pointing up at drunken angles.

Six more hours of this, he thought coldly. As well it had not started earlier; they would never have survived.

4:45 A.M.
The English Channel

"Break left!" Adolf Galland shouted into his mike. It was going to be a fight after all. He pulled his Me-262 into a sharp banking dive as he tried to line up on the British Meteor that was in turn trying to line up on his wingman. The RAF had been waiting for them. The Meteor broke away, but he could not follow; another Meteor was on *him*. He managed to jink away. What a furball. How much nicer it had been last time, when they'd caught the RAF napping.

He could sense already that the German attack was falling apart. By now they should already be over the coast, turning in to hit the airfields that ringed the southeast coast. He saw a plume of smoke and fire tumbling down, an Arado 234 breaking up in a fireball. Seconds later another plane plummeted past his portside: another Arado.

The Brits were focusing on the bombers. Well then, that meant they weren't focusing on him. He pulled up sharply, aiming at a Meteor that had slipped onto the six of an Arado and fired off a burst. Lucky shot: part of the Meteor's tail assembly flew off and the plane spun out of control. It was his first kill in three years, but he felt no elation.

It was going to be a long, bitter day, the hope for an easy victory already gone, the hope for any victory at all beginning to glimmer as well.

10:50 P.M.
Oak Ridge

Otto Skorzeny guided the Piper Cub across the baseball diamond, braking it to a stop. Flinging open the door he swung out.

A grinning Captain Ulrich, dressed as an American MP, came running up and saluted.

"Report, Captain!"

"Sir! First Platoon is moving north into the town, Second Platoon is swinging down to secure the airfield. Third Platoon is in reserve here along with the headquarters and heavy weapons sections."

"What about the others?"

"Richer reports a successful drop on the north side of the town. They're sweeping up hundreds of civilians. The damn fools are running straight to them, crying for help. They just have to wait till they've collected a batch, kill them, and wait for new fools!"

"K-25 and Y-12?"

"On K-25 both teams missed their target by more than a kilometer. At Y-12 one drop landed straight into the fires. Almost everyone in the group was killed. The other drop landed successfully and is now sweeping the buildings."

"And Radl?"

"Nothing. Something's wrong with their radio. But they are in contact with the gunship, which reports that they're inside the building."

Skorzeny nodded.

"Now we must secure the administrative building. Where is your headquarters?"

Ulrich nodded toward a baseball dugout that now bristled with antennas.

"Once it's secured, we'll shift into the administration building. Now move it!"

Ulrich, grinning, called for his platoon and started off at the double toward the target.

Skorzeny looked over at Gunther, who smiled and said, "So far so good."

Skorzeny spat on the ground. "We could still fail."

10:54 P.M.
Oak Ridge

"The reactor is definitely running hot," the physicist shouted, trying to be heard above the staccato of explosions detonating outside the building. A sudden spray of bullets slashed through the corrugated walls, across the face of the reactor, and ricocheted off. The two ducked down. There was an explosion outside and the firing stopped, replaced by a high piercing scream that was finally cut short by another explosion.

Schiller looked over at Radl, wide-eyed with fear. The weapons fire had bothered him no more than it had the others, but this was different, and he understood it too well. "For all we know it's melting down as we speak."

"Just keep pulling the rods and packing the plastic in," Radl shouted.

"You have no idea what you're playing with here."

"The only thing I know is that I'll leave this place a smoking ruin!"

Radl stood up and walked over to a rod sticking out from the wall, pulled it out, flung it to the floor. "Was that uranium or was it a control rod?"

The physicist looked at him gray-faced. "Graphite. But if you pull them all, it will run away on us. The gunship blew out all the instruments. I can't follow what the reactor is doing. It could go at any second. When it does the explosive will go too, at that very instant."

"Then we'll pull some, pack in the explosive and then pull the rest. Perhaps the explosive will do the job of the graphite!" Radl nodded to several of his men holding the tubes of plastic explosive and motioned to them to slide them into the holes left by the graphite.

Schiller found his voice. "You're going to kill us all!"

Radl turned on Schiller, gun raised.

"The rest of us are dead men anyhow," Radl snarled. "Even for those of us who survive this one, there'll be another and another until we're all dead. You just do your job and go home the hero. That, or I blow your brains out here and now!"

10:55 P.M.

Martel raced up the steps to the main entrance into the administrative building. Turning, he waved on the straggling crowd following behind him. Small-arms fire was already starting to lace through them; half a dozen had fallen before the rest could huddle at the side of the building.

"Inside, inside, down into the basement!" he kept shouting the command over and over, pushing men through the doorway.

"It's a death trap if we're caught down there."

Martel turned. It was Marshall.

"Sir, you're the one who pointed out that the Germans were avoiding the admin buildings. Besides, what else can we do? It's either that or get mowed down in the open. It's one of the few strong points we have. Damn near every other building is temporary, above ground and no basement. This is not just an air raid; it's a killing mission, and these people are the targets. We've got to get them into a place we can hole up till help arrives."

Marshall nodded slowly. It seemed that he too could see no other way to stave off immediate annihilation. The last of the scientists came through the doorway, followed by half a dozen Rangers and MPs.

"We'll set up our first line right here," Marshall said, implicitly accepting Martel's plan. He began detailing off the Rangers to rooms on either side of the doorway and sent two more down the corridor to cover the back approach.

Then Marshall cocked his carbine and laid down by the door. Martel looked down at him. "Commander Martel, decide for yourself how long to stay on your feet, but if you don't get down you're not going to last very long," Marshall said quietly.

Jim, not quite certain if he were the victim of gallows humor, but unable to suppress a wry grin, dropped prone by Marshall's side and waited with him for the onslaught that was coming. Harriman, who had taken it upon himself several minutes before to begin organizing the building, was now crouched at Marshall's other side.

Seconds later, from around the side of the building, several figures in MP uniforms appeared, crouching low. Marshall got up on his elbows and peered out at them. "Hey, you men, over here!"

One of the MP's helmets swiveled directly toward Marshall. The man waved and trotted toward them. Jim watched him carefully as he mounted the steps, sensing that something was wrong but not quite grasping what it was that bothered him.

"Who's in here, sir?" the strange MP asked.

Marshall stood up and the MP slowed and then snapped a salute.

"We've got some of our top scientists down in the basement," Marshall said. "Get your team up here now."

The MP looked intently at Marshall, eyes flickering across the five stars on each shoulder. A look of delighted recognition started to form as he began to swing his weapon, previously held out of sight, to the front. It was a Schmeisser. Jim started to bring his M1 into line, but he knew that with his bad shoulder he was far the slower, and that he and those with him were about to die—

A sharp *crack!* followed at even intervals by two more spun the "MP" around and flung him down the steps. As that one tumbled, Harriman shot the next in line. The third MP backed away, firing wildly. Braving the scattered fire, Jim caught him on the shoulder, knocking him down but not killing him, since he rolled behind the side of the building.

"What the hell?" Marshall looked at them as if he thought they'd gone mad.

"Nazis dressed as MPs!" Harriman explained, pointing to the dead man sprawled out on the steps. "Look at the jump boots! Plus he's carrying a Schmeisser. Besides," pointing at the direction from which the trio had come, "there's nothing but Germans in that direction."

"You OSS gentlemen really do seem to have all the answers, don't you," Marshall said in tones of wonderment. Following some train of thought of his own, he added, "Where's that Grierson?"

"Still in the parking lot, most of him," Harriman replied.

11:10 P.M.

"Gunther, you stay here at the command post! I'll be back."

Gunther looked over his shoulder from the transmitter from which he was calling in another gunship. Sporadic firing was still preventing the transports from landing at the airstrip. "Sir? May I ask where are you going?"

"The people we want, including Marshall, have organized resistance. I'm going to take care of it." Motioning for his reserve platoon to follow, Skorzeny ran toward the administration building.

11:15 P.M.

Richer, dressed as an American MP, walked down the middle of Georgia Avenue.

Outer Drive had already been taken care of, his second platoon was further east, his third was scattered out to the west.

The homes in this area were E and F class housing units, dwelling places for middle and upper level scientists and managers of the project. Hundreds of them were burning, bodies littered the street, and staccato bursts of machine-gun fire echoed as his team systematically slaughtered its way across Oak Ridge.

A door swung open. From a small house a gray-haired man half-carried a younger woman. Her clothes and body were lacerated by flying glass. He staggered toward them. "Help us, for God's sake!" he screamed. "She's bleeding to death!"

"Glad to," Richer responded calmly. He walked up to the couple, lowered his gun and shot the woman in the forehead, splattering her husband.

The man looked at him, paralyzed with shock.

Without a word, Richer shot the man in the stomach, then turned and walked away, smiling to himself at the kind of noises the man was finally giving voice to.

The American attitude toward uniforms was a strangely trusting one. More often than not they simply ran to him, begging for help. And not one of them had had a weapon, for weapons were forbidden within the confines of Oak

Ridge. Nearly all of the few MPs and security guards encountered out here in the residences were taken completely by surprise, and the few alert or paranoid enough to suspect were quickly eliminated. So far he had taken more casualties in the jump itself than from actually performing the mission.

A gunship roared in low overhead. A stream of fire spewed from it, followed by a ripple of secondary explosions as fuel tankers on the targeted rail-siding went up. It made a pleasant backdrop to his work.

11:19 P.M.

"Slide those tubes in!"

"We're close to meltdown!" Schiller shouted, trying to be heard above the steadily building firefight outside the reactor.

"Shove them in!"

"Major!"

Radl turned and saw one of his lieutenants standing by the door into the reactor building. He ran over.

"A Ranger unit is deploying east of us, two hundred meters up the road. There are at least a hundred of them."

"How many do we have left?"

"Not more than forty on the perimeter."

"Hold for ten more minutes!"

The lieutenant saluted and Radl started to turn back. He wasn't sure if at that instant he actually saw the wall of the reactor bursting open or not. One second he was standing, turning—an instant later he was flying out the door. The entire east side of the corrugated outer wall was peeled back by the force of the explosion, which vented out of breaches in the reactor wall like hot exhaust from a rocket.

A searing wave of heat washed over him and he rolled away from it, curling up, covering his head. He felt the skin on his hands blistering. As if from far away he thought he heard screaming, a high keening wail. The heat washed over, dissipated, and he sat up. From out of the door he saw someone emerge, his clothes flayed from his body, blood oozing out through blackened, cracked skin.

The man sagged down in front of Radl.

"I told you," Schiller gasped. "The reaction started to go critical, and the explosives were touched off by the heat." He hunched over, gasping.

Radl looked back at the plumes of fire and smoke filling the inside of the reactor building, venting in plumes from the holes lacing the rest of the building and billowing from the blown-out east wall.

The physicist looked at him and tried to laugh.

"I'll see you shortly in Hell, Radl; you've killed us both." With that the physicist collapsed into unconsciousness, his breath coming in ragged wheezes.

Radl stood up and edged over to the open side of the building and looked in. The east wall of the reactor was torn wide open, littering the interior of the building with fragments of concrete, twisted hunks of metal, and less identifiable materials, as well as with the torn bodies of the team he had walked away from only seconds before. Then he noticed a strange unearthly glow issuing from within the reactor, and he knew he was looking straight into the heart of Hell.

He shielded his face and turned away. Funny, he didn't feel any different. He had not been vaporized, or melted, or even changed into a pillar of salt for daring to look into the holy of holies of a dark new age. He had only been killed.

For a random moment silence returned as the battle began dying down. From a building to the south he could hear voices, American voices, shouting in panic. Civilians began pouring out in spite of the risk of being shot. He did not even bother to raise his gun.

Now the roof of the building was peeling back from the

intense buildup of heat inside, revealing a fiery glow rising up from within. Flames consumed everything that was flammable, including the graphite core. Coils of dark and deadly smoke swirled up and drifted off to the east and south.

"Major!"

Radl turned and saw his lieutenant coming back.

"Are you all right, sir?"

Radl forced a smile. "It is time to leave. We have worn out our welcome, I fear."

11:22 P.M.

Martel clutched the Schmeisser that he had taken from the dead SS captain along with his ammunition and two grenades. Marshall, beside him, continued to scan the ground ahead, clearly illuminated by the inferno consuming the town. Five "MPs" lay sprawled on the ground before them.

"Welcome to Hell," Jim whispered.

A burst of machine-gun fire rattled across the doorway, then flayed the corridor behind them.

"They're in the building — " The shout from further down the corridor was cut short.

Jim looked back over his shoulder. "We better head downstairs."

Another burst of fire swept overhead. Marshall fired off a quick reply and then started to crawl backward.

There was a dull thud and then a sound like a snake hissing.

"Grenade!"

Harriman, on Marshall's other side, leapt over the general, attempted to scoop the grenade up but fumbled, grabbed again, and then simply fell on it. A muffled *pfoomph* lifted Harriman into the air.

Marshall started to turn Harriman over.

Jim grabbed Marshall by the shoulders and pulled him away. "He's dead, sir!" Jim shouted in a voice that was almost a sob. "Come on!"

Marshall nodded and the two started down the corridor, crouching low. Two Rangers joined them from the side rooms where Marshal had detailed them. They turned from the corridor into the stairwell and raced down the stairs, stopping short on the bottom level at the sight of a nervous MP looking at them over a leveled M1. Fortunately, the MP recognized Marshall.

"They're right behind us," Jim hissed, urging the MP through the doorway.

The corridor, illuminated only by an emergency lamp at the end of the hall was packed with civilians.

"Is there a secured area here?" Marshall snapped.

The MP just looked at him, speechless with awe.

"Snap out of it, soldier! *Is there a secured area here?*"

"Ah, sir. Down the end of the corridor. Records storage area. A single big room. Real big. This corridor is the only way in."

"Unless they come through the ceiling," Marshall said. "But if they have time to figure out which floor matches where we are, and then do the demolition work, we're dead anyway. Let's get these people in there. The Nazis will be coming down this corridor any second now."

11:30 P.M.

"Sir, we're starting to have problems!"

Skorzeny slowed on the steps into the administrative building and looked back at his radio operator.

"What is it?"

"Gunther just reported back in, sir. The transports are landing now. But they've picked up a scramble alert from several American air bases. Fighters are coming this way. If they catch the transports on the ground, we're trapped."

"How much time?"

"Half an hour for the first of them."

Skorzeny looked down at his watch. They'd only been on the ground for fifty minutes. He'd planned for a minimum of two hours.

"What else?"

"A number of armed civilians, many wearing bits and pieces of uniforms, were seen coming in through the east gate. Gunships are still sweeping the area, but they're running low on ammunition. The team at K-25 is running way behind schedule and we have no report at all from Radl, but the orbiting gunship reported a major ground explosion about five minutes ago."

"The reactor?"

"I don't know, sir."

"Never mind."

If the reactor had blown at least the second most important part of the mission was a success. The wind was west-northwest. That meant the radiation would blow toward Knoxville. Good. Keep them excited.

"All right, tell the teams to hurry up. Forty-five minutes and we start to pull out. And make sure they keep the landing area blacked out!"

Following his team in he started the sweep through the building, room after room. There was only scattered resistance. Behind him the intelligence team came tearing through. He decided for the moment to stay with them while the assault team pushed ahead. There was a shout of triumph when they found Groves's office. A minute later they exited the room and stood pressed against the wall. There was a muffled explosion, and they poured back in. The team started to scoop papers out of the safe, sorting them out as they did so. Just as they had rehearsed, some of the papers were spread out one after the other on Groves's desk, one of the team members photographing each sheet while another swept that sheet to the floor as a third man slapped down yet another in its place. Other team members began to grab documents and load them into oversized backpacks to be taken out.

"We've found the door to the basement!"

Skorzeny backed out of Groves's office and followed a sergeant who turned a corner and then pointed to a doorway at which several men were crouching.

"Well damn it, what are you waiting for?" Skorzeny shouted.

One of the men popped the door open and another hurled a grenade down the stairs. After the explosion had slammed the door back on its hinges, one of the men leaped through, firing as he darted down the steps. He made it to the bottom and was turning the corner before an M1 cracked and he crumpled.

Another man started down the stairs, leaned around the landing to throw a grenade, and then pressed himself up against the wall. When the explosion swept back up he raced around the corner, machine pistol low and firing. Two more followed him. A moment later Skorzeny had joined them. The point man stopped by the shattered door into the basement corridor, pulled out another grenade and tossed it through. There was a shout of warning from the other side, followed an instant later by an explosion.

The point man leaped through the doorway, turned right, and fired. Answering fire caught him from behind and he collapsed. The next man of the team now leaped forward, throwing a grenade through the doorway so that it bounced against the far wall and rolled up the corridor to the left. Almost before the explosion, he was through the door, crouching low, firing. The next man in covered to the right.

Skorzeny was next and last. He looked over his shoulder. A squad had finally caught up with him. Crouching low he went through the door. His two men were half a dozen meters up the corridor, lying on the floor, weapons poised. A dead MP was sprawled in the corridor, blood oozing out from under him.

The long corridor which ran down the main axis of the

building was lined with office doors. Skorzeny motioned his squad in, and pointed down the corridor to the left. "Check each office. If possible, take some prisoners, especially any ranking officers. Marshall is down there. It would be better than Koniev if we bring him out still breathing. Now move it!"

The team started down the corridor, moving swiftly but cautiously. They stopped at the first door, kicked it open and swept in. Empty. Seconds later they were doing the same at the second room, and then the third. At the fourth, a pistol cracked as the door was kicked open, punching the lead man backward. Preceded by two grenades, the others swarmed in, Schmeissers chattering. Then they were back out, the squad leader signaling that there had been only the one man in the room.

Skorzeny snarled with impatience. This was taking far too long. He sprinted back up the stairs, shouted for a second squad to join the one in the basement. Then he went outside. Overhead a gunship was pulling up and banking after a strafing run against the buildings just north of them. Clearly its pilot was intent on wheeling around to do it again.

He spied his radio man. "What's the latest?"

"Y-12's on fire and Radl reports that the reactor is blown. The team is getting set to pull out."

Skorzeny grinned like a wolf. The entire town seemed to be going up in a raging firestorm, the rattle of gunfire sweeping across the hills. If the reactor was blown as well, all that was left for a perfect mission was to finish off K-25, kill the scientists—and get the hell out.

"What's happening at K-25?"

"They're running behind."

Not so good . . . Well, Holzer would do the job or die trying. "What about those fighters?"

"The bomber stream is already into North Carolina. Two have been shot down. It's getting confusing. We're not sure if we have any fighters coming here, or if they are all going after the bombers." That was as it should be. Some of the bombers were supposed to climb and make a high-altitude run-out with the intent of drawing off fighters from the rest of the stream—and also from Oak Ridge itself.

As they spoke, Skorzeny continued to watch the gunship wheeling up out of its strike. Suddenly there was a burst of fire from out of the darkness. The gunship continued its turn, but the tracers followed. Then, ever so gracefully, the gunship's turn tightened so that its wings pointed nearly up and down, and then it started to roll over on its back as it arced into the ground. An instant later it impacted into a hillside, adding its fuel and explosives to the inferno that had become Oak Ridge.

A P-51 fighter came racing in low at barely tree toplevel, and then pulled straight up and disappeared into the darkness. Skorzeny watched it, saying nothing. He looked over at his radio operator, who was gazing up in astonishment.

"Signal back to Gunther that American fighters have arrived, and have him relay it out to the teams. Tell them to get a move on."

Skorzeny waited impatiently while the radio man carried out his instructions. Next he said, "Find out if the reserve bombers are still orbiting."

The radio operator relayed the inquiry and a moment later looked back up at Skorzeny.

"One has been shot down." Clearly the fighters were not equipped with radar; the bombers would be in far worse shape if darkness could not cloak them.

"Tell the team at K-25 to pull out of the building and mark it with flares. Send the rest of the bombers in—wait! Divert one bomber over to the reactor and have it drop its load there."

Even as he turned back into the administrative building he could feel and hear the ripple of explosions and gunfire coming from the basement.

11:45 P.M.

"Get down!"

Jim ducked down behind the barricade of filing cabinets that Marshall had ordered to be piled up a dozen feet back from the door. The cabinets had been knocked over and piled up two high, with traverses laid out dividing the defensive line into half a dozen small cubicles, with more piled up further back into the square room with its forty-foot sides. The scientists who weren't armed were now in the back corner behind a wall of cabinets, with a single Ranger as their final line of defense. Everyone else with a weapon was lined up behind the barricade, barrels leveled toward the door.

Suddenly, to the accompaniment of exploding HE, the heavy steel door was smashed open as by an angry giant's fist. The cabinets that had been set to block it skittered and tumbled into the room and against the far wall. Two commandos flung themselves into the room diagonally left and right, quartering the room with machine-gun fire as they did so. After a split second's shock the defenders opened up, and the two Germans were cut apart by a torrent of fire. A grenade rolled in, coming to rest against the barricade in front of Jim, who ducked down low. The explosion was strangely muffled by the contents of the stuffed file-drawer. For once, all the paper generated by a government agency had served a noble purpose.

Another German tried to come through and was cut apart in turn. Having learned the hard way that a single grenade did not answer their needs, the raiders now sent in a flock of them, some of which arced over the barricade, bursting toward the back of the room. One bounced off the front of Jim's barricade and went spinning into the defensive cubical next to him, where it detonated.

Jim pulled out one of the two precious grenades he had taken from the dead SS officer, pulled the ring at the bottom of the handle, and threw it into the corridor. At the very instant he did so commandos poised outside the now-empty door frame lunged into the room as a follow-up to their own grenade toss. Jim's grenade caught only the two who would otherwise have been last in.

Three more Germans were dropped coming through the door, but the remaining two managed to leap over the barricade, firing their weapons at point-blank range, sweeping the line. A Ranger, using his rifle like a club, smashed one of them down, while one of the scientists managed to drop the other with either a lucky or a well-aimed shot from his forty-five.

Ignoring the action, Jim kept his weapon leveled on the doorway. No one else came through. An MP jumped over the barricade and went up to the door, grabbing the machine pistols from the dead Germans and tossing them back to the surviving defenders. Jim vaguely recognized him as the one who had been awed speechless by Marshall's presence.

Just as Marshall realized his intent and shouted "Don't be a dead hero, boy!" he slipped out the door and kicked one more weapon back through. Then he was down, jerking spasmodically from the rain of bullets that hit him.

"General Marshall!"

The voice echoed from down the smoke-filled corridor.

Marshall remained silent.

"General Marshall!"

It was Skorzeny.

At Marshall's nod, Jim shouted, "What's the matter, Skorzeny? We playing too rough?"

There was a pause.

"Ah, Martel. I was hoping we'd run into each other again, but I didn't expect it to be so soon."

"Come on in, Skorzeny, any time you want!"

"*Mano a mano*, is that it Martel? You know I'd have you; you're no match."

Martel bristled, even though he knew Skorzeny was

right, especially with his shoulder all gummed up.

"Martel. I know Marshall's in there. Also Oppenheimer. Tell the two of them to come out, and I'll let the rest of you go. That's the deal. Otherwise we come in and everyone dies. Take a minute to think it over."

Martel looked at Marshall, who looked like he might be considering it, and shook his head in violent negation. "Sir! The bastard wants all of us," Martel hissed. "You two will be prisoners and then he'll kill the rest of us anyhow. Don't *you* be a hero, sir."

"Is that an order, Commander Martel?"

Martel forced a smile. "Damn right, sir."

"Martel! How about it?"

"You can kiss my ass!"

Skorzeny, crouched down at the edge of the corridor leading into the storage room, looked back at the one surviving member of his assault team. "I need another squad. You go round them up. Then, find the headquarters team. If they aren't still in the field, they're somewhere in this building. Tell Gunther I need more men. Also tell him to find me a couple of Panzerschrecken. Move it!"

Skorzeny looked down at his watch. Time was running out.

11:59 P.M.

Since there had been no possibility of breaking through the Ranger force east of the reactor, what was left of Radl's team had been forced to backtrack north and then pick up the main Oak Ridge turnpike for the run back to their rendezvous. The road was chaos leading to an inferno. Refugees fleeing west to supposed safety clogged both sides of it, leaving only the narrowest possible corridor for traffic heading east, back into the madness. Now eastward movement was grinding entirely to a halt as cars backed up

before the security gate ahead. Frantic, carbine-brandish-
ing MPs were ordering cars off the road. Slowly, one after
the next, each driver was leaning out of the window trying
to make the case that he, if no others, should be allowed to
continue on.

Radl's truck, and the two behind him, contained all that
was left of his team. As the trucks inched forward, Radl
cocked his Schmeisser.

The driver of the car in front of them was approached by
an MP, as another stood with carbine leveled. "My family's
back there, we have a new baby! I've got to get back!" The
screaming argument was brief, being settled by a forty-five
pressed against the temple of the driver. Weeping now, the
man backed the car off to the side of the road.

"Get ready," Radl whispered.

His driver let in the clutch slightly, edging forward.

"All right buddy, who are you?" the MP shouted.

The driver, wearing an American helmet taken from one
of the Rangers back at the reactor, leaned out.

"Reinforcements for the town. Get the hell out of the way."

"My orders are to stop and check every vehicle," the MP
shouted back. "Now get your ass out and let's see your
identification."

"We're ordered to move! Get out of the way!"

The MP shouldered his weapon, pointing it straight at
the driver.

The driver looked sidelong over at Radl.

Radl started to bring his machine pistol up.

"Duck!"

The driver did so as Radl pointed his Schmeisser
straight at the windshield and fired. The glass in front of
him exploded, rounds pocking the pavement. One of the
MPs, firing wildly, shot back and then spun around. Radl
heard his men pouring out of the back of the truck, racing
up to either side, storming the concrete bunkers of the
checkpoint. An American machine gun opened up,
dropping several of the men. Then they had gained the

bunker, shoved in a grenade through the firing slit.

Radl jumped out of the truck and ran across the road, heading for the other bunker. By now civilians were piling out of the cars and running panic-stricken in every direction. A woman slammed headlong into Radl, tripping him, which saved his life as a machine-gun bullet on its way to where he had stood a split second before killed her instead.

Men from the second and third trucks were now out and pouring in fire on the bunker. The position was overrun and the gunfire slacked off.

Radl came back up to his feet, breathing hard. Trembling, in a cold sweat, he leaned over, gasping for breath, and vomited. When the spasming didn't stop he squatted down on the pavement, head lowered. Finally it passed. A cold chill seized him and he started to shake uncontrollably.

"Are you hurt, sir?" asked one of his men.

He looked up, smiled weakly, and shook his head—but when he tried to stand he found he couldn't. He raised his hand and the soldier, filled with concern now, pulled him to his feet. Radl looked around and saw that one of his men was down on his knees, doubled up and vomiting.

"Stephan's sick like you," the soldier said nervously. "A couple others are vomiting as well. Are we poisoned, sir?"

Radl shook his head. "Just a flu or something." He laughed weakly and waved the man off. "Let's move it!" He started back to his truck and then cursed. Steam was billowing out from under the engine, and a pool of water was spreading out underneath. The other two trucks, thank God, were in better shape. All three had been targets of the American fifty-cals, but only his had been subject to prolonged attention.

He looked back at the row of cars that were now backed up in the opposite direction, the remaining drivers and passengers still piling out and fleeing.

"Those who were riding with me, grab those cars! The rest of you, into the trucks."

Radl went up to the truck and pulled the driver's-side door

open. The boy that he had been riding with slumped out, bleeding from the mouth. He was dead. Another wave of nausea hit Radl and bending over he convulsively vomited. With tears in his eyes he gasped for air until the attack passed.

The soldier who had helped him get back up was looking at him, wide eyed.

"Help me to one of the cars," Radl ordered.

Obediently the soldier came up to his side and, putting an arm around him, he half-carried Radl over to a Ford that was sitting in the line of cars, the motor still running.

"We're poisoned, aren't we?" the soldier asked again. "I heard one of the men say that the Americans were running in panic once that building blew up. Am I going to get it too?"

Radl looked over at him and forced a smile. "Don't worry. Tomorrow you will bask in the praise of the Führer himself."

APRIL 21, 12:01 A.M.

"General Groves!"

Leslie Groves looked up at the MP who came in through the door, not even bothering to salute.

"What the hell now?"

"Sir, we just got a report from the east gate. One of the surviving MPs there reports a couple of hundred armed civilians in the area. Most have already just pushed their way through. They're mostly vets wearing their old uniforms. They had organized themselves under a couple of sheriffs and came down when they saw the bombing going on and heard a radio report. I don't know why they had assembled in the first place."

For a moment Groves could only look wonderingly at the MP, then he found his voice. "Get them in here now! I'll meet them on the turnpike!"

"Most are already up in the residential area, sir."

"Bring every man you can find back here. Move it!"

Groves turned back to the Ranger he had been speaking to when the MP arrived. After a few moments they went out onto the street. To the north, up in the residential area, the sound of gunfire still crackled. The reports coming in for the last half hour had numbed him. Nazis, dressed in American uniforms were systematically executing everyone they met. To the south and west he could see the fires from Y-12 and K-25, and confirmation had just come in that the reactor was blown. If the wind shifted to the southwest, Oak Ridge would be a graveyard and the Nazis could spare themselves a lot of trouble. Of course, they'd be dead too. . . .

All outside communication was still down except for one radio link. In the last hour he'd managed to gather a small force, but in spite of the agonized pleas of his civilian police chief and the MPs, he was not sending them up to the civilian living quarters. It was a coldly pragmatic decision: They could perhaps save some middle-echelon people, or they could marshal a counterstrike to retake the administrative building. Oppenheimer, Teller and the others holed up in there were worth far more than all the rest of the personnel combined now that there was a war on. Well, even if not many of those armed locals rendezvoused with him here, maybe they could do at least a little about the atrocities taking place in the residential areas.

An ironic complicating factor suddenly occurred to him. Several of his security personnel, unable to bear the thought of what was happening in the housing complexes, had simply gone AWOL, and were currently engaged in their own private wars. He hoped they would be able to link up successfully with the civilians, even though they and the invaders wore the same uniforms.

He couldn't blame them for caring more about the women and children they saw every day than about a bunch of middle-aged dome-heads from out of state, and part of him was glad they'd "deserted" in a good cause. He'd skin those who survived though.

12:05 P.M.

Richer popped the magazine out of his Luger as he gazed tenderly down at the half-dozen girls he had just talked out of their hiding place and then killed. It had felt so wonderfully good, especially when the extremely pretty one started to cry as, after first forcing them to kneel, he systematically shot her five friends, one after the other. She had looked quite a lot like another girl from Tennessee, but that one had been laughing. This one had not found him so amusing; after she learned what was going to happen to her, she begged to be shot like the rest. With a knife he would never be a failure again.

As he absentmindedly reloaded his pistol he could still feel that delicious chill from gazing into her terror-filled eyes as they finally glazed into nothingness. What a relief to once again be able to give this side of his nature free rein. After the Armistice, even in Occupied Russia his favorite sport had to be practiced in secret, or in the camps. How stupid the law was, Richer thought as he holstered his pistol and walked back out to the street where his personal squad of three waited, looking at him wide eyed.

"Don't approve, Peter?" he asked his radio man. Peter hadn't served with Richer before, and was an odd combination of soft and outspoken.

"Sir, they looked like *gymnasium* girls. No more than seventeen. There was no reason for that. Especially what you did to the last one."

"Hmm. Perhaps you're right. I'll remember that, Peter," Richer said calmly as he sensuously wiped his bloody hand along his trouser leg. It was good for morale for the troops to know you *listened.*

Richer looked down at his watch. The fun was almost over. It was time to order the teams to the rendezvous. From around a corner he saw three figures approaching. "Hey! Come over here!" Richer shouted. He waited.

The three slowed.

"Come on, I don't have all night; get your asses over here!"

"Call in the platoon leaders," Richer said over his shoulder to Peter. "Rendezvous at the command post in fifteen minutes."

The three civilians remained where they were.

Richer unslung his machine pistol and strode briskly in their direction. Ammunition was running low; no sense in spraying them from a distance. Besides, up close was more interesting.

As he was bringing his Schmeisser into line, Richer was suddenly aware of a rifle barrel angling up from hip level. The next instant he felt a terrific punch to the shoulder. He was vaguely aware of two more rifle shots and the deeper blast of a shotgun, followed by the clattering sound of equipment-laden bodies collapsing to the ground, his own and others.

Now a man wearing a US Navy blouse over striped gray pants was staring down at him. "I told you they was Germans, Al," the man dressed as a sailor announced, chambering another round into his rifle. "You could have got us killed, making us wait that way till you were sure."

"You are awful doggoned easy about maybe shootin' Americans, Lloyd," the one addressed replied. "Besides, I had at least a quarter second even after he started swinging that midget machine gun of his around."

Frank, dressed like Al in a US Army jacket with corporal's stripes looked at his cousin unbelievingly. "A whole quarter second. Hell, I guess I could shoot the whole German Army in a whole quarter second, Al." The words were ironic, but the voice was filled with rueful admiration. "Now what we gonna do with this live one?" He pointed the gun straight down at Richer, the muzzle a few inches from his face.

Instinctively, Richer interposed his bloody hand.

"Let's hog-tie him and let him lay," said Al. "The brass is

gonna want some prisoners, and this one's an officer. That's why I was careful not to kill him in the first place. I wouldn't a' killed the other one I got either, except he was farther away and startin' to move," he added apologetically.

Frank laughed. "Well, don't you worry about that, Al. Me 'n Lloyd, we sure as shootin' shot to kill."

"Jesus mercy, come over here!" Lloyd, who had left the cousins to their friendly squabble, shouted.

For a moment Richer was alone. He turned his head slightly and saw the three of them standing off to the side of the road, staring wordlessly at the covey of dead girls, paying special attention to the one he had not shot. Suddenly the sailor turned away from the others and gagged.

A few moments later the three loomed over him again.

He tried to move, rolling up on his right side.

Frank Watson, a sheriff who firmly disapproved of police brutality, kicked him in his wounded shoulder so that he slammed back against the pavement with a keening gasp of pain.

"Monster," Lloyd hissed, bringing his rifle to bear, so that it touched the lashes of Richer's left eye.

"No, wait," said Al. "You know I don't hold with shootin' prisoners of war. Soldiers shouldn't ought to do that to each other. Besides, if we shoot theirs, they'll shoot ours . . ."

Lloyd looked ready to mutiny.

"'Course I don't see any enemy soldiers around here," Al continued, "just this puddle of filth." He gazed straight at Richer. "I'll be scouting a bit. Meet you down by that corner," he said, pointing. Then, with an attempted ironic nod to Richer that was spoiled by the look of loathing he couldn't suppress, Alvin York turned and moved on down the road.

Free at last, Frank knocked Lloyd's rifle away with his shotgun, then centered it on Richer's chest.

Richer, as he was meant to, saw the trigger finger slowly start to tighten.

"Come on fellas," he gasped. "I was just having a little fun. It got a little out of hand, is all. I got excited. You know how it is." The finger relaxed. Lloyd looked at him speculatively, as if trying to imagine what exactly the words he had just heard could mean. The shotgun's muzzle drifted downward.

"Yeah, 'yer right. There ain't nothin' like havin' a little fun," he finally replied thoughtfully, the muzzle having drifted farther yet.

"I wasn't the only one!" Richer's voice was high-pitched as a girl's.

"The other ones didn't have blood on their hands," the sheriff replied, then added calmly, "Now you see if you think this is fun, you Nazi bastard."

They left Richer lying there, his groin a red mass. He was still alive, but he wasn't having any fun.

12:20 A.M.

"Howdy boys. What took you so long?" York called to the other two when they finally found him.

Rather than answer they continued to stare dumb-founded at the array of scattered dead and neatly arrayed living-but-hog-tied Germans on the street before them.

Finally Lloyd looked at him sternly and said, "Alvin, now don't make any jokes and don't tell me any lies. How did you *do* that?"

York smiled modestly. "Well, that's a funny story. . . ."

12:21 A.M.

As the assault team formed up in the corridor Skorzeny

went back to the stairwell and started up. His radio operator was at the top of the stairs.

"What news?"

"We just lost contact with Richer. All hell broke loose on K-25. Three more bombers are down, and the second strike hit the wrong part of the building. Holzer just called in and said the hell with the pickup, he's staying on to finish the job."

Skorzeny nodded. Holzer was the sort to do something like that rather than admit defeat, and his men would follow him to Hell—literally in this case.

While they were talking three men came running up, one with a Panzerschreck, the other two carrying an MG-42 machine gun and ammunition.

"I know you said two, sir," the one in charge said hurriedly, "but we only had one."

"Well, we'll have to make do. Come with me."

"Something else is developing," the radio operator called out before they could leave. "Increased counter-fire coming from the east end . . . reports of armed figures moving this way . . . they just overran our antitank gun and mortar crew blocking the road in."

"You men, downstairs. I will follow you shortly. Wait for me," Skorzeny called. Then, to the radio operator, "All teams are to initiate pullback to the pickup point *now*. Get the intelligence team packed up and out of here. Just ten more minutes here, that's all we need!" Even as he turned and started back down the stairs he heard a sudden increase in firing from outside.

Going back down into the smoke-filled basement he caught up with the Panzerschreck team.

"Give me that," he snapped, and grabbing the shoulder-launched rocket he made his way down the corridor, stopping just short of the turn that led to the storage room.

"Martel!"

"Come on in!"

"Martel, I'm giving Marshall and the rest of you one last

chance, tell him he's got two minutes. Either he comes out or we come in and kill you all."

"We've been waiting for fifteen! What's the matter, getting a little nervous about what happens to people who come through this door, Skorzeny? I'll be real disappointed if you turn coward." Martel laughed sardonically. "Big brave commando faced off by a bunch of desk jockeys! How will *that* read in *Signal*, hah?"

Skorzeny looked back at the fifteen men of his assault team. "Forget the two minutes. It's now. If you can locate Marshall, grab him. Shoot everyone else."

He pulled the safety release on the rocket, hoisted it to his shoulder, and kneeled in the middle of the corridor.

Martel, peering up over the side of the barricade, saw no reason to assume that they actually had two minutes. He looked at the scientists who had picked up the weapons of the fallen MPs and were now on the firing line. Some of them were trembling, but all were as ready as they could be, and needed no admonition.

Suddenly a spear of fire was flung from the end of the darkened corridor. It roared over his head, shrieked the length of the room, and impacted on the far wall with a thunderclap roar. Since a Panzerschreck's shaped charge was designed to penetrate armor, most of this one's explosive force was wasted in blasting a crater into the concrete wall, but enough blew back to fill the room with a cloud of wall fragments and noxious effluvia.

Still groggy from the blast, Martel forced himself up — then ducked back as a heavy machine gun coughed. There were no direct hits, but the rounds ricocheting off the back wall added to the rocket's contribution with a howling blizzard of steel and concrete.

When he realized the machine gun was firing high Martel popped up and tried to return fire, but he was driven back down as the stream of bullets lowered, slashing into the filing cabinets. Some of the rounds finally cut clear through the government red tape to tear apart the men crouched on the other side, and the room echoed with screams of death and terror. Then the machine gun cut off, and half a dozen grenades bounced in.

Martel, arms covering his head, crouched over Marshall as the grenades exploded in a nearly simultaneous roar that was followed up almost instantly by the high-pitched ripping snarl of Schmeissers. Knowing that they must, Martel and Marshall came back up, weapons leveled and firing.

For a short time that seemed very long the room was an inchoate maelstrom of smoke, flames, and stroking flashes of gunfire. Then a flare went off. Suddenly it was brighter than day, and Martel was horrified to see that several Germans had joined them. But three died as he looked while another sprinted across the intervening space and leaped atop the barricade — and then tumbled onto Martel. Marshall grunted in satisfaction as he dropped his revolver and reached over to snag the fallen German's machine pistol. Marshall popped up and fired a burst — then dropped like a sack, his face a bloody mask.

The remaining two invaders were crouched behind the cabinets that had been scattered by the blown door. Marshall was not their only victim, and under cover of their fire five more Germans burst through the door and systematically started to fire at the crowd of scientists huddled behind the secondary barricades. Two of the new intruders fell, but the other three followed up their initial fire with a coordinated rush, leaping atop the first barricade, shooting downward at the remaining armed defenders as they did so.

Momentarily no longer targets, a desperate frenzy took hold of the surviving scientists and they scrambled over their barricade and charged madly forward. Since the three atop the cabinets were otherwise engaged, the disorganized rush was partially effective—several of the unarmed civilians died from the careful covering fire from the two still crouched in the corner, but all but one of the Germans quite literally fell back from the barricade, to be dispatched one after another by armed defenders in what had become a one-sided exchange.

For Martel the action suddenly freeze-framed: the man still standing on the barricade was—

"*Skorzeny!*"

Only when the figure suddenly looked down at him with an expression of joyful recognition did Martel realize he had shouted that name aloud.

"*Martel!*"

As his own weapon swung toward his enemy, Martel saw that the muzzle of Skorzeny's machine pistol had already gone from narrow oval to full circle, and he was staring at his death—or would have been had Skorzeny's Schmeisser not chosen that moment to jam. As Martel's weapon came in line, Skorzeny's foot lashed out quicker than thought, knocking the barrel high, and before Martel could bring it back down, two hundred and fifty pounds of human attack-dog was on him.

Martel was naturally a strong, athletic man—before the age of powered control devices fighter pilots didn't come in any other variety—and since the crash of his Corsair his initially therapeutic weight-training regimen had made him very strong indeed. But he had suffered greatly this night and soon the other's tiger strength had borne him down. Their short, fierce struggle ended with Martel's wounded arm pinned under him and the other in Skorzeny's iron grip—which left one of Skorzeny's hands free to pluck a dagger from his boot.

"Good game, Martel! And now—"

It hadn't been *that* hard a night. With strength amplified by pure desperation, Martel's captured right arm jerked to parry the descending dagger. Rather than pushing through the bridge of his nose and on into the brainpan, the plunging blade merely sliced the side of his forearm to the bone.

As Skorzeny attempted to draw the dagger back for

another stroke, Martel snatched at the German's knife-hand, momentarily immobilizing it as he scrabbled backward with his free arm, trying for leverage, for a roll to the side, for a moment more of life. Then his hand closed on something roughly rounded, warm and metallic. Marshall's discarded forty-five.

By now Skorzeny had jerked his knife-hand free. As he raised himself for a lunging stroke that would never be deflected, his eyes widened in astonishment and he jerked his head aside, almost far enough, as the revolver had its say. With the aid of Skorzeny's convulsive leap the shot flung the German backward against the side of the barricade, where he somehow found the strength to flip himself over it before collapsing, hands clenched to the left side of his face.

Martel stood up, leaned over the barricade, aimed—and as he squeezed the trigger a German soldier leaped between Skorzeny and Martel's pistol, taking for himself the bullet meant for his commander. Before Martel could fire again he was forced back to cover by renewed machine-gun fire that continued for some little time. When next he could look up he saw three black-clad figures stumbling around a corner to the stairway, covered by two more walking backward, machine pistols poised, behind them.

The room was suddenly quiet, except for the cries of the wounded and dying and the crackling of the fires. The entire action had taken perhaps two minutes, his hand-to-hand with Skorzeny no more than fifteen seconds.

Jim peered into the confusion. Skorzeny was nowhere to be found, nor any other living German. Among the defenders only he and a single Ranger remained armed and at least somewhat dangerous.

"Come on!" Jim said to the Ranger, who was standing there dazed. He started for the door. After a moment the Ranger followed. Together they moved cautiously down the corridor, which was carpeted with German dead, the floor slippery with their blood. Coming at last to the corner, Jim nearly lost his footing on the hundreds of shell casings from the heavy machine gun sitting in the center of the hallway.

Thoughtfully, Jim stripped a grenade from a dead soldier. Discovering that his left arm would barely answer, he handed the grenade to the Ranger, who pulled the ring, swung the grenade carefully around the corner without exposing himself, and let fly. After it exploded the Ranger launched himself in a rolling dive across the opening, firing a burst as he did so. When there was no answering fire he rose and motioned for Jim to follow.

They continued down the corridor, passing half a dozen more dead Germans, the Ranger kicking their weapons out of their reach just in case. Finally they came to the gaping doorway leading to the stairs. The door itself lay broken where it had come to rest after being blown off its hinges. Now Jim could see that the opposite wall of the stairwell was shimmering with reflected light from above.

"They're burning us out!" the Ranger gasped. Jim stuck his head through the doorway and looked up. The top of the stairwell framed an inferno.

12:30 A.M.

"Sir, sir! I must!"

Skorzeny forced himself to allow the medic to draw his hands away from what he knew was a terrible wound. When the site was cleared the medic peered at it for a moment, then upended a canteen of water to wash the blood and detritus away. The stream struck like a slashing razor. For a moment he thought he'd faint from the pain, then it ebbed to mere agony. He'd taken four serious wounds in his career, of which the worst had been to his leg. Even that had not hurt, compared to this.

"Sir, let me give you something for the pain. You're out of this one."

"No. I won't be out of this one till it's over, and I can't afford to be stupid. . . . I only have one eye now, right?"

The medic nodded.

"Bandage me up. There's work to be done."

The medic reached into his pack for a pair of medical scissors. There was a brief *scritching* sound of meat being cut away.

"What'd you do?" Skorzeny asked.

"It was hanging out of its socket, sir. There was nothing else to be done."

As the medic pressed a pad against the wound, Skorzeny remained steady and stolid as a rock, but his world went gray as the shattered bones of his cheek grated against each other. The bullet had just touched the left cheekbone; hydrostatic shock had done the rest. Any change at all in angle or position and he would have been as dead as Martel had intended him to be.

Forcing himself back into the world, Skorzeny focused on the burning building on the far side of the baseball field. "Who set the fires?"

"Gunther ordered it. He's the one who pulled you out. He came in to get you and ordered the building fired when the defense perimeter at the other end of the building collapsed. Suddenly the men started dropping dead with no enemy in sight. Then, when somebody said it was Alvin York come for revenge, the rest panicked. Of course there were only three or four alive by then. Sir . . . ? Who was Alvin York? Somebody said he single-handedly killed or captured one hundred and thirty-nine Germans in one afternoon in the last war. But that's impossible."

Skorzeny said nothing. York had been a figure from the Great War of some little interest to him, one of the few individuals of any army worthy, in his limited way, of comparison to himself. He tried to remember the details that had seemed irrelevant at the time . . . Alvin York . . . didn't he . . . ? Yes, he lived in this state. There was no doubt then. Combat soldiers slaughtered as if by sorcery, probably with neat little bullet holes in the centers of their helmets . . . the ones left alive bereft of all nerve . . .

Alvin York had emerged from the mists of legend to screw up his operation with his magic sharpshooting. Life just wasn't fair. Forgetful of his injury, he started to shake his head, until a lightning-flash of pain reminded him. Well, he consoled himself, York or no York, "Manhattan" was *kaput*, and Otto Skorzeny was the one who had done it.

"Where is he?" Skorzeny asked.

The medic hesitated. "Sir?"

"Gunther. Where is he?"

Wordlessly the medic pointed over to the side of the baseball dugout which had served as headquarters. Gunther was stretched out on the ground, looking almost as if he were asleep.

"Just before you regained consciousness a sniper got him." The medic looked around nervously. "Why didn't he kill us, too?"

Skorzeny looked over at the body of his friend and shrugged, saying nothing. There was nothing worth saying. The gallant York had spared a medic and an anonymous casualty with half his face blown away.

A stream of tracers etched a curved line across the field. The remainder of Skorzeny's personal team returned fire. They were all gathered together now, those who were still alive, waiting for the pull-out.

The medic finished tying off the bandage and Skorzeny, waving off the medic's offer of assistance, stood up.

The administrative building was now fully ablaze, adding its light and smoke to the inferno of Oak Ridge. A fighter plane came sweeping in low across the field and then arced back up into the darkness.

"Let's go," Skorzeny announced. "We've finished here."

After two of its members carefully helped Skorzeny aboard, the team loaded itself into a captured truck, taking nothing but weapons and ammunition. As the truck gathered speed Skorzeny took a last look at his friend, and then at the burning administration building.

Bitterly Skorzeny contemplated all the harm that Martel had done him. Without Martel's intervention the operation would have gone flawlessly, As it was—half his force dead, *all* his remaining friends dead. Worse, had he been a little more practiced, or a little luckier, or had a touch more support, Martel might have stopped him cold, in fact had very nearly done so. And Martel was really nothing but a pilot. An amateur had almost defeated the great Otto Skorzeny, and *had* left him a friendless wreck.

As the glow of the Admin building faded behind them, Skorzeny whispered softly, as to an intimate, "Martel, I hope you burn in hell forever, just as you are burning now."

12:45 A.M.

Jim hugged the corridor floor, coughing, struggling to take another breath, wondering what the hell to do. Further down the hallway nearly twenty yards of the corridor ceiling had collapsed. They were cut off, and the fire was coming for them.

Suddenly there was a puffing explosion of hissing steam from the gutted stairway, followed by a slowly building cascade of frothing water. Then, like a disapproving Saint Peter at the Gates of Heaven, General Leslie Groves stood looking down on him, offering reluctant salvation.

"On your feet, Martel."

Martel struggled erect, as did the Ranger.

"Where are the rest?"

"Down the corridor to your right, sir. Can't miss it."

Groves looked at him sharply. "Well get a move on, damn it. The rest of the ceiling is about to cave in!"

Actually there wasn't much for Jim to do, nor for the MPs Jim was suddenly aware stood behind the general. The men he had left in the storage room, the battle room, were now flowing down the corridor toward them. He stepped aside as the first of the scientists staggered unceremoniously through the door and up the stairway, which was clouded in a mixture of steam and damp dark smoke. After the first few had disappeared into the billowing smog, a sort of controlled panic ensued. With no regard for rank at all the crowd of physicists and engineers pushed and shoved its way through, those more or less whole helping their wounded comrades, as well as, to Jim's amazement, a few Germans who had indeed been not quite dead after all.

Physicists. They just couldn't keep track of who the enemy was.

Bringing up the rear was General George Marshall. Groves silently saluted.

Ignoring his fellow general, Marshall said with a grin, "Well Commander Martel, we did it, didn't we? Now let's get out of here. You first this time." With that he gave Jim a friendly shove through the doorway.

Under that five-star impetus Jim ascended to the main landing where a fireman grabbed him by his wounded arm and pulled him along. Manfully resisting the urge to add yet one more to the casualty list, Martel let himself be led outside. The several dozen survivors of the attack, the men who would rebuild "Manhattan," were sprawled on the ground. Except for those nearly comatose from their wounds, all were coughing and gasping from the effects of the smoke. A number of armed civilians carrying an assortment of hunting rifles and shotguns moved among them, offering what aid they could.

One of them, carrying a battered old Springfield and a holstered pistol, offered Jim a hand. About to tell the fellow that he was too busy to rest, Jim suddenly realized he was at loose ends. Looking around, he saw that Marshall had relented and was deep in consultation with Groves. Jim supposed he was once again an onlooker.

"You're pretty beat up," his helper announced. "Let me get somebody to look at you."

"It'll wait. Got anything to drink?"

"You put that bandage on yourself? It looks about ready to come off, and then you'll start bleeding again," the stranger insisted as he reached into his pocket, where he found a pint bottle. "Reckoned someone might have a use for this," he said, smiling. First uncorking it, he passed it over, and Jim took a long, grateful slug of bourbon.

Exhaling mightily, he passed the bottle back. "Good whiskey!" he wheezed. "Strong, anyway. . . . You used to be a soldier? You carry that rifle like you know how to use it."

"Yeah, I was a soldier last time, in Europe," the man replied as he gently took Jim's arm and started rearranging the self-applied rag bandage. "Medic!" he suddenly shouted.

The passing medic paused, assessed, shook his head. "Man, I got people dying here. This one can wait."

"Well, spare me a roll of gauze, okay soldier?"

The corporal shrugged and tossed him one.

Without comment, the civilian pulled out a hunting knife and cut through the rags around Jim's arm, cut off the sleeve of his shirt, and slit the yoke so that the shoulder was exposed as well.

"Belleau Wood?"

"Huh?"

"We were talking about where you saw service," Jim said.

"Oh. Uh . . . yeah. And the Argonne. And other places." Carefully he tied off the bandage on Jim's forearm and began the more complex task of cleaning and bandaging the shoulder, continuing the conversation as he did so. "Now, I'm a sheriff a ways up the road. I was here visiting my cousin. He's a sheriff too. We heard on the radio about the bombing, and we could see it, so we came on down. As a matter of fact we'd gotten this strange phone call an hour or so before, so we'd already organized some vets."

He hesitated and looked back at the firestorm consuming the town to the north. "I reckon we done some good," he said quietly. "Not nearly enough, but some." Finishing up the rough field dressing, the normally teetotaling sheriff paused to take a sip from the bottle, corked it, and handed it back to Martel.

Martel did not comment on the phone call, merely said, "Well, my friend, you sure saved me from getting cooked —and see those guys on the lawn, the ones in civvies? By saving them you just might have saved your country. And here's to you." As he took another slug of whiskey, Martel again noticed Marshall and Groves, still conferring as they walked toward a jeep. A major and a captain hovered nearby, close enough to take and relay orders without interfering in their talk.

Suddenly, as if telepathic, Marshall swiveled his head and, gazing directly at Martel, gave a small peremptory gesture that brought Jim to his feet. Taking a final slug, Martel nodded his thanks to the civilian, handed him back his bottle, and returned to work. As he was leaving he turned and said, "By the way, I'm Jim Martel. What's your name?"

"York. Sheriff Alvin York. Pleased to meet you, Jim Martel."

Nodding, Jim turned away. There was something about that name. . . .

"Commander!" Marshall called as Jim approached. "They're withdrawing toward the new airstrip. They must have some planes landing there. I'm trying to get word to those fighter planes overhead but it's absolute chaos. They can't see the strip, and so far we haven't been able to organize a force to punch through and light it up. Plus our only communication is through a single phone line running through Knoxville. We're looking for some ham radio operators, but with Oak Ridge in flames we're having to look pretty far afield. Damned security radios won't talk to the damned fighter-plane radios. Do you believe that? Well by God it's going to change, but for the moment all we can do is go after the Germans the old-fashioned way. We're heading down there now to try and cut them off."

While they were talking Groves had climbed into the jeep and turned the ignition. Without waiting to be asked, Martel climbed in behind him, leaving shotgun for Marshall. When Marshall was aboard Groves pulled out and the jeep began to travel on the road that ran southwest parallel to the open field behind the administrative building. Behind them, six truckloads of armed men pulled into line.

"Sir! Pull over here for a second!" Martel shouted.

"What now, damn it?" Clearly, though he could hardly admit it, Groves had seen enough of Martel for one day, or one lifetime for that matter.

"That Piper Cub. Please pull over to it. I have an idea. Just take a second."

"We don't have time for your bullshit, Martel. Just because—"

"Pull over, General Groves," Marshall interjected flatly.

Without a word, General Groves did as ordered.

Martel climbed out of the jeep and ran over to the Cub's side, while the convoy waited impatiently. He came back a minute later. "I met that Piper" — Christ, was it only yesterday? — "It had a radio. I just managed to get into direct contact with the military in Knoxville. They're relaying the information up to the fighters. At least I hope they will."

12:47 A.M.

"Here comes the X-10 team!"

Skorzeny turned and saw several autos and two trucks leaving the road and coming straight at the airstrip. That had to be Karl; the survivors of the Y-12 team and Richer's group had already come in, and the K-25 team wouldn't be coming in at all. Those who had come in had boarded the first three transports, which were already lined up on the runway. The only thing that remained to be done after loading Karl's people would be to set the triggers on the thermite grenades in the planes that were being abandoned because there were no passengers for them. With any luck that would prove quite diverting for the frustrated Mustang pilots ghosting around up there.

Skorzeny looked over at his anxious radio operator who had just overheard a contact between the American fighters and someone who was all too near to their own location. Whoever it was had the German take-off plans down pat, and so now the fighters did too. Indeed, as he was digesting this a fighter came streaking in, but it was flying by dead reckoning; its machine guns plowed a furrow parallel to the landing strip, and it disappeared into the night.

Had that furrow been on the other side of the strip—the two trucks and several commandeered autos had come to a halt and men started to scramble out of the vehicles when the Mustang interrupted the process. Now they were crawling out from under the trucks and from behind the cars. Several of them were moving slowly, walking with strange shuffling steps. One of them collapsed as Skorzeny watched. A familiar form began to slowly and painfully extract itself from the lead auto.

"Karl!" Skorzeny trotted toward him, but Radl held his hand up.

"Don't come near me."

Skorzeny slowed.

"We're dead men, Otto. The reactor blew with us right next to it. Maybe some of the men were far enough away, I don't know." He leaned forward, vomited a black gush of blood.

Gasping, Radl looked back up. "Get my boys who are still mobile out of here. Maybe some will live."

"Come on Karl, we're going home."

Radl weakly shook his head.

Probing fire, originating a hundred yards or so down the access road, burst out of the night. The security team answered it.

"We were trailed! Get out of here!" Radl paused to

vomit again. His next words came out in a muttered gargle. "We'll hold them back. Let your men" — Karl waved toward the security team—"Fall back to the planes."

Skorzeny looked at his oldest friend, a man who had been with him from the very beginning, before war had made of him . . . what he had become. For the first time in a decade he let emotion overcome reason, and stepped forward, arms outstretched.

But his friend staggered backward: "I'm covered with the stuff. Touch me and you'll get it too!"

Skorzeny felt restraining hands grabbing him from behind.

Radl looked up at him, smiling wanly. Then, as ever doing his job, he added a distraction. "Looks like you picked up a hell of a scar this trip, Otto."

Another burst from out of the darkness tore up the ground less than a meter away, but Skorzeny didn't move.

"Good-bye Karl," he whispered.

The medic, still holding Skorzeny, tugged gently at his elbow. Finally he let himself be turned. Tears blinding his one eye, he followed the medic back toward the waiting planes. Walking backward, firing into the gloom, the security team fell back with him.

Skorzeny climbed into the plane waiting first in line, its engines howling at the delay. As the medic entered behind him and slammed the door, Skorzeny climbed up to the cockpit and sat in the jump seat behind the pilot.

"Go."

Instantly the pilot simultaneously released the brakes and hit the ignition button for the rocket-assisted-take-off packs. The plane leaped forward, twin tongues of fire jetting out from beneath the wings. Save for a single faint flare at the end, the runway was pitch black, the pilot steering by feel, while the copilot shouted off the rapidly building airspeed.

"One hundred and sixty!" the copilot roared, and both he and the pilot pulled back on their yokes. There was a jarring blow as the bottom of the plane struck something. Skorzeny waited for the impact, but they kept climbing. Then came the twin thunks as the spent rocket packs were jettisoned. Skorzeny signaled for the pilot to bank the plane hard to port so that he could study the inferno he had created.

In the middle of the turn the pilot shouted, "Plane Two is taking hits!" Skorzeny peered out the portside window. The second transport, its rocket packs still firing, was being laced by a stream of tracers coming in from its starboard side. Suddenly it fireballed. Seconds later the third plane burst through the conflagration, still climbing. A moment later its rocket packs flamed out and it was shrouded in blessed darkness.

The fourth plane, the one carrying the survivors of Radl's team, never left the ground. The fire from a P-51 caught a wing during take-off, and the transport tilted over and pinwheeled down the runway, finally exploding in a smeared fireball that was answered in counterpoint by the timer-fused thermite grenades inside the planes abandoned for lack of passengers. Plane after plane exploded in flames, though not with the fully fueled enthusiasm of those with men aboard.

As the plane finished its turn and followed the Clinch River north, Skorzeny looked down upon the visible evidences of his visit. Though few who followed him here were returning home, still he had won a famous victory. Next year on Victory Day they would sing of it, and him.

12:58 A.M.

Karl Radl watched as the plane carrying his men exploded in a blinding flash. Perhaps it was a mercy, he thought. Perhaps for all, certainly for many. There was a sporadic flurry of shots over by the trucks as the last of his doomed and dying rear guard collapsed, from weapons fire or nuclear poisons he wasn't sure. With a sigh of release he allowed himself to slide down the side of the car he had been leaning against, dropping his weapon as he did so. Strangely, the awful burning inside had become a warming glow, as if the invisible fire that had entered him had consumed all there was to consume, and was flickering down to a final charred ember.

"Here's another one!"

Radl looked up. Interesting. The stars were still out, the Moon—yes that was the Moon—was high overhead.

"He's still alive . . . sort of."

Someone was blocking the light and he wanted to protest but the words somehow wouldn't come.

Words were being spoken. English. Yes, he could speak English . . . or could he? Not just now, perhaps. How odd. He could understand it, but he couldn't remember how to speak it.

"Who are you?"

The other replied in German. Good. It was soothing to hear one's own language, here at the end. In gratitude he responded by looking up. The face before him flickered and glowed from the light of the funeral pyre of 264s on the runway.

"Radl—aren't you Karl Radl?"

"Yes . . . how do you know me?" Radl asked, using the intimate form, as if speaking to a friend.

"Jim Martel, American Navy. We met on Victory Day."

Radl smiled. "Victory Day . . . day of victory. Whose victory? Not mine. Not even Otto's, this time."

"Skorzeny. Where is he?"

Radl nodded to the airstrip.

"He got away, he always does. He always does."

He saw Martel leaning down, reaching toward him.

"Don't, and I speak as a friend. I'm dying from radiation, a very great deal of radiation. Don't, or you'll die too." Martel drew away.

Radl laid his head back, trying to see the stars just once more. But there was nothing there now, only darkness, and then, finally, a soft gentle light. He imagined himself moving toward it.

1:05 A.M.

Martel rose from Radl's side. As he stood, he realized that Marshall was standing at his side.

"What did he say?" Marshall asked.

"Skorzeny's alive. They got away."

"Well, that doesn't matter now," Marshall said. "It's what happens next, and what we do, that matters now."

Jim Martel turned and looked back at the fire that seemed now to spread from horizon to horizon, filling all the world, and all the future as well.

INTERLUDE

2:35 A.M.
Knoxville Airport

Lieutenant Commander James Mannheim Martel and General of the Army George Catlett Marshall were pressed gently back into their upholstered seats as the DC-3 that had been commandeered for their use lifted off from the Knoxville airport.

"Wondering why I dragged you along, Commander Martel?"

Jim hadn't really been wondering about much of anything. So much had happened to and around him in the last twenty-four hours that he was just observing without judgment. In his hypoadrenalized condition a surprise trip in an overloaded helicopter, followed by a quick transfer to an executive aircraft hardly counted as interesting.

"I figured you would tell me, sir."

"We'll be seeing the President this morning."

"Sir?"

"Do you recall the story of Saul of Tarsus?"

"Yes, sir, I do," Jim replied, puzzled. "I'll probably get this wrong, but as I recall, on the road to Damascus, Jesus appeared to Saul, saying, 'Why do you persecute me so?' Saul was so impressed he changed his name to Paul. Changed his whole way of thinking, too . . . Oh."

"Well, I'm not about to change my name, but my 'whole way of thinking' has just undergone a major shift. Listening to the dome-brains gathered in Oak Ridge was part of it, that and realizing just where we would be without them. Another part was watching you and Skorzeny—"

Jim snarled unconsciously at the name.

"—in action. Almost like mirror images of each other, but both so very good at what you do. Him as a super-commando, you as a superb improviser in an impossible situation, countering his every move, almost stopping him cold. But the clincher was realizing that we are in a de facto state of war with a power that makes the Japanese Empire at its height look like a Gilbert and Sullivan threat."

Jim, who would bear the scars of the Great Pacific War to his grave, was not pleased at this demeaning of a fierce and powerful enemy, but he took the General's meaning.

Marshall looked at Jim speculatively. "What chance do you think an unbiased oddsmaker would give us in the coming fight, Commander? One in three? Two in five?"

Jim shrugged. "We always start behind, sir. It's a national tradition by now."

"Not this far, Commander. Not this far." Marshall shifted in his seat, leaned his head back and closed his eyes. He was silent for long enough that Jim began to wonder if he had gone to sleep, but apparently he was merely gathering his thoughts.

"When I spoke to the President, your name came up, probably because Donovan was with him. I recommended you for the Medal of Honor."

Jim's eyes flew open.

"But never mind that now."

"Uh . . ."

"It turns out you're not just a hotshot pilot and fast on your feet, but an acute technical military theoretician as well."

"Me, sir? I've thought about things a bit—"

"You're trying to tell me your father really wrote the piece in *Defense Review Quarterly* on 'Carrier Reaction Times and the Jet Threat'?"

"Er . . . he had a big hand in that one, sir."

"How about the one on airborne radar-vectoring?"

"That one was pretty much mine."

"The one on aircraft as 'weapons platforms'? 'Stand-off and Deliver' was the title, as I recall."

"Guilty as charged, sir, except for the title."

"Right, I just wanted to be clear. Not that the job you did wouldn't qualify you for a spot on my team anyway. I can always use somebody fast and brave and smart, someone who isn't afraid to talk back but usually doesn't. But those articles that got you in so much trouble . . . did you know I'm familiar with them? Irritating as the devil, a couple of them. But even the ones that I disagreed with at the time I now see to have been spang-on. I'm told that your analyses of German weapons while in Berlin also had that intriguing/irritating, spang-on quality. That makes me interested in you on a whole different level. In a Saul of Tarsus kind of way, if you see what I mean."

"No sir, I'm not sure I do."

"Hmph. Maybe I've left a few steps out. Look, I don't suppose the whole thing really came to me in a flash last night as I watched X-10 head for the stratosphere — the notion is too detailed and polished for that—but I do have a new model — a new paradigm — on how a modern democratic state should organize itself to make a surge-effort in war. This is radical stuff, Jim, and I'm going to need a cadre of thinkers, thinkers, who can take my ideas and run with them and build on them. And that's why I'm dragging you along to Washington."

"Sir, I'm all ears."

"In a nutshell, I want to, as it were, give them an unlimited charge account, and toss them into Macy's Department Store."

"Sir?" Then Jim recalled the joke about every woman's dream and nodded politely for the General to go on.

Marshall paused in thought. "By that I mean, give them the greatest possible freedom to shape the very goals they pursue . . . or to put it yet another way, to *call* the shots, not just make them. Consider: We won the Great Pacific War as fast as we did by assembling first-rate teams without regard for the organizational provenance of the team members. Then we set them goals and arranged things so that they could charge forward full-bore, with no bottlenecks, or bureaucratic jerks, or surprise budgetary constraints allowed to get in the way. That was enough to whack Japan pretty good. It wasn't really a contest except in the very short run."

"Not after Midway," Jim agreed.

"This time, this time will be different. The Germans have plenty of industrial depth — and a truly wicked immediate military potential." Marshall paused for a moment. "We could lose, you know."

Jim nodded grimly. Down deep he couldn't really integrate that idea — after the invariable rough start, America won, always—but intellectually it was awfully easy to paint a victorious Nazi scenario.

"It may seem I'm being unfair to you, Commander Martel, since you saved your country once today already—"

"Sir, I was just one man. If any of us, you included sir, had failed in his duty, to say nothing of York and his militiamen, we would have saved nothing."

"Entirely true, Commander. But you and only you saw the truth and acted on it. Without your 'interference' every one of us who was at Oak Ridge last night would be dead this morning." Marshall paused, seemingly at a loss for words, then added, "Lieutenant Commander Martel, I am not by nature a person given to over-familiarity, and in fact I regard this modern instant-intimacy as deplorable. Yet that said, I do wish you to understand that while it may not seem so, I am very much aware that without your efforts both in general and particular, I would have met my Maker around 10:15 last night."

Jim in his turn was puzzled for a response that was neither fatuously self-deprecatory nor presumptuous. God forbid that he should seem "overly familiar"! Yet to tell the General that there was nothing personal in what he'd done, while true, did not seem to quite fit the moment either. He settled for what he hoped was an encouraging nod.

"Well then, as long as we understand each other, we can

continue," Marshall said rather more brusquely than he'd probably intended. "Furthermore, and more to the point, Groves tells me that without the scientists and engineers he wouldn't have any idea how to go about restarting Manhattan. The Nazis would have had time to build dozens, hundreds of atomic bombs before we produced our first, and that would have been the end of us. Thanks to you we're still in the race. Behind, but still in the race."

Jim wasn't at all happy at the notion that if it hadn't been for his entirely fortuitous intervention the United States wouldn't stand a chance in the coming war. He knew well enough that sometimes one man did make the difference —Civil War buffs generally agreed that the untimely death of Stonewall Jackson from friendly fire had doomed the South, for example — but he didn't like it. What if he'd failed?

Seeing that Jim had nothing to say, Marshall continued. "As I was saying, it may be unfair to ask you to save your country two days running, but there it is."

"Sir," Jim said carefully as he composed his thoughts, "if I understand you, you are telling me that watching me has led you to radical ideas for winning the war. Industrial-organizational ideas I assume, since that is your forte. Then you tell me that this inspiration consists of throwing our best and our brightest into some upscale department store with unlimited charge accounts."

"Macy's, I believe I said," Marshall corrected.

"Yes, sir. And then you tell me that not only did I and I alone save my country from utter disaster yesterday, but that I must do so again today. Frankly, sir, I'm having a little trouble digesting all this."

Indeed he rather marveled at the General's resilience. All that mortal peril and physical stress, and the only outward sign was a certain quirkiness. Of course Marshall hadn't already been through the mill once when the bombs started falling, Jim consoled himself.

Marshall grinned. "I can see you're tiring, Commander,

so I'll give you the short-course version now, and let you catch forty winks. Last time out we took the people we thought could perform, gave them specific goals, gave them everything they needed to meet those goals, and then got ourselves and everybody else out of the way. This time we'll do the same—except we will go one step further: the very best of them will set their own goals."

8:00 A.M.
Washington, D.C.

"Martel, you look like hell," Donovan said pleasantly as he personally ushered Jim into his office.

Jim forced a half-smile. Without, as far as Jim could tell, saying a word, Marshall had somehow arranged for fresh uniforms to be waiting for them when the plane set down, but he still bore the evidences of a very hard night, nor had he had a chance to do more than splash water on his face when he switched into the uniform.

"Nah, let's sit over here," Donovan said, gesturing to an arrangement of a worn but solid leather couch with facing easy chairs and coffee table. "You get any sleep on the way up?"

Jim nodded. "Some. An hour maybe." He allowed himself a sigh as the easy chair took the burden. "Marshall and I talked for a while. Then I fell asleep, but they woke me up to take out some bits of this and that."

Donovan looked a question.

"I was a little too close to a grenade that lost its temper. Among other things. I wouldn't mind a chance to take a shower."

"Well, in this line of work there are days like that—at least one per customer. But I'm afraid you can't stand down quite yet. In two hours we're meeting with the President."

"General Marshall told me about it. Said I'm supposed to be there. Frankly I'm too damned tired to be as impressed as I should be." After the surgical procedure he and Marshall had spent the rest of the flight deep in conversation.

Donovan looked at Martel speculatively. "Tired or depressed?"

"Both, maybe. I knew something bad was coming, knew it from the beginning, and I didn't stop it."

"How do you think I feel, Jim? Or the President? You were one man, totally untrained for the situation. For us, the failure is much, much deeper, and I promise you we feel it. While you, in the face of ridiculous blindness and resistance, saved all you could. You should be proud, James Martel."

To the extent that he could feel any emotion right now, such praise from this man left Martel uncomfortable. Besides, it was a crock. He'd run through the situation a hundred times in his mind on the way back, and had seen a dozen places where with just a little more brains he could have nailed Skorzeny cold. If he'd just been a little firmer with Johnson, for example, or had quietly withdrawn with Wayne, rather than try to go one-on-one in the woods with Germany's top commando. That last thought left him more wretched than ever. He'd as good as killed his best friend. Dragged him from the loving arms of his true love and thrown him to the wolves. God, how would he ever be able to face that young woman? He hadn't even met her — he hadn't wanted to deal with people, even a friend like Wayne, after the FBI let him go.

After looking at Martel closely Donovan added, "Jim, it won't improve your mood to tell you things will look better after you've had some rest. But consider this: at this very moment Otto Skorzeny is cursing you as the man who ruined the culminating operation of his life."

Jim shrugged indifferently. The more he thought about it, the more he was certain that stampeding everyone into taking up a defensive position in a cellar had been less than brilliant. What if the enemy had simply called in an air strike, as it had done so effectively against the fabricating facilities? Contrary as it ran to instinct, they should simply have scattered, maybe with a screening force of whatever size they could manage fighting a delaying action. True, he had taken notice when Marshall pointed out that the bombers were scrupulously avoiding the administration building, but still it had just been dumb luck that Skorzeny & Co. had found the combination of records and scientists so tempting a target that—he shook his head angrily.

Donovan tried another tack. "C'mon, Martel, in three, maybe four hours you can cry in your beer if you want to, but you're not done yet. And this next part may be the most important of all."

Jim stirred. From earliest youth he'd been taught that duty's call must always be answered. "What do you mean?"

"I mean that General Marshall is about to attempt to convince the President that to beat the Germans we need to create a new paradigm of national R & D and production. You're part of the presentation."

"Hey, the General told me to be there, but just as an observer, an aide or something."

Seeing that Martel was safely re-engaged, Donovan snickered. "Oh, you poor, fair-haired boy."

Alarmed enough to momentarily forget his depression, Martel asked, "Why me? What do I have to offer on their level? I'm a pretty good analyst, a fair pilot—and I've just proved I'm a piss-poor field operative. How does that qualify me for anything but taking notes at a meeting like this?"

"Try any of that false-modesty crap where we're going and they'll hand you your head. Like the General no doubt told you, what you were was *right*. Everywhere we look, you called the shots as you saw them, and you saw them the way they turned out to be. That makes you New Paradigm Exhibit Number One." Donovan grinned. "I might also add that for some folks that makes you real obnoxious to have around. For example, I hear that General Groves just loves you to itty bitty pieces."

The third time Martel opened his mouth to speak and nothing came out, Donovan laughed again as he checked his watch.

"But wait! There's more!"

"More *what*?"

"More fun for me, watching you," Donovan replied as he touched a buzzer on his desk. "Dave—"

"Yes, sir?" said the box next to the buzzer.

"Send her in, will you?" In response a door on the far side of Donovan's office opened, and a beautiful woman entered, hesitantly, as if unsure of her welcome.

"What the hell . . . ?" Jim whispered. "What are you doing here? And where were you when I—"

"When you needed me?" Betty McCann asked sadly, as she approached.

Jim nodded mutely.

"I know how it must have seemed to you. I wanted to follow you back to the States, but—"

Jim could only look at her, his mind a whirl of emotions. He had given her up and even managed to wish her well. But he'd been hurt, savagely hurt, he now realized, by the way she'd left him to fend for himself after his run-in with the Bureau. Now —

As the two of them stood there, motionless, speechless, not touching, Donovan thought it might be time to intervene. "Why don't the two of you sit down — no, together there on the couch, of course," he added when Jim made to take the easy chair opposite the one Donovan had been sitting in.

When the three of them were settled, Jim and Betty rather stiffly, Donovan went on. "I felt really bad about it, Jim, but just as it was important for you to stay in the doghouse with the Navy, so that if anybody was watching you they wouldn't twig that somebody might be listening to you, we thought it was important that you also seem to be abandoned by your girlfriend. If you weren't even able to convince her you were clean, then they had nothing to worry about. Anyway that's how I saw it."

"You could have just told me," Martel replied with an expression that was not quite a snarl.

"You were just an anonymous pawn, Jim. Who knew how you would react? It isn't easy to hide joy. The whole point was to try to make the other side believe we all bought it about the leak being at the Embassy and not in Washington. It was better for you to be crushingly depressed."

"And he made it stick, too, the rat," Betty added, trying to smile. "Two of his goo—er, operatives were waiting for me at Templehof when I—"

"Yep," Donovan interrupted. "About three weeks after your big day with Grierson, Betty tried to jump ship. She'd grabbed a bunch of documents she thought would exonerate you and was headed in your direction. Lucky for her my boys were the ones looking over her shoulder; some of that paper was classified. She knew it, and didn't care. She was ready to risk time in the slammer just to make you look good. Don't let her get away, Martel, or you're a fool."

"My husband-to-be is not going to be ruined just so that the FBI can shovel their mistakes under a rug," Betty said defensively.

Though she was joking, suddenly Jim realized that their running gag about his career prospects was not entirely a joke to her. That his perfect, perfect angel had such a human foible warmed him even more. The last of the ice melted.

Donovan continued. "Anyway, my boys accompanied her on her plane ride—and brought her to me instead of to you. So I told her what was what, and why she—and you— had to wait, and sent her back to Berlin. Trevor made a couple of adjustments in her folder that made it look like she had merely taken a little accumulated vacation, so she was in the clear. Except Acres got a little too curious, so we had him reassigned to the Pentagon. He still thinks it was on account of you, which it was in a way." Donovan laughed. "Since the only guy I had available to send in was a field operative, it was a good thing that Betty had been doing most of Acres's job all along."

"So now maybe she can have the recognition as well as the work?" Martel asked dryly. The disparity between what his girl accomplished and what she got in return had bothered him since before she was his girl. She was the kind who should be giving orders—and at a very high level —not taking them.

"Well, I certainly recognize her," Donovan said, "and the guy I sent in pretty much took her orders and passed them on, so he must have recognized her too. If you're talking about suffragette stuff, I basically agree with you, but you're in the wrong department to get anything done about it. We're at war and I'm in charge of covert ops."

Martel nodded, sorry he'd brought it up.

"But that's only the beginning of the Betty story: you want to hear the rest?"

"Of course," Martel said quietly. "If there's time."

Donovan glanced at his watch again. "Barely. Anyway, on April 19th Betty jumped another plane at Templehof. Care to guess why?"

Martel raised an eyebrow, hoping that would be enough.

"Because," Donovan continued obligingly, "of your cousin Willi."

"What?"

"Sometimes the oddest coincidences turn out crucial," said a man who'd had his share of experience in that line. "You recall the time you and Willi were setting up a meet, and Betty happened across you while she was shopping?

"Yeah. What a pain. Acres had a kitten."

"Well, be glad it happened. Willi had a message to pass on, and he knew there was a major leak Stateside, and that it was as much as his life was worth to communicate through the Embassy. The only person he was sure he could trust was you. You, that is, and your secret fiancée who only he knew was your fiancée. Apparently as far as your cousin was concerned, Betty was already family."

Betty blushed prettily. So did Martel. Donovan grinned.

"It seems," Donovan continued, "that Willi spent a full week lurking outside, and finally caught Betty on another shopping expedition."

"I didn't recognize him at first," Betty interjected. "I thought he was trying to pick me up. If he hadn't looked so worried I'd have given him the brush-off."

"Well, thank God you didn't," Donovan said. "Because the message he gave you will win the coming war for us—if we win — and if you had refused to speak to him we wouldn't have gotten it."

"'Look for Otto Skorzeny on an airfield from thirty to one hundred and fifty miles east-northeast of Manhattan,'" Betty said. "What it meant was as much a mystery to Willi as to me. Why would Skorzeny be running around Long Island Sound? When I told him, Mr. Donovan seemed to be able to make something of it, though. I thought he was going to arrest me."

Donovan grinned. "Well, I was a little excited for a minute there."

"So you called Harriman, and he told me and Wayne to check every airfield within one hundred and fifty miles of Oak Ridge. And we did. And there he was." Jim shook his head wonderingly, then looked rueful as he turned back to Betty. "And I thought you'd dropped me."

His gaze held hers for a long moment. Basking in the warmth he was now feeling made him begin to realize just how cold his world had been without her. Their hands touched, clung.

The main door to Donovan's office opened slightly and an aide peered in. "Sir? They're here."

Donovan nodded. "Ask them in." Then, turning his attention back to Betty and Jim, he said with mock severity, "Let go of each other, you two. Time to get to work."

Donovan got up from his desk and moved toward the door as two men entered.

One Jim instantly recognized. He didn't know the other but he rose eagerly to seize Congressman Brian McDonnell's outstretched hand.

"Well Martel, you've certainly managed to insert yourself in the middle of things—and from what your boss here's been telling me, it's a damned good thing you did."

"Thank you sir."

"By the way, I took the liberty of calling your dad to let him know you were in that scrap last night, and that you're okay — but from the look of you, I think I may have reassured him a bit more than was strictly accurate."

"I'm glad you did, sir. It'd be like him to put two and two together and figure out where I was and who I was playing patticake with. His heart being the way it is, I don't want him to start worrying."

McDonnell, old friend of the family, nodded acknowledgment and found a seat.

"Uh, sir, I'd like you to meet Betty McCann. My . . . fiancée."

McDonnell leapt back up. "Delighted!" Turning to Martel, "She's obviously much too good for you, you know."

Martel said in all seriousness, "Yes, sir, I do."

"I am not," Betty replied, pretending to continue McDonnell's joke, "I'm just right for him."

As he gestured at the visitor who had entered with him, Donovan said to the congressman, "I gather you and Kelly have met?"

"Committee meetings," McDonnell said succinctly, then added, "Jim, this is Kelly Johnson. He's a designer with Lockheed."

"Kelly, meet James Martel."

Jim was more than a little impressed. Though still a relatively young man, Kelly Johnson was already something of a legend.

"Kelly and I have worked together before," Donovan

said. "When General Marshall explained what he has in mind to present to the President, I figured he'd be just the man to have sit in." Obscurely to all but Jim, he added, " . . . as Exhibit Two. He's been in town reviewing OSS files on German aircraft design, so I grabbed him."

Betty, Martel and Johnson sat themselves on the leather couch. Donovan and McDonnell took the facing easy chairs. After a bit of shuffling they all took steaming mugs of coffee from a tray that an aide brought in.

While they settled, Donovan looked at the GI clock on the wall, then unconsciously checked it against his watch. "In an hour and a half we leave for the White House. Jim, before then I'd like you to go over exactly what you and Marshall talked about. I've heard the gist of it already, but maybe I'll get some new insight. And for the Congressman, Kelly and Betty, this will be their first time through. If we're going to help in this we need to get our ideas in synch."

Jim hesitated.

"Don't worry, Jim. First off, General Marshall and I have already spoken about all this. Secondly, he understood when he spoke to you last night that you work for me. Thirdly, we are all of us—" He gestured broadly to include the group sitting before him " — on the same team. Marshall's team, really. Or maybe the President's if this works out as the General intends."

McDonnell stirred slightly. "Bill, as it happens I too have spoken with George Marshall this morning. That's why I'm here. And while I may not be on the General's 'team,' or the President's, you may rest assured that I find his ideas on a national surge of creative and industrial strength most intriguing, and that if I too find this coming presentation persuasive, I plan to support them in every way I can."

Donovan paused for a moment at the not-quite-rebuke, then said, "Point taken, Congressman. My apologies if I seemed . . . presumptuous."

McDonnell waved the matter away.

Though horrified at the prospect of bringing Donovan up

short a second time, still Jim hesitated. Marshall hadn't explicitly authorized him to repeat their private conversation, and—as he looked from the head of OSS to the Chairman of the Armed Services Committe he realized he was being ridiculous. If they'd said they'd talked to Marshall, they'd talked to Marshall, and Donovan was his boss.

"Yes, sir," he said simply.

"As soon as you have briefed us all, we'll try to brainstorm for a while. That ought to leave us with just enough time for you to grab that shower, which you do need. . . ."

Jim looked over at Betty and smiled a bit sheepishly.

Suddenly Donovan seemed struck by a thought. "Betty, do you take shorthand?" he asked.

"Yes, but it's not what I do, not anymore," Betty replied, a little taken aback at the question.

"Perhaps just this once," Donovan responded cryptically.

The Oval Office

Moments after the receptionist spoke into the box on her desk, John Mayhew appeared at the door and gestured for Donovan's group to enter. As they filed in they saw that the President was not alone. On three of the nearby easy chairs were seated George Marshall, his arm in a sling, Douglas MacArthur, and Bill Halsey. Apparently the four of them had been deep in conversation for some little time. There were also two secretaries seated at a desk in a far corner taking notes,

Harrison rose, smiling. "Brian!" As political protocol and wisdom demanded, he spoke first to the Chairman of Armed Services. "Good of you to join us on such short notice. General Marshall promises me you'll be glad you did, though."

"I'd have bought a ticket, Mr. President," McDonnell assured him. "This promises to be historic."

"That's what George tells me," Harrison agreed. "Bill, I suppose this must be Commander Martel, but perhaps you could introduce your other friends to me?"

"Mr. President, may I present Kelly Johnson of Lockheed, and Miss Elizabeth McCann, who until recently was for all practical purposes in charge of military intelligence at our Berlin Embassy."

Only a lifetime in politics allowed Harrison to maintain a look of polite friendliness as he absorbed this rather astounding assertion while gazing upon the twenty-seven-year-old girl before him. He did allow one eyebrow to raise a trifle.

"A peculiar set of circumstances, sir. Miss McCann was Administrative Assistant when the man in charge was suddenly recalled. Because things were rather . . . strange just then, I thought it best not to rock the boat."

The President was intrigued. "And how is it that you have just now returned, Miss McCann? Awfully lucky for you, I must say."

"More than luck, sir," Donovan answered for Betty. "She took it on herself to hand-carry a vital piece of information. The final piece of the puzzle that allowed us to locate Skorzeny."

The President winced at the name. "In that case, Miss McCann, you are very welcome indeed."

Normally unflappable, Betty for once was overwhelmed. She could only smile and nod.

"And Mr. Johnson?"

"He builds airplanes. I very much hope his role here will shortly be made clear."

The President shrugged. "Very well. Please, all of you, be seated." He gestured toward the well-appointed furniture placed within comfortable speaking distance of his desk as he returned to it and sat.

"General Marshall and I have been reviewing the general situation at Oak Ridge for the last hour, so assume I'm up to speed on that. We have also discussed his ideas for a radical shift in part of our military R & D procedures. I must say that there aren't many from whom I would have listened to such a scheme. On the other hand, by the time he was finished, he had made me a provisional believer. Who better to set goals than those who can set the highest possible reachable ones? Reachable in terms of time and money as well as simple feasibility, I mean. But note I said provisional believer. General Marshall has promised me a chance to watch his new system in operation. In retrospect I must say that as convincing as it was when he laid it out, it is already seeming a bit like voodoo."

Marshall spoke up from where, a wounded warrior, he had availed himself of the privilege of remaining seated. "Mr. President, the results will seem like voodoo too. Voodoo that works."

"Well. I await my own amazement, General Marshall. If this . . . demonstration is as successful as you lead me to hope, there will be more such meetings as this."

Marshall smiled, confident of his magic. "Truth, sir, is an amazingly powerful tool, when used with discretion."

"Especially among politicians, eh?" the President added lightly.

Donovan chose this moment to break in. "Speaking of discretion, Mr. President, since we are hoping that this meeting will not merely involve secrets, but maybe even generate one or two, it is crucial that what gets said not be passed on. As you know, Edgar and I agree that there must be a leak somewhere in this building." He glanced significantly at the two secretaries sitting in the corner.

The President shrugged and nodded to Mayhew, who had settled himself inconspicuously in a chair just within hearing range. Mayhew rose, walked over to the secretaries and murmured something to them. As he made to return to his chair, Donovan spoke again. "Mr. President, nothing personal here, but no one has been ruled out in this investigation."

Mayhew stopped short as every eye in the room turned to him.

"John . . . ?" the President said gently.

Eyes downcast, Mayhew unobtrusively left by the same door that had just closed on the two secretaries.

"I'm sorry to have discommoded John like that, sir."

"Yes. Quite. Is there anyone else here you do not trust fully?" Since Andrew Harrison was the only person in the Oval Office not there at the express request of Marshall and Donovan, this was a rather loaded question.

"No sir," Donovan said with careful neutrality.

"I must say, though," Harrison went on thoughtfully, "that John took it very well. He's generally terribly solicitous of his own prerogatives. He's really not been himself lately. . . ."

A delicate cough from Marshall broke the ensuing silence. The rest of the group returned to the moment, only Donovan remaining lost in his meditations. Unobtrusively he fished a notebook from his jacket and wrote, *"Mayhew*?? *Talk to Edgar soonest."* As he did so, Betty stood and went to the desk the two secretaries had occupied.

"Ah, Miss McCann?" the President said gently.

"Sir? Mr. Donovan said I might be asked to keep a record of this meeting. I'm more than happy to—"

"Oh, quite. I just thought it might be better if you did so from where you were sitting before, so that you remain part of the conversation."

Almost regretfully Betty returned to sit next to Martel. She'd always been ambitious, both for herself and her sex, but this! Couldn't she at least have had a chance to prepare by hobnobbing for a week or two with the head of General Motors, say, or the Speaker of the House?

"Very well, then," the President said by way of bringing the meeting to order. "As I said, General Marshall and I have been reviewing the entire situation, not just Oak Ridge, but our overall military posture as well, particularly as it relates to the current invasion of England. Since all of this is highly relevant to our little experiment here, let's make sure we are all working with a sufficient knowledge of particulars. Also it will give me a chance to correct myself if I've misunderstood anything."

One of Andrew Harrison's many virtues was an unself-conscious modesty most becoming to the mighty. Along with an intelligence greater than its possessor gave it credit for, it went far to explaining his assumption of the highest office in the land. The fact that the only participants who might not have a full knowledge of particulars were the meeting's three junior members had honestly not occurred to him, and if it had it would not have mattered. FDR could have done a lot worse in his search for a consensus heir.

"First, Oak Ridge," the President continued. "Bill, you of course vouch for everyone here."

"Absolutely, sir."

"Very well, then. Correct me when I go wrong. First, for our current purposes an atomic bomb may be simply understood as an explosive device with the equivalent force of five thousand bombers each carrying five thousand pounds of high explosive. More than that, it's as if all five thousand of them were delivered magically to a single point in space at a single instant in time."

"Simultaneity is always a force enhancer of course, Mr. President," Marshall commented, "but the desirability of putting all that force at a single point depends somewhat on the target."

"So I'm told," Harrison agreed. "But be that as it may, a single atomic bomb would take out most of Lower Manhattan — the financial district — or all of downtown Washington from this office to the Capitol building."

Marshall nodded. "Please go on, sir. Sorry I interrupted."

"Our plant at Oak Ridge was within a few months of producing the first such weapon. Now, that isn't going to happen."

Marshall stirred, looked uncomfortable.

"Have I got my lesson wrong, General?"

"No sir. But it may be important to note that if absolutely necessary we might be able to maintain some production from the gaseous diffusion plant. We're not certain yet."

"Yes, so you said. But we certainly can't depend on it."

"No sir."

"So for the purposes of this conversation Oak Ridge is a write-off. We won't discuss the horrible damage, the slaughter of tens of thousands of our citizens, the poison cloud moving toward Knoxville, or anything else we now owe to Germany, but I will mention that there was a second strike, this one at Los Alamos. It too was quite successful. Several hundred scientists were murdered, most facilities destroyed. Gentlemen, we have lost at least a year. Add to that another six months to get to production. . . ."

The President took a breath. "Still it could have been worse. Thanks to the heroic defense that you two organized" — a nod to Marshall and Martel — "and to General Groves having extinguished the final blaze in the administration building, it looks like we will be able to re-create a more or less complete set of records for Project Manhattan. Without the records and the scientists you saved we would be very nearly starting from scratch.

"As for the German program . . ." For a moment the President sagged, his air of smooth control and competent bonhomie slipping like a mask. "Bill?" he said to Donovan. "You stand by your earlier estimate?"

"Yes, sir. With the records they stole, twelve months to production. We can't count on more. They're ahead of us now."

"And it might be less than twelve months?"

"Only if they get lucky, sir."

"Even you may not be aware of this, Bill. I've just been informed by Winston that the Germans are moving in great force on the uranium mines in the Congo, and the British don't have much in place to hold them back. I'm told that the ore from those mines is about a hundred times richer than that available to us. Would that constitute 'luck,' Bill?"

Donovan paused. "I don't know, sir. I'll check."

"Please do. I'm shortly going to have to decide whether

to divert resources from the English invasion to deal with that, and I don't know how we can do both."

Donovan nodded and made another note. "How are they doing, sir, if I may ask?"

"The bad news is that as of approximately two hours ago a German invasion force has established a bridgehead along the Firth of Forth, and is already sending out flying columns to link up with air-dropped forces that have captured various outlying supply depots and airfields. It turns out that the British have stockpiled huge supplies of both avgas and regular gasoline up there. Though Winston did not put it quite this way, the British seem to have been overly focused on the fleet assembled in the Channel, and did not think through the ramifications of a thrust from the north. As Winston said, their attention has been focused wonderfully now."

MacArthur, who had been carefully silent so far, could not resist a murmured "My God . . ."

The President looked at him. "General, I know that officially you and Admiral Halsey are 'not here' but perhaps you would share your thoughts on this development with us."

"Well," MacArthur murmured, "it's a masterstroke. If the Brits wheel to meet it, it's a feint drawing off defenses from the real threat to the southern coast. If they don't treat it seriously, it becomes a dagger plunging for their industrial heart in the Midlands. Damned if they do, damned if they don't." He shook his head in professional admiration. "It will take a very careful calculation to allocate the proper amount of force to deal with it while leaving sufficient defense for the south. Furthermore, if the Germans manage to seize those depots the British navy will thereby be evicted from the Channel." He looked at Halsey. "But that's not my department."

Halsey glanced at Marshall, shook his head ruefully. In this circumstance even he had to admit the superiority of land-based air. "With airfields so close and fuel for their planes, they can pound and pound and pound until nothing is afloat at Scapa Flow. Since there is no other tenable base on the eastern coast they have no choice but to take to the high seas. I expect they will group southwest of England, just out of range of the Luftwaffe, prepared to lunge back in for a final fight when the Germans launch their southern invasion."

MacArthur looked at Marshall, who nodded.

Tacit permission granted, he said to Halsey, "Bill? You know there is another factor to the north."

Halsey just looked at him, cocking his head a trifle, so MacArthur continued. "The German navy. It has control of the North Sea. Now the Brits have to keep it out of the Atlantic. Once in, we wouldn't be able to resupply the British until we'd chased it down and sunk it—and by the time we managed that . . . well, England would be just another occupied country. So the British have to block the northern entry—and I just don't see how they can do that *and* loiter with significant strength to the south."

Halsey remained silent. He was professional enough to have known that Scapa Flow was vital, but he'd also thought it was invulnerable, and hadn't really considered the consequences of its falling except as part of a general British collapse. "Doug, I think you're right," he said at last.

MacArthur smiled and turned to the President. "Sir, may I ask one question before turning invisible again?"

Smiling in return, the President nodded.

"Who's in charge of this northern thrust? Do they know?"

"British intel thinks Rommel."

"Ah . . ." MacArthur sat back in his chair, satisfied. So it would be Rommel versus Patton. Wasn't that interesting. . . .

Harrison gazed around at the solemn faces. "So. The bad news is the British must meet an already entrenched thrust from the north. The good news is that this time the RAF was virtually lying in wait when the Luftwaffe arrived. Despite being outnumbered two to one they have maintained a slightly better than one-to-one kill ratio throughout the day, which is even better than it sounds, since unlike the Germans they get most of their pilots back to fly another day. They project a total of only seventy-five pilots dead, if you can believe it."

Martel nodded knowingly. At least the RAF would not be threatened with running out of pilots before running out of planes, nor forced to send up untrained teenagers in a last-ditch defense. The RAF would make a good account of itself right to the end . . . which at that rate would come in about ten days.

"Of course," Harrison continued, "the Luftwaffe can't maintain today's torrid pace for very long. After this initial surge, Winston tells me, the RAF expects to lose perhaps thirty to forty planes per day net, including newly manufactured replacements. At that rate the collapse will come in approximately thirty-five days. I do not need to explain to this group that without England our strategic situation becomes untenable."

Nods from Martel and the senior officers.

"In a nutshell, if England falls, we fall. Therefore we must arrive both in time and in sufficient force to save her. Clearly these are opposed criteria, and we must find a viable balance between them." Turning to Marshall the President said, "General Marshall, I believe it's your meeting now."

"Very well, Mr. President." Marshall leaned forward, drawing attention to himself in a way known only to generals. "First we need just a little more technology review on current operational German state-of-the art weaponry. That is, what we will face over England, and what the British are facing now." He looked at Martel. "Commander Martel, that's your specialty, I believe."

"Yes, sir, it was. I haven't been able to keep up since leaving Germany, of course. . . . but I'm sure Miss McCann will correct me if any of my six-month-old projections go off track." After thinking for a moment, he added, "In fact,

I think Miss McCann is in a better position to bring us up to speed than I am."

Betty looked up from her notepad, appalled. Twice her mouth opened silently. Then, "Gentlemen, because the Germans were beginning to ramp up for production in their latest weapons-development cycle we have not had any reason to adjust the projections that Commander Martel helped develop prior to his return to the United States. We've seen hints of some astonishing developments in aerial reconnaissance, and of course their next cycle of combat aircraft will be very formidable indeed. But neither of these subjects seems germane to the current context, and in terms of what is relevant to the coming battle, the projections with which Commander Martel is familiar remain current."

Marshall smiled. "Commander Martel, I guess you're still on the hook."

"Yes, sir. By now the Luftwaffe should have about twenty-five hundred Me-262s and approximately one thousand Gotha 229s on line. After attrition in this new Battle of Britain, they should be down to maybe one thousand 262s and six hundred Gothas. When replacements are taken into account that means our fleet, when it arrives, will face sixteen hundred 262s and eight hundred and fifty Gothas with approximately . . ." He nodded deferentially to Halsey. "Please correct me if I'm wrong on this sir, four hundred and fifty Phantoms."

Halsey nodded in affirmation.

"As for our Bearcats," Martel continued, "they're about as good as prop-driven fighters are ever going to get, and we have plenty of them. But frankly they won't even be able to take care of themselves, much less provide effective cover for the fleet against 262s and Gothas. Except when they're lining up to shoot them down, the German jets will simply ignore the Bearcats, while the Bearcats will have to position themselves to intercept incoming dive bombers and torpedo planes if the fleet is to survive. That will make them little more than meat on the table for the German fighters."

Harrison shook his head somberly as he shared a glance with McDonnell. Both men understood too well the nature of the budgetary follies that had left them in this plight. Had the Congress in its wisdom seen fit to spend the money, the Navy would now have a thousand, two thousand jets. And had Harrison been willing to expend all his political capital on the risk, he might have been able to persuade them to do so. How many, that shared glance seemed to say, would die due to their combination of indifference, sloth, lethargy, ineptitude, and the insensate desire to cling to political power?

Aloud, the President said hesitantly, "That would hardly seem to leave the fleet in a position to play a serious role in this fight, then."

Halsey stirred, but at Marshall's glance remained silent.

"Not in the air war, sir," Martel confirmed. "At least not while the Luftwaffe has plenty of fields within range of it. But Admiral Halsey is much more qualified than I am to discuss that aspect of things."

Marshall shook his head decisively. "No, Commander. General MacArthur and Admiral Halsey are here strictly as observers for this part of the show. You keep on going."

"Yes, sir. As I was saying, the role of the fleet is to keep the seas clean of enemy shipping, and our own convoys safe. Attempting to go head to head with the air force of a land power such as Germany would be suicide even with a full complement of modern aircraft."

It was a credit to Marshall's force of personality that Halsey did indeed keep silent at this assessment of his precious carriers; he seemed ready to burst. Still, silent or not, the daggers flying from his eyes toward Martel did not go unnoticed. Martel thought for a moment. "That's not to say, of course, that the fleet could not provide significant assistance to the RAF, but only while the carriers are kept out of range of land-based planes." Still conscious of Halsey's burning gaze, Jim paused again, then said, "But I repeat, my area of interest has always been naval air technology and its effective application. I really shouldn't be the one briefing you on fleet actions."

Halsey's gaze flamed down a notch.

"You're doing fine, Commander," Marshall said quietly. "We don't want excessive detail at this point anyway." Marshall turned to Halsey. "Admiral, have you heard anything here you think is wrong?"

Free at last, Halsey prepared to ventilate. "The US Navy will do its job! There is no enemy so powerful we can't face it. None! I admit that—"

Marshall leaned over to Halsey and said very quietly, "Admiral, let's keep it light. My demonstration is doomed if Commander Martel gets too inhibited to think straight."

For a moment Halsey looked as if he had a gas bubble. Finally he relaxed and smiled in the manner of a family guest who would really like to give Junior a much-deserved thwacking, but knows it's not his place, and that it would be hopeless to discuss the matter further with the doting parents. Ironically, as was obvious from an unconscious change in his stance, that attitude could not have been better designed to bring out the intellectual combatant in James Martel.

Marshall sat back with a look of satisfaction as Halsey continued:

"Hrmph. Well, I think your emphasis is off, but I don't argue with your basic facts. Just remember that the fleet is a very powerful weapon."

"Yes sir. Properly used it is the most powerful instrument of war ever conceived. Which is another argument in favor of using it properly."

Halsey's eyebrows went up at this hint of counterthrust. Though his hand happened to be covering his mouth at that moment, Marshall's eyes danced.

Martel continued, speaking directly to Harrison. "Sir, given our weapons limitations, it is my opinion that the fleet's role in this first phase of the war is to secure the sea-lanes and allow for maximum flow of men and materiel to England. As to how to best use the fleet to counter the

Luftwaffe in the final stage of the passage from our ports to theirs, I have an idea or two, but I don't like them much. If they are the best we can come up with, a lot of good men will die for only a small additional advantage."

"Well, then," Marshall said, "let's save them for later. For now I'd like you to go into a little more detail on what we're facing."

"Sir? With Kelly Johnson present wouldn't it be better to get it straight from the source? Furthermore, since he's been busy in the OSS files—that's what he's in Washington for, I believe—he's bound to be more current than I am."

Marshall smiled. "Tiring of the limelight so soon, Commander?" He turned to Kelly. "Mr. Johnson?"

"Commander Martel is a much better speaker than I am, General. I think it would be better if I just sit here ready to help out when needed. You should have had Dutch Kindelberger here. He can build planes *and* talk." Kindelberger could indeed talk. He was also the man who had taken the P-51 Mustang from back-of-the-envelope to test flight in just over four months—just as Kelly Johnson and his Skunk Works had done with the P-80 Shooting Star in just under five.

"You were in Washington, Mr. Johnson; Mr. Kindelberger was not," Marshall replied. "Otherwise you would both have been here." Turning back to Martel, he added, "Just give us the basic performance characteristics, and the implications in terms of our own weapons. Nothing fancy."

Wondering again just what he had done to deserve this, Martel prepared to continue lecturing the President of the United States, the Army Chief of Staff, the two officers in primary charge of the Great Pacific War, the head of the OSS, one of the world's most brilliant aircraft designers, and — Betty. Thank God for Betty. For all too brief a moment his mind wandered to the many hours, sweeter still in retrospect, that they had spent with their heads together poring over grainy photos, roughly copied schematics, and occasionally a genuine fresh-stolen blueprint.

Strengthened by that momentary respite he went on. "The Gotha 229 is their most current operational fighter," Jim began quietly. "As I said before, by now they will have started producing them in quantity. Our projection at the time was one thousand on-line by this spring. Their 262 is in the process of becoming the old warhorse of their fighter force, but it is nearly a match for our Phantom and perhaps a bit more than a match for our Shooting Star."

Betty and Kelly Johnson both nodded.

"As for bombers, their four-engine Arado 234-C bomber can outrun every prop fighter we have. We also expect their Ju-287V3 to start coming on line soon."

"That's their jet bomber with the forward sweeping wings," Kelly interjected.

"The same. Intel says the Germans expect it to cruise at thirty thousand feet at over four hundred miles an hour."

"Remarkable," Kelly commented. "We tried the forward wing sweep; couldn't get rid of the turbulence. I don't understand how they got past that."

"Within the year we'll see supersonic fighters start coming on line as well."

Donovan, Johnson, and Betty nodded in unconscious unison.

"Right. I've been briefed on all this, of course," the President commented. When Jim stopped in confusion, Harrison hastened to add, "But go on, Commander. Assume that I am missing just one piece of vital information, and you don't know which it is. That's a big problem in my line: nobody wants to insult me by assuming I'm not omniscient."

Jim took a deep breath. "Yes, sir. There are a number of other areas where they've grabbed a long march forward. Their peroxide-powered subs are fast, silent, and even when submerged can match the cruising speed of nearly any target. They've already got surface-to-air missiles, air-to-air wire-guided missiles for use against bombers, and a nasty package called the Henschel 300, a television-guided rocket bomb with a range of twenty-five miles and a payload of half a ton — enough to ruin any ship and sink most." Jim paused and looked at Donovan. "One thing I doubt anyone here is familiar with is their air-launched jet-powered glider — a glider for most of its flight time, I mean — that can cruise as high as seventy-five thousand feet for recon. When I was . . . recalled from Berlin we hadn't decided if it was real or we'd just been given the schematic for somebody's pipe dream. It looked buildable, though."

The President and Donovan shared a glance. Then, as the President nodded, Donovan grinned sourly and said to Martel, "From now on call that pipe dream the DFS-228. They've been flying a few of them since '43, and it performs as advertised. Frankly, we just plain missed it."

For some reason Kelly Johnson seemed riveted by this particular piece of news. "That's nearly into space!"

Harrison looked at Kelly speculatively, but remained silent.

"Nothing we have can touch it, sir," Martel continued. "As Mr. Johnson says, it might as well be in space. They could put one up over Southern England and cover the entire country from one end to the other with a single camera pass. For that matter, if they manage to seize and hold Greenland — which they might well do if England falls — they could stage it out of there and sweep recon flights right down our coast. We won't be able to hide anything from them. And speaking of space, there's the V-10, a ballistic missile designed to hurl a projectile across the Atlantic. Mate that to an atomic bomb and twenty minutes from launch time they could indeed wipe out lower Manhattan or downtown Washington. It would also be possible to use the V-10 to put a payload in orbit."

"What for?" Harrison asked. This was apparently one of those vital facts that had slipped by.

"Reconnaissance satellite," Kelly interjected. "Let it do

several orbits, photograph what they want, then drop the satellite back down and pick up the film. They could keep track of everything we're doing anywhere in the country— anywhere in the world, for that matter." Johnson paused for a moment. "I don't know if they've thought of this, but they might even be able to mount a variant of that rocket-glider of theirs and do actual eyeball observations from space. Then we would really be naked."

"And they can do this?" the President whispered.

"It would depend on the wing structure, mainly," Kelly replied abstractedly. "They would need special reinforcement . . . the weight would be a problem . . . titanium air frame, maybe deployable wings. . . . Well, given the missile and the rocket-glider, we could do it, sir, so we have to assume they could. And will." Kelly glanced at Donovan. "How much does one of those atomic bombs weigh?"

Donovan glanced in turn at the President.

"If anyone here was not cleared to hear anything we want to talk about when they walked in, they are now," Harrison said dryly.

"Uranium or plutonium?" Donovan asked.

"Whichever would make a lighter bomb," Johnson replied.

"About five tons for a plutonium bomb, but we're not sure the plutonium bomb will actually explode. Also keep in mind that the explosive material only constitutes a small part of the weight. I expect that if really required, even the uranium bomb could be made much lighter than five tons."

"Well then, it ought to be possible to stow something like that aboard a beefed-up version of the rocket-glider, then use television guidance to put it just exactly where you want. Atomic bombs aboard ballistic missiles aren't good for much but mass murder; this way you could put one in a latrine window, so to speak. The pilot would have to walk home, but so what?"

"Even the Hanford reactor won't be safe," Harrison said numbly.

The gloom in the room was thick enough to cut with a knife.

"Well sir, I don't believe they have any such capabilities yet," Martel said into the silence.

"How long will it take them?" Harrison asked.

Martel and Johnson looked at each other, then at Donovan and Marshall.

"It would take me about a year, I think, if I already had the V-10 and the rocket-glider. It would be a real pilot killer at first, though."

Jim nodded somberly. Marshall and Donovan did not disagree.

"Is that it?" Harrison asked. "No German invisibility cloaks? No secret rays that can set off explosives from a distance?"

"That's it sir, assuming they don't have secrets we don't know about," Donovan deadpanned.

Suddenly the President looked very tired. "General, this meeting is being held at your behest. I'm waiting for that voodoo you promised."

Marshall leaned forward. This was it. "Yes, sir. That's what I'm here for. Obviously there will be a lot of philosophy and detail to go through before you can sign on, but for the moment let me keep it short and sweet."

Harrison seemed amenable to this.

"What I'm proposing is that we take our very best performers from the Great Pacific War research and development surge and let them use their own brains to decide on how to maximally contribute to the war effort. The total input from above will be go/no-go after the design phase is finalized. If no-go, the proposer comes up with a new idea. Oh, and of course supposedly 'failed' designs will be handed out for peer review, so the people who veto new designs had better have good reasons."

Marshall paused to look around. Only MacArthur and Halsey had not had a chance to consider the bare bones of the notion already. They both seemed confused, but a large part of their reason for being here was to play audience. Though they didn't know it, Marshall regarded convincing the pair of them as his primary goal. If he could convince the President, he could go ahead. If he could convince such as Halsey and MacArthur, it would work.

"General, Admiral, something like this can only work if the men in charge believe in it. I'm not asking you to suspend disbelief. I am asking you not to reject it until you have good reason. And remember: the Germans have too big a margin right now. We have to get outside the model, break the paradigm. This is how we'll do it."

"General Marshall," Halsey said, "I'm not sure I understand how we're supposed to trust a bunch of creative types to come up with something sensible. How can we hope to give them their heads and keep them focused? Give those crazy scientists an inch and they're off in cloud cuckooland before you turn around."

"Not just any creative types, Admiral. Creative types who have produced. Men like Mr. Johnson, here. You too, Commander. Men who have performed way over expectations, men who even under our old system provided miracles that astounded the world. Let's see what they can come up with on their own. That's all I'm saying. And I guess it's time for our demo."

Everyone sat expectantly, looking for the hat, waiting for the rabbit.

"Mr. Johnson," Marshall said, "I take it that you agree with Martel on the inadequacy of the Navy's aircraft to deal with the Luftwaffe within range of a large number of their airfields?"

"Yes sir, I do."

"Well, do something about it."

"Sir?"

"You, sir, are one of the world's foremost technologists. I want you to come up with something to give the Navy a chance against the Luftwaffe. The fleet will consist of approximately twenty carriers and various escorts. Keeping the oceans safe for our convoys is all very nice, but by the time the fleet arrives England will be in the final stages of the fight of its life. If the RAF is about to be suppressed, and the landing barges are spewing out German soldiers, what good will supplies do? As of now it looks like the Navy will literally be sunk if it attempts more than providing port-to-port protection. Unfortunately we are arriving so late that that won't be enough. We have to be able to deal with German air power in a better way than simply skirting it.

"One more thing: The fleet sorties in three weeks."

Even a man as confident of his powers as Kelly Johnson could be taken aback. "Three weeks? I could about start to assemble a team in three weeks, sir."

Marshall leaned forward and looked Kelly in the eye. "Wrong answer, Mr. Johnson. Let's try again. You can have anything you want or need. If you tell them to, men will sprint from place to place following your orders. The President backs you one hundred percent, and whatever you want, I will make happen. In about twenty-seven days our fleet will be fighting an enemy with more and superior aircraft. If the fleet loses, England is conquered. If England goes, well, so do we. We could lose our country. Only you can save us."

"Three weeks," Kelly mumbled. His face took on the slack look of someone very bright whose entire mind is engaged. "Nothing. It's just not enough time."

There was a collective exhalation of disappointment from around the room.

Marshall was the first to speak."Well, that was a longshot. Three weeks is hardly a fair — "

"Well, maybe one thing," Johnson said.

"What?" repeated three times from three different throats.

"Well, we've got a whole slew of just about useless P-82s, and another whole slew of P-51s in open storage that we can't use in a serious fight."

"So?" Jim asked, after noting his superiors' continued silence. Perhaps better than anyone else in the room Jim knew just what Kelly was talking about. The P-82 was about the oddest plane ever built. It was essentially a pair of Mustangs glued together, sharing the inboard wing and horizontal stabilizer. For stupid political/budgetary reasons it was powered with the very same unsatisfactory Allison engines that had limited the original P-51 Mustang to ground-attack roles until the RAF tried replacing the Allisons with Rolls Royce Merlins. A hangar-queen abortion of an aircraft that pilots loved to hate, its only saving grace was that on the rare occasions it actually flew it flew for a long way, and was sort of a fighter plane when it got there. It had been conceived as an intercontinental escort for the B-36 bomber expected to roll out in a year or so.

"So, we take a bunch of Merlins out of the P-51s and drop them into the P-82s we have gathering dust out on the Consolidated-Vultee ramp at Downey. We can also set up a line to turn pairs of P-51s into P-82s. We can have five, six hundred planes rendezvous with the fleet as it goes into action. Since they are double-piloted they wouldn't even have had to land first. If the action started late in the day, the first thing the Germans would know of them was when they saw them coming out of the sun."

Harrison looked inquiringly at Marshall, who turned to Martel. "Commander? What do you think?"

"I'm not sure, sir. Even with Merlins, the P-82s are not going to last long against 262s and Gothas. And of course I'll take your word for it that we could actually have the work done in time."

"Oh, I'll see that the work gets done," the man who had buried the Japanese Empire under American ordnance said grimly. "But is it worth it? That's the question."

Jim said unhappily, "Anything is better than nothing, I suppose."

The President looked at the engineer. "Is that all you have for us, son?"

"Well sir, we might soup up the P-82s a little."

Marshall interjected. "You already told us about the Merlins. . . ."

"No, not Merlins—well, yes Merlins, but not just Merlins."

"What then?"

"Rocket boosters scabbed into the tail sections."

"RATO pods?" Jim asked dubiously, but with a dawning hint of hope.

"Not exactly," Kelly said. "An internal booster. Aerojet came up with it for a Northrop project that "— his broad face broke into a grin—" never got off the ground. We've been fooling around with the notion out at the Skunk Works. It'll add some weight, but no drag to mention, so it won't hurt the range much at all. We have the specs already. Aerojet's actually built a few. Each unit'll give two thousand pounds of thrust for as long as it burns." He sobered and added, "That's if it doesn't blow up instead, which it will, sometimes."

Jim shrugged. "Blowing up won't kill the pilots any deader than 262s will if those P-82s go in without the rockets. Can you really fit them in three weeks?"

"If we can get the boosters built in time. Aerojet isn't expecting a big order, you know." He paused. "Or any order at all, for that matter."

It was Marshall's turn to look dubious. "I said I could get them built, and I can. But again, would it be worth it? How long will the rocket pods keep thrusting?"

"The ones we played with were limited to three minutes," Kelly responded.

"And you think that would be worth the effort?"

Now, Kelly, perhaps the greatest aircraft designer the world would ever know, was in his element and answered confidently. "Absolutely."

"Why?" the President asked.

Unable to contain himself, Jim answered for Kelly. "Because, sir, for those three minutes the RATO'd P-82, or whatever you want to call it, will be the fastest thing in the sky."

"Speed increase will be about a hundred miles an hour," Kelly added. "In six months I'll build you a swept-wing, Nene-powered screamer that will outfly a Gotha and maybe break the sound barrier." He looked at Marshall. "But a RATO-boosted P-82 powered with Merlins is what I can give you in three weeks."

President Harrison's expression was an odd combination of relief and disapproval. "Why didn't I know about this? If we had this stuff on the shelf, why aren't we already using it?"

Jim answered hesitantly. "Well, sir, this is a stopgap measure. We weren't expecting to need anything like it, and, I guess, nobody really thought about it." Jim paused to look at Johnson. "Well, from the look on Kelly's face, I guess it's passed through his mind, but not seriously, or he'd have had it on the tip of his tongue. Actually, I guess I've thought about it in general terms — from my Berlin days I know that the Germans had been playing around with this technology too, mostly for launching, but some in-air stuff too. They started losing interest as they got going on jets in a big way. Frankly, I figured that we would be wasting our time too, and never recommended anything beyond trying to keep track of any new German developments. By 1950 any prop plane, no matter how goosed up, will be obsolete in a serious war, and who thought we'd be fighting the Third Reich in 1946?"

"I want to emphasize one thing again," Kelly said soberly. "These rockets are dangerous and I don't mean a little bit. They burn fuming nitric acid and aniline. Any leak, any flaw in a combustion chamber—" He snapped his fingers. "And something else. When those rockets fire off, these planes will suddenly be flying at velocities way outside their design parameters, and there won't even be time for practice."

Jim winced at the sudden mental image of shuddering breakups, spinouts, and explosions, but again answered for his peers. "You tell a prop-plane fighter jock that if he lives through the startup he'll have a shot at waxing the ass of any jet-powered Kraut he meets, and just try to keep him out of that cockpit."

"Just so everyone is clear," Kelly said doggedly.

"Have the test pilots power down the Merlins before

lighting up the first couple of times," Jim suggested.

Kelly shrugged his assent. Apparently that much was obvious.

Marshall began to turn toward the President when impulsively Jim said, "But wait, there's more."

Donovan did a double take and grinned.

"Yes?" Marshall prodded.

"Unless there's something funny I don't know about the structure of the Bearcat, we can also switch out every Bearcat in the fleet for a RATO'd model, and then start on Mustangs."

Kelly looked troubled. "I don't know how many Bearcats we can have retrofitted before the fleet sorties," he said. "There will be some startup time. We'll do as many as we can, of course, but with their shorter range the logistics are more difficult. With the P-82s we can just fly 'em to meet the carrier group wherever it happens to be. That gives us an extra ten days . . . well, eight days more if you're willing to fly the Bearcats out to it while the fleet is still in range."

Jim smiled triumphantly. "We can keep switching them out right up until contact with the enemy. Past contact with the enemy! And when we finish with the Bearcats, if there's time we can start stashing RATO'd P-51s on the left coast of England!" He looked around, realized he was getting a little excited, decided to hell with it. He *was* excited. He turned to Halsey. "Sir, if we're only going to have twenty carriers ready for fleet action, that must mean that at least ten more could be gotten far enough out of mothballs to steam, as long as they aren't called on to fight or run their elevators, right?"

Halsey nodded. "I expect half of them could run their elevators well enough, as long as they weren't hurried."

Jim continued. "So here's what we do: Five of the not-quite-demothballed carriers will form a bridge to the fleet, one carrier every six, seven hundred miles. The 'Cats land, they fuel up, they take off. One every five minutes or so ought to be feasible. We won't even need to fit them with drop tanks! So it won't be just a wave of six hundred or so P-82s come roaring out of the sun that the Germans will have to worry about. Twenty-five hundred . . . call them *RatCats* will light up just as the Germans see the P-82s." Martel grinned. "We're going to give those Kraut sons of bitches a surprise!"

Admiral Halsey was so enraptured by Martel's vision that he forgot to be offended by a lieutenant commander telling him what they were going to do. A slow beatific grin began to spread itself over his beefy features.

A thoroughly vindicated George Marshall looked to the President for silent confirmation.

Speechless, Andrew Harrison could only nod. He did so for quite a long time.

Speechless also, Betty looked at her man with eyes shining.

Caught in the moment, or perhaps unhappy on the periphery, General Douglas MacArthur broke the spell of silence. "That's great for the Navy. How about the Army? We'll be landing in England while all this is going on, maybe in the face of German resistance. What have you got for us?"

Martel was on a high, and didn't bother to come down. "Plenty! First, any extra Bearcats can continue straight on to England, if the Brits have kept their air-fields open. Second, the Germans think that by taking Iceland and Greenland they've interdicted fighter-ferry-ing to England. Not enough range. Wrong! Remember those other five carriers? They're going to cycle back and forth from East Coast ports to about five hundred miles out loaded with RATO'd Mustangs. From there the Mustangs can fly nonstop to England as long as they have a place to land. Each carrier can handle one hun-dred and fifty planes in a ferry mode. Call it eight hours for loading and fifty hours for the round trip and that's seven hundred and fifty RATO'd Mustangs every three days or so. Say the flow starts in two weeks. That leaves two weeks before contact. Six, seven thousand RATO'd 'Stangs." He paused, thought. "We don't have that many.

How many do we have?" he asked, turning to Marshall.

In his own tribute to the moment, Marshall grinned and said, "About two thousand, sir."

"Damn. We're gonna run out of planes." Suddenly Martel heard that 'sir' from Marshall and recollected how and to whom he was speaking. Strangely, when he looked around he saw that no one seemed to have minded. Perhaps the fact that he and Kelly Johnson had shown how to upgrade and position every single Bearcat and Mustang in inventory into a pseudo-jet ready to take part for a magic three minutes in the Second Battle of Britain had something to do with that.

Marshall turned to Harrison. "Mr. President, I think that concludes my demonstration."

"General Marshall, it does indeed. And you have made a sale. And do I get to keep the free sample?"

"You do indeed, sir." Marshall replied, then added thoughtfully, "We have to work out the details, of course—most importantly, Aerojet's capacity to turn out those RATOs. The whole scheme depends on that. I'd better fly out there personally."

"Shall I join you?"

"I don't think so, sir, but a phone call might be in order."

"Very well. Set it up with Mayhew."

As Marshall hesitated, Donovan broke in. "Sir, I think we should maintain the same security precautions for a while."

Harrison frowned. This was growing inconvenient.

"I can take care of that for you, sir," Betty offered.

Harrison's face cleared. "That will be fine. Ah, Miss McCann . . . ?"

Donovan spoke for her. "I'm sure Miss McCann would be delighted to serve as an unofficial administrative assistant while we sort things out—wouldn't you, Betty?"

Betty nodded solemnly.

There was a knock on the door and Mayhew's pained face appeared. "Mr. President, there are several people here who really need to speak to you right away."

The President glanced at his famous mantel clock and stood. "General Marshall, I'm going to have to do other things for a while. I really don't have a choice. Tomorrow I'll be addressing a Joint Session and demanding a declaration of war. Let's meet here at six this evening." As he started to stride from the room the President paused and glanced at Martel, who was visibly swaying as the adrenaline suddenly left him. "General, I want you and Martel to spend the intervening hours in bed here in the White House. Miss McCann, perhaps you could find someone to escort Commander Martel to the third floor. Then have whoever you find send a physician. General, you take the Green Room. Betty, have a physician attend General Marshall as well, if you will."

When Marshall made to demur, his Commander in Chief said simply, "That was not a request, General. I need you well."

As the meeting broke up, Kelly said disconsolately to Donovan, "And I didn't even get a chance to mention the Shooting Stars. We can strengthen their nose gear and launch them off the carriers."

Donovan smiled happily. "Oh, I don't think your idea will have been had in vain. Just wait for this evening."

Comforted, Kelly Johnson accompanied the small crowd as it exited the Oval Office in the President's wake.

1:00 P.M.
Lincoln's Bedroom

"Amazingly, there is nothing terribly wrong with you that a week in bed wouldn't cure," the attending physician told Martel. "But do not let that blind you to the potential seriousness of grenade fragments. In future avoid them if you possibly can."

Martel was almost certain the man was joking, his deadpan way of taking his patient's mind off the process of probing and prodding of the affected areas. That had not been a lot of fun, but it was over now, and the good doctor was busying himself with dusting, injecting, and rebandaging. Soon he would be gone.

Betty stood behind him, a little to his right, as if supervising. Framed by the early-afternoon sunlight streaming in behind her, she glowed like a creature from a higher plane, or so it seemed to Martel. Would the two of them really be alone at last? It hardly seemed possible. . . . And yet, *snap*, the black bag achieved closure, and with a final admonition that Martel was to avoid any exercise, the good doctor walked the considerable distance to the door to Lincoln's bedroom, and was gone, leaving the door discreetly ajar.

With a barely visible hesitation Betty sat beside Jim where he lay gazing at her. Their hands sought each other, clasped. They drank each other in.

"I thought you dropped me, girl."

"No, never, Jim." Carefully not letting go of his hand, Betty leaned over and kissed him softly for a long time. Jim felt a single tear fall from her cheek to his as, exhaustion finally having its way with him, he sank into reverie, and then sleep.

6:00 P.M.
The Oval Office

As the group was ushered in, each taking the same seat as the time before, the President spoke somberly. "There is more bad news, I'm afraid. German forces have completed their seizure of Greenland and Iceland. It will take us months to extract them. For a while we thought they were going after Bermuda as well. That turned out to be a simple airfield seizure, part of the Oak Ridge operation. Apparently the idea was to provide a refueling base for the bombers. We've captured the lot of them. They blew up their planes though. Other than that not much has changed in the last few hours. The country is going crazy of course."

The President shook his head, then continued. "Well, let us turn to the matter before us. General Marshall, rather than deal immediately with the underlying philosophy of your proposal or the details of execution, I would like to continue the demonstration just a little further."

"I'm not quite sure what you're after, sir," Marshall said after a puzzled moment.

"Well, we've seen the results of rubbing a few very sharp minds together here. I'd like to continue the process with focus on exactly how to apply our new-old weapons to best effect."

Marshall hesitated, clearly troubled. "Sir, I will if you insist. But I'm not sure a technique conceived to generate wild and woolly notions and extract the best of them is really suited to strategic analysis in a command situation. It certainly would never have occurred to me to use it for that."

MacArthur and Halsey both sat glowering. There was no need to ask them their opinion of this new development. Martel sat frozen in place; the faintest hint of receptivity to the notion would land him in very hot water indeed, and he had no wish to be a lobster for his country, especially since he understood and shared his superior's attitude regarding an intellectual free-for-all in the venue of command decisions.

Harrison, aware that somehow he was suddenly faced with a united military front, preemptively surrendered, but on his own terms. He supposed that such instant agreement on the part of all four of them — the lowly Martel seemed as negative as the others — probably had some basis other than prejudice.

"I seem not to have expressed myself well. I merely want to listen to your group—including General MacArthur and Admiral Halsey, of course—consider the tactical implications of these weapons and procedures. I've been thinking about this off and on throughout the day, and it occurs to me that at least half of the effectiveness of what you propose will depend on surprise, and therefore none of what we have discussed here should be revealed in a piecemeal fashion. But I suppose that is obvious to the rest of you."

Marshall nodded encouragingly. "Yes sir, any weapon will be most effective the first time out, and since we have the option of a strategic-level rollout, we should take it." He looked at Martel. "Commander Martel? Any counter-analysis?"

"Well, sir, as a pilot I want the best I can get every time I go up. As an analyst . . . the only counterargument for using these weapons as soon as we have them would be air-bridging them to England for use before the fleet gets there. The RAF will need all the help we can give it, and I expect we could have carriers waiting in place for them as soon as the first RATO'd Bearcats are ready. Conceivably two hundred juiced-up Bearcats might keep England in play while we finish gearing up."

Marshall smiled lopsidedly. "And do you believe that, Commander?"

"No sir," Jim answered promptly. "I think the Ratcats should be kept under wraps until we use them all at once. With a weapons development like this, with such obvious tactical counters, surprise is everything."

Marshall nodded and looked to the President. "Anything else, sir?"

"Well," the Commander in Chief said slowly, "I'm no strategist, not even an amateur one, but this begins to remind me of politics. I know Martel said before, and you all agreed, that the fleet mustn't go up against the Luftwaffe. But now I'm hearing that we actively want as big an initial air battle as possible."

Heads nodded thoughtfully.

"So what better," Harrison continued, "to tempt the Luftwaffe out over the water than twenty carriers and their attendant vessels?"

MacArthur laughed. "Since we can anticipate that the Germans will be doing their level best to tempt *us*, all we have to do is pretend to fall for it and go charging up the channel. Pure Plan Five, eh, Admiral?"

Admiral William "Bull" Halsey just smiled as he contemplated the prospect of Luftwaffe butt scattered to the four winds as his fleet steamed up the English Channel like they owned it.

While Halsey contemplated his version of Heaven, a place where subtle strategy and brute force were connubially intertwined, Jim, with a sudden sense of vertigo, looked over at Kelly Johnson. Kelly was looking at him with an expression similar to his own: It began to look like the better part of the US Navy would be going head to head with the Luftwaffe on the basis of what they had said here this day.

MacArthur spoke again. "There's about a fifty-fifty chance we'll arrive after the RAF has been knocked out, but with British ground formations still fighting. A surprise bloody nose to the Luftwaffe could make all the difference in a landing. If it gave us time to ferry in some jets it might win us the war."

"This would be a good a time as any to mention your other thought, Kelly," Donovan said quietly.

"What? There's more?" asked Harrison.

Martel and Donovan carefully did not look at each other.

"Just one thing, as far as I've come up with, sir," Kelly said.

"Which is?" the President gently prodded.

"Shooting Stars, sir."

"That's the Air Force's P-80 jet fighter that nobody seems to like very much, right?" The President asked.

"Yes, sir. The first version was underpowered and the newer one has control problems. But it is a jet, sir, and certainly good enough that pilot skill and surprise would be more important than specs in a fight with a 262. Anyway, we could catapult them from the carriers. They'd have to land on RAF fields, of course, but if the British are still fighting they will surely control some airfields even if they can't get planes off them."

"How many Shooting Stars do we have available?"

"Approximately three hundred by the time we sortie,"

Marshall said. "We'll want to spread them on-deck throughout the fleet, since they would take up too much room belowdecks. That's fifteen per carrier, and one launch only, since they can't land on a carrier deck. But if the fight goes on long enough they can refuel in England and return for another round. Admiral Halsey, what shall we do with the Bearcats the 'Stars are replacing?"

Halsey had the unbelieving look of a man who hears reindeer on his roof. "The jeep carriers were earmarked to carry our entire inventory of Shooting Stars, sir. We'll just swap in Bearcats. In fact after the 'Cats launch off the jeep carriers they can rendezvous with the main carriers. There'd be no trade-off at all!"

Martel stirred. Marshall looked at him inquiringly.

"Uh, Kelly, you're sure the noses can be quickly reinforced to stand up under the catapult launching?" Jim asked.

Kelly shrugged. "Lockheed builds 'em, so I'd better be."

"Of course. I just wanted to be sure." Jim paused, then dove in. "The thing is, with P-80s in the picture the optimum disposition of the fleet changes."

Halsey started to swell dangerously.

"Not the fighting ships," Jim added hurriedly, "just the jeeps and the lame-duck carriers. What they're going to carry."

"Right. Just don't tell us how to fight the battle, Commander," Marshall added.

"Wouldn't dream of it sir," Jim replied fervently, "but I do think that given the time constraints we ought to look at our logistics very carefully in light of what we've come up with here."

"Go on."

"Well, I was suggesting before that we use the lame-duck carriers as bridges, but maybe that job would be better handled by the jeeps, and we send in the lame ducks with the fighting ships."

"They'd be more than 'lame,' Commander, they'd be *sitting* ducks. It's not just that they'll be slow. They'll be running with skeleton crews."

Jim shrugged. "Yes sir. War fighting is a dangerous job, and sometimes you have to do what you have to do." He pushed away an image of Trevor Harriman voluntarily absorbing the blast of a grenade. "Or maybe fifty miles behind the fighting ships. That should be close enough."

"Close enough for what?" Halsey asked suspiciously.

"Close enough to launch the P-80s and get the hell out of town," Jim said simply. "That way we could have a lot more jets in the air a lot faster, and if a problem cropped up with the nose gear it wouldn't be a problem in the main battle group."

"A problem in the main battle group would be a problem over the side," Halsey said dryly.

"Exactly, sir. Since the backup group would have nothing else to do, the flight crews could take their time if they needed to and fix whatever it was that came up."

"Well, maybe," Halsey said. "What about your 'Bearcat Bridge'?"

"Jeep carriers for that, sir."

"Hmm. That works. We had jeep carriers ferrying the P-80s anyway, so a couple of them will be free."

"Gentlemen," Marshall intoned, "perhaps the President doesn't need to hear this level of detail."

"Perhaps not," the President agreed. "But would someone like to summarize what we've come up with here? Miss McCann?"

"Yes sir," Betty said, flipping through her notes. "Twenty-five hundred RATO'd Bearcats, some of which will sail with the fleet, some of which will rendezvous with the fleet *en route* via the 'Bearcat Bridge.' Two thousand RATO'd Mustangs will fly to England, launched from carriers five hundred miles off the coast. They will not, I gather, see action until the fleet arrives. Three hundred Shooting Stars will accompany the fleet on partially activated carriers for one-time catapult launch at the onset of battle. Four hundred and fifty Phantoms."

"Plus whatever the RAF can send our way," Jim added.

"We won't want to depend on them for anything," Marshall said. "They will be in a bad way by the time we get there."

"And the Luftwaffe?" Harrison asked. "What exactly do we anticipate facing from them?"

Betty consulted her notes. "After a month's fighting with the RAF we figure they'll be down to around sixteen hundred and fifty 262s and eight hundred and fifty Gothas."

Marshall said thoughtfully to Halsey, "This will need careful analysis of course, but here's my dream scenario: The Phantoms and Bearcats fly normal Combat Air Patrol in forward-defense mode, well ahead of the carriers; the Germans jump the CAP; the Shooting Stars arrive on the scene to make things a little more interesting — and after the Germans have lost airspeed dogfighting, the P-82s swoop by and tear some of their heads off. That causes the Germans to break off to regroup; while they're separating, the Bearcats fire off their RATOs and slaughter them to the last plane with the aid of the two thousand Mustangs that have just arrived."

"I like your way of thinking, General," Halsey grinned.

MacArthur looked at them with raised eyebrows.

Marshall smiled. "It won't work out just that way, of course. But while it's true that no battle plan ever survived contact with the enemy, it is also true that no enemy survives contact without a battle plan."

They all laughed.

The red phone rang.

In the silence that followed the President picked up the receiver. "Harrison here."

"Mr. President."

"Winston. How goes it?"

"We have beaten them off for today, Andrew, and given better than we received. In the north, though, Rommel's forces have gained a solid foothold. It begins to look like he will manage to keep the fuel depots."

"Will you throw everything at him?"

"We cannot. We await a second invasion to the south, probably around Dover. It will be the main thrust. We must hold Rommel at a line running from Newcastle to

Carlisle with as small a force as possible as we await the southern onslaught."

"Is there anything we can do for you, Winston?"

"Come soon, Andrew, come soon. Do you hear the bombs? It's not like last time, Andrew."

"I've consulted again with my people, Winston, and thirty days is the best we can do."

"Then we will hold for thirty days. But there won't be much left of us."

In the background Harrison could indeed hear the sound of numerous explosions, some very loud. For a moment it seemed that the connection had broken up entirely, but then the roar again became a hiss.

"Winston. I do have some good news for you."

"Good news is always welcome, never more than now."

"We've been doing some thinking here, and when we arrive it will—"

Donovan's hand clamped on the President's wrist. "Sir! Security!" he whispered desperately.

After a brief moment of outraged tension, the President relaxed and nodded, and Donovan sagged away from him.

"Winston, I'm afraid the exact contents of our present must remain a surprise for now."

"Come soon, Andrew, with all the presents you can."

Again the sound of a nearby explosion was followed by a crackling roar that overwhelmed the line, and this time did not recede.

In the nearby communications room, John Mayhew flung down his headphones and snarled with frustration and despair.

TO BE CONTINUED . . .